# Those Rosy Hours at Mazandaran

## Marion Grace Woolley

**GHOSTWOODS**

# THIS IS A GHOSTWOODS BOOK
2 3 4 5 6 7 8 9 10 11 12 1

Copyright ©2015 Marion Grace Woolley. All stories, artworks, fonts, and textures appear under license.

**Executive Editor**: Salomé Jones
**Cover**: Gábor Csigás
**Image Credits**: *To the End* (girl) by Babak Fatholahi; *Abbasi House* (arches & pool) by F. Dany www.fabiendany.com; *Décor du harem de Tash Khauli* (tile pattern) by Jean-Pierre Dalbéra; *Il ridotto* (Pantalone figure) by Francesco Guardi.
**Fonts**: *MKorsair* by Manfred Klein (www.moorstation.org/typoasis/designers/klein02/text/index_t.htm); *Nymphette* by Lauren Thompson (www.fontsquirrel.com/fonts/Nymphette); *Fanwood*, by Barry Schwartz (www.fontsquirrel.com/fonts/fanwood). *Monospace Typewriter* by Manfred Klein (www.fontsquirrel.com/fonts/MonospaceTypewriter); *Zapfino Ornaments* by Hermann Zapf via Linotype; and *Garamond* by Claude Garamond via Christophe Plantin and Adobe.
**Gábor Csigás** can be found at gaborcsigas.deviantart.com

**ISBN-13**: 978-0-957627-16-1

**This edition published February 2015 by**:
Ghostwoods Books
Maida Vale
London W9
United Kingdom
http://www.gwdbooks.com

**British Library Cataloguing in Publication Data**
**A catalogue record for this book is available from the British Library**

Obviously, we can't stop you pirating this book, but we hope you don't, unless you're in serious financial trouble. Ghostwoods Books is an independent, fair-opportunity publisher, and 50% of all proceeds, before our costs, go to the authors. The rest is used putting our books together and keeping us going. No shareholders. No fat-cats. No rampant profiteering, we promise. If you have pirated this book – and if you enjoyed it – please consider buying a copy!

If you are interested in writing for Ghostwoods Books, please head to:
**http://www.gwdbooks.com/submission-guidelines.html**
for details of our submissions policies.

# Those Rosy Hours
# at Mazandaran

Marion Grace Woolley

*For Kirstin*
*Unconditionally*

♦ 1 ♦

Those days are buried beneath the mists of time. A lake of memory, distorted by ripples of remembrance and youthful uncertainty.

I was the first, you see. The very first daughter. There would be many like me to come. Svelte little figures, each with saffron skin and wide, dark eyes. Every one possessing a voice like honey, able to twist the *santur* strings of our father's heart. With his sons he was a committed teacher, quick to turn the back of his hand. They were born to rule. Although he neglected to teach us anything, neither did he raise his voice or his fist.

Like the first of all things – the first flower, tree, or vine – I soaked up the lion's share of sunlight. I bathed in adoration every day of my early life, growing strong and assured. I did not know then what I know now, for I could not count. Though my name has since been removed from the annals of history, it was Afsar. Afsar. You remember that, and tell any who deign to ask. For I was she, and no other.

That name belongs to me.

How the years slide by, and what we thought so solid, so everlasting, simply shifts like sand beneath our feet. All that we hold dear turns to ash. All that ever was disappears in the darkness that follows. Yet even in the darkest night a few stars are brave enough to shine. Pinpricks of cold recollection in the yawning abyss.

It began with a rumour.

In the balmy air of late afternoon, I sat on the balcony of my room, pressing my head against cool, white marble. One of those endless evenings, still and relentless, without the slightest breeze blowing in from the Caspian Sea.

The heat made me sleepy. The sound of children laughing and peacocks mewling on the lawn put me in poor temper. Though it sounds strange to say now, there seemed so many children then. I was hardly more than a child myself, and it felt as though it were our palace. As though we had taken it over. Some of them were my brothers and sisters, others belonged to the cooks and the cleaners, the guards and visiting dignitaries. I couldn't tell whose blood I shared, and little did it matter.

Şelale entered my room. I could always tell when she was near. Even when the air was perfectly still, and with her feet bound in silk, a faint zephyr accompanied her. That subtle scent of snow on the Alborz mountains, the cascade of water that was her namesake.

"*Sultana*," she cooed. A Turkish title, in her thick Turkish accent. I preferred to be addressed as *Shahzadi*, but, from her alone, I would allow it. "There is a man come. He entertains in the courtyard. Your father wishes you present."

"I am too tired. This heat drains me."

"He insists, Sultana."

With a heavy sigh, I allowed her to pull me to my feet. She guided me, like a limp blade of grass, to a block of stone overlooking the forest. Returning with a wooden pail, she began to sponge my head and face. Rivulets trickled down my back and the smooth, flat landscape of my chest, pooling between my feet on the rough granite. When all the water had gone, and with my white cotton shift plastered to me like a second skin, she led me inside and peeled it over my upstretched arms.

Naked, I sat on the end of my bed and waited whilst she combed out my hair. Every *Shah*'s daughter is considered a national beauty. Who, after all, would risk offending such a man? I am led to believe, however, that the rumours of my beauty were a matter of public consensus. I was beautiful. *Truly* beautiful. They likened my eyes to the graceful gazelle, and my movements to those of the agile lynx. Even at ten years of age they understood me for what I was: Death, disguised as Grace.

Şelale finished with my hair. She rubbed a little jasmine oil through, to make it shine, then fastened it with a silver grip. I was starting to feel more alert and stood to allow her to dress me.

From one of many chests against the far wall she brought a skirt in the Gilani style, woven in bands of red, white and black. The material fell full and heavy around my ankles. To cover my torso, she pulled over a white shirt, tucking it into my waistband. The outfit was completed by a sleeveless embroidered jacket, its red flowers glittering with golden thread which caught the light as I turned, allowing her to fasten my headscarf.

"There," she murmured, sweeping an errant strand of hair beneath its fringe. "Perfect."

We left my room and walked along the hallway to a set of steps. At the bottom of these steps the walls arched and gaped, revealing a small, cobbled space. In the centre of this courtyard stood a perfumed fountain, leaping in the glory of Allah like a joyful fish. Mirrors, beneath high windows, caused fragments of light to dance between noon and nightfall. People who had never seen this miracle became frozen in wonder, uncertain whether they had mistakenly stepped into a *jinn*'s lair.

I, however, had witnessed its magic since birth. It held little interest for me. I walked across to the far wall where another towering archway opened onto a vast lawn. Turning, we continued along the wall some distance before ducking beneath a second archway into a much larger courtyard.

My father sat on his replica of the great Peacock Throne of Nader Shah, a gilt platform supported by four sturdy legs, shaded from the sun by a painted paper awning. He wore his father's tall, black hat and a regal shirt of butterfly blue, bejewelled with silver disks. He was laughing and talking animatedly with mother Ezzat. Of all my mothers, she was the one I liked the least. She had recently birthed him a son, and you would have thought the great Goat King, Takam, had sired it himself from the ridiculous grin on her face.

Ezzat was one of those women who swooned and smiled in my father's presence, yet grew sour as milk when his back was turned. Several of his wives were like that. Jealousy, I suppose. But those sows were the exception. My father inspired loyalty and trust in all he met, male and female alike. As such, most of my mothers were the type of women capable of mirroring such qualities. Their doors were always open. As children, we roamed freely between them, certain of a cup of milk or a sweet fig in any direction.

Beside my father's throne sat my brother, Mahmoud, and sister, Fakhr. Born to separate mothers, these were my closest siblings in age. Six years old, both. My father had sired them the year before he ascended the throne. Then it did not strike me as odd that, for four years, between my birth and theirs, my father had ceased to procreate. Neither did his own years cause me to question.

When you are ten, twenty-one seems like a very grand age indeed. More than a lifetime away.

He looked up and saw me. With a wave of his hand, the crowd parted and bowed respectfully. I strode forward, head held high, befitting the eldest child of the Shah. In the centre of the throng stood a towering, meaty man with thick arms that rippled in the sweaty heat. He wore an open jacket of wolfskin, his loose trousers ending in a pair of expensive leather boots.

"My daughter, my daughter. Come," my father beckoned.

As I arrived by his side, a serving girl produced a wooden stool for me.

"Listen to this – just listen!" He motioned to the man to resume speaking.

"Well," growled the fur trader, flexing his muscles. "I tell you this as I've told a thousand before you. I had never seen such a sight! Ugly? Like a *gallu* it was. I watched soldiers draw back in fear! Hardened men who had fought with their bare fists and killed like lions, unable to cast their eyes upon it!"

"What is he talking about?" I whispered.

"Shush, shush – listen." He waved me quiet, eyes fixed upon the storyteller.

"Oh, we were ready to run all right! We were halfway out the tent by the time he opened his mouth. Just as you've never seen anything so ugly in all your life, I swear to you, you have never heard an angel, either. Not until that moment. It opened its mouth and the bells of heaven rang forth. The sweetest, saddest songs you have ever heard in all your born days. It made the heart weep."

"What else did the creature do?" someone in the crowd cried out.

"What else? Well, as though that weren't enough, the creature could make its soul leave its body! It could whisper in your ear from a hundred paces. It could call invisible animals out of the sky, make you turn your head to look for them."

"A *daeva*!" a woman shouted excitedly.

"That's what we all thought at first," the man nodded. "Some evil, escaped from the underworlds."

"And was it?" the Shah asked.

"No, *Shahanshah*." The trader shook his head. "I am convinced that it was not. Not after I heard it sing. No evil could sing like that."

"Then what was it?"

"I do not know. I honestly could not say. Some unfortunate, perhaps. Maybe a disfigured *peri*, here to work off its mortal debt on earth before ascending back to heaven."

My father stroked his beard thoughtfully, then leaned back his head to mother Ezzat and asked for a cup of milk. She served him with her own hands.

"You tell an interesting tale," he said at last. "I shall see you are rewarded for it. And I will reward you double if you can find me the whereabouts of these gypsies."

The bear of a man grinned. "That is easy. I rode with them from Nijni-Novgorod, until they turned off the trail at Ak Mola. We travelled together for a month along the Russian trade routes. When I left them, they said that they were continuing south, towards Kabul."

My father stroked his beard again. "And you, where is your home?"

"The great stone fort of Samarkand."

"You have come a long way."

"And further yet to travel."

Taking a sip of milk, he seemed to come to some conclusion. "I shall buy ten of your finest furs. Show them to me. There is the price of twenty more if I find your circus at Kabul."

They smiled at one another and the man left to fetch his wares.

"There," my father said, turning to me. "You'd like that, wouldn't you?"

I didn't understand, so he explained to me as though speaking to a damaged child.

"That man has been all the way to Russia. They have a circus there, so famous that we now know of it all the way down here in Persia."

"I would like to see that very much," I admitted.

Anything to break the monotony of those long, hot summers.

"And you shall! It will be my gift to you on your birthday."

"Father, I do not turn eleven until next year."

"Kabul is a long way," he laughed. "Even further if they are still on their way there. Better I make promises I can keep than promise you what I cannot deliver." He smiled and reached out to touch my cheek.

I saw mother Ezzat's eyes narrow.

So it was settled. He paid the fur trader handsomely for what I thought to be goods of only average quality. Then he dispatched a messenger for Kabul to summon a bunch of gypsies who, by the time they arrived, I would have forgotten were even coming.

And the days rolled by. And the heat stuck to my skin. And the flies buzzed through the open arches of my window, keeping me awake at night.

Sari is older than time, this great city of my father's fathers. We know how it came to be because it is written in the *Shahnameh*, the history of our people. Sometimes travelling scholars and poets would visit, and my father would employ them to read from it.

One summer, a troop of musicians came to sing the entire saga. My father was so impressed that he wanted to keep them permanently, but they refused to stay. They said that the stories of our history belonged to all people, and all people should have equal chance to hear them.

It was a brave stand on their part, sadly.

The *Shahnameh* says that long, long ago, a terrible demon threatened our homeland. Zahhak, the Arabian Dragon King. A homicidal patricide, his lust for death was legendary. Enchanted by wicked magic, two black snakes burst through the flesh of his shoulders. These serpents threatened to feed upon his brain. In order to stay alive, he fed them the brains of others. Each night, two men were chosen at random and sacrificed to sate the lust of these bloody demons.

For a thousand years Zahhak ruled the world. He invaded our lands and slaughtered our people. It seemed as though no one could stand against him until, eventually, the blacksmith Kaveh raised his apron in a sign of defiance. Waving it like a flag, he rallied an army and set forth for the Alborz mountains in support of Fereydun, the Boy King.

Fereydun fulfilled the prophecy that had set Zahhak against him. He struck him down with an ox-headed mace and imprisoned him in a cave beneath Mount Damavand. With no servants to bring his serpents fresh brains, there was only one left to feast upon.

The spirit of the blacksmith lives here still, high in the mountains of Northern Iran, running through the rivers of Mazandaran. Fereydun established this city in gratitude, so that he could live out the rest of his days close to his champion, Kaveh.

We were of proud heritage. Iran owed us her loyalty for the part our region played in her survival. Without those great men, who rose up like gods, her people would have been overrun by their foe.

From the top of the highest tower, I could look out and see the city sprawling in the distance. A smudge of white between the trees. On a quiet evening, I swore that I could hear its pulse beating. The sound of bare feet on dusty roads, of laughter and music, carts, markets and mosques. I was sure of it. I could even smell her: fresh roast fish, fried squid, rice boiling in sweet milk, and sour yoghurt, tart to the taste buds and yellow with saffron. Some nights I dreamed that I was wandering her streets. Sari welcomed me with open arms. Her sound and light engulfed me, calling me to play amongst the shadows of her houses.

When I awoke from these dreams to find myself alone, deep sadness overwhelmed me.

One particular morning, I woke in such sadness. The sharp crack of powder ripped me from the embrace of sleep like a whip flaying my soul. In the instant that my eyes opened, I swear there were celestial tears behind them.

Şelale stood by my balcony, staring out across the forest.

"What is it?" I asked.

She did not answer me.

Throwing aside my covers, I pulled yesterday's skirt and blouse over my shift. I covered my head with a green scarf and wrapped its tail around my neck. A second volley of gunfire tore through the morning. I wasn't afraid. If danger were afoot, Şelale would have woken me. There would have been an alarm.

As I strode purposefully towards the door, she called out to me. "Don't go, *çocukcağız*."

Ignoring her, I ran to the top of the stairs and descended to the fountain yard. I paused to dab its rose-scented water beneath my chin, ashamed that I had not washed.

A third thunder of firearms spurred me on.

Breathless, I continued through the opposite arch, along the wall, past my father's own courtyard where the fur trader had once stood, still further to a third, smaller yard, which was usually gated by high wooden doors. Today these doors were drawn back, revealing a shaded square. There was an overhanging parapet to the right, and a towering brick wall to the left.

Against that wall, three men stood.

By their feet, six more lay dead.

Those three men had been required to climb over the bodies of their friends in order to stand in the line of fire themselves. I studied each one carefully. The one in the centre was fat. He wore a white smock to his ankles, which strained visibly around his gut. It made me giggle. He looked like he were with child. If Ezzat had grown a beard, that is exactly how she would have looked the month before her son was born.

The two on either side were younger and much slimmer. The one to the right was almost handsome in his way. I recognised them instantly as Bábí. All of them wore strange, triangular talismans around their necks. The sight made my skin crawl.

"Afsar, did I wake you?" My father turned to me with a look of apology.

I shook my head and took a step closer. Two of the men kept their eyes to the ground, but the handsome one raised his a fraction. I felt him staring, and wondered what he thought. Did he see my beauty? Or did he see his last moments drawing near? I could not read his expression.

"Here," my father said, handing me his own gun. It was a work of art. A Persian *miquelet* from the beginning of the century. Its light wooden handle had been decorated with fine brass inlay. It felt comfortable in my grip. Almost familiar.

As I turned towards the men, I noticed that one of the bodies by their feet was twitching, its hand outstretched as though reaching for something just beyond grasp. My father noticed too, and knelt down beside me. Carefully, he slid his right hand beneath mine, helping me to steady the barrel. "Take your time," he whispered, tilting the weapon at a sharp angle. "Can you see him?"

I nodded.

"Ready?"

I nodded again, one eye closed in concentration.

Placing his thumb above, he drew back the hammer, and together we squeezed.

I watched as the man's head opened like a pomegranate. Pieces of him scattered as ruby-red seeds in all directions, peppering the white smocks of the three Bábí as they flinched. Their turbans and their faces looked as though someone had dusted them with paprika.

"Very good," my father said, and I felt his arm tighten around me. "Let us hope that Mahmoud learns from his elder sister. A strong ruler needs good aim."

I smiled, though his words stung. My name was Afsar. It meant Crown. Unbefitting for a girl, who is born to breed and nothing more.

The Darougheh stepped forward. He had come with my father from his birthplace of Tabriz, a huge city to the North. Two years ago, in the same city, they had executed a man who called himself 'the gateway to truth'. He had claimed to be the Hidden Prophet. His followers had named him Báb, and took the name Bábí for themselves.

They had risen up against traditional Islamic law, threatening the stability of our great kingdom. It was our duty to rid ourselves of such vulgar self-interest and to protect those who deserved our protection.

Father handed his gun to his chief of spies, who reloaded it and added more powder to the tray. He was older than my father. Thin lines webbed his eyes and flecks of grey were starting to show at the sides of his face. I could not guess more than that. At my age, he could have been as old as the hills. He had been favoured by my grandfather, continuing to serve after his death.

Once the weapon had been reloaded, I was disappointed that my father seemed to have forgotten me. Without turning from the Darougheh, he lifted his arm to the side and shot the fattest of the Bábí without even aiming. Two simultaneous cracks sounded. Guards at either end of the square had fired their weapons and all three traitors fell to the ground.

"What news of the gypsies?" my father asked, flashing a broad smile.

"Our messenger in Kabul says that they are expected."

"Good, good. Let me know how that goes." He handed the gun back to his trusted servant, then turned and strode out of the yard.

I stayed for a moment, watching the way in which the fresh blood seeped between the cobblestones, creating miniature islands in a sea of cochineal. I was a little surprised. I had expected the blood of traitors to run black, or not at all. I asked for a small vial in which to collect some of it, to remind myself that our enemies are closer than we think, in every sense.

Back in my room I asked Şelale to wash me properly. She had already warmed a pail of water on the balcony. As I stood in the wooden tub, she expertly cleaned my skin with a soft sponge. She brushed out my black hair and rubbed sweet violet oil against the insides of my elbows and thighs. She hummed softly as she worked, and we did not mention the events of that morning.

I took my first meal of the day on the lawn. There was a makeshift awning to shade me from the sun, and a folding wooden table with three stools where I sat by myself. It felt as though I were always by myself. Mahmoud and Fakhr had each other, and the younger ones were incapable of conversation. I had no one of my own age. My servants were old, and they always masked their thoughts as though afraid of me. Even Şelale carried herself with an air of caution.

Once the imperial capital, my father kept Sari as a place of peaceful retreat. Whilst I wanted to explore the world, he was intent on keeping me from it, never knowing how deeply I resented his long absences.

I reached out for a ball of sticky *kateh* rice, rolled with *panir* and garlic. It tasted plain in my mouth. A salty spoon of fresh caviar from the Caspian depths only caused my nose to wrinkle in disdain. Every day the same, unending, food. Thick *āsh* soup, vegetables pickled in vinegar, lamb meat and spiced *baqala* beans. Even the sweet sesame *halva* that I adored in my infancy seemed sickly to me now.

Was this to be my life in its entirety? Like a fat, juicy grape perched precariously on the edge of an overflowing bowl, was I destined to shrivel and wither here in obscurity, my youth and my brilliance lost?

I would be eleven in a few months. After that, twelve, and then older. Sometimes I felt as though my chest were itching, as though two horned bumps wished to tear through like tusks. I detested women's figures with their full curves and ridiculous buttocks. If I could bind my form with rags, I would do so, simply to stop its mutation.

It seemed completely unfair that the caterpillar, an ugly, maggoty worm, could seal itself away and return as a glorious butterfly. Yet I was destined to transform in the opposite direction.

Despairing of the human form, I went to my chamber and called Şelale to me. She brought the painted *nard* board, with its cylindrical counters of jet and ivory. We set them out and began to throw dice in turns.

"Are you well, Sultana?"

"Yes. What makes you ask?"

"You seem quiet today."

"I am perfectly fine."

"It's just, after this morning–"

I stared at her until she lowered her gaze.

"Perfectly fine," I repeated.

We played on in silence. I was winning, and she was losing gracefully.

"We should place a forfeit," I suggested. "To make the game more interesting."

"But I am already ruined."

"Oh, so I see. Still, should you lose–"

"I cannot win."

"Then you will go to the stables, to my brother's horse, and you shall piss in its trough."

She blanched. She knew not to answer back, not to allow a glimmer of incredulity to cross her face. She understood that my games were all too credible. My commands, law.

"That would not be good for the horse."

"No, it would not." I smiled.

"Has it harmed you?"

"Never." I reached for the dice.

"Then why do such a thing?"

I used the line that my father had voiced so many times before. "Do you question me?"

She shook her head slowly, returning her attention to the board.

"Oh, look," I said, moving my counter and collecting hers. "I have won."

We descended the steps and I paused by the fountain to sprinkle rosewater on my headscarf. Then we set off across the lawn, around the back of the firing range, to the stables. It was gloomy inside. As I entered, I dismissed the guard with a single word. He looked uncertain, and I knew that he would not go far. Just far enough.

He feared me, but he feared my father more.

At the back of the stable a chestnut colt was tethered to an iron ring. It turned its docile eyes towards me and I patted it, reassuringly.

A long wooden trough ran along the wall for the animal to drink from. Reluctantly, Şelale placed a foot either side of it and steadied herself against the stone.

"Don't watch me," she said quietly.

"I have to, otherwise how will I know that you've done it?"

Even in the shadow, I could feel her burn with shame as she hitched up her skirts and squatted over the water. A steaming stream of urine flowed from between her parted legs. She hastily straightened and replaced her clothes, stepping down onto the hay-strewn ground.

Satisfied, I dismissed her and returned to my room. I didn't know what would happen if a horse drank human waste, but I hoped it would make its belly bloat and its hooves heavy. That would teach my gloating brother. He wasn't really big enough to ride yet, but my father liked to pretend that he could, holding him on and parading him about the grounds. Well, we would see if he could parade him on a sickly mule.

I dozed until late afternoon, when Şelale returned to cool me with water and change my clothes. She was tall and graceful, though her eyes were like the cow, not the tiger. Sometimes I wondered what she would say to me if our roles were reversed. If I were a child like the child of a cook. I'd seen adults scold children every day, sometimes even thrash them with strips of cane. It amused me, for I had never been thrashed in all my life. The first adult to raise their voice to me would soon find themselves without a tongue.

Yet I did wonder, just for a moment. If Şelale could talk freely, what might she say to me? I had no doubt that she disapproved of some of the things I had her do. I probably wouldn't have liked it in her place either. Even so, I felt there was a bond between us. She must have cared for me at least a little.

After I had changed, Shusha came to deliver my Latin and Arabic lessons. I never did learn his true name. Everybody simply addressed him as Shusha because that is where he came from, a great cultural city in the South Caucasus. His people had fought against us twenty years before, and relations were still guarded. Nobody was entirely sure how Shusha had come to be at our palace in Sari, or why he chose to remain instead of returning to somewhere more favourable, such as Armenia.

I mentioned that my father neglected to teach his daughters. Unlike many, neither did he seek to suppress our learning. He simply turned a blind eye to our ambition. It was left to each of us what we wished to know. All of us were forced to marry young, and many chose to pass those precious years of freedom in idleness and leisure. I could not blame them for that, yet I had a different mind. Mine was sharp and creative. I had to feed it or risk slipping into despair.

I liked to read and to write, even though my father never knew that I could – at least, not to such a degree. I often composed poems in secret, then burned them. I don't think he would have minded, but it was not good for a woman to become too clever. It might have raised questions, and my father craved public approval. If I wished to keep my hobby, I had to practice it in private. I knew the value of keeping to myself and, besides, who else was there to share such things with? Şelale was ignorant. She could barely sign her own name, and only then because she had painstakingly copied the letters I had given her.

Shusha was perhaps the cleverest man I had ever met. He knew languages that I had never even heard of before. He could read and write Russian, whereas I kept my learning to Arabic and Latin. At least those I could practise. I was most comfortable in Mazandarani and Farsi, and spoke a little Turkish, Turkmen and Lori, as we had servants of those tongues.

Although Shusha was patient with me, he was still a man, and many years my senior. His white hair was long and his beard thick. He spoke quickly in whichever language he chose, eyes glistening, lips moving as though his mouth found it difficult to keep up with all of the ideas inside his head. I looked forward to our lessons. We held them three times a week. On the days he did not come, I tried to memorise what he had taught me.

That evening we practised Latin tenses and then the *qanun*, a table of strings to be plucked between fingers with nails that had been allowed to grow long. I was not as gifted in music as I was languages, and soon dismissed him because I had grown tired of it.

By evening, Şelale and I were back to playing nard by the light of scented oil lamps. I think, if there was one thing that I had to pick to describe the passage of time, it would be the *click, click, click* of counters moving around that board. After all, it was never-ending. Someone lost, someone won, and the pieces were reset.

Over and over and over again.

❧

When the month of *Muharram* came, my father chose to spend it in Tehran with his brothers. This was our most sacred month, when we remembered the martyred Husayn ibn Ali, and in which no food could pass our lips before late afternoon. I typically cared little for food, yet being denied it made me crave it.

My father had chosen to take Mahmoud with him on this occasion, rendering Fakhr inconsolable. She cried incessantly and I made her mother take her to the far end of the palace. In my father's absence any domestic issues were referred to mother Arezoo, his eldest wife, or to myself, his eldest daughter. Matters of greater importance were referred to the Darougheh.

We had just entered the year 1268 *anno Hegirae,* and, along with an empty, aching belly, the rains came. I sat in my room listening to the downpour against the forest canopy. It was cold, so I wrapped a thick woollen shawl around my shoulders.

I had started to compose a poem, but the shadows cast by the candlelight stole my attention: the flash of a dragon's claw, the whirling blade of a Sultan's sabre, and the rising smoke of villages alight. The wind proved an eerie puppeteer.

I should have written those words, rather than watched them.

After a while, my fingers felt too cold to grasp the pen, a wooden-handled implement with a steel nib I'd claimed from a high shelf in a neglected room. When my fingers grew cold, I would make mistakes, ruining my work or coating my fingers in ink. So I had to stop. Ink on my fingers would bring me into trouble.

As Heaven's tears drummed down against the acer trees, I heard another sound. It was faint at first. I thought perhaps a peacock crying. As I listened, it came again, and then again, and I realised it was a woman.

I wrapped a second shawl around my shoulders and set off down the hall. At a certain point, the covered section of my own rooms was separated from the main palace. I had to brave the rain to dash between the overhang and the door opposite. It was only a very short distance, but the sky was bleeding heavily enough to soak my headscarf.

Passing through the corridors and rooms of the main palace, the face of every servant confirmed my suspicion.

It was Sarvar, my father's second-newest wife. She had been with our family for less than a year, and had fallen pregnant almost immediately. She was not the prettiest of my mothers, for that was Azin, and she was not the most practical, for that was Arezoo. She was not even the most ambitious, for none other than Ezzat could fill that esteemed position. She was simply Sarvar, and none of us knew her.

As I approached her chamber on the east side of the palace, where most of the wives at Mazandaran lived, the scent of sweat and frankincense became overpowering. For a moment I thought to turn back. Then another scream came, and I found myself drawn.

She lay there, on a damp mattress in the centre of the room. Arezoo was beside her, and Bousseh, the best midwife in the North of Iran. She had delivered me, Mahmoud and Fakhr. My father had enough wives to fill his courtyard thrice over. Whenever one went into labour, it was Bousseh they cried out for. Her face resembled leather left out over winter and dried in the sun: coffee-brown and thickly wrinkled. Yet her hands were as soft as Chinese silk, and she sewed stitches finer than the coats of the richest princes.

Şelale knelt by her side, a bowl of water and strips of clean cloth to hand. There were perhaps as many women in the room as caged birds in my father's private garden. In the far corner, I was surprised to see Ezzat. She was resting against the wall, crouched on her heels, her black *maghnaeh* causing her round face to float like a moon in the shadows.

There was a strange weight to the air. Usually the women of my father's harem spent hours before their mirrors, each one trying to outdo the other, vying for his approval. Yet however much my many mothers pecked amongst themselves, however many feathers they plucked or wings they clipped to get the cock's attention, each of them knew that one day they would end up in a room just like this, legs spread wide on a soaking mattress.

They would end up here because of him.

My father's loins spurted children like fish leap from a stream. Like his wives, the later children were left to jostle amongst themselves. It was a good thing their mothers remembered their names, for no one else ever would.

Sarvar's scream brought me back to myself.

"Mop her brow," Bousseh instructed, changing places with Şelale so that she could push her fingers up between Sarvar's legs, feeling for the crown of the child.

"Afsar, what are you doing here?" Mother Arezoo came towards me, arms outspread to block my view.

"Let her watch," Bousseh called over her shoulder. "It is best she knows what to expect."

Arezoo hesitated for a moment. I could see that she wasn't sure, so I gave a smile to show that I was all right and that I wanted to stay.

She nodded and returned her attention to Sarvar. The woman's head was bare and her hair plastered itself to her face in wavy lines, like newly-hatched snakes escaping over her skin.

Time passed.

Eventually we heard the call to *Fajr*, the first prayer of the day. The sound of the *muezzin*'s voice rose and fell as he greeted the dawn. Although it was still dark outside, we knew that it would soon be light. We had been absorbed in our task. None of us thought to bring food. It was too late now to prepare any.

Sarvar had grown paler by the hour, her groans weaker as she tried so hard to push. I waited to see what the mothers would decide. Would Bousseh remove her fingers from Sarvar's legs, wash them clean and prostrate herself, or would we silently agree to hold Fajr later in the day?

The decision was made for us. With a blood-chilling cry, Sarvar pushed and the baby's head appeared. I was frozen to the spot, hardly believing my eyes, that something so large could suddenly appear where once only folds of flesh had been.

It happened far quicker than any of us expected. One moment there was a white ball rimmed with red, the next an entire face: eyes, lips, chin. Then a thick rope, like a string of animal intestine. She screamed again, and something extraordinary happened. She began to convulse. Head thrown back, teeth tight as a wall of ivory. I saw Bousseh falter, unable in that very moment to decide which end of the woman to attend to. She chose the head, slopping a sodden cloth across Sarvar's brow and speaking quickly.

Even I could see that it was the wrong decision. Me, with no knowledge of how these things should progress. As she mopped away at Sarvar's waxen face, the child between her legs began to turn an unusual shade of blue.

I looked around to see whether the other women had noticed, and caught the gaze of Mother Ezzat. She was still sat, pressed against the far corner. From that place, there was no way that she could have seen the things I saw, yet, as though watching the reflection in my eyes, she came quietly forward, removed her maghnaeh, and draped it over the half-born infant.

The room fell silent, as though the veil of death itself had fallen. Sarvar made no more sound. On a table set back from the bed stood a silver bowl filled with sacred clay, ready for the baby to suck from its mother's finger. Next to that, a safety pin, endowed with all the blessings of the *ayatollah*.

It had not managed to ward off this evil.

"Take Afsar to her room," Arezoo said, turning to Şelale.

We walked back without a word. Neither of us ran between buildings to avoid the rain. I arrived in my room soaked to the skin.

As Şelale began to undress me, replacing my sodden fabric with soft, dry cotton, I could not help but ask her:

"What will they do with the baby?"

"Hush now, çocukcağız. Don't think of that."

"I want to know."

With a sigh, she sat me down on my bed and began to comb out my hair.

"They will push it back inside her. So they can be buried together."

"Why didn't Bousseh save it?"

She paused for a moment, brush held in midair.

"She couldn't."

"She didn't try."

"She has delivered enough children to know what is possible and what is not. Please, do not upset yourself."

"I'm not upset."

Şelale was quiet for a moment, listening to the sound of the sky beating against the roof. "They will light candles now, and stay with her until the sun is up. They will sing the Prayer of Fear so that she will not be afraid. Then they will take her to the mosque."

"What shall you do?"

"I will remain here for as long as you need me."

"I do not need you."

She placed the brush in her lap.

"Then I shall return to help wash the body."

I waited until she had gone before admitting my lie. It did upset me. Each time I closed my eyes, all I could see was that grotesque skull, white as bone against her brown thighs. The smell of salt and blood and excrement blurred together like paint in a cup of water.

It made my skin prickle.

That weight to the air that I had felt on entering the room. I knew what that was now. It spoke of the presence of Death. Allah had abandoned her bedside long ago, leaving the way clear for *shayatin*, those devils which feast upon vulnerable spirits. He had forsaken her, for what reason?

The rain eased beyond my window; Sarvar's screams were replaced by the sharp ululation of my grieving mothers. Even as a very small girl I had understood that sound. It was so loud and so keen as to cause all heads to hurt, all eyes to note that you were crying out for the loss of your sister, or your brother, or your child. You were marking the passing of one of Allah's creation with the flicker of your tongue and the air in your lungs.

You were seen to be good in your grief.

Meanwhile, in their heart of hearts, I was sure that it was not only Ezzat who was smiling peacefully at the loss of another rival. *If only*, I could hear her think, *more births would end this way*. Perhaps then my father would count his losses and content himself with those wives he already had, those who had proven their ability to take his seed and bear his children without the expense of a funeral.

And what of the child? Stuffed back into its mother's belly, wrapped in white and plunged into the earth.

That fragile skull, red with blood, brown skin rent apart. Had it felt anything? When weighed in proportion, had that brief moment of panic and pain been worse than a lifetime of such? We would never know.

I did not pity the creature.

♦ 2 ♦

Many weeks passed before she arrived.

My grandmother.

I had not seen her since I was the same height as Fakhr, for she rarely visited this far north. She came in a horse-drawn carriage from Tehran. The rains had made the roads treacherous. According to the driver, it had taken several days and at least two wheel changes to make it as far as Sari. Yet my grandmother descended the steps of her carriage as though she had been carried there by a great bird. Not a bead of sweat shimmered against her lip; not one strand of hair peeked from beneath her scarf. Dressed entirely in silver-threaded blue silk, the colour of midnight, every inch of her bodice and skirt confused the eye with its miniature flowers and its climbing vines. The ivory blanket that covered her head fell like a frozen waterfall to her ankles, where socks of the same colour fitted neatly into black velvet slippers.

It took me a moment to remember myself, so dazzled had I been.

My feet came to their senses before my mind, taking me to join my mothers, sisters and brothers in a line outside the palace. We had all been taken unawares, stumbling clumsily into place. As the eldest of my father's children, I stood proudly beside Arezoo, his eldest wife. Fakhr stood beside me, followed by five or six other children who were old enough to stand. The rest of my mothers lined up behind us, cradling those still in their infancy.

On the other side of the entrance stood the men of the household: my cousins, my father's clowns, and the servants. I was having difficulty remembering the last time we had all turned out in this fashion. It surprised me to see just how many lives hid behind our walls.

A natural silence fell as people began to settle. The Darougheh stepped forward to greet Mahde Olia, the Sublime Cradle of our nation, my father's cherished mother. She smiled at him, a fleeting flash of teeth that disappeared as soon as I blinked, leaving me to wonder whether I had indeed imagined it.

I am not sure what I had expected. Not to be singled out or spoken to, certainly not that. What I had not expected however was to be ignored entirely. For Mahde Olia to walk past us all, eyes fixed firmly on the door to the palace, until it swallowed her whole.

Later, in my room, I asked Şelale why my grandmother had come.

"I think perhaps she is waiting for your father to return."

Part of me wanted to protest at my father's absence. He was only supposed to have been gone for Muharram, yet we were well into Safar and there was still no word from him.

"Do you think her arrival means that he will be here soon?"

Şelale shrugged and began to fiddle with the strings of my qanun. Ever since the incident with the horse trough, she had been reluctant to lay out the nard board.

"I cannot say, but I would think that it is a good sign. He cannot be long now."

I watched her fingering each thread for a moment, doing what Shusha had told me time and time again never to do. He said that the oil from my skin would distort the sound, dull it, though I did not chastise her.

"She did not look at me," I said.

"What is that?"

"Mahde Olia, she did not look at me as she entered the palace."

"Did she look at anyone?"

"No," I said carefully. "I don't think so."

"So why does that upset you?"

I could think of no answer, so I gave none.

"Do not worry, Sultana," she continued. "You must understand, a woman like your grandmother, she fought hard to gain her position.

She is not so different from Ezzat or Azin. Though probably younger than Arezoo."

We smiled at this.

"You can't expect her to see every face that she passes. She was born a princess, yes, but one of many. It is her ambition only that singles her out. Women like her, they only see in others their own achievements. You are still a girl, and your mothers are merely wives. What is there to see in them?"

She did not look at me as she spoke, focusing her attention on the strings, playing them with her eyes. For a servant who could barely write her own name, Şelale always managed to cut to the bone beneath the meat.

"Leave me," I told her.

I wanted to hurt Şelale then. Her face showed that she did not understand what she had said to offend me; another display of her bountiful ignorance. Yes, my mothers were simply wives, not one of them clever enough between them to claim the position of Consort, to be my father's favoured wife.

But I was not like them.

I was alive with fire, like the desert sands that shift, restless and rebellious. Or, better yet, the winds that blow those sands and tear through the trees on a stormy night, stripping their leaves and howling at the frightened forest.

Could my grandmother truly not see that?

That she and I were so much alike?

I would have to show her.

That evening, I ate with my siblings and mothers as usual. Only, this time, instead of returning to my own quarters, the Darougheh himself came to fetch me. He came also for Fakhr and my second oldest brother, Zhubin.

We walked towards the interior room in silence. Even Zhubin, who was only five, seemed cowed by the weight of my grandmother's presence.

She was a stranger to me, to all of us. A stranger who I dearly wished to impress.

Rumours of Mahde Olia were richer than the fabric of legends. She had single-handedly brought my father to the throne.

"The truth is, there was no love lost between your father and his father," Shusha explained to me once when I asked. He switched to Arabic, and then Latin, making me work for every snippet of information. "Shortly after your grandfather came to the throne, his brother, Ali, stole it from him for forty days and forty nights."

This sounded very much like part of a story I had heard before, but could not quite place.

"So, my grandfather did not trust his sons?"

"Not particularly. Though, by all accounts, he disliked your father most of all."

"And my grandmother?"

"Ensured that he became the next Shah. She sat upon the throne like a nesting hen from the moment her husband died to the day your father was old enough to reign."

"How old was he?" I asked.

"When he became Shah? Seventeen."

It had seemed an impossibly grand number. I was still considering it as we emerged from the corridor into a large room deep within the palace.

The walls were tiled white, rich blue and gold, vaulting up towards the sky. In the centre, half a bubble of clear glass allowed the light in. Clouds passed swiftly overhead, yet I did not stop to appreciate them.

My eyes were fixed on my grandmother, seated on a wooden chair in the centre of the room, her feet resting on a tower of woven rugs. There were few others present, only a couple of servants who sank into the shadows as I stepped towards her.

She was all there was.

"Zhubin, Afsar and Fakhr," the Darougheh announced, indicating each of us in turn.

Zhubin tottered towards her leg and placed his sticky fingers on that fine, embroidered fabric. I expected Mahde Olia to smack his hand away. Instead, she reached down and lifted him onto her lap with a smile as bright as daybreak.

Fakhr hovered by my side, sheltering behind my skirt with her thumb in her mouth.

Mahde Olia looked to her and reached out a hand.

"Fakhr, my daughter. Come."

With an encouraging nod from the Darougheh, a man who inspired trust even in those he had never before met, she stepped out from behind me and made her way forward. When she arrived, Zhubin reached down to give his sister's hair a loving tug. She looked for a moment as though she might cry, but Mahde Olia stroked her cheek and she was distracted.

"Where is Mahmoud?" my sister asked, removing her thumb from her mouth just long enough to be heard.

"Mahmoud is her brother," the Darougheh obliged, as my grandmother looked to him for an explanation. "He has gone with your son to observe Muharram. They are close in age."

"Ah, ah, young one," she crooned, continuing to stroke Fakhr's cheek. "You miss him?"

My sister nodded.

"Ah!" my grandmother said again, reaching down and lifting her onto her other knee. Zhubin erupted into a fit of giggles to see his sister fly up next to him, both ensconced upon the magic flying carpet that was Mahde Olia's lap. "My dear daughter. You must not miss people who are destined to go away. Your life will become one long river of missing, flowing to nowhere. Love those who are with you when they are with you, and when they are not, find another to love." I could tell by the look on my sister's face that she was struggling to understand.

I waited patiently for my turn. I listened to her whisper soft, intimate words into Fakhr's ear, and endured the screeches of my brother as she bounced him from time to time. Eventually, she lifted them back to the floor, where neither was in any hurry to leave her.

"Go now, my children." She smiled. "Fill your bellies and your beds."

Once again, with the Darougheh's gentle encouragement, my siblings turned from our grandmother towards me.

Mahde Olia raised her eyes and they met mine.

She was old, yet her eyes shone like polished labradorite, that greenish stone that glosses milk-white in the light.

"And me?" I heard myself ask, impatient for my turn to step forward.

"I know who you are," she answered, with the slightest of nods.

Arm outstretched, the Darougheh came to shepherd us away but I remained frozen to the spot. I could barely turn, convinced that there must be something more. As I found myself swept away on that tide of abandonment, I looked back one last time, certain that she must have something to say to me, that I had not been called before her simply to watch my siblings bask in her glory.

She had already turned her head.

It felt as though the whole world were spinning out into the universe, the sun's light extinguished, enveloped in the depths of an everlasting darkness.

In my room, I sat staring as the lone candle guttered in the evening breeze.

*She knows who I am? How does she know who I am when she does not even speak to me? What did I do that offended her?*

I ran through everything in my mind. The slow walk down the corridor from the harem, behind the Darougheh in his stiff, blue uniform. In her presence, I had been silent. I had not spoken a word. Therefore I could not possibly have said anything to affront her. Perhaps that was it. Perhaps I should have spoken more. That would have been out of place, but perhaps that was what she wanted, to see my defiance of the rules.

What was it Ṣelale had said? "Women like her, they only see in others their own achievements." Maybe, in her eldest grandchild, she had expected to see the same confidence that had crowned her ruler of our dynasty?

I repeated this to myself several times for comfort, yet still it did not ring true. There had been something in the way that she dismissed me. In her voice, and in her look. In that slight nod of her head as she turned away.

What did she know of me that I did not know of myself?

That night, it happened. Sitting on my bed, as the final ember died on its wick, I felt a little something die inside of me, too. As the last of the greasy smoke curled into the air, my heart began to harden with the wax. Only a little at first. It remained warm, soft, and malleable for several months to come, yet I can identify that night, that precise moment in time, as the one in which the last vestige of my childhood dissolved.

When blossom falls like snow, and all the world is white with hope, then comes the New Day, the start of *Nowruz*. The Spring Equinox marks the end of all that is dark and cold in the world, and the rebirth of fire into the sky. My father used to tell me that this fire was brought by a winged dragon, with teeth of Caspian pearl and claws as sharp as the Darougheh's sword. I delighted in going into the gardens to watch the sun rise on that day.

This year felt colder than those before. I found that I was holding my breath as the first trees became visible that morning. Like thoughts forming, their shapes became clearer with every passing moment.

I had not seen my father in more than five months, since he'd ridden off with my brother to celebrate Muharram at his great palace in the capital. My grandmother had stayed no more than a week before loading up her carriage and leaving again. In all that time, I saw her on just one more occasion. She had been talking to a man with a scarred face in the main hall. I almost stopped to listen, but the Darougheh caught my eye, and I knew that my presence there would not be welcomed.

I do not think that she noticed me at all.

Şelale found me after final prayer that night, standing on the roof of the palace above the harem, staring out towards Sari.

I felt her presence before she spoke.

"What are you doing here, çocukçağız?"

"Listening."

"Ah. *Bijî Newroz!*" She smiled and came to lean against the wall beside me.

Through the darkness, I could make out the faint yellow glow of candles in the windows of Sari's many shops and homes. In my mind, I could reach out and run my fingers through her streets, tasting the grit that had been trampled by generations of children's bare feet as they raced to mosque, to school, and to supper.

Unlike most nights, that night Sari answered back. She clamoured across the fields between us, raising her voice in a cacophony of pots and pans.

"Do they do that where you're from?" I asked.

"Chase out the bad luck? Of course."

"And jump the fire?"

"Yes, always. We have many fires. The men, they like to show off."

"There is no difference, then."

The day had begun with large bonfires on the lawn. Men, women, and couples, hand in hand, leapt through the flames to raucous applause. The chant grew louder and louder: "My yellow is yours, your red is mine," as people cast their sickness into the flames in return for its strength.

Around the fire, my father's Hajji Firuz kept watch. Dressed in red satin from head to foot, with his face blackened for good luck, he symbolised the ancient Keeper of the Fire. From time to time he would dance and leap, smashing his tambourine against his thigh whilst singing silly songs. Other times, he would offer thirst-quenching cantaloupe juice to those drooping from exhaustion. The juice was offered in a carved elephant tusk, said to be the cup of Jamshid, the greatest of the Creator Kings, who held sway over all of the angels and demons of this world. When he was not the sacred overlord of fire, he was simply Behrang, one of my father's clowns.

I'd learned this when I ran up to my father to tell him that the Hajji Firuz had frightened me with his rolling eyes and bloated tongue.

"Who? Old Behrang?" he had laughed. "Don't be afraid of that fool."

It had seemed such a natural thing for my father to say, yet for me it was the first time that I had truly understood the meaning of disguise. If I wore a paper mask with wide eyes and whiskers, my father would always laugh and my mothers would shoo me playfully away saying "Go hunt mice, Afsar. Go be a cat elsewhere." I may have pretended to be a cat, but they always knew me for exactly who I was.

I had not known Behrang for who he was, and this was a revelation. Once my father had made that connection for me, I spent half the day stalking him and staring whilst he rehearsed his tricks with Emad. Even though his face had been washed clean, with his red satin clothes exchanged for brown ones, I could, with practice, still make out those wild and fiery features. Slowly, I came to accept that Behrang was both the fool and the fire.

"Where do you think the bad luck goes?" I asked, turning to Şelale. "Sultana?"

"If they are chasing the bad luck out of the village, then it must go somewhere. Where does it go?"

She frowned, drawing her shawl around her shoulders.

"I do not know."

The thirteenth day of Nowruz was called *Sizdah Be-dar*, a day dedicated to chaos.

It was also my birthday.

Because of that, and because I was the eldest daughter, it fell to me to carry the bad luck out of the palace and throw it in the river.

Şelale and I began our procession from the mosque shortly after second prayer. Dressed in blue satin, I made one full circuit of the palace before entering the main hall through my father's court. As I walked, all those who were staying at the palace, either because they lived there or because they were visiting relatives, gathered behind me like the twisting body of a snake. When I entered the hall, they waited in the courtyard behind me.

The main hall was a long room, decked in Allah's green with gold gilt edging the ceiling and the chandeliers. In the centre, the dining table had been pulled back to allow for a smaller table to take pride of place.

This was the *haft-seen*, our New Year altar. It smelled of rose-water, which had been collected from the dancing fountain beneath my quarters. Candles blazed, symbolising the four elements, as well as plants, animals and humans. A silver mirror reflected the sky, set beside apples as round as the earth. There was also a glass bowl containing Daric, the fat royal goldfish named by Mahmoud for the coins of the ancient kingdom. Beside Daric's bowl sat another, which was full of sprouting barley. All around the base of the haft-seen, in woven willow baskets, were the most beautifully decorated eggs you could ever imagine. Hardboiled and dipped in dyes, wax patterns peeled back to expose each hidden layer of colour; one egg representing each member of the family. So many, it was impossible to count.

I knelt before the altar and recited a brief prayer to Allah, and to the barley. It had been seeded here at the eve of Nowruz. As its sprouts grew, they sucked up the bad energies that had become stagnant in the palace over the past year. I asked Allah, and the barley sprouts, to hold those energies tight and not to let them return to the palace.

Then, I carried the seedlings to a small stream on the far side of the North Lawn, and threw them in.

As I watched them sink beneath the cool waters, a huge cheer rang out behind. Women and children ran to me, asking me to unknot their handkerchiefs in the hope that the year ahead would prove brighter. By picking apart these knots, I was releasing their fears and their troubles, leaving space in their lives to be filled with love, and joy, and happiness. If such a simple thing as unknotting a handkerchief could achieve twelve months of heaven, I wanted to ask why they came again and again each year, clutching tightly to new knots. If it hadn't worked the first year, why would it work the year after or the year after that?

"Allow them their simple ways," my father once told me. "What is the other option? To believe in a year full of difficulties and heartache? To believe that there is nothing you can do to change your future? That you can only look behind and expect more to follow? No, that would be unkind."

Perhaps I was not a very kind person.

The rest of Sizdah Be-dar was spent on the lawns, sitting beneath painted canopies, eating *baghlava* and sesame halva, fish stewed with herbs in its own juices, rice, and mixed nuts. As Pisces dived beneath the ocean of last year, and Aries raked his hoof through the dust of the stars, readying himself to charge forth the new day, the universe paused for breath.

This was the day of chaos. The day between years.

Everybody lied to one another on that day, trying to trick their friends and loved ones into believing fantastical tales. The fires were stacked even higher, the young men even bolder in their displays of daring.

It was believed that the thirteenth day was a day of trickery and bad luck. The only way to avoid its mischief was to create even greater mischief of our own. Behrang and Emad performed cartwheels and backward springs across the lawn, whilst women danced in their most colourful silks, and anyone who could bash a tambourine or blow into a flute was encouraged to rouse up their instruments in a cacophony of wrong notes and enthusiastic pandemonium.

Sizdah Be-dar is a loud, lawless day.

Even I could not help but enjoy it.

Şelale had outdone herself with my headdress that year. I had strands of jasmine looping behind my ears, whilst tulips and wild hyacinth formed a coronet on top. One of the gardener's boys, who had stopped to stare at me the day before on the lawn, was bold enough to approach. It was only on Sizdah Be-dar that a boy with mud beneath his nails would be permitted to address me, the eldest daughter of the Shah of Iran.

I watched as he twisted the end of his green *kamar-band* between his hands. In the fading evening light I saw beads of moisture appear on his upper lip, where smooth skin darkened slightly with strands of fine hair. His eyes were unusual. Brown as dates, yet warm as nutmeg. They shone with flecks of gold.

Although I never admitted it to anyone then or since, his wringing hands mirrored the nervous twist in my own stomach.

Şelale brushed my shoulder lightly from behind, encouraging me to step forward.

As the boy held out his hand, I lifted mine to take it.

And that is when my world changed.

As the crowds parted, I could not be sure at first.

It could have been a cousin arriving from Shahi, or an officer from Sari.

Yet the moment I saw his tall black hat, I knew that it was my father.

The gardener's son forgotten, I began to push my way through the throng of excited wives and curious guests. My father always knew how to make an entrance. At a casual slump, with his pelvis thrust forward, disks of silver and gold shining against the breast of his jacket, he led his entourage across the lawn toward me.

At first, he was all that I could see. I had missed him these past months, though I had not dared to hope that he had missed me as much, and would certainly never have dreamt a scene in which he might single me out in a crowd as the first person to greet on his return.

People were beginning to draw back, allowing me to pass, when suddenly my feet sank into the earth and I found that I could not take another step.

In the wake of his horse's frisking white tail, there was an elephant.

I could hardly believe my eyes as it followed him across the lawn. It was much paler than they appeared in books. The great war elephants of Persia are always painted in black ink, but this one was light grey, like the sacred clay that babies suck after they take their first breath. Its tusks had been cut short, its ears pressed neatly back against its giant head.

As though the world could spin any faster, the elephant reared up on its hind legs, causing people to stumble backwards as they tried to hide behind one another. The tide that had been flowing towards my father now fell over itself to retreat. They must have thought the animal was about to roll on top of them.

Instead, it paused there, trunk snaking up like the neck of a swan, forefeet raised in perfect balance. At this point I became aware of the person sitting on top, legs squeezing the beast's neck. He was a Moor, his pearl-white grin bright as the mask he wore, trimmed with feathers and droplets of colourful glass.

I laughed out loud and clapped my hands as the elephant lowered itself gently to the ground.

I had never seen anything so breathtaking in all my life.

"I found them, my dear. Your circus."

My father's horse came to a square halt beside me.

His steady hands took me beneath my arms and lifted me up to join him.

"Happy Birthday," he said, placing me upon his lap and kissing my cheek.

I could smell something sharp on his breath, and knew it to be wine.

"Come, let us chase out the chaos!" he laughed.

The crowd drew back once again as my father kicked his horse into a steady lope, angling the reins with one hand to steer it in a tight circle. I clung to his jacket, breathing in his sugar-spiced scent as his medals chimed in my ears, feeling myself every second giddier and more likely to fall.

When he eventually came to a standstill, I hardly knew which way was up. Every inch of my body rang with disorientation and delight. He held me in his arms as he dismounted on the pathway outside the palace, his own legs faltering for a moment, causing him to lean back against his horse's flank to steady himself.

We both laughed as he lowered me to the ground.

By the time I had caught my breath, I realised that he had turned away. Beside him stood a lady unlike any I had seen before. She was tall, perhaps only a few fingers shorter than my father, dressed from head to toe in layers of transparent black gauze that dripped with tiny silver disks. She sounded like rain as she walked.

"My sweet," he chimed, drawing back the edge of her veil to kiss her on the cheek. "This is my eldest daughter, Afsar."

The woman smiled down at me and bowed her head.

"Afsar, this is my wife, Shokuh."

I felt ice water down my back. How could he? The entire palace stank of women: their hair oil, their kohl sticks, even their monthly blood. The halls of the palace ran thick with it. How could he bring us another?

By the time I could bear to look back at her, she had returned her attention to my father. They were moving, her hand on his arm, away towards the fires on the lawn.

My eyes stung. I bit the back of my hand to stop my rage from escaping. Around me, white horses danced with pink plumes of ostrich feather for crowns; my father's clowns were in their element, performing tricks through flaming hoops, tricks on trampolines, and even tricks with dogs; the elephant was once again squatting on its hind legs, trunk raised, this time wrapped around its rider's waist and holding him aloft.

I took joy in none of it.

It was all an illusion.

The stream stung me with her chill as I reached beneath her shallow surface for a stem of barley. I plucked it from its siblings and tucked it amidst the flowers in my hair where nobody would notice it.

In my father's bedroom, I slipped the fragile stem inside the pillow case on the opposite side to the table with his books and his drawings.

For the rest of the evening, I watched my father and his new wife lying on a sea of pillows beneath an orange awning by the fire. She sprawled across him, slim and pale, lips the colour of carmine parted to receive his kisses.

I watched, also, the reaction of the other guests. Many of the men, those who had ridden with him, were becoming loud in both voice and expression. They flung their arms wide, laughed with their heads thrown back, and more than once made comments to women that caused them to blush.

Some of my father's wives remained by the fire late into the night. Arezoo was one, and the ever-present Ezzat, whose eyes screwed so narrow that I'm sure she could hardly see through them. The rest of my mothers had shepherded their visitors away, ashamed by their husband's lack of piety.

The longer my father remained at our palace, the more he turned towards Allah. When he returned from long absences, it was almost as though a stranger had come in his place, someone who had forgotten Islam.

Bored of this, I made my way towards the palace.

"Afsar! Eh, Afsar!"

I turned to see Uncle Ja'far coming towards me across the lawn. He was my father's uncle, and much older than him. Whereas my father was handsome and glowing with youth, Ja'far's jowls wobbled when he spoke, and the sides of his beard had turned grey. He also walked with a limp, which they say was given to him by the British during one of my grandfather's attempts to capture Herat. The shot was rumoured to have passed straight through his leg and killed his horse.

"It has been too long, Afsar. Where are you going? Do you not like the circus?"

"I am tired," I told him.

"Tired? Ah, but the night is young." He smiled and put his hand on my back, turning me towards the house. "Come," he said, "I have something for you."

In my father's study there were many books. Large manuscripts edged in gold and silver, with thick leather bindings embedded with semi-precious stones. There was also a desk with a secret drawer. It had a dial to open it, which could only be reached by sliding your hand up under the part where you usually put your legs. I had found the dial shortly after I was old enough to crawl, but had never known the combination.

Uncle Ja'far did, and from the drawer he drew a long-necked bottle. It was made from dark-green glass and sealed with a cork.

"How old are you now?" he asked, polishing the glass on his jacket as he came towards me.

"Eleven, today."

"Today?" His eyebrows lifted in surprise. "A woman at last. Well, that certainly calls for a celebration. Here." He sat down beside me on the divan and leaned in to show me the bottle. "Do you know what this is?"

"Wine," I replied.

Shusha had told me all about wine. How it had been made from pomegranates in Armenia, transported in great ships by the Romans, and used to bless the vines of ancient Greece during *Dionysia*. I also knew that it belonged to Shaitan, as a tool through which to turn us from Allah.

"The best the fertile land of Shiraz has to offer. Have you been there?"

I prickled with irritation, for he knew that I had been nowhere.

"Ah," he continued, "the parties we used to have there, your grandfather and me. Great sin, and some profit. Here, try."

He gripped the top of the cork through his shirt and twisted until we heard a squeak followed by a pop. The air became heavy with the scent of sharp fruit, like cherries that have been left in the sun for a day.

I drew back a little and he laughed.

"Ah, Afsar. You do not approve?"

I shook my head.

"Here." He leaned towards me again, lifting the bottle a little. "Just a sip."

Again, I shook my head.

"For your Uncle Ja'far."

He smiled, and pushed the mouth of the bottle against my own.

The liquid caught the back of my throat. I closed my lips tightly, causing the rest to spill down my dress, staining the satin as I choked. I pushed his hand away and stood, but he grasped my wrist and pulled me back down.

"Not so fast, little bird. You owe me a kiss."

I tried to snatch my hand back, but he was too strong. This old man, who smelled of boiled rice and walked like a cripple, had the strength of the mountains within him. He grasped me by my waist and pulled me towards him, flattening me against the couch with my arms pinned beneath me. Before I could even scream, he had clamped his hand across my mouth.

"That's it, just a little kiss," he rasped in my ear.

Surprise gave way to panic. I could hardly fill my lungs with his hand across my mouth and his weight pressing down upon me. Without the use of my arms I was paralysed, as helpless as a fly wrapped in the spider's silk.

If he had removed his hand even for a moment, I know to this day that I would have pleaded. I would have begged him to release me, to let me go to my room. I would even have given him a kiss to allow me to do so. I would have bent down on my knees, bowed my head, and told him that he was more exalted than Allah himself, if only he had let me.

Instead, I shivered like a frightened animal as I felt something smooth and hard press against the inside of my leg. It caught for a moment on its own moisture, before sliding up, like a fleshy snake, towards the centre of my parted legs. With his free hand he pulled up my skirt and pushed my undergarments aside.

I could not move.

I could not scream.

I saw Uncle Ja'far from a point very far away, as though I were watching the circus performing on the lawn from the highest roof on the palace. I could see myself, too, lying there, eyes wide and glistening, struggling for breath. Because I was above, I could hardly see his expression at first, but as he flew away from me I clearly saw shock in his eyes.

It took a moment to return to myself. I came back from a peaceful place to find my ears ringing and my chest crushed with pain.

It was only then that I saw the Darougheh.

He held Uncle Ja'far against the wall, one hand holding Ja'far's own hands behind him, the other arm pressing Ja'far's neck so that his cheek was pressed flush with the marble. As I struggled to sit up, my arms numb to the point of being unable to support me, my uncle pushed the Darougheh away and turned, fire in his watery eyes.

"What the hell do you think you're doing?" he bellowed. "Do you know who I am?"

"Yes, exalted *Mirza.*" The Darougheh stepped back.

For one dreadful moment, I thought he might leave the room.

"And do you know who she is?"

Holding the Darougheh's gaze, I saw my uncle's jaw flex. He nodded slowly and drew himself straight, brushing down the front of his jacket.

"Very well," Ja'far said.

"Be assured, this will go no further."

My uncle snorted. "I'd expect no less."

Without looking back, he left the room.

The Darougheh followed him to the door and shut it.

It took him a long time to turn back to me. When he did, his eyes were kind.

"Can I get you anything, Shahzadi? A glass of water?"

I shook my head, unable to hold his eyes for the shame.

He knelt down beside me and gently pulled my undergarments up beneath the hem of my dress, smoothing down the skirt to cover my legs. There was something gentle in the way that he did this for me. Natural. As one might pick up a dead bird after the cat has left, and pity the poor thing even though it is too late.

"Are you... whole, Shahzadi?" he asked, staring only at the fabric of the couch.

"I am," I managed.

He swallowed, and then nodded. "I am glad."

Rising to his feet, he suggested that it was time for me to retire. He told me that he would send Şelale to take me to my room.

In the quiet after he left, I focused on a corner of one of my father's bookshelves. That is all I can remember about the end of that day. A perfect, mahogany corner, with two finger-sized steps running along it, one on top of the other. Not a fleck of dust to be seen, only a minor chip against the left-hand side of the near edge.

Hardly even noticeable.

If it weren't for the corner of that bookshelf, I would have gone mad.

♦ 3 ♦

The morning after my assault, I was excused having to attend mosque. Şelale told the imam that I was unwell, and then returned to wash me and pray with me in my room. We did not speak of what had happened.

I did not know whether she knew, or how much the Darougheh had told her.

I remained in my room until shortly after *Dhuhr*, when my father sent a note. He hoped that I was not too unwell to enjoy the circus, and requested my companionship in the main hall.

My stomach knotted itself at the thought of seeing Uncle Ja'far again, yet I need not have worried. As I crossed the space between my quarters and the main palace, Şelale met me with the news that the Darougheh had requested she deliver a message:

"'Kindly tell the Shahzadi,' he said, 'that her uncle has had to attend urgent business in Tehran and regrets that he will be unable to meet with her again.'"

My relief was palpable. Şelale saw me smile, but did not ask why.

When we reached the main hall, we discovered that we were the last to arrive at the party. It seemed as though every member of the palace had managed to squeeze between its pillars and its high, domed roof. As I stepped forward, people parted to allow me to pass. My father had positioned rows of seats towards the front so that members of his close family might have a better view.

"Afsar! We have been waiting for you," he said as I sat down beside him.

"I am sorry, Father."

Ignoring my contrition, he stood to address the crowd.

"Friends, family and beloved wives," he announced, clapping his hands for attention. "Today is a special day. Our eldest daughter is another year taller, by the grace of Allah!" A cheer rose. "To celebrate, let us enjoy this spectacle which has been brought to you from lands as far as Russia–" a loud boo chorused around the room, "and India." A cheer went up. "Behold, the greatest show on earth!"

As he returned to his seat, I noticed that Shokuh was sitting beside him, dressed the same as she had been the night before, only this time in midnight blue. She turned her head and smiled at me with those painted red lips of hers. My own smile was brief as I turned my attention to the performance.

A large space had been cleared at the end of the hall. Against the walls, several men and women were positioned. They were dressed in drab greys and browns, hardly the colours for clowns. Yet each one had a task to perform, and that task was unusual. One woman was lying on her front, resting her chin on her hands, whilst her legs snaked up and over the top of her head, casually rotating squares of cloth with the tips of her toes.

One of the men, with bronze skin and a turban, sat cross-legged with his back against the wall. In front of him stood six short wires, each supporting a porcelain plate. Whenever a plate appeared to wobble, he would reach out and flick the wire in one, quick, movement. The plate would immediately resume spinning, defying gravity on top of its wire.

At the very back, I noticed a girl with charcoal skin and long black hair. She wasn't very old, a little older than Fakhr, I assumed. She was also lying on her front, arms splayed out to either side, her legs bent double and her feet solidly planted either side of her face with her toes pointing towards us. As I watched, she raised her feet onto tiptoes, showing the soles, and I saw that there were large eyes painted on each one. Shockingly grotesque, yet enthralling.

As we were taking this in, our eyes roaming from one strange display to the next, the saddest, slowest note began to rise. It was soft and haunting, echoing from every pillar of the room. It was so sad that it made it hard to concentrate on what the performers were doing, calling to something deep within the heart.

What I had thought to be a ball of rags beside the little black girl slowly unfurled itself with infinite care. As it straightened, it turned to reveal a person playing a wooden flute. The note was followed by another, and another, until the notes soared like birds towards the great dome above. As the musician stepped towards us, we could see that his face was hidden behind a brown leather mask with a long, beak-shaped nose.

Closer and closer he drew.

Then, with one foot poised ahead, ready to meet the ground, the music suddenly stopped. As he lowered the flute from his mouth, a deep hush spread. Even the lady spinning her cloth had become still. It was as though both the audience and the performers were leaning in closer, expecting him to speak.

A crow cried from the back of the room.

Shock rippled through every person, our eyes turning in surprise to look behind.

When we looked back, he was gone.

A murmur rose, but did not travel far. Consternation turned to delight as the women in the troop stood and pulled away their drab over-clothes to reveal brightly coloured silks and shimmering scarves. The old man with the plates was drumming away on a *tonbak*, whilst Behrang and Emad appeared beside him bashing tambourines and torturing a reed *duduk*. The women swirled and somersaulted across the stage, the little black girl performing three back-flips, and the one who had been spinning the squares of cloth on her toes was now spinning and spinning on the spot, her face always facing forward. It seemed an impossible feat.

For a long time they entertained us, first the women and the musicians, then the specialty tricks. A man with bulging muscles, and tattoos all over his arms and face, lay down on a bed of nails whilst a dwarf performed somersaults on his chest. When he turned to leave there was blood running down his back, but he didn't appear to notice.

At one point, the little black girl returned with two older girls who looked much like her. They entered the space with a live tiger! Lined up tightly in front of my father, their backs to the tiger which sat patiently waiting for them, they gave him a little red ball and asked him to tuck it inside the belt of the girl he thought the sweetest.

This raised a chuckle from the audience.

My father chose to tuck the ball into the belt of the second tallest girl, who was standing to the left. He did so subtly, whilst looking at the girl on the right, in case the tiger was watching. Then the three girls lay down on the floor and performed an intricate trick of rolling and bouncing over one another. They looked like lace bobbins. Had you tied thread to each of them, they would have woven a pattern.

When they finally became still, the tiger approached, stepping over them one by one. When it reached the end of the line, it turned and walked back to sit on top of the girl beneath whose belt my father had placed the ball.

As she stood up to reveal it, the crowd lost itself in deafening applause. It was a marvellous trick, though I would have applauded simply for the chance to see a tiger so closely.

As well as the acrobats and the jugglers, the dancers and the animal tamers, there were several grotesque spectacles. There was a fat white woman with a grey beard to her knees, teeth missing, and tattoos of dragons up her sagging arms. There was a skinny man with slanted eyes whose head was completely shaven except for a black braid as thick as my arm which hung down his back. His special gifts were being able to hammer an iron nail into his nose, and eat fire!

These formed only the prelude. The little girl with painted eyes on her feet returned leading a boy on a lead. The boy was covered from the top of his head to the tips of his toes in thick, black hair, yet he was still distinguishable as human. This caused a collective intake of breath from the audience. Releasing the boy's collar, the girl produced the same red ball from earlier. She threw it, and the boy chased after it, letting it bounce once before catching it between his teeth and performing a backwards somersault. The onlookers were beside themselves, some laughing so hard they could barely stand up.

By far the most monstrous of these many curiosities was the Kicking Boy. He was very young, no older than Zhubin, though he came in front of us quite willingly. We could tell immediately that we were about to witness something unusual, as his shirt pointed out in front of him as though leading the way. With a little smile, he casually lifted it over his head to stand dressed only in his *şalvar*.

From just above the right of his navel, a small yet perfectly formed leg protruded, along with a tiny, crooked arm.

Horrified, yet unable to look away, we watched as the leg began to kick!

Some of the women turned away and covered their eyes, cooing sympathy for this poor, deformed creature, whilst the men jeered and shouted for him to replace his shirt.

After several moments of this loud reaction, the boy replaced his clothing, made a short bow, and left the room, still smiling. It was the most peculiar thing to witness. It was almost as though he did not understand how his deformity made us feel – that it sickened us.

As we sat there, fearing what might be inflicted upon us next, that same, sad flute struck up. It lulled us all to silence. We were certain it came from the front of the room, and waited expectantly for the musician to step through the door which had been used as the entrance for performers and their animals.

Instead, a slow commotion spread from the back of the room. Having swapped his dull rags for a hooded cloak of many-coloured patchwork, the beak-nosed Mask arrived before us. When he had completed his procession, he slowly turned and took a step towards us, then another. Lowering his flute, his foot hovered before him, just as before.

From the back of the room, a crow cried.

But this time we knew the deception. We had all looked before, and there had been no crow. None of us would be fooled a second time. Instead, most of us laughed in the awkward silence of a trick gone wrong, and some of the men shouted out, calling the Mask a charlatan and a fool.

Before they could draw breath to shout again, a thousand crows filled the hall!

They flooded forward from the coloured cloak like a river of ash, their black hoods thrusting forward beaks as sharp as daggers, their wings a frenzy of discarded feathers. That is how we knew that the crows were real. They vanished almost as soon as they had arrived, yet they left behind a shower of down. As soon as I regained enough sense to move, I reached forward and plucked a piece from the floor.

The coloured cloak had disappeared in the chaos of that moment, and the Mask stood before us dressed in a skin-tight costume of scarlet, with a black cape and a miniature *fez* clipped at an angle. Without the hood to shadow his face, the coffee-brown mask looked even more sinister. In texture it reminded me of Bousseh, the midwife, wrinkled and weathered. It covered his face from the line of his hair, down, over his nose with its huge hooked beak, then further still on either side of his cheeks to the line of his jaw. The only point of visible flesh was his chin, leaving his mouth free to blow the flute.

There was an uncomfortable silence in the room. Those of us who at first thought him a cheap illusionist, or some sort of clown sent in between the main performers, suddenly realised that we were in the presence of a master conjurer.

Anything was possible.

His hand flew to his chest as he dropped to his knees in a fit of coughing.

He coughed and coughed to the point we started to believe this was not part of some trick, and that he was in real distress. One of my mothers, far along the row, rose from her seat to offer her assistance. She had not taken two steps when a white rose appeared on the ground in front of the Mask. One white rose, then many. Every time he coughed, another rose appeared, and then another and another, until the floor was strewn with them. As he took a shaky breath, he clutched once again at his chest and fell to a final coughing fit. With each crack of air from his lungs, the white roses began to turn red.

At this point people began to laugh and hoot their appreciation. For my part, to say that I was mesmerised is to speak only half a truth. I could no more turn my attention away than a rat can turn its attention from the hypnotic stare of the cobra. I would have continued to watch even had he swallowed me whole.

When the performance came to an end, my father called the Mask to him. Instead of leaving through the door with the other performers, he was stopped by the Darougheh, who held out his arm to indicate that my father wished to make his acquaintance.

For a moment, the Mask paused. I observed the briefest of frowns cross my father's brow, which melted to a smile as the Mask came towards us, still in his scarlet costume with its black cape and Turkish cap.

I felt a flutter through my own heart. He was more than a foot taller than me and the fabric he had chosen for an outfit contoured his slim figure, leaving little to the imagination. Growing up in a household of modest dress, I found it difficult not to stare. Memories of the night before plagued me with a mixture of curiosity and revulsion. More frightening than his masculinity was his magic. I had never seen anybody perform the type of tricks he had so effortlessly performed that day. To my mind, I doubted whether they were tricks at all. I looked upon him as some sort of sorcerer.

"Pantalone, I presume?"

The Mask's lips tightened in a smile as he bowed stiffly before my father.

I became aware that his eyes were ringed in black. They looked extremely deep-set: small chips of onyx reflecting back light that danced off our jewellery. I did not know who Pantalone was, and assumed that someone must have informed my father of the performer's name.

My father's white teeth flashed behind his beard. "Well, don't be shy now. Remove your mask and let us take a look at the man who has so enchanted us this past hour."

The Mask did not respond. My father's face began to darken once again, until the Darougheh leaned forward and whispered that the boy did not speak either Persian or Turkic.

"Ah," he nodded, and then proceeded to smile broadly at the Mask whilst miming the motion of removing his disguise. "Yes?"

Still, Pantalone hesitated.

I saw those sunken eyes glance towards me, and then further, to the crowd pressing themselves against one another for a better view.

"Oh, for goodness sake. What language does he speak?" my father growled.

It did not prove necessary for anybody to find the answer to that question. The young man slowly returned his attention to my father and performed the action he had recently mimed.

There was a collective intake of breath as the mask came loose. Once again, women turned their faces away and covered their eyes with their hands, whilst men clucked and shook their heads in wonder.

Myself and my new mother were the only two women to remain unaffected. The sight was indeed a terrible one, but hardly more terrible than the Kicking Boy, or a human dog. His disfigurement was far less entertaining, though.

The kohl around his eyes had enhanced their mystery when covered by the mask. Now, it only served to frame the fact that they were sunken far back from his brow, which hung like a mantelpiece above. More disturbing was the fact that he had no nose, simply two slits in his face where a nose should have been.

What none of us had realised was that his mop of black hair had also been part of the mask. It was sewn in along the top of the leather, and meticulously positioned to disguise the fact that the creature had only a few tufts of his own. It grew in patches from skin so tightly drawn across his skull that he looked for all the world like a living skeleton.

The most curious aspect was that the right side of his face seemed almost unaffected in comparison with the left, where his deformity was further enhanced by the presence of blood-red welts the shape of worm casts, which marred the landscape of his features from his temple to his cheek.

I imagine the correct response ought to have been pity.

After a moment's consideration, my father raised up his hands and began to clap. Encouraged by his example, others did the same. Even those ridiculous women who had hidden behind their hands, peeking out through the gaps between their fingers, now lowered them to applaud.

All the time, I watched the Mask carefully. His expression remained stoic, that same tight-lipped smile which could hardly be called such a thing. He took the clapping as a sign that it was time to replace his mask. Although no one ceased to clap, there were visible signs of relief among the audience.

My father nodded his head. The young man returned the gesture, then turned to leave.

"The fur trader was not lying," I heard him say as he sat down beside me. "Ugliest thing I ever did see."

When I returned to my room that night, I was greeted by an unexpected gift.

There, on my pillow, lay a little doll made of hay. Its arms and legs were fashioned from the plaited stems, whilst its featureless face was a ball of the same. It seemed so crudely made that I thought it had to be a present from Fakhr.

I felt differently when I saw that it wore a simple brooch: a twisted green barley stem, pinned to its heart.

Two things happened that week to make it one of the most memorable and unhappy of my life.

The morning after finding the doll on my pillow, and one day after Uncle Ja'far held me down and taught me what it was to be powerless, I awoke to find the sheets stained with my own blood.

At age eleven, I experienced menarche.

Only, I did not know what that was.

On waking, I knew that something was wrong. I could feel the hot, wet mess between my legs. When I pulled my hand from beneath the covers to find it covered in blood, I began to shake. I truly believed that mother Shokuh's doll had placed a curse on me. I believed myself to be dying.

My breath tightened as I turned my face into my pillow. I was afraid to scream out loud because if someone came they would ask me why I had been bewitched, and I would have to tell them that I had cast the first spell, placing chaos beneath my mother's pillow. I knew that I would not be forgiven for this, and so no one must ever know.

Şelale was my saviour. She came to wash me and dress me for second prayer, and discovered me white as my own sheets, unable to move with fear. When she saw what had happened, she collected me up in her arms.

"Ah, çocukcağız!" she cooed. "My little thing. Please don't be afraid."

She hugged me for a long while, kissing my temple and smoothing back my hair, all the time reassuring me that this was not some deadly curse but instead a sign of life. A sign that I was capable of bringing life into this world. Something natural to all women.

It took a very long time to bring me back to myself. Eventually, she washed me down, taught me how to wrap a pad of clean rag between my legs, and took my soiled sheets away to be washed. I made her promise that she would wash them herself, and that she would tell no one of what had happened.

The second thing that disturbed me that week was that I witnessed my father crying for the very first time. I had been excused from prayers for poor health. All that time, I dreaded that my father would call me to him, to enjoy one of the performances that the gypsies were giving to entertain the palace in my name. Thankfully, he did not, and I was left to empty my womb of its life-giving content in privacy.

On the fourth day, the cramps and the blood subsided, and I found that I had developed a pressing hunger. After noon prayer, I left my room and headed towards the kitchen in search of something to eat. So many people lived within the palace walls that my absence at prayer was hardly noticed. Those I met in the hallway nodded and smiled at me just as they would on any other day, although I lowered my eyes quickly, feeling self-conscious about my new body, especially around the men. I felt that they could see it in me, this difference, as though they could hear the change in me when I breathed. In thinking this, I found myself holding my breath as I passed them.

It was with this irrational mood for company that I made it to the kitchen. I took several flat pieces of *barbari* bread and a hunk of white cheese made from ewe's milk. My plan was to return to eat them in my room.

Halfway down the corridor, I passed my father's study. I would never have stopped had it not been for the sound of someone crying. I was used to my mothers with their wailing and their false compassion, yet this was a sound altogether deeper.

Through the half-open door I could see my father, the Shah himself, head-in-hands behind the desk with the secret drawer. He clutched great fistfuls of his hair whilst Shokuh stood behind him, her hand gently upon his shoulder. She wore that same style of wrap that so suited her slender figure. This time it was dyed deep purple like the robes of the Roman Emperors. It chimed as she leaned to place her cheek against my father's neck. She whispered something I could not make out.

A sound in the corridor caused me to start. It was one of the male servants coming from the kitchen. Reluctantly, I tore myself away and made for my room, where I devoured the bread and cheese with a passion, as though eating away my confusion.

I had never seen my father weak before. To me he was Kaveh, the mighty blacksmith, his apron held aloft to rally his troops, his resolve as strong as steel. If my father had been broken, what hope remained for the rest of us?

That was a dark week for me. I understood very little of the world at that point and could find solace in neither my family nor my own body. Even Shusha, ever ready to help me learn, would not tutor me on my father's business. When I asked he simply replied, "It is a political matter," and would say no more.

By the end of the week, the wound inside of me had healed. I no longer bled, and I no longer craved treats from the kitchen. Şelale took away the last of my rags without a word, and returned with a clean pile of undergarments. From that day on, she knew my cycle better than I knew it myself. Without fail, there would be clean strips of cloth by my bed the night before I bled. I never had to ask her for them, they were simply there.

We met one evening shortly after *Maghrib*. I had just returned from the mosque and the sun was falling softly to its bed. It was a warm afternoon and I had planned to bathe before making my way to the lawn to watch the circus. Şelale had told me again and again about the beautiful horses and the women who stood on their backs.

"They are made from the wind!" she laughed. "Now that you are better, you must come and see for yourself."

I was removing my headscarf when I heard a turtle-dove at my balcony and turned to look. There, sitting on my stone seat, ankle resting casually upon one knee, was Pantalone. He wore loose black şalvar, tied at the waist with a kamar-band. A tight-fitting jacket covered his torso, ending several inches above his waist. It was also black, and sewn with mirrors that flashed like eyes in the last of the light. Around his shoulders he wore the same cloak that he had worn during his performance. This is how I was sure it was him, for the mask was very different. I found myself staring into the perfectly pointed heart of an ornate ivory face, its eyes framed with black diamonds. Gold leaf curled in the pattern of a climbing vine around the temples and the cheeks, but continued further, touching his fleshy lips which were golden too – a mask within a mask.

I was speechless for a moment. Such perfect poise, he looked almost like a painting.

Then I remembered the face beneath that mask, and I remembered what it was to feel powerless.

"What are you doing here?" I cried. "Get out."

He tilted his head.

I turned to my dresser, grabbed the closest thing to hand – a heavy glass paperweight – and hurled it as hard as I could.

He caught it without even flinching.

I opened my mouth to scream, but no sound came as I watched my paperweight transform into a bouquet of flowers before my very eyes.

There were no words inside my lungs. All the air had left me. I simply stared at what could not possibly have happened. Somehow it seemed even more impossible to be happening here, in my room, where no one but my maids should ever be. The circus had owned my father's hall for an evening, turning it into everything they wished it to be. Yet these were my private quarters, somewhere I had assumed safe from all magic and sorcery.

Apparently, I was wrong.

From between the petals of a dozen red roses emerged beautiful white butterflies, so delicate they floated like snowflakes. I took a step closer and held out my hand for one to land on.

I heard the door open behind me and turned.

"Şelale," I called, half laughing. "Şelale, come see!"

"What is it, Sultana?"

"Come see—"

There was no one there.

I would have doubted there ever had been were it not for a handful of forlorn butterflies that remained, looking for flowers in a room without roses.

"Oh. How pretty." She smiled.

For three days I waited in my room between prayers for him to return, but he did not. With every day that passed, I started to doubt what I had seen more and more. When my doubt became unbearable, I went in search of him.

It was late afternoon. The sun had set and fires blazed on the palace lawns. Beneath awnings, my mothers and their children lazed on embroidered cushions whilst servants brought a never-ending supply of dried fruit and nuts. I took a handful of almonds to chew as I explored.

The horses were grazing, docile on their tethers. The tiger was in its cage. The elephant drank from a large pail of water that somebody had brought from the stream. I stopped to watch, and it raised its trunk as though saluting.

At the far end of the South Lawn, a small city of tents had been erected from white canvas and coloured silks. This was where the gypsies lived, and where I felt sure that I would find Pantalone.

I had dressed entirely in black so that I could slip between the tents unnoticed. It was difficult in the dark to avoid the guide ropes and their hidden pegs. More than once I tripped. The tents were so close together that I had to hold my breath to squeeze through the spaces between.

In each tent a different scene was unfolding. I heard babies wailing, and men and women squabbling. I heard musicians practising their flutes and strings, their drums and tambourines. I witnessed between the gaps a man throwing knives, another wrapped in a giant snake, a woman dancing in a line with three dogs that were mimicking her, and a boy balancing a chair on his chin. I must have heard five or six languages and seen almost as many skin colours. It was a rag-tag collection of vagabonds.

Eventually, I came to a small, round tent. I peered in to see the Mask sitting cross-legged on the floor with Shusha. He wore his black costume with the leather, hook-nosed disguise from the hall. My tutor's eyes were shining as he dealt cards into four piles on the ornately woven *gelim*. When he turned them over, one was a pile of Kings, another Queens, the third Jacks and the fourth aces.

"Well done, old man," said the Mask in perfect Turkish. "You could teach me a thing or two." They both laughed as Pantalone collected up the cards and shuffled them into a single deck. "But can you do this?" he asked, flicking his wrist so that the end of his hand formed a perfect fan of the deck, all hearts and diamonds.

Shusha shook his head in wonder.

"That really is quite amazing," he replied, also in Turkish. "Where did you learn all of this?"

"Ah, well–"

I let out a shriek of terror.

Standing right beside me was a black Moor, white teeth gleaming in the dark. He placed his hand on my shoulder and pushed me into the tent.

"Shahzadi!" Shusha exclaimed, scrambling arthritically to his knees so that he could press his head to the floor.

"Get your hands off me," I hissed at the African.

He held them up and took a step back, laughing. There was a bull ring through his nose and the lobes of his ears were stretched in wide Os, like gaping mouths. I recognised him to be the elephant rider I had seen when my father first led the circus onto our lawns.

"Shahzadi, forgive us. We were simply–"

I waved my hand at Shusha. I did not wish to cause him trouble, I simply wanted to see what they were doing.

"Come, will you sit with us?" he asked, straightening and indicating a spare cushion on the rug. I settled myself and they did the same, except for the Moor who had already left.

"He speaks Turkish?" I asked, staring at the Mask.

"And Russian, Latin, and a little Greek. The boy is a polyglot, he has many tongues," Shusha explained.

"Yet you chose to deceive my father? You pretended that you did not understand him when he told you to remove your mask?"

The Mask did not respond. I felt myself shrink beneath his gaze. Those eyes of his, I don't know how to impress upon you just how deep they were. It was as though you were looking at that point in the night sky, the midpoint between stars, where the darkness seems to swallow the light.

"You must think yourself very clever, Pantalone."

He let out a short, humourless laugh.

"Ah, Shahzadi. I believe you may be mistaken," Shusha whispered, leaning carefully towards me. "You see, Pantalone is a character."

"A character?"

"Yes, from the *Commedia dell'Arte*. It is a form of theatre from Western Europe."

"I was dressed as Pantalone," the Mask elucidated. "I am not he."

"So, what is your real name?" The irritation was plain in my voice, for I felt myself the fool and hated it.

"You may call me what you like," he shrugged.

"Fine. Then I shall call you a liar for your tricks."

"If you'll forgive me, Shahzadi, I do not believe that I deceived anyone. It was your father's officer who saw me hesitate and made the assumption that I did not understand."

"You could have corrected him."

"Wouldn't that have been impertinent of me?" The Mask smiled a wide, perfect smile that was quite disarming.

"Still, you should not have hesitated to obey my father's command."

He did not respond to that, but we both knew in that heavy silence that someone with features as fine as his own would always hesitate before unveiling them in public.

Shusha walked me to my room that night, in time for final prayer. As we walked, I wanted to ask him again about my father, about what had caused his distress. However, I was not someone to try the same approach twice. Knowing that I would only receive some partial answer, I found myself telling him that I wished to be educated in Politics.

"That is a weighty subject," he said, stroking his silver beard. "What interests you?"

"Everything," I replied. "I hear that in some countries in Europe people are allowed to elect their own leaders? They say that the Queen of England is not truly her own mistress?"

He laughed at this and shook his head. "Little one, no ruler is absolute."

"My father is."

"Your father–" he paused then, measuring his words. "Yes. Your father is." He uttered this with a slight sigh that suggested he would rather agree than go further. "Shahzadi," he said, after a moment. "Forgive me, but I do not think that your mind is suited to politics."

The next afternoon, the Mask appeared in my room again.

"I do not recall inviting you," I said, walking in to find him silhouetted against my balcony.

"Why do you always remain in your room?" he asked.

"I don't."

"Your father brings you the greatest circus in all the kingdoms, yet you spend every night in your room."

"I have been unwell."

As my eyes adjusted, I saw that he was dressed as the first visit, with his ivory mask, the one with delicate trails of gold across it. For some reason, his presence did not alarm me. I suppose that must seem strange, that a young woman should walk into her private quarters to find a man on her balcony, and not be alarmed? Well, perhaps I was not like other women my age.

"My father would kill you if he knew you were here. Men aren't allowed in the harem."

"You are not in the harem."

"Would you like to tell him that?"

The Mask laughed. "Shahzadi, I assure you, I am far too ugly for your father to consider me a threat. Every woman in the palace saw my face that day. They have hardly been beating down my tent to get a second look."

"Then show me a trick," I said, taking a step towards him.

"Ah. You like those, do you?"

I shrugged.

He stepped into my room and held out a clenched fist towards me, turning it upright.

"Here, see what I have in my hand."

Cautiously, I began to peel back his fingers, then leapt back with a shriek.

My hands were still clamped over my mouth as he wiggled his fingers in front of me. I know what I saw, and he knew that I had seen it. There had been a hole through the middle of his hand! I had clearly seen the floor through a circle in his palm. Yet there he stood, his hand perfectly whole.

"How did you do that?" I demanded.

"Do what?"

"How did you make a hole through your hand?"

"What hole?"

I glared at him.

"You are not natural," I said.

"You are seeing things. Too much time in your room. You should get out more, enjoy the sunshine and the sea air."

He said this flippantly, to tease me, but deep down it stung. It was easy for him to say, this *ayyār* who could travel between cities and even continents, stealing what he needed to survive. How many mighty palaces had he slept behind, and how many rare animals must he have seen? In that moment, I envied him more than I envied Mahmoud his fine horse.

"Take off your mask."

I watched his smile fade. "No."

"Take it off, I say. I am your Shahzadi, and I demand it."

"I will not remove my mask, and you do not rule me."

"I shall have you flogged!"

"You would need to catch me first."

I lunged at him, catching the edge of his cloak. As I pulled, it unravelled in my hand and he was gone.

Someone laughed in my ear.

I turned and turned, but could not see him.

"Come out! Show yourself!"

That laugh again, louder and louder.

"Come out!" I screamed.

My scream was cut short by the tightening of my throat. I reached a hand up, but could not pull the cord away. He stood directly behind me, so close that I could smell him, a heady mixture of sandalwood and myrrh.

As I stopped struggling, he released the pressure. I could feel the heat of him against my back as he whispered in my ear.

"Shall we start again?"

I nodded, but continued to hold to the cord for a moment before allowing him to slip it over my head. It was a red cord, one that I recognised from the curtains in my father's study. He had fashioned it into a noose, the very sight of which caused my eyes to widen.

"A little trick I picked up in the Punjab."

He smiled again, and the sight of this figure in black, clutching a red noose, stirred something deep within me. I told you that I was not like other women of my age. That is true. Whereas they would have called for their servants and had him strung from the balcony with the self-same rope he had used to assault them, I found myself ringing with deeper desire.

For nights afterwards, I would wake sweat-drenched between my sheets, my hand pressed to my neck, delightfully dreaming that he stood behind me once again, that his scarlet cord held within its mercy my life or death. Whenever I awoke to this fantasy, the smell of him was always thick on my pillow. Looking back, and knowing him as I came to know him, I would not be surprised if his own desires caused him to sit there of a night, my sleeping head resting against his lap, his Punjab lasso wrapped across my throat.

It was the next night that we went to Sari for the first time. Although we would go many times over the coming year, this was the one night that I will always recall most perfectly. For him it was a simple journey along a road to visit a village that he had never been to before. For me, it was my first night of freedom.

"Perhaps this one," the Mask said, holding up a hooded cloak made from simple brown cloth.

I held it between my fingers and announced that it felt itchy.

"If you wish to look common, you need to dress like a commoner."

"Is this really what they wear?"

He laughed and held up a black baize cloak instead. "What about this?"

I allowed him to place it over my shoulders, then I wrapped my arms inside and pulled it across my front to make sure that it would cover me entirely. "This will do," I conceded.

"Make sure your ṣalvar aren't too loose. Wear a dark shirt and tuck it into the top of them, then tie with a kamar-band. If you don't have one, I'll bring you one. You need to be able to run fast, like a boy."

"Run?"

"And climb." He smiled.

I didn't ask any more than that. I trusted him implicitly. After all, he had travelled the world, and where had I been?

He came after *Maghrib*, and I told Şelale that I would pray last prayer alone in my room, so there was no risk of being found out. The greatest problem was sneaking out of the palace grounds without being seen by my mothers or the servants. I begged my friend to turn us both invisible, but he told me that I should learn that trick for myself.

He wore a simple leather mask that covered all but his mouth and chin. It was smooth, without Pantalone's large hooked nose. In the dark, with his hood pulled up, you could not tell that he did not have a face. For my part, I wore my hair pinned and wrapped beneath a simple black cloth. He smeared my upper lip with kohl so that I would look like a boy from a distance.

"Stay close, and do exactly as I say," he told me as we stood at the border between my father's lawn and the dirt track that would eventually lead us to Sari. He could not believe that I had never been before.

"I went to Tabriz once, when I was a very little girl. That is the problem, though. I was too young to remember," I said.

That was the night of a million wonders. It took almost an hour to walk from the palace into Sari. With every footstep the air became thick with the smell of charred dough, sweet, boiled rice and *esfand* seeds, which the townspeople burned to ward off evil eye.

My great-great-grandfather had made Sari his capital many years before, but fighting amongst local tribes and the people of the hills forced a move to Tehran. Now it was simply the capital of Mazandaran. I had heard Shusha say that it was nothing compared to its former glory, yet to me it was everything.

Everywhere I heard Persian and Mazandarani being spoken, and stopped to listen to the conversations.

"...owes me money for the carpet he bought last week..." one angry woman in a green scarf was telling a trader selling fried squid, with no small amount of finger wagging.

Another woman, round and fat like mother Ezzat, was hurrying her children home with threats of Allah's disapproval, whilst a young girl looked up at her father and asked: "Will Mama be home soon?" The look on the man's face spoke of something uncertain, or sad, but we moved on before I could decipher what it meant.

"Here," the Mask said, pushing a paper cone of squid into my hands. I had not even seen him steal it. I crammed the crispy pieces into my mouth, chewing as the oils ran down my chin. It was the most delightful meal I had ever eaten.

Horses, goats and chickens vied for space between the sandaled, shoed and barefoot people they shared the roads with. Everywhere there was noise. Along with familiar languages, I heard many others that I did not know. Rather than one city, Sari seemed to me to be a patchwork of different foods, clothes and customs. I had always assumed my father's palace to contain a diversity of people, with mothers from all over Iran, and our servants from even further. Yet, in experiencing Sari for the first time, I realised just how small my world truly was.

I did not want that night to end. We walked until our feet were sore, and the candles in the windows had all burned out. It was only when I saw the faint glow on the horizon that I realised we should turn for home. We arrived just before second prayer. I would have gone straight to mosque if my friend had not stopped me and wiped the fake moustache from my lips. I returned to my room to change. However, the moment I sat on my bed to remove my sandals, my eyes closed and I fell asleep.

We did the same two nights later. This time, we stole food from a family's kitchen whilst the wife was berating her husband in another room for being lazy. How mad she must have been, returning to find their supper gone.

I stepped out of the shadows once, to play a game of *naqala* with a young boy. He had hollowed cups in the earth with his hands and filled them with tamarind seeds. My friend stayed in the shadows, unwilling to play, and the boy seemed happy simply to have company. He looked a lonely child there by himself. I would never have played such a game with Mahmoud or Fakhr, yet there was something enchanting about playing with this boy. He had no idea who I was. To him, I was anybody.

That night, when we returned to my room, my friend lay down next to me for a while.

I asked this time, rather than demanded, and he allowed me to remove his mask.

In the dark, lit only by the fading moon, I struggled with myself. I wanted to touch his face, to explore with more than merely my eyes. Yet what little I could see caused my gut to twist. It was painful to look upon him, as though I had swallowed glass. I raised myself up on one elbow and leaned in closer.

There was no smell to his skin, like you would expect from rotting flesh. His skull was terribly misshapen, as though it had collapsed behind his left temple, bulging towards the back. Without the bright blood-red of the worm casts, and the blue-black peeling of his scalp, the most noticeable thing in our half-lit world was the absence of his nose. Grotesque is not even a word for it. I could have placed two fingers over the cavities and prevented him from breathing, yet the thought of touching that face was more than I could bring myself to countenance.

"Where do you come from?" I asked, lying back beside him.

"Europe."

"Yes, but where in Europe?"

He took a breath, sighing as though this were a tiresome thing to ask. "France. Near Rouen."

I laughed. "Near where?"

He smiled in the dark as he repeated the word, his thick accent making it sound like a soft jumble of vowels. I tried to repeat the sound and we both ended up giggling. Then he spoke more in this way, and I closed my eyes, each syllable tickling my ear as his voice wrapped itself around me, thick and rich and golden.

"*C'est un p'tit oiseau qui prit sa voleé, La branche était sèche, l'oiseau est tombé, Je m'suis cassé l'aile, Je veux me soigner et me marier...*"

"What does that mean?"

"It is a cradle song. One that mothers sing to their children."

"I know one like that," I said, and sang him a little in Persian: "*la la la la, gole poneh, bekhab bach'che, delam khune.*" *Sleep my child, my heart is broken.* I felt my eyes flush hot and sore, and so I stopped.

"Did your mother sing that to you?" he asked, smoothing my hair from my face.

"No," I replied. "My mother died."

"Well, that is something. My mother wished I had."

"What is your name?" I asked. "I cannot keep calling you for your mask."

"Then call me Vachon, it was my father's name."

"You do not have a name of your own?"

"If I had, I have forgotten it." He saw me frown and sighed again. "I left home many years ago. My father thought it would be best. He tried, but my mother..."

"Where did you learn your tricks?"

He remained silent for a while, until I thought perhaps he would not tell me.

"The first circus I joined was a small sideshow in Paris. They exhibited me..." He paused again. "They exhibited me as The Human Corpse. When that is your future, you search for something better."

"So, you became a conjuror?"

"I became many things."

I still could not bring myself to touch his face, but I pulled him a little closer and rested my head against his chest.

In the morning, he was gone.

For the next three days I was a victim of my father's will. As we had just celebrated the New Year, he decided to buy all of his women new outfits. A camel train of cloth merchants arrived from Tehran, and all of us were gathered into the main hall to choose our fabrics and to have our measurements taken.

Most all of my mothers seemed in character that day. Mother Arezoo, being the eldest and most responsible, chose dowdy grey silks with ordinary silver trim. Mother Tala, befitting her precious name, dressed herself and her twin girls head-to-toe in golden fabric which shimmered in the light. She did not seem to care whether she cost her husband a fortune, so long as everybody knew that he could afford it. Mother Nazgol, one of my father's less enlightened conquests, showed enthusiasm rather than taste, opting for some ghastly European print with white daisies set against gaudy pink. I couldn't imagine any cut that would make that cloth look flattering.

The only one of my mothers to act strangely was Ezzat. She approached me whilst I was sifting through green and blue lace. She held up a malachite bracelet next to the sample I was considering.

"Here," she said. "This would go nicely, do you think?"

I levelled her with my gaze, but she took no notice.

"You're such a pretty girl," she continued, touching my cheek with the back of her hand. "You deserve pretty things." She placed the bracelet on the table beside me and walked away.

Mother Ezzat had never given me anything without granting it in full sight of my father, to win his approval. I picked the bracelet up and turned it in my hand. Then I placed it once again on the table and moved toward aquamarines.

When you grow up in a palace full of jealous women, you learn to mistrust kindnesses offered too freely.

♦ 4 ♦

On the first day that my father's enthusiasm for clothes began to wane and he left us alone in the great hall with our buttons and our lace, that was when I made my escape. I had finally settled on plum purple with gold trim. The best I could do to help the tailor transform my material into a dress was to leave him to it.

Of course, my first thought was to find Vachon.

I made my way to his tent, through the city on the South Lawn. He was not there, nor in any of the other tents that I had become familiar with. I was about to give up when I heard laughter and decided to follow it. As with the North Lawn, the South Lawn had a stream running beside it, though much smaller. There was a dam built from sticks and pebbles, to pool the water so that the performers could lower their buckets and collect enough for their needs.

By this pool, I saw Vachon with the little Indian girl, the one with charcoal skin and eyes on her feet. I watched them rolling by the water. He tickled her, and she cupped her hands in the pool and showered him with water.

I felt my cheeks redden.

At first, I thought about confronting them. I had not seen Vachon for days, and here he was, flirting with a circus whore. No, I needed time to consider this. To decide the right form of punishment.

Quietly, I slipped back through the city of tents. Once I was free of the ropes, I began marching across the grass, carried forward on a tide of furious energy. I'm not entirely sure what caused me to look up. I think I must have seen her in the corner of my eye.

She saw me, too.

Mother Azin, the prettiest of all my father's wives, caught and held my surprised glance as she stepped from the palace roof, plummeting to the ground, where the hard earth opened her delicate face like an egg.

I was too stunned to move for several moments. If it had not been for the crowd that gathered around the wall, I might almost have believed that what I witnessed had not actually happened. But there were people, lots of people. There were cries from the women and shouts from the men.

I decided to slip away to my quarters.

Şelale found me there some time later.

"Oh, çocukcağız. What a terrible thing!"

"Mother Azin is dead," I stated.

"Yes. How did you know?"

"I saw her fall."

"Oh! My dear, dear one."

She came to the bed and bundled me up in her arms, as though she had forgotten I was her mistress. Her eyes were red-raw from crying and her hair slid from beneath her headscarf, causing an unruly mess of curls to plaster themselves to her forehead.

"Why did she jump?" I asked.

"Oh, such a sad, sad thing–"

I slapped her hard across the face, and she drew back.

"I'm sick of it, you hear me? I am not a child any more. You all tread around me as though I need protecting. Well, I don't. What is going on that I do not know? I will have an answer."

She simply stared at me, wide-eyed. "I do not know," she said eventually. "I do not know why she jumped."

"Then what use are you to me? I am the first-born of the Shah's children. I have a right to know what happens beneath his roof. From now on, you are to be my eyes and ears. Do you understand? I want to know every detail."

She did not respond, so I repeated myself until she nodded. Then I dismissed her.

I was angry at the secrets all around me. Why did my father cry? Why did Mother Azin take her own life? Why did Ezzat bring me gifts? What comfort did Vachon find in his little Indian slut?

For two of these answers, I did not have to wait long.

I returned from Maghrib to find Ezzat sitting on my bed. She had lit my lamps and the smell of their scented oil made the air between us heavy. I felt as though I had walked into a dream, for Ezzat had never visited my quarters before. Few of my mothers ever did. They used to come by when I was younger. When they thought perhaps I was lonely here by myself, or when they were looking for their own children and wondered if I might be playing with them. They stopped once they realised that I loved my own solitude and despised their offspring.

"What do you want?" I asked, with no formality.

Ezzat's fat round face looked pinched in the glow of the lamps. The shadows fell into the wrinkles around her lips, causing her to age by a century.

"We need to talk."

"We need do no such thing. You may leave now."

Her shoulders rose as though she were about to retort. Instead, she lowered her gaze to the floor and continued in a measured voice. "Are you not at all curious about today?"

"Azin? No, what business is it of mine."

Of course I was curious, but I had already sent Şelale to find the answer for me. I was not about to barter information with that div. It would probably cost me more than I was willing to pay.

"More of your business than you know."

"What do you mean by that?"

She shifted slightly on the edge of my bed, then looked up. Her eyes had changed. They seemed almost desperate.

"Afsar, I know that you and I have not always seen eye-to-eye—"

I snorted. That was putting it mildly.

"But you must believe me. Both of our lives are on the line. Last night, your father signed a death warrant for Azin."

"Why?" I asked, genuinely surprised. "She was the prettiest of you all."

Ezzat flushed at this and glanced down briefly. I'd noticed that this was her way of controlling her temper. "I think that is precisely why. Your father came to believe that she was impatient with him. That she had found love with another man. Perhaps even with a servant."

"Who?"

"No, that is just it, Afsar. She had not. I know she had not, because I truly knew her. Azin was beautiful, yes, but she only had eyes for your father. She would no more take a common lover than you would–"

"Than I would what?"

"Never mind. It is not important. What I am telling you, is that someone told lies about Azin to your father."

"It wasn't me."

"No, I wasn't suggesting that you had. Who else might your father trust enough to stone one of his own wives to death for?"

It slowly dawned on me.

"Shokuh?"

"I fear so."

"Why are you telling me this?"

Ezzat sucked her tongue for a moment as though it were hard-boiled sugar.

"You and I are not friends, Shahzadi. We never have been. But we are family. I would no more hurt you physically than I would expect you to hurt my son. Your mothers are worried, child. We have seen this new wife, Shokuh, and there is much to be afraid of. Your father loves you, Afsar. If he will listen to anyone, it is you. You can protect us."

Later that night, Şelale came to tell me the same story. A rumour had begun that Azin and a servant had been caught cavorting, though no one knew the name of this servant or how long the supposed affair had been going on. My father had signed her death warrant, and another of the staff, a serving girl who was close to Arezoo, had told my eldest mother before it was served. Arezoo had broken the news to Azin, who was inconsolable. Rather than suffer the bloody humiliation of a public stoning, she had climbed to the top of the palace and chosen a quick death by her own hand.

It was clear that my father did not know who the informant had been, otherwise she would have been whipped. After Azin's death, the girl had simply fled. One of many young girls working at the palace who would never be missed. Before leaving, she had apparently told Mother Arezoo that it was Shokuh who had told my father of his prettiest wife's deceit. The girl said that my father had been reluctant at first, but that Shokuh had warned him of the damage it would cause to his reputation if he was not seen to be strong on this matter.

"Do you want your wives to play you for a fool?" she had asked him.

When Şelale came to the end of her story, I asked her this question:

"Do you think that Mother Shokuh is like my grandmother?"

Her dull brown eyes held mine for a moment, uncertain how to respond.

"Yes," she said eventually. "In ambition, very much so."

The events of the rest of that week are as much a blur as the view from a speeding carriage.

My first fall.

I went to my father's office at a time when I knew that he would be there with Mother Shokuh. She had cast aside her dark silks in favour of brash red. There was no doubt any longer who my father favoured most.

"I have heard what you have done to protect my father's reputation," I told her, in plain view of the Shah.

Shokuh's eyes narrowed. This witch who had returned my curses manyfold, who had killed one of the kindest of my own mothers, now dared to show disdain for me. Was she expecting a scene? Was I to scream like the child she thought I was? Should I call her a liar, and implore my father to come to his senses?

She waited for the challenge.

"Though I can barely overcome the sorrow it causes me to say this," I began, "I believe that Mother Ezzat knew of Azin's lies. I believe she helped her to keep them."

My father said nothing, he simply stared at me from behind his desk. Dark rings beneath his eyes suggested that he had forgone sleep in favour of the contents of his secret drawer.

"I see," Shokuh said quietly. "Thank you, Afsar, for your loyalty. It means a great deal to your father and to me."

Her voice was thick as honey. It must have seduced my father like a peri. This dark-winged angel, fallen to earth and unwilling to leave again without him. Sucking the energy from the palace to feed her own bright blaze.

I admired her for it.

Who holds to a tiresome past when the future could be glorious? Certainly not I. Ezzat disappeared from our happy little home some days later, I am not entirely sure when. Her son, the great goat-god heir of forgettable progeny, was given to Tala to finish raising. I think he lived to at least nine.

My second fall.

I somehow found myself by the pool behind the tent city one day. By coincidence, that little black girl was there also. Her name was Ishya, and she was not as young as I had thought. She was almost my age, only small for it. Our conversation was stinted as I spoke no Marathi and she spoke very little Farsi. I managed to discern that she was from Nagpur in central India and that she was not related to the other two girls who performed the tiger trick with her.

I invited her to come to Sari with me the next night.

We left under cover of darkness, shortly after *Isha*. This was the first time that I had been to the town by myself, and I had made her promise to tell no one. She was so trusting, like a little lamb. I almost changed my plans when I saw how excited she was. Her teeth flashed every time she smiled, and she smiled a lot. Perhaps if she had been like me, I would not have done what I did. But she was not like me. She may have been my age, yet she had travelled half the world already. She had eaten foods I could not even pronounce, seen wonders I had only imagined in dreams. A life is not measured in years but in experiences, and she had lived enough.

It was easy once I had made up my mind. Azin had given me the idea. We crouched in a tree to look through a window as a woman breastfed her baby, trying to stop it from crying.

Ishya turned to smile at me, and I pushed her.

I didn't even have to push very hard. The branch was narrow and her grip had relaxed. She was so surprised that she didn't even scream, hitting the ground with a dull thud. When I climbed down the tree to check that she was dead, I saw that her head was bent at a funny angle. Shusha had taught me that there are certain things in the human body that, once broken, cannot be repaired. The back is one, the heart another, and then the neck.

I knew that it was done, so I dragged her body into the bushes and covered it with fronds. I was careful, but perhaps not as careful as I should have been, for I reasoned that nobody would ever be able to identify this little Indian girl.

She came from nowhere. She had no family. She returned to nothing.

It was not the next day, but the one after that when I was woken by screams.

I had returned to bed after first prayer and it was only just starting to become light outside. The screams were so loud and went on for such a time that the whole palace was woken. By the time I reached the South Lawn, my father was ahead of me, tying the sash of his sleeping jacket as he ran.

You cannot begin to understand how I felt that morning, standing there before the tiger's cage. At first, I thought there had been some terrible accident. The beast sat there, dopey as the day he sat waiting for the girls to lie still so that he could sniff out the ball. Vachon had explained that trick to me. He found it so easily because they kept the ball with the dried fish that he was awarded for good behaviour. The scent was not strong enough to offend the audience, but the tiger, with its animal knowledge, could find it hidden in a tub of offal. He had also informed me that Eirik, as the tiger was named, was perfectly harmless because he had no claws and no teeth.

That is why the scene before me made no sense, and why the events that followed were so terribly tragic.

Eirik's chops were soaked with the little Indian girl's blood. She lay between his massive matted paws like a discarded doll. Her throat was open from one ear to the other. Eirik would dip his head now and then to lick the cut, perfectly unaware of the horror his natural thirst instilled in those who saw it.

I was frozen to the spot. How had she come to be in the tiger's cage when she had died so far away? How could she be covered in blood when her heart had long ceased to beat?

My father called for silence.

The men of the circus held their wives' faces away from the gruesome spectacle. They parted to allow the Shah to approach. He stood, staring for a moment, taking in the full extent of what had happened.

With a look of resolution, he turned towards the Darougheh, who handed him his miquelet. I opened my mouth to cry out – to tell him that Eirik was innocent – but before I had time to draw breath, my father had fired with perfect precision.

The tiger slumped forward, his head pressed against the iron bars, lips curling against them as his face slid down, creating the type of obtuse leer that men develop when they drink. There was so much blood that it was impossible to tell which belonged to the girl, and which to the beast.

"Oh, Eirik," I whispered.

I knew that I could not tell anyone. What good would it do? How could I ever make anybody believe that the girl was not killed by the tiger without implicating myself? Even if I could, the animal would remain dead and nothing I said would resurrect it.

I found myself searching the crowd, wondering who might call me out. Since I had thrown in my lot with Shokuh over Ezzat, I strongly suspected that she may have had me followed. Sometimes I would return to my room only to ask Şelale whether she believed anything to have been moved.

"I do not think so, Sultana," she would say, frowning at my comb, or my bed sheets, or whatever else I happened to be frowning at.

In truth, I think my own conscience had been casting a shadow on the wall, causing me to see things that were not there. I did not feel good about what I had done to Ezzat, or to Ishya, but Shusha had been wrong, you see. I was good at politics. I knew when to smile and when to act. And I knew how to win.

Long after the bodies had been removed and the cage washed down, I stood on the roof, watching the scene below. The other two girls who had performed the ball trick came to lay flowers. Even Behrang and Emad, the clowns, came to sprinkle blossom and say their prayers. There was a subdued atmosphere in the camp after that. A strong wind blew in from the north, causing the city of tents to flutter like restless doves.

An argument ensued between some of the men from the circus and Farzan, my father's treasurer at the palace. The men wanted payment for the tiger, who they said had been a valuable asset to the show. The argument was really only for display. Nobody truly believed that they had wanted to retain a man-eater, but Farzan played along, reciting the words he knew were expected of him, telling the troupe that they would receive not one penny, and if they didn't like it they could leave.

That was what the men had really come for: permission to leave. I heard the argument from the lawn, where I sat watching the sky darken as a storm approached. Goosebumps rose against my flesh but I did not move. I listened as the men grumbled and gave in, telling my father's long-suffering go-between that they would never again grace the lawns of Mazandaran, and that they would be gone by the next afternoon.

Thunder clapped across the sky as they uttered that last word, just as the heavens opened. First one drop, leaving a dark blot on the dust, then a thousand drops, turning the dust to mud.

I pulled my headscarf as far forward as I could, draping it across the backs of my hands like a porch. My sandals slapped against puddles as I ran to the back of the palace, desperate to find Vachon. The circus could ride their pink-plumed horses into hell for all I cared, but he could not leave.

I wouldn't allow it.

I searched until it grew dark, the muezzin's cry rising and falling with my own hope. My clothes were soaked through. I had peered behind the flap of almost every tent, tripping once or twice on the ropes, landing on my knees in the mud. All of the tents were packed with gypsies. Vachon may well have been among them, but I could not see him, and I could not go in to ask. The mood of the circus had changed dramatically since my father shot their tiger. Those who did brush past me in the rain only scowled and continued on.

When I arrived at the mosque for Maghrib, I was admonished by Arezoo.

"Afsar, is that any way to greet your Lord?" she asked, frowning at my sodden, mud-stained dress.

"No," I admitted, slipping off my sandals and continuing through to the women's side. I did not care. I needed Allah's forgiveness for what I had done. Perhaps if he forgave me, as he must forgive a daughter of Islam, then he would also return Vachon to me.

The next morning, after Fajr, I climbed to the top of the palace and huddled there in my blanket. Few of the gypsies were Muslims, and even those who professed to be paid little attention to our mosque. By the light of the moon, I could already make out shadows moving between the tents. The sound of small children wailing for more sleep. The members of the circus were beginning to pack their things.

By the time second prayer was called, half of the tents were folded into neat piles on the lawn. I had watched carefully from my position, but there was no sign of my masked friend.

After second prayer, I sat on a bench along the wall so that I could better see the faces of the people who came and went. I thought perhaps Vachon might be avoiding me and that he was hiding behind a disguise.

As the last cart was loaded, with the help of the elephant's strong trunk, I felt a heavy sensation in my heart. Some of my brothers and sisters had come to walk the caravans to the gates of the palace, but I could hardly find the strength to stand up.

Returning to my room, I found a single scarlet curtain cord lying on my pillow, twisted into the shape of a Punjab lasso.

I knew in that instant that he had left me, and that he had done so without a final goodbye.

Lying on my bed, clutching that lasso to my chest, I cried myself to sleep and did not wake until evening.

For the next week, I practised with that lasso. There was a private garden behind my father's courtyard that few people visited. In it there stood a worn stone plinth whose statuette had long since left for better climes. I placed various objects on top of this plinth, from shoes to books, and tried to hook them through the hole. It was harder than I had anticipated and more often than not I would miss, gathering only grass.

I ignored all calls to prayer that week, performing only Fajr and Isha in my room. When Şelale asked, I told her to tell the imam that I had taken ill. That is the week I came to know how little my father truly cared, for he sent no one to check upon me and my lie was never discovered.

With each failed throw I grew angrier. There was a fire burning in my belly and I could not put it out. I hadn't loved Vachon, for who could love a face like that? But he had been my friend. He had come to see me when others did not, and he did not come to ask for anything, simply to entertain me, to fill my room with butterflies and turn my paperweight to roses. He had been more interesting than all the rest of the palace put together, more complex than Shusha's encyclopaedic knowledge of languages, funnier than mother Ezzat in a temper, softer than Ṣelale's skin and more mischievous than Behrang. He had been all of them, only better.

The cord whipped through the air, scuffing dust from the plinth and separating wildflowers from their stalks as I dragged it back towards me, empty.

Again, and again, and again.

"What are you trying to catch?"

I turned to see the gardener's son standing beneath the archway in the hedge, the one that ran all the way around the secret garden and hid it from the palace. I pulled the back of my hand across my upper lip to wipe away the beads of sweat that had formed.

"What do you want?" I snapped.

"I am sorry for disturbing you, Shahzadi." He bowed his head and turned to leave, then turned back. "Would you like me to teach you?"

Crossing the space between us, he held out his hands and I placed the lasso in them, stepping away. He held the end against his palm, beneath his thumb, then coiled the rest of the rope loosely around his hand. In his other hand he held the loop, throwing it into the air a couple of times to feel the weight of it. Studying the silver jug I had placed on the plinth, he waved the noose over his shoulder three or four times before throwing it forward, lunging on his right leg. As it flew forward towards the plinth, he opened his other fist, all but the thumb, allowing the rope to uncoil.

Placing the silver jug in my hand, he bowed again with a shy smile.

"Where did you learn to do that?" I asked.

"It's just a game we play, my brother and I, with the cook's sons."

"Do it again," I said, replacing the jar on the plinth.

When he handed me the jug for the second time, I agreed to let him teach me.

All that week we practised. I learned that his name was Shahab, like the shooting stars that fall on winter nights. When the sun caught his eyes, their rich brown glittered with gold, and I remembered how nervous he had been that night before my father returned, when he asked for my hand in a dance.

His own hands were rough, and there was still dirt beneath his nails, but I did not mind him touching me to show me how to hold the lasso. I improved quickly under his tutelage. Before long, I was able to snap an apple from the plinth to my hand. Not at all easy, as the noose of the Punjab lasso does not close around its victim. Moving a small object relies on the speed of its momentum. Killing someone relies on their surprise to allow you to get close enough to twist.

Though that was a detail I would not learn until some weeks later.

We practised and practised, Shahab and I. Within two weeks I could hook a ball, a cup and a melon. Within three, I could drop my noose around a stuffed goat and a hat stand. On the fourth week, Shahab allowed me to practise on him, standing still at first, and then running and ducking around the plinth.

"Very good!" he laughed, pulling it back over his head as he walked toward me. "But keep hold of the other end."

"You moved too fast."

"Things will, when you try to catch them."

We sat in the shade of a silk flower tree. He pulled a brown paper parcel from his bag, two apples and a flask of water. Unfolding the parcel, he held it up, offering me one of the honeyed dates inside. It tasted so sweet on that first summer day.

"What's it like?" he asked me. "Being a princess?"

Nobody had ever really asked me that before. Almost everybody I came into contact with already was a princess or a prince.

"It's all right."

"You don't get lonely?"

I stared at him.

"Sorry. It's just, I see you sometimes in your window. I wonder why you don't live with the other women?"

"Because I am the first born."

He hesitated, conflicted over something more he wanted to ask.

"That makes sense," he said, looking down at the dates.

"And, no. I am not lonely. I like my own company."

"I see that."

After we had finished the apples and the water, we returned to practising.

"May I try?" he asked with a smile, coiling the cord around his hand. "I've never caught a princess before."

I laughed and ducked behind the plinth.

"You won't today," I shouted, popping my head up for only a second.

As my head bobbed back down, I heard the noose land above me. "Missed!"

I gave him a moment to wind the rope back in, then bolted like a wild horse, attempting to run a full circle around him and get back to the safety of the stone.

"Missed again!" I laughed, as I completed my mission.

"I don't want to throw it when you're running so fast. I might hurt you."

"What an excuse! You would prefer I stand still and *allow* you to capture me?"

"It would help."

I peered over the top of the plinth.

"Well, that's hardly a game, but if it's the only way you can–"

"It is not the only way! If I hurt you, even by accident, your father would have me shot."

"Very well."

I stepped out from my refuge and stood perfectly still, arms straight by my sides.

The noose whistled through the air and landed in a perfect O around my neck. I couldn't help but clap my hands.

Before I could raise them to remove the cord, Shahab had wound in the rope, standing before me with a smile on his face. The sun hit his eyes and they glowed golden in its light. I thought how handsome he looked.

"I've caught my princess," he smiled. "What shall be my ransom?"

There were no words in my mouth as he leaned in to kiss me.

I was wrong about women's bodies! I was wrong about breasts and buttocks and bellies. I wanted them all, immediately.

Shahab's kiss was like a meteor, its impact blowing my past away and leaving only a crater of pure longing deep inside me. When I opened my eyes, he was all that I saw. Beautiful, handsome, glorious Shahab with eyes like the sun and lips like the heavens.

When he pulled back he looked serious, but all I could do was smile, which, in turn, cause him to smile, until we were both laughing. He leaned in to kiss me again, and again, and again.

For six perfect days our games with the Punjab lasso were forgotten. Even my fury at Vachon's abandonment was forgotten. We took long walks through the woods, out of sight of the palace, we bathed our worn feet in the cool stream, and we told each other stories in the shade of our secret garden. I would rest my head on his chest and listen to his voice, warm and gentle, rolling up from within him. More than anything, I loved the way he smelled. There was nothing artificial about him. He did not powder himself with styrax like the carpet traders' sons, or in frankincense like a prince. He simply smelled of the earth.

On the seventh day, I waited for him to appear beneath my window, our sign that he had finished his chores and was free to go walking. Only, on the seventh day, he never came.

I looked for him at prayer, but he was not there.

Shortly after *Asr*, Şelale came to my room.

"Your father wishes you present in the lounge," she informed me.

When I arrived in the lounge, I found it to be crowded. My father sat, a little slouched, in a large gilt chair. I could smell as I walked in that they had been drinking alcohol, and a large decanter of something Shusha had described as 'Scotch' sat on a table by the far wall. Several of my uncles and cousins were present, as were the Darougheh and a number of servants. I was the only female.

The Shah patted an empty chair and I went to sit beside him.

"Afsar, my dear. Where have you been these many days? We have missed you around the palace."

"Nowhere, father," I said carefully. "Walking."

"Well, if you were walking, you must have been somewhere?"

My smile felt strained.

"A little bird told me that you have a new trick, eh?"

I shook my head, slowly.

"Don't be modest." He clapped his hands and called for the table which held the decanter to be cleared and placed in the centre of the room. "My little girl has been inspired by the circus!" he shouted, causing everyone in the room to turn and look at us. "Come, show us what you have learned."

"Really, I—"

"Put that book on the table," he called to one of the servants. "Stand it upright." He grabbed me firmly by my wrist and threw me to my feet. "Here, this is right, isn't it?" My father handed me a lasso, tied from a black curtain cord. "Have I done it right?"

I nodded and took the rope.

This was not the first time in my life that my father had asked me to perform in front of an audience. When I was six or seven, he had me sing an entire saga from the *Shahnameh*, and when I was ten I gave a brief performance on the qanun. Brief because I was so terrible at it. He wished to praise my limited achievements whilst sparing the ears of his guests.

This felt like something altogether different.

"Come, Afsar, don't be shy. Your family are waiting to see what you can do."

I turned to the table and began to wind the cord around my sweating palm. The book looked impossibly far away, and when I threw the noose it missed by a good hand. Dragging back the empty loop felt like dragging it across the salt desert of Dasht-e Kavir. I was aware of every eye fixed upon me as my mouth grew dry with nerves.

I wrapped the cord around my hand again, and again it missed.

"All those hours practising, and still you have not mastered it?" my father cut in, to save me listening to my cousins' smirks. "I was led to believe you were better than this."

"I beg your pardon, Father. I will try to do better."

"As well you should. Where is your tutor?"

I was about to tell him that I had no tutor, but the look in his eyes told me this was not a question I should answer. I followed his gaze, astounded as Shahab was pushed through the crowd to stand before me.

He looked as confused as I must have.

"Ah," my father leaned forward, resting his chin on the back of his hand as he scrutinized my friend. "You are the son of Vafar, the gardener?"

Shahab reddened with embarrassment, bowing his head to cover his loss of words.

"Afsar, give him your rope."

I did so willingly, and returned to sit by my father, grateful that the attention had passed to another.

"Be a good boy, and hook that tome over there," my father smiled, flicking his eyes to indicate the target.

Shahab swallowed and turned to the table, wrapping the cord around his hand. He licked his lips nervously, then took a deep breath before swishing the noose over his shoulder three times. When he released it, the only sound to be heard in the room was the whistle of the rope through the air.

After the applause had died down, he handed the book to my father.

"Very good!" laughed the Shah. "Very good indeed!"

He pointed to the decanter, which had been moved to a bookshelf. One of the servants immediately made his way through the crowd to collect it, placing the object on the table in the centre of the room.

"Do you know what that is?"

Shahab shook his head, mystified.

"Very expensive," my father enlightened him.

Twice as nervous now, the gardener's son coiled the rope around his dirt-stained hands for a second time. He pressed the back of his hand against his nose, took another deep breath, and prepared himself.

A deafening cheer went up as the noose dropped around the decanter, whipping back to Shahab's hands so fast that he caught it without spilling a drop.

"Quite incredible," my father laughed. "Tell me, where did you learn this trick?"

"Just a game we play. Me and my brothers," he said, much the same as he had once told me.

"That you should achieve all of this whilst I am paying you to tend my lawns," my father replied. "Such an accomplishment."

A chuckle went up from the crowd.

I saw Shahab swallow, as though trying to suck back his answer.

"My daughter is not such an easy pupil to teach, eh?"

"She does very well, when we are by ourselves."

I winced inside at this blunder. The mind of every man in the room sank to the level of Ja'far, I could feel it. Their eyes rubbed across my body as they contemplated what a young daughter of the Shah might be doing alone with a servant boy. His honesty was painful, and I willed him with every fibre of my being not to say any more.

"Hmm." After a pause, my father leaned forward. "I'll tell you what, how about a real challenge? Someone to match your admirable skill?"

Shahab frowned slightly, but nodded.

The crowd parted again. To my utter disbelief, I recognised the figure that stood by the door. I knew him instantly, though he was draped in a long dark cloak, his face obscured by a Pantalone mask.

"Vachon," I whispered.

A little flicker of lightning shot up my spine, causing the hairs on the back of my neck to rise.

Shahab turned to look at this elegant, imposing person who walked towards him, one foot perfectly placed in front of the other, silent in his thick stockings and velvet slippers. He glanced back at my father as if to ask what he would be expected to do, but in the instance it took him to avert his gaze, Vachon unleashed his red cord. It did not miss Shahab's neck, for it had not been aiming for his neck. Instead, it clipped the side of his ear, making it bleed.

Shahab looked back, shocked. He raised his hand to his torn lobe. When he saw the blood, his fingers began to tremble.

Vachon did not give him a chance to collect himself. He stepped forward, cast a handful of glittering sand into Shahab's eyes, then punched him solidly in the stomach whilst he was blinded. The young man went down like a sack of rice, doubled in agony.

I saw my father raise his hand to say *halt*. Vachon walked to the bookshelf where the servant had replaced the decanter, and poured himself a glass of Scotch. He took his time, smelling it and then sipping; swilling it around his mouth before swallowing.

Whilst he was doing this, Shahab managed to straighten himself. To his credit, he did not cry. Instead, he coiled the black cord around his hand as he rose, turning and unleashing it towards Vachon.

The second it dropped over Vachon's face, two things happened.

Firstly, Shahab pulled as fast and as hard as he could. Secondly, before he'd even begun pulling, Vachon had turned towards him and grabbed the cord with his hand, exposing to the crowd the fact that the noose had been prevented from closing around his neck because it was stuck above the great beak nose of his mask.

The crowd greeted this with great hilarity as Vachon ducked his masked head out of the noose and began pulling on the cord hand over fist.

Shahab tried to stand his ground and a tug of war ensued, which Shahab seemed at one point to be winning through sheer brute determination, until Vachon let go of the rope, catapulting him into the crowd.

Battered and bleeding, Shahab scrambled to his feet.

I saw the end coming even before it happened. With no lasso, the young man took a more visceral approach. With fists clenched, he lowered his head and charged. Vachon simply stepped aside. As Shahab sailed past, a flicker of red, like a snake's tongue, caught up with him.

I closed my eyes for only a moment. When I opened them, Vachon stood before us with Shahab in front of him. He twisted the noose so tightly that his opponent could not even choke. In fact, Shahab could not breathe at all. His eyes rolled in his head, resting on me for a second before moving up to the ceiling – to Allah – as his bladder emptied.

"Oh, really," my father sighed.

As Shahab kicked out his last before the Shah of Iran, the spectators moved towards the door, adjourning to a cleaner space – one unsoiled by common blood.

"You may return to your room," my father told me.

I did not hesitate.

He did not come to me until much later.

I lay on my bed with my knees tucked up to my chin, holding myself. There had been nothing I could have done for Shahab. I knew my father, and I knew my family. We were cruel people, there is no denying it. Once it was in my father's head to torment someone, or to bankrupt them, or to take what they once owned, there was nothing that could be said to change his mind. It was rare that he took against one so young though, and rarer still that he should choose to torture me.

Though there was more to it than that. Something deep, and dark, and desirous, which walked in the form of Vachon.

I sensed his shadow fall across my room before I heard his silk-stockinged feet tread softly towards me. The bed depressed as he sat down, then lay beside me. His hand rested gently on my shoulder and I turned towards him.

By the light of the moon, he must have seen that my cheeks were wet with tears.

"Why?" I asked, my throat hoarse. "Why did you do it?"

"You took something of mine that was very precious," he replied. There was no reproach in his voice. It was simply a statement, as though providing the answer to a mathematical problem. "It was only fair that I take something of yours."

He wore a different mask to the hook-billed Pantalone. This was a mask of pure, polished ebony. Rubies encrusted its eyes, and the upper lip was formed of brass. Golden but cold, a reversal of my bright-eyed love with his warm lips.

I felt as though I were about to cry again.

"Hush now," he said, reaching his hand to my ear and plucking from it a beautiful white butterfly. "Let us talk no more of things that hurt."

As the delicate insect beat its wings and took flight in the dark, I couldn't help but smile.

"Now we are both alone," I told him.

"Everybody on this earth is alone," he replied. "Company is just an illusion."

"I did not feel alone when I was with Shahab."

"Nor I, with Ishya. We had travelled far together."

"I'm sorry for what I did."

"I am not." His eyes held mine, and I swear I saw a flash of fire there. "From now on, you shall call me Eirik. I will not answer you otherwise." I opened my mouth to protest, so he placed a finger across my lips to silence me. "What you did was a very stupid thing. You and I are too alike to be parted, but from this day forth I want you to think upon your actions every day. I will stay with you, and I will be your friend, but with that you must always remember the loss of that animal's life. It died for your thoughtless fancy, and your family's murderous, unthinking rage."

It took me a moment to regain my voice.

"I did not put her in that cage."

"Do not lie to me again, Afsar. I know that you killed her."

"I killed her, but I didn't put her in that cage!"

"Then it must have been someone else."

"Who? Who else knew? Why would they do such a thing?"

I struggled to sit up as he laughed.

"Your tutor was right. Politics is not your forte."

This time I did cry. Confusion and shame melted down my face. I bit the back of my hand, trembling with anger at what I did not understand.

"Oh, hush, hush," Eirik said, rising and holding me close.

I sobbed into his chest and he let me. When I eventually calmed, I drew back. He waved his hand across my mouth and I found a lump of halva on my tongue, its sweet, comforting flavour reminding me of childhood and bringing fresh tears to my eyes.

"Afsar, your innocence is charming."

I chewed quickly and swallowed so that I could breathe more easily.

"You have outgrown your lessons," he continued. "Will you let me teach you?"

"What could you possibly teach me?" I snapped, regaining a little of my courage.

"How the world works."

He held me with his eyes and I felt a steady calm wash over me. The death of my first love had come as a shock to me. For the second time in my life I had known what it was to be utterly powerless. My future had been dictated by others. Only, unlike before, the person who had decided my fate was this time willing to offer it back to me.

"Very well," I conceded.

He smiled. "Good. Here, dance with me."

He stood from the bed and held out his hand, pulling me up to face him. I did not understand what he meant at first, as he held me close and positioned my hand around his waist whilst holding the other aloft. I was about to protest when the sound of a string quartet filled the room, echoing from the marble walls and the tiled floor.

We began to move, slowly at first, and then a little faster, swooning and sighing in a circle, our reflections moonlit and pale in the mirror. Around and around we went, like black silhouettes in a daedaleum.

♦ 5 ♦

That summer went by so fast.

Eirik left me that night, promising to return in two weeks with a surprise he assured me I would love. Without Shahab to walk with, I immersed myself once again in Shusha's language lessons, and in fumbled attempts at the qanun. When left to myself, I tried to write poetry, but the verses no longer came to me.

Life in the palace was certainly simpler without Ezzat's constant scrutiny, and with my father once again on matters of state that took him far from home. He had taken both his new wife and the Darougheh with him, which left myself and Arezoo to run the palace as we pleased. As I recall, it was a time of peace. An uncomplicated season of sunshine and easy pleasures.

When Eirik eventually did return, it was in a magnificent carriage, drawn by two black horses with scarlet plumes. I recognised it as my father's *tarantass*. During the war with Russia, my great-grandfather, in a fit of rage, went about burning all things Russian, including most of his wives' carriages. My father said that this one was saved, hidden in a hay barn. It held special significance to one of my grandfather's conquests, who had given birth to a son in it. My grandfather inherited it and decided to keep it for its amusement value. He had the carriage painted and furnished with soft cushions and a low silver table in the centre for sweets. I believe my father had seduced half his harem in the back of that thing.

"Come, get on!" Eirik called from the driver's seat.

It was unusual for the daughter or wife of a Shah to ride at the front of a carriage, rather than safely inside. It was more unusual still for her to be seen driving one.

"Take the reins." Grinning, he passed them to me before I could protest.

"I can't! I don't know how to—"

"Don't worry. Pull left to go left and right to go right. Nothing can happen."

There came the most incredible sense of freedom and power in taking control of those horses. I felt as though we could go anywhere, just keep driving until the horses collapsed from exhaustion. I laughed aloud as we made for the gates.

"Where are we going?" I asked.

"You'll see when we get there."

My laughter was cut short by the stony face of Vafar, Shahab's father, who knelt tending flowers along the path.

It was more than I ever could have imagined, this dust bowl of a citadel in the heart of my homeland. If I remember the details correctly, the area had formerly been a stone quarry, mined by locals for their houses and for walling the vast terraces of rice further up the hills. It provided the perfect shelter to undertake such a project, as the cliff behind hid the foundations from the grassland where the tribespeople sometimes hunted, and it allowed for the building to expand not only upwards, but backwards, into the cliff itself, like the ancient churches of Armenia that Shusha loved to talk of. Places where choirs would sing deep within the sacred caves, drowning people in sound.

I didn't understand what it was supposed to be at first. This was very early on, and men were still digging the pits for the base to be laid. Mostly, they worked topless, their tanned muscles rippling beneath the relentless sun. They worked with simple tools, the same pick axes and wooden shovels that generations of men had used before them, erecting the great palaces and mosques throughout our nation. Their hypnotic movements and the continual crunching of dry earth made it seem a desolate place.

"Come," Eirik said again, holding out his hand to guide me around the lengths of string and stick-drawn lines by which the workers were measuring their days. Even then, at that early stage, Eirik could look at those faint outlines and envision entire worlds. I genuinely believe he intended it to be his life's work.

In honesty, I did not wish to follow him. In my desire to retreat, I shouted out to him by his old name. "Vachon!" I cried, but, true to his word, he kept walking. I forgot myself several times over that first summer, yet he never once forgot himself.

"Eirik, wait!"

By the cliff, the men had erected a pulley system which raised a flat square of wood to an alcove almost at the top. There were no railings to hold onto. I sat, my nails digging into the planks and my head swimming with the height, whilst Eirik stood tall beside me, holding to one of the support ropes, laughing at my discomfort.

"We're perfectly safe," he chided.

We weren't, of course. All it would have taken was for one of those men on the ground to falter, his sandal sliding on the dry dust, or the sweat of his palms allowing the rope to slip through, and we would have plummeted to our deaths.

Eirik never thought that way.

When we shuddered to a halt beside the alcove, he helped me shakily to my feet and pulled me inside. It took a moment for my eyes to adjust to the gloom, but what I saw enchanted me. Somehow, he had managed to carve a little room for himself out of the cliff face. It was cool in there, shaded from the heat outside, and it held a perfect view of the work taking place below. From there, he could keep an eye on construction whilst planning out the next stage at a little desk that stood in the centre. Most impressive of all was that everything was lit in beautiful colours: blue and green and red. Even though we were still several feet from the top of the cliff, he had constructed a round shaft, capped at the base with a dome of stained glass. Using a system of mirrors, he reflected light from above down into the cave. When he was working, he could lower the dome and flood the room with daylight.

On the desk sat an intricate paper diorama of his plans. Every day it would change a little, losing a turret here, gaining a storey there, expanding further out from the cliff face, shrinking back against it. Yet it always, more or less, resembled a sturdy square palace, with flying buttresses and a domed centre. His design combined the best of European and Middle Eastern architecture in a jumble of elegant disorganisation.

It took my breath away.

"How do you know all of this?" I asked him, sweeping my hand to encompass the model and the open entrance, which in its turn encompassed all of the men working beneath us.

He told me that his father had been a Master Mason. His mother had apparently been too ashamed to hold him to her, so he had been raised sucking on the teats of sheep. His father had taken pity on him, wrapping him up in swaddling and laying him beside him as he worked. As Eirik had grown in size, he had watched more keenly the work his father did.

"I was eight or nine by the time I left," he confessed. "My father tried, but they were all the same. He was the only person who ever truly seemed to care for me, so it was the least I could do to make sure he never had to."

"You learned everything from your father?"

He snorted and went on to tell me about his travels. How he had left his esteemed position as Human Corpse at the circus near Paris and made his way further into Europe.

"There were times when there were no shows hiring, and times when I did not wish to make a spectacle of myself just to earn enough to eat. Then I would take building work. I would lay walls, mix cement and chip rock down to size. I wore a scarf across my mouth to keep out the dust, and bandaged the rest. There were men missing fingers and men with thick scars across their arms and chests. Building is a dangerous profession, and no one asked to look at me."

He talked of the first independent school of architecture that had been opened in London five years before, and how he had met a cousin of Robert Kerr's at the opening night of Verdi's *Macbeth* in Florence a couple of months prior to that.

I had no idea who either Robert Kerr or Verdi were, but apparently the latter had been a good friend of Eirik's, and through that introduction he had gone on to study in London for a term.

"In secret, of course," he said, pointing to his face with its smooth, beakless leather mask. "They thought a lot of me," he went on, "but eventually the heart calls. It is a horrible existence to be only half a part of what you know yourself to be the entirety of."

I listened as he talked of nights at the opera, of chorus girls and ballerinas, of champagne receptions and late-night intrigues; as he talked of London and Rome and Paris, then of circuses in India, Russia, Egypt and China.

It seemed inconceivable that one person could have travelled so far. At nineteen he was younger than my father, nonetheless he had travelled further than he, my grandfather, and his grandfather put together. Yet we were the ones with the wealth and the power to do so. It was a bittersweet realisation that money could not buy us freedom, and freedom had not brought him wealth.

It was early July when my father returned. He had been gone for many weeks but, like the rain, he never missed the feast of *Tiregan*. Not everywhere in Iran celebrated this day, but in Mazandaran it was one of our primary festivals. Much like the story of the blacksmith Kaveh, who sleeps beneath the Alborz mountains, our lands celebrated the fame of another hero, Arash. In the month of the archangel Tishtar, lord of lightning, Arash loosed an arrow that drew a border between the land of drought and the land of plenty, our own land. In so doing, the rains came and washed both worlds with fruitful bounty. Never again did people thirst in Turan; never again was there need to fight or to war.

Our midsummer water festival was spent by the streams, our hair decorated with rainbow ribbons, splashing one another with water. Many of my mothers went to the coast to paddle in the sea and to buy fresh fish for their supper.

Having spent all week with Eirik at the cliff, I was grateful to lie in the stream and scrub myself free of the grit that caked itself to me like a second skin. Mostly, I stayed in the cave and helped him to cut out walls and roof tiles. My small, feminine hands meant that I could hold the razorblade more delicately as it negotiated complex curves. At least, that is the reason he gave me.

I think, in truth, he simply took pleasure in having someone to share his dream with. A magician as skilled in legerdemain as he, had little need for my handicraft. More than once I raised my eyes to catch him watching.

In truth, I enjoyed being there too. How could I not? It was as different from palace life as cattle are from doves. A hot, dusty environment a world away from marble corridors and scented fountains. Most of all, it meant being close to Eirik, and hearing his many stories of sword fights and sailing rigs, railways and runaways.

However, that July morning was a welcome break. I submerged myself in the pool behind the dam, allowing the cool water to block out the sound of my shrieking siblings. The world around me gave way to the beating of my own heart. For a moment, that was all I could hear.

My heartbeats merged into hoof beats as I broke the surface of the water.

This time, my father rode from town with a circus altogether more familiar. He brought with him an entourage of brothers and cousins, half-cousins and half-forgotten cousins. Shokuh rode in a fine gilt carriage which opened to reveal that she travelled with a companion: Mahde Olia.

My grandmother was helped from the step by the Darougheh. The river of familial blood flowed towards the interior of the palace grounds, to sit beneath canopies on my father's private lawns and admire his collection of rare and extraordinary songbirds.

I did not see most of them again until that evening, when a banquet was held in the great hall. Silks had been hung from the ceiling, and expensive rugs on the walls. So that my grandmother could sit more comfortably, she had been provided with a high-backed wooden chair, and so that she did not seem out of place, so had we all. Half the Royal Family were seated at a long table in what Shusha referred to as 'the European style.'

In recent years, Uncle Taqi, one of my father's younger brothers, had cultivated an obsession with medieval history, particularly that of Western Europe. He had taken to collecting chainmail and suits of armour. Having run out of places to keep them in his own modest apartments in Tehran, he had gifted a large number to my father. As Taqi was there that night, so were a selection of his gifts. They stood against the walls watching us eat, harshly at odds with the soft silks.

My heart sank as I found myself seated at the opposite end of the table to Mahde Olia and Shokuh. They were both dressed in emerald green with gold detail. Cut from the same cloth. My grandmother nodded slowly and attentively as Shokuh spoke to her throughout the meal. I watched every exchange, feeling the acid rise in my stomach. She was my grandmother. I should have been seated beside her.

I heard Uncle Ja'far before I saw him. He had gained a little weight, his cheeks and his nose shot through with broken vessels. I smiled to myself that his wickedness was so apparent that people could read it on his face, and hoped that it was a sign he might die soon.

He was very much alive when he cornered me in the space between the hall and my quarters.

"Going to bed so early?" he asked, appearing like a fat, old panther from the night, wheezing and slow-eyed.

"Let me be, Uncle."

"Let you be? Oh, Afsar." He tutted at me and wagged his finger. "Still sore about your peasant boy?"

I glared at him.

"Don't be shy, little bird." I pressed myself against the palace wall as he came closer, the smell of stale cigars and half-digested food on his breath. "Rumour has it he made more than your heart sore." He slid his hand down between my legs.

I waited until he leaned his face against my shoulder. Then I turned my own face and bit his cheek so hard that I could taste blood. He roared in pain as he pushed me away. Without waiting to see the damage I had caused, I ran for my room, bolting the door and dragging a clothes chest across it for good measure.

That night, I sat there on my bed, hugging my knees to my chest and watching to see whether he would come for me.

The party continued for almost a week. I ventured out of my room only to attend mosque. Nobody sent for me. Shusha and Şelale were the only two who came to my room. Even Eirik was too busy with his project to visit. I thought at the time he was avoiding me because he was afraid that my father would announce him to my family, and force him to unmask himself again.

It was only after Mahde Olia left that I discovered the true reason for his absence.

"Your father has been in a terrible mood all week," Şelale said, shaking and then folding the skirts in my clothes chest. "He's locked himself away in his library almost as much as you have in your room."

"Who upset him?" I asked.

"Your grandmother," she confided. "I overheard talk that she pressured him to sign the death warrant of Prime Minister Kabir."

I had heard the name. An image of a fat man with a thick black beard and tall hat came to mind, though whether from a visit or a portrait, I could not recall.

"What is a Prime Minister?" I asked.

Her eyes opened for a moment, before returning to the clothes she was folding. I knew that look on her face. It meant that I had surprised her in some way, but that she did not feel it her place to say so. She was right. It was not.

"The Prime Minister is someone appointed by your father to help him to run the country."

"What happened to him?"

"He was executed last year, at the bath house in Kashan."

I considered this for a moment, whilst Şelale busied herself all too readily with re-packing the chest.

"What had he done wrong?"

"I could not say."

I would have pressed her further, only I heard a flute outside my window.

"Eirik!"

He wore a brown half-jacket and wide şalvar, showing a little of his midriff and displaying his slim yet muscular arms. It was clear that he had been working hard, for the sun had turned his skin the colour of an Arab.

"Come down," he shouted, staring up at me from behind his plain leather mask, the one as smooth as polished wood. He wore this almost every day, complementing it with a wig of chestnut horsehair, tied in a ponytail at his back. At night, though, he would wash himself off in the stream and give play to more theatrical tendencies. Plain brown gave way to mahogany and rubies, or black, white and gold, cloaked in velvets of midnight-blue or blood-orange, and always with an oiled wig of jet-black human hair.

"Sultana, you should stay. Your father–"

I did not wait to hear the rest of what Şelale had to say.

Instead of driving directly to the construction site, we came off the road a little early and down a narrow path into thick jungle.

"I have a surprise for you," he told me.

We were in a smaller carriage this time. The tarantass had only been for show that first time, a flashy status symbol that showed not only the breadth of my father's wealth, but also the depth of his trust in Eirik, that he would lend him such a precious heirloom. Once that had been established, he had changed to a two-seater *ekka*, drawn by a single white horse. It was comfortable enough, like a high-backed chair, with two poles at the front supporting a thickly woven canopy. It was also intimate. I was acutely aware of Eirik's thigh pressed against mine, and the way the weight of his body shifted against me whenever the horse changed direction.

Despite being much lighter than the tarantass, its wheels soon began to struggle in the soft, mulchy ground. When it became apparent that it could go no further, Eirik brought it to a halt in a clearing by a stream. After helping me down, he unhooked the horse and pegged it beside the water, where it drank thirstily whilst swatting flies with its tail.

"This way," he said, beckoning me to follow.

Instead of continuing along the dirt track, we stepped off onto a deer trail. I could hardly make it out through the overgrown ferns and dead leaves, relying on Eirik to show me the way.

"Where are we going?" I asked.

"Don't worry, you'll like it. I promise."

I believed every word he told me, and followed him further and further, until, eventually, we came to another clearing. It was much smaller than the one in which we had left the carriage. Barely a clearing at all, simply a gap in the canopy above a circle of swept ground. In that circle, a tall wooden box stood, built out of planks which had been nailed together and stuck with tar.

"What is that?" I asked, taking a few cautious steps towards it.

Walking around the box, I saw a ladder propped against one side, the one furthest from the path.

"Take a look."

Carefully, I planted one hand on either side of the rungs and made my way to the top. The roof was flat, so I stepped onto it. In the centre was a long wooden pipe that drew level with my shoulders. I went to it, examined it, and peered down it.

What I saw left me speechless.

The pipe gave a perfect view of the inside of the box, bending the walls around in a panorama so that it seemed as though you were looking in every direction at once. Mesh slats in the corners of the roof allowed enough daylight through to make out the figure of a man slouched in the corner. He sat with his legs pulled up to his chest, his hands behind his back. I guessed that they were tied, as he didn't look particularly comfortable. He wore a buttoned shirt, white with blue stripes, torn open at the top and brown with dirt. A black kamar-band had been used to blindfold him, and a strip of cloth had been tied across his mouth to keep him silent.

Instantly, I recognised him as Uncle Ja'far.

I stared so long that when I looked up, Eirik was standing beside me. He didn't look smug or proud of what he had done. Instead he looked at me with such heartbreaking reserve, uncertain whether I would be pleased with him or not.

"You did this for me?" I asked.

"Do you like it?"

There was little else I could do but nod. The back of my throat tightened slightly, and breathing in sharply, I felt my eyes burn. Nobody had ever done anything like this for me before. Certainly, I had a palace and a room filled with fine clothes and rich fabrics. I wanted for nothing, but that was simply the fortune of my birth. Nobody had ever done something simply for me, because they wanted to please me. Even my father looked upon me as one of many children. Whereas Eirik saw me as Afsar. And he had seen enough to know that Ja'far wished to harm me.

"Wait, there is more," he said, holding up a finger. "Keep watching."

I pressed my eye again to the viewing pipe whilst he descended the ladder.

A moment later I heard him hitting the side of the box with a stick.

"Stand up. Stand up and answer for your crimes!" he shouted.

Starting around with blinded eyes, my uncle scrambled to his feet. It was not easy for him with his hands tied behind his back and his injured leg, but he was clearly afraid enough to try.

"Is he up?" Eirik called.

"Yes."

I felt a sudden jolt. Holding on to the pipe with both hands, I became aware that the room in which my uncle stood was gradually shrinking. His head was getting closer, until he looked like a stretched beanpole of a man. Like people who have grown fat with age look in old mirrors that offer only a distorted reflection.

Through the mesh slats, I could hear my uncle's muffled cries of distress as he crouched down on the floor and eventually pitched back, flattening himself against the ground. When I looked up, I realised that I was almost at ground level myself. I could simply step off the roof of the box onto the soft earth.

It was a marvel of engineering. By winding a wheel attached to the outside of the box, you could raise it up to be three times the height of my father, or shrink it down to merely the height of my own knees. There was another wheel next to it that brought two of the opposing walls together like butter boards.

"See?" Eirik grinned. "He has no room to lie down. All he can do is stand. You could leave him like that for days."

And we did.

Another thing we did was to turn up the temperature in the box using a mirror and lens contraption that fitted to the mesh slats. Eirik understood the mathematics of it, but Ja'far understood the results. Sweat would pour from his forehead. He had to wipe it on his raised knees because he could not free his hands to use his sleeves.

From the smell emanating from the slats, and the flies that hovered above them, it was clear that Ja'far had already been there for some days. I did not ask exactly when he had disappeared, but I suspected it had been the same night that he had put his hand between my legs.

Ja'far lived for two weeks in that condition. We would pincer the sides together so that he could only stand, then leave him that way for a day or two. Other days we'd open the box up to its full height and angle the lens to increase the temperature, closing off the slats so that air became scarce and he suffocated in his own stench.

94

"He will die soon," Eirik said at the end of the second week. "I've only fed him scraps, and he's taken to licking his own arm for the salt. We can't let him go, so we should probably kill him."

It was my idea, I will admit it. I was the one who suggested we give him the choice.

Eirik lowered a fish hook down into the box and used it to pull Ja'far's blindfold off. He screwed his eyes shut, protecting them from the little light that entered. It took him several minutes to be able to open them fully.

"Hello, Uncle Ja'far," I said, smiling down at him through the mesh.

He already knew I was there, for he had heard my voice many times. Yet seeing me seemed to turn him an extra shade paler.

"You don't look well, Uncle. Is the accommodation not to your taste?"

Of course, he could not answer me with the gag in his mouth.

I had already made up my mind when I turned to Eirik and asked, "How should we end his life?"

"By the lasso."

"Perhaps. Or perhaps we should let him choose?"

Eirik's expression was unreadable beneath his mask, yet his eyes seemed to latch onto me, like the hook on his fishing line digging deep into living flesh.

"Here's your choice," I said, returning my attention to Uncle Ja'far and holding out my hand for Eirik's lasso. "There are three ways you may die, Uncle, and you must choose one, for there is no going home. Firstly, you may choose to die standing up. We will sandwich you between the walls, on your feet, and leave you there to rot. Secondly, you may choose to die from the heat. We will angle the lenses and increase the temperature until you cook. Finally," I waved the lasso above the slat for him to see, "we will lower this into your chamber and you may choose to take your own life. It is the quicker of the three options."

I heard the faintest intake of breath from my friend. When I looked up, those coal-black eyes of his sparkled as though I had crowned him a prince.

It was harder to arrange a suicide than I had anticipated. Not only did we have to tie a rope long enough to secure it to the viewing pole, but we also had to provide a stool for him to stand on. In addition, we had to lower down a knife on the end of a stick to free my uncle's hands. It was too tricky for him to secure the noose with them bound behind his back.

At Eirik's suggestion, I allowed him to hook off my uncle's gag before he died. The barb caught in Ja'far's cheek as it rose, drawing a thick scarlet line.

"Do you have any last words?" I asked him.

He stood for a long moment with the noose resting around his shoulders. When he looked up, his gaunt face twisted into an expression of pure hatred.

"You are a fucking bitch," he spat, and kicked the stool from under himself.

That is how it began. After Ja'far had stopped twisting on his rope, Eirik drove me home to the palace, where I called Şelale to wash me in cool water. I was tired and dusty from the day, but also afire with something as hot as burning embers in my head and my heart. I felt like a tigress. As though nothing in this world could touch me.

I did not ask what happened to the body, and we never returned to that place again. Something had changed between us, though. An energy, thick and palpable, crackled in the air whenever we were in the same room together.

My father spent many days away from the palace at that time. More often than not, Shokuh would go with him. I was lawless, left to my own devices. I'd spend hours each week in that cave at the top of the cliff, cutting out paper shapes for Eirik's model palace, each day seeing nuances I had missed in the early stages. Such as the way in which tiles in the larger rooms slid back to reveal secret passageways, and bookshelves swung on hinges, opening into cubbyholes and mysterious tunnels.

As time passed, he began to paint the rooms he was satisfied with. The colour brought out the boundless splendour of his mind, until such a palace as I had never thought possible materialised in that lofty room above the world. No longer white on white, more and more details became visible, elaborate and intricate in their ambition.

"It's a magic box," I exclaimed, punching open a tiny wooden door with a toothpick, setting in motion a system of tiny folds which created a floating pathway between two ledges, high above a hidden moat.

"And it will be a reality," he smiled. "What you see today as a doll's house shall soon be a king's abode."

"My father commissioned this?"

"He realised he wanted it, yes."

"I don't understand. You came to us as a circus performer, and now you are building the Shah a palace. How did he come to know that you could build?"

Eirik simply shrugged and returned to gluing a joist to the upper floor.

"Did somebody tell him how good you are? Did you have references?"

"He asked about my lasso, and I did him a favour," he said, not taking his eyes from the task at hand.

"What sort of favour?"

"What sort of favour would you expect from a lasso?"

It dawned on me slowly.

"You killed somebody for him?"

"One or two."

"You are my father's assassin?" The thought seemed so absurd that I couldn't help but laugh.

He looked up sharply. "Yes. What is so funny about that?"

"Nothing. Only that I thought the Darougheh did my father's work on that score. Why does he need you?"

Eirik shrugged. "The Darougheh has certain principles, I suppose. Your father admires him, and he needs him, but sometimes he needs me also."

"Well, who did you kill?"

"It was an old score, I think. I don't know. Your father and I have an arrangement."

"He must have told you something?"

Eirik sighed and straightened, laying his glue brush down.

"Last year, your grandmother persuaded your father to have his Chancellor assassinated."

"Kabir? I've heard of this. Wasn't he Prime Minister?"

"Ah, so you do know something of politics?" He smiled, and I remained silent. I did not wish to tell him that the only thing I knew of politics was the one thing I had just told him, and that this single scrap of information came from none other than my illiterate servant. "Well, I think he was sore about that. From what I could tell, he was fond of the man. Your grandmother was, too, at one point, but he went too far with his scheme of eradicating some religious sect—"

"The Bábí."

"That was it," he said, clicking his fingers. "Something about the Gateway of, to, or from Truth. Anyway, the man who killed Kabir."

He ended the sentence there, whilst I continued to wait for more.

"That was the man you killed? The man who killed Kabir?"

Eirik shrugged again, prodding his joist with a toothpick to make sure it had set. "Your father said, to quote: 'My mother may have her way, but I shall have my vengeance.'"

"Oh."

"And then he broke down in tears."

"What?"

"He was drunk at the time. Your father has a way with words when the wine gets to him."

I felt my cheeks flush. "We're Muslim. He does not drink."

Eirik looked at me, derision plain to see. "No, of course not. Neither does he smoke tobacco when his wives are not watching, or gamble on the racehorses his cousin does not keep."

"Hold your tongue," I snapped, pricking my finger with the razor I was holding.

A single drop of blood landed on the white paper that I had spent the past hour cutting into the shape of a window casement.

"Ah, my vicious princess," he sighed, taking my finger to his lips and kissing it, licking away my blood with his tongue. "There is no need for that. Fighting against what is true will only ever lead to a lifetime of contempt. Fight against injustice, fight against what is wrong when you know it to be wrong, but, when it is true, simply accept that it is true and do not be angry."

I struggled with his words. My father was still my world at that age, and any insinuation that he should be less than absolutely perfect roused my rage.

"Look at me, my dear. I am uglier than sin. That is a fact. I could choose to scream and shout about it all my life, but it would not change that fact. Just as my face is a fact, so are the skills I possess, and it is with those truths that I shall overcome the disadvantages of the first truth."

He put his fingers to his mouth and pulled out a giant red lotus flower. When I reached to touch it, each petal came loose, falling to the ground.

I could not help but smile.

That evening we went to Sari.

Our trips there had grown less frequent since the circus left. It was not easy to return after what I had done, but it was Eirik who suggested we should. That was the funny thing about him. Something might happen that would destroy any other human being: the disfigurement of his birth, some public ridicule, the death of his friend at my hands. Yet it almost seemed as though it were forgotten about as soon as it had happened. He never once referred to Ishya whilst we were there, and he never allowed the silence between us to become uncomfortable. It was as though she had never existed. As though there had never been a circus or a former life for him.

Sari was still a beehive of activity. Ten years before my birth, the great plague had arrived here from Russia. Shusha said that it wiped out almost the entire population of Sari, and that the subsequent wave of cholera did for the rest. He told me there had been no more than three hundred people left standing, yet you would never have known it now. Its people bred faster than rats, and every day new immigrants came to set up stalls and shops. No two people we passed seemed to speak the same language or wear the same clothes.

I loved it there, truly I did.

That particular night, I left the shadows to purchase fried squid from a street vendor. Eirik and I sat in a tree eating it whilst watching the world pass beneath us.

As we started to make our way home along the dirt track that would eventually lead to the palace, I turned to ask him something, only to find that he was gone. Standing there, alone on the road, my senses shone alive. It was as though Zam-Armatay, the Earth herself, had lent me her eyes, for I could see so clearly by the light of the stars, my ears as sharp as the fox's.

A figure was walking towards me from the direction of Sari. I slipped my hand beneath my cloak and grasped the handle of my knife, for I never left at night without one. "Come no closer," I said, my words ringing loud in the frog-chorusing night.

"It's okay," the young man said. "I wish you no harm. Don't you recognise me?"

I squinted until a voice whispered in my ear that it was the squid seller I had bought our meal from.

"Oh," I exclaimed, then realised that the man had not heard Eirik tell me this. "Yes, you served me food earlier?"

"Yes," he smiled, taking a step closer. "I hope you do not mind, but I saw you walk this way. Are you alone?"

"It would appear so," I replied, glancing around.

"A woman should not walk alone at night."

"I will be fine."

"I'm sure," he said. "It is quiet here at this hour. I often come to get some peace after my stock is sold. If you don't mind me asking though, where are you going to on your own in the middle of the night?"

"Home," I said, unprepared for such questions.

"The only thing down this path is the–" He paused as the realisation struck him. "You live at the palace?" he asked.

"Yes."

"Are you a princess?" he laughed.

"Yes."

His smile froze in place whilst his eyebrows slowly journeyed to a point in the centre of his brow. He must have thought I was joking: a princess walking alone along a dusty road at midnight.

"Oh," he said eventually. "Well, that would explain your beauty." He paused for a moment more before asking whether he could walk me there. "I can see you safely to the palace gates," he said.

"That would be very kind of you."

We began to walk, side by side along the road.

"Are you really a daughter of the Shah?" he asked me.

"His eldest," I confessed.

"You are Afsar? I have heard of you. There is a children's song they sing in the villages, have you heard it? It goes 'The Shah's eldest daughter has eyes like the tiger.'"

"What else do they say?" I asked, amused at having the opportunity to hear about myself through the eyes of a peasant.

"That your heart is cast of gold, and your lips are set with rubies." He laughed, embarrassed.

"What a disappointment I must seem in the flesh."

"Oh, no!" he said. "No, not at all."

We stopped then as a shadow appeared on the road ahead.

"Who's there?" my companion called out.

The shadow simply stood, illuminated by the slim scythe of a crescent moon.

The young man took a step forward, instinctively holding out his arm to keep me behind him. I thought that it was very sweet of him to be so protective. He reminded me a little of Shahab.

"We only wish to pass. We are going to the palace," he said, a slight tightening in his voice.

Still, the shadow did not move.

A crow screeched in a tree by the road. His fatal mistake was to look for it.

In the second it took him to turn his head, a thick red cord embraced his neck and pulled him to his knees. By the time he thought to cry out, Eirik was behind him, tightening the noose. The young man was clever, though. Instead of straining forward and clawing at the rope like most victims would, he smashed his head backwards into Eirik's nose, connecting both elbows with Eirik's ribcage.

I bit the back of my hand to hold back my laughter. It was the most undignified thing I had ever seen happen to my friend. He lost his footing and ended on his buttocks in the dust.

The young man climbed to his feet, towering over Eirik.

"Run," he shouted to me. "Run home as fast as you can."

As he lifted his hands to remove the noose from his neck, Eirik's feet shot out, knocking him clean off his. I could hear the crack of bone as the squid seller landed. This did cause me to laugh. I couldn't help myself. Firstly, that two grown men should find themselves in such a state, and secondly, I must admit, because one of them still did not understand the joke.

The sound of my laughter caused my gallant rescuer to glance towards me. Some people do not learn quickly.

Eirik shot forward and tightened the noose again, dragging him to his feet. This time he kept the young man at arm's length, so that he couldn't kick back with his head or his elbows. Eirik did learn quickly. I never saw him repeat a mistake.

"This pretty young lady was walking home," Eirik said, pushing his victim along until he stood before me. "What right have you to harass her?" He loosened the noose just enough for the young man to reply.

"I was not harassing her–"

Eirik cut him short with a twist of the rope.

"Really? Did you not think that I could protect her? Was she not safe with me?"

"I didn't see you with her. I thought she was alone," he gasped.

"Exactly. You saw a pretty lady on her own at night and you followed her. Why? Did it make your manhood hard? Did you think about all the things you might do to her with nobody watching?"

"No!" he cried between clenched teeth. "I only wanted to–"

"I only wanted to, I only wanted to," Eirik mimicked in a high, squeaky voice. "I dare say you did."

Tears were streaming down the young man's face as his eyes bulged and he struggled for breath.

"Is this true?" I asked, holding up a hand for Eirik to relax his grip a little.

"No," the young man moaned.

"But you did wish to walk me home in the dark."

"Not for that."

"Then, for what?"

"I just – I just thought you were pretty."

"Ah. And what do you do with pretty girls?"

He shook his head, tears and mucus spilling from his face.

I leaned in slowly and kissed him.

I felt his confusion. I could taste it on his lips as he returned the kiss, drawing away and then pressing hesitantly against me.

That sharp intake of breath.

I could not pull the knife out immediately. The blade had pierced his heart and thick gushes of hot blood flowed from the wound. The ivory handle became butter between my fingers. I tugged, and he simply fell forward. First onto his knees, then onto his chest, driving the weapon further into his flesh.

Eirik was staring at me. I could feel him, but my own heart was racing a thousand times faster than my mind. All I could do was stand there and watch. He quickly took control, turning the body over, placing his foot on the squid seller's chest and using his own weight to lever the blade out. As he did so, a spurt of blood caught him in the eye and he turned away, fist pressed to it.

"Quickly," he said, clicking his fingers and pointing to the ditch that ran alongside the road.

We rolled the body into it and ran for home.

That night, we washed blood from one another by the stream in the woods. Eirik went to my room and returned with a fresh set of clothes for me, so that no one might see evidence of my kill.

In the canopy-covered darkness, I stripped off my clothes and stood before him, naked. I cannot describe to you the thrill of murder, not in a way you would understand. You are invincible. Knowing that we would escape, blameless, made it all the more seductive. Our veins ran with molten iron that would set over the days and months to come, until our spines rivalled the great pillars of Islam.

Besides, I had seen him in all his nakedness, stripped of his mask in a hall of spectators, and, in his turn, he had seen the deformity of my own soul. I felt then that there was no level of shame we could ever sink beneath.

I watched him watch me as I dressed.

It pleased me that he watched.

♦ 6 ♦

Eirik and I honed our skills in the streets of Sari. Twice a week, some-times more, we would go to the town. At first we would steal vagrants or stray animals. Things that people would not miss. Over time we took to hunting our prey more languidly. We would observe potential victims over a week or more, learning their habits and watching them whilst they slept. We would tailor their deaths to make them unique.

It was the beginning of autumn that I returned one night from Sari to find the Darougheh in my room.

"Shahzadi," he said, turning from my balcony to greet me.

I stopped where I was. If someone were in my room, I would have expected Şelale to warn me, yet I had not seen her since that afternoon at the mosque. Of all the people in the palace, the Darougheh of Mazandaran was someone who evoked calm in me. I had seen his face every day since my birth. Unlike Shusha's, which had always been lined and framed with silver, I remembered a time when the Darougheh's hair was as thick and black as mountain grass. Age had favoured him, though. The lines that were starting to become visible around his eyes, and the salting of his temples, lent him an air of authority which was required in a job such as his.

Thinking on it, I am not sure that I ever knew his name. Naser, or Namdar, perhaps. Everyone simply called him by his office. A distant cousin of a cousin of a cousin's, like everyone in power throughout our nation. He had been married, once. I remember a lady in a bright red headscarf, with smiling eyes, though what became of her I could not say. I must have been very young when she died.

"Darougheh," I nodded, stepping a little further into the room. "It is a strange time of night to be making inspections."

He walked to my dressing table and lit two of the lamps there, illuminating his face before dissolving once again into shadow.

"I apologise for the hour, but I think that there are pressing matters we must address."

That was the funny thing about the Darougheh, you see. He stood so straight and stiff, yet spoke with such soft elegance, never a word out of place, never raising his voice. He could have whispered and you would still have been able to hear him. He almost possessed Eirik's skill for ventriloquism, though he never appeared to be aware of it. Such a gentle, unassuming man. I never could bring myself to think of him as others saw him. Those who could not pay their taxes, those who were caught stealing from the palace, or those who insulted my father in some other way. It was very difficult to imagine this man, almost a second father to me, presiding over the tortured screams of men and women who had fallen foul of my family.

We all have our second lives.

"Please," I said, gesturing to a chair by my bed, and seating myself on the latter. "What is so important it cannot wait until daybreak?"

He smiled slightly as he took the chair, crossing one leg carefully over the other and lacing his fingers above his knee. He was dressed in a plain blue suit, devoid of his favoured *karakul* hat. That night he came as a friend, to discuss matters that only the walls would remember.

"I see you so rarely around the palace these days. How have you been keeping?"

"Well," I replied, offering no more than the question required.

He took a moment to absorb this, nodding slowly before continuing.

"There have been such funny stories of late. Have you heard them?"

I shook my head.

"Strange occurrences in the forest. A wooden crate that appeared and then disappeared, leaving behind a distinctly unpleasant smell, according to the villager who lives nearby."

"I had not heard that one," I said calmly, cancelling his green eyes with my steady brown stare.

"No." The foot he held aloft, twitched. "I would not have expected you to."

"What was in the crate?" I asked.

"Oh, nothing of importance," he replied.

There was a long moment of silence between us. I knew then that the game had begun. I knew also that he had shown his hand too early. There was no doubt in my mind that he had looked inside that box, and that he had seen Uncle Ja'far.

And that he had left him there.

"Is that what you came to talk to me about in the middle of the night? Some superstitious villagers and their fears?"

The Darougheh sat up a little in his chair.

"Yes, it is rather late, isn't it? Have you been taking the night air?"

"I couldn't sleep."

"A long walk, then?" he asked, glancing at my dust-caked sandals.

Şelale herself had commented whilst washing my feet on how hard they had become. She rubbed them with pumice stone and massaged them with almond oil, but, unlike the Darougheh, she never questioned what had caused this.

"Yes. To the woods and back."

"You really shouldn't walk alone at night."

I could not tell in that instant whether he knew that I walked with Eirik, or whether he was testing me to see. With the Darougheh, it was always wise to assume he knew everything, and offer him nothing.

"You are probably right."

He rested his elbows against the arms of the chair, raising his hands and tapping his steepled fingers against his lip.

"Well," he said, eventually. "So long as the Shahzadi is safe."

He rose to his feet and walked to the door. Wrapping his fingers around the handle, he turned before opening it.

"There has been a spate of disappearances in town recently. People who have gone missing, only to turn up dead. It has the people worried."

"I'm sorry to hear that."

"It has your father quite upset."

Was that a veiled threat? Did he know, and would he tell my father? Or was he fishing for truths, hoping I might rise to swallow his baited questions and in so doing snare myself upon their hook.

"It would be my considered advice," he continued conversationally, "that a young woman of the Shah's household avoid placing herself in such danger. Stay indoors at night, and don't go walking alone."

After he left, I sat very still for a long time, watching the oil lamps flicker and twist on their wicks.

There was a long period after that when I did not see Eirik.

The words of the Darougheh could not be ignored. He knew something, but the extent of that something was unknown. It was not safe to test him.

Eirik's palace at the cliff kept him occupied all summer, though whether he was there or not, I could not say. It was only later that I discovered the extent to which my father had employed him.

Starved of entertainment, I spent my own days in much the same way that I had before the circus arrived. I played nard with Şelale late into the evenings, attended prayers, practiced the qanun when I was sure that no one would be listening, and resumed my language lessons with Shusha.

With every hour, I felt time passing.

The sense that I was walking slowly towards my grave almost drove me mad. Life had seemed so vibrant before, emotions had been strong enough to taste, and those first stirrings which Shahab had elicited, lingered like a ghost in the cool coastal air.

When the attack happened, it was as though Allah had heard my prayer and answered it with a gift. It was the festival of *Mehregan*, marking the celebration of the harvest, the Persian festival giving thanks for abundance and for friendship. I was seated in the main hall, at a table dressed in shimmering fabrics that reflected the light in dazzling silver, green and red. All of the ornaments, from candlesticks to crockery, were formed of burnished copper, the colour of falling leaves. In the centre, half a giant watermelon had been stripped of its skin, its pink flesh scored in a paisley pattern.

The hall was packed to bursting with my mothers, for it was our Mehregan tradition to dine together as women before the main banquet. I was lost in my thoughts, trying to blot out their incessant chatter and the smell of sour breast milk, when the door exploded.

Through it fell a young man dressed in black, followed by twenty guards. Chairs upturned as my mothers shot to their feet. Siblings screamed, candles blew out, and plates crashed to the floor. In the midst of this pandemonium, time itself seemed to slow. I sat, watching the whirlwind around me, safe in the eye of the storm.

Though there was much conjecture afterwards, I can attest to the fact that there was no knife. He carried no weapon, at least by the time he entered the hall. Those who say that his face was painted with the blood of Twelver children, or that his eyes burned with the flames of hell, were simply victims of their own imagination. He was no more than a man, dressed in the clothes of a man, wearing the expression of a man.

Before the guards overpowered him, he managed to scream:

"My son, in his name—"

What he was doing in his son's name, we never found out, for the Chief of Guards stepped forward from behind and slipped his steel through the man's windpipe.

The event itself had been noteworthy only insomuch as it had not been related to clothes, childbearing or the quality of the food. What followed, however, was far more interesting.

My father had been gone for weeks, as had the Darougheh, yet Shokuh remained. She had been sitting at the head of the table, the only other woman to remain seated throughout. Afterwards, she sent a messenger for the Darougheh, who returned within a day. He organised an interrogation of Sari, hauling in every man, boy and goat that might offer intelligence on the incident.

He soon discovered what any person with eyes might have seen had they taken the time to watch the assailant, rather than imagine him the Devil incarnate.

The man had worn the triangular *haykal* of the Bábí.

"Did nobody tell you?" Eirik asked, appearing on my balcony one evening. "It was revenge for revenge. Politics, my dear."

I did not understand.

"The Shah and Kabir killed the Báb, so the Bábí attempted to kill your father."

"Kill him?" I was horrified.

"Where do you think he's been this past month? Three men ambushed him near Niyávarfin. They say he hasn't left his room there since."

"Have you seen him?"

"Briefly. He'll live."

"But why come here?"

"Why come here to attack the Shah's wives, his most precious possessions, proving that you can infiltrate even his most private quarters? I have no idea."

I glared at him.

"Don't talk to me like a child, Eirik. I am not stupid."

"Far from it," he said, stroking his hand against my cheek. "Your father and his former Prime Minister embarked on a – how shall we say? – cleansing operation together. They sought to remove many of the Bábí from Iran. The man who interrupted you so rudely at dinner had lost–"

"A son," I completed.

"Actually, no. His entire family."

"That serves him right for betraying Islam."

Eirik laughed. "I am not a Muslim. Would you have me hanged?"

I had never thought of this. Dressed in ṣalvar and speaking Persian, it had almost slipped my mind that he was not from Iran. Cold horror swept through me.

"You are a Christian?" I asked, astounded.

"No." He laughed again.

"A Jew?"

He shook his head.

"Then what?"

"I don't believe in anything."

Now it was my turn to laugh. "How can that be? You must believe in *something*."

"Human nature," he shrugged. "Death – now that is a certainty."

"And after death?"

"Oblivion."

At that age and, if I am being truthful, for the rest of my life, Eirik's outlook on existence was beyond my grasp. A Christian I could understand, a Jew, even, to some extent, a Bábí. But *nothing*? That I could not comprehend.

I was quiet for a moment. Then, as happened on several occasions when I did not understand him fully, he rescued me by changing the subject.

"Would you like to see something?" he asked.

"How can I answer you that when I do not know what you wish to show me? Would I like to see a magic trick? Yes. Would I like to see the Russians invade? No."

He stared at me as if to ask whether I had finished.

I sighed and followed him from the room.

Down a dirt track about a mile long, at the furthest reaches of the palace, hidden from the West Lawn by a border of evergreen trees, my father kept a stable as a prison. It was an enclosure of three sides framing a cobbled square. The fourth side was made of a high brick wall with shards of broken bottle embedded along the top. Outside, several guards were resting, their guns slung casually over one shoulder as they passed the time playing cards for coins.

As they saw us approach, they scrambled to their feet.

"How are the natives today?" Eirik asked.

The head guard smiled and waved him through, bowing his head to acknowledge me.

I had never seen the prison from inside before. Each of the three sides contained fifteen horse stalls, each able to hold twenty people when packed to their full capacity. The upper half of the doors were open, crisscrossed with barbed wire to prevent anybody from trying to climb out. I saw eyes staring at us from behind those lengths of wire.

"Who are these people?" I asked, confounded by the sheer numbers. I rarely ever came to this part of the palace, and had thought it abandoned.

"Bábí," Eirik replied, walking from stall to stall, staring back at the occupants. "This one!" he shouted, and a guard appeared by his side. "See – that one there." He pointed.

The guard undid the bolt from the outside and I saw the inhabitants of the cell draw back.

"Which one, sir?"

"That one, with the squint-eye."

The guard drove forward into the room and returned pushing someone before him. He was a scrawny man, possibly underfed. His moustache looked like two black rats' tails hanging limply from his upper lip, his teeth were crooked, and his right eye had gone to sleep. Staggering forward, he looked almost drunk.

"You choose one," he said to me.

I approached the door and peered in. It was like leaning into a wall of stench, which reminded me of Ja'far in his box. The animal house scent of dung, sweat and urine.

"That one," I said, pointing to an elderly gentleman in the corner. He was wearing a white turban, and had a white beard to match.

The guard dutifully brought the man forward. Then, at Eirik's request, a cart arrived to drive us to the palace with our hostages.

We unloaded them into the firing square, where my father had first taught me to shoot so many moons ago. I still possessed the vial of blood in my room, though it was darker now that it had dried.

The men must have known what awaited them, yet they never showed signs of panic. Dressed in their simple clothes, reciting prayers beneath their breath, they simply stood there and waited.

It began quietly. Eirik with his red cord, and me with my black cord. We circled the men, occasionally loosing the rope to whip at their legs or their backs. Testing the reach of our throws and taking the men by surprise.

They drew closer together, until they stood back-to-back, turning as we circled them, keeping their eyes on us whilst protecting themselves with folded arms.

It didn't take long for people to gather at the parapet above. Word spread quickly through the palace and soon an audience of cousins and mothers had gathered. Shokuh arrived at the central window, flanked by the Darougheh. By the archways, servants crowded. I saw Shahab's father, Vafar, and his brothers, as well as the cooks and cleaners with their children.

A great excitement began to build.

"That's it, my daughter," Mother Tala shouted down. "You show them that we are not afraid! You show them that they cannot intimidate us!"

"Make it slow!" another called down. "Make them suffer!"

As the crowd whipped itself into a fury, we slashed our cords back and forth, licking their faces red with blood. Eirik even managed to lasso the old man's turban, yanking it clean off his head and delivering it to an upstairs window.

The spectators roared their approval.

"Your Gateway to Truth is a gateway to Hell!" someone shouted, an egg landing squarely on the rat-tailed man's forehead. He raised one arm to wipe it away with his sleeve. As he did this, Eirik's noose landed squarely around his neck. Because the man's arm had been raised, he was able to lift the rope and duck beneath it, returning it empty.

When my turn came, I hesitated. My heart thundered. I had never felt so alive, yet at the back of my mind I recalled the day in the study with Shahab. I remembered the sounds of disapproval from my cousins as I cast my cord and missed. There were so many people now, I was almost afraid to throw. I listened hard for a moment, absorbing their cheers of support.

My noose found its mark. I pulled, and the old man fell to his knees, shins cracking against the cobbles. Another chorus of approval swept the overhang, my mothers ululating themselves into a frenzy. Yet, now that I had hit my target, I was uncertain what to do. I had never killed in front of anyone except Eirik, and never with the cord. My arms simply weren't strong enough to twist the life out of a person. Instead, I fell back on what I knew. I reached for the dagger sheathed in the sash of my şalvar. Walking cautiously forward, as though the old man might rise up and attack me, I drew back my arm and embedded my blade in his throat.

As his life pooled at my feet, I looked up to the windows above, to Shokuh's satisfied smile, to the Darougheh's passive stare, and to Mother Tala's triumphant grin.

Then I looked to the arches, and I saw Vafar.

His expression left me cold.

Those were rosy hours at Mazandaran.

Every week, the Darougheh interrogated more families and brought fresh traitors to the makeshift prison. Hunting them down became a common form of entertainment. My cousins made our games with the Punjab lasso look amateur by comparison. Mahmoud learned to fire his first gun in much the same way that I had learned with our father.

My cousins from Tabriz came for the weekend. They lined up a row of men in white turbans and forced them to run across the lawn towards the woods. Then they helped my eldest brother to line up his shot and reload the chamber on his rifle.

None of them made it.

They came to be known as rosy hours because Bábí blood blossomed crimson across the palace grounds. They were hanged from the rooftops, lassoed in the square, and shot on the lawns.

We had been possessed by a madness, and I had never enjoyed myself more.

These events did not come without consequence, however.

Shusha was the first to leave. I do not believe he was even going to say goodbye, but Şelale came to tell me. When I went to his room, I found him packing his meagre belongings into a leather case. He looked older than he ever had.

"Where are you going?" I asked him.

"Away."

I laughed. "I forbid it."

He sat down on his bed, shoulders sagging, eyes devoid of that sparkle they once held.

"Afsar, do you not see what is happening here? Those are people out there."

"The Bábí attempted to kill my father," I said. "They must be punished."

He sighed, long and drawn-out, as though the winds of the Dasht-e Kavir were leaving him. When he finally regained the strength to speak, he looked up as though seeing me from a very great distance.

"It is my fault," he told me. "I should have taught you politics. I should have taught you history as it truly happened, not as the victors wished it to be written. There is so much more you should know, Shahzadi. Perhaps then you would have compassion."

"You are saying that I do not feel?" I asked, anger sharpening my voice.

"Do you?" he replied, calmly. "That man whose life you ended the other day, do you not think he looked like me? I watched you. I saw the pleasure you took, and I thought to myself that could be me."

"Oh!" I said, sitting down beside him and taking his hand in mine. "No, teacher. Never think that. You have taught me so much in my life. You have known me since I was very young. You are a good and loyal servant of the Shah. I would never cause you harm."

"That is it, though, Afsar. That man that you killed, how many children did he see into this world? How many people had he taught?"

"What could a Bábí teach anyone?" I snorted.

"Oh, Afsar." He sighed again. "You do not understand, and I fear you never shall. It is for that reason that I must leave."

For a moment, I thought to forbid him again. Threats came thick and fast to me. I would have him executed, I would have him strung from the roof, or placed in the prison. All of these options ran through my mind, but were prevented from reaching his ears by my heart.

In honesty, I loved Shusha.

He was perhaps the only person in the entire palace who had read my poetry, and who understood how important it had been for me to have an education. He had spent hours teaching me languages and encouraging my music, even though he knew that I was not gifted. A threat is only worth something if you are prepared to carry through on it, and I was not.

He was not the only one to leave. Other members of staff seemed to slip away in the night, never to return. It mattered little, as they were soon replaced by others. There were always people who required work. It simply meant that we gained a more wholesome type of servant: ones loyal only to Islam and to my father.

Nowruz 1232 was overshadowed by a catastrophic event that would change the course of our family, and history, forever.

Two days after the Equinox, whilst the palace was in a frenzy of feasting and good cheer, Shokuh, my father's favoured wife, gave birth to a son, Mozaffar.

By this time, my father had returned to the palace, apparently no worse for the failed attempt on his life. Indeed, his spirit seemed redeemed. He commended the Darougheh for his work in rounding up the traitors. He watched a few displays of lasso in the shooting yard, and publicly extolled the progress I had made, for my noose never missed any more.

A few days later, the prisoners in the stables mysteriously disappeared. I doubt anyone but the Darougheh and his men knew where they went, and they would never tell another soul.

That marked the end of the rosy hours, those months in which we had all shown ourselves to be Caspian tigers, protecting our territory and felling our enemies.

Towards the end of Shokuh's pregnancy, she was instructed by the physicians not to move too much, so my father called upon Eirik to entertain her. Instead of the packed audiences he had drawn in the hall, he now performed to a select group of family in the lounge. He would frequently appear dressed in his black and white mask, summoning invisible crows and brilliant butterflies.

I would often attend these displays, marvelling at how this man, with a face like a gallu, could construct a palace from solid rock and the very next moment dance about the room as delicately as a Darvesh. My father took to calling him by alternate names, one day his 'Prince of Conjurers,' the next his 'King of Stranglers.' Whatever task he was called upon to do, he executed faultlessly.

When the baby came, Mother Shokuh spent more than an entire day in labour. My father left for Tehran to escape her screams.

Shokuh had called for her own family's midwife. Because of this, rumour soon became rife amongst my mothers that her slighting of Bousseh would cause the child to be born with two heads, or chicken claws for feet.

None of this was true. When it came my turn to hold the bawling bundle of flesh and fat, I could see that it was perfectly healthy and full of life.

"He will be Shah some day," Eirik said, looking at it over my shoulder.

"Mahmoud is the eldest."

"Shokuh is his favourite." He smiled and walked off, leaving me staring into the red cheeks of destiny.

What did I care? That would be years away. Let Mahmoud and Mozaffar fight it out when the time came. They'd probably both be beaten by Rahim, who hadn't quite been two years of age when he'd discovered the effects of lens glass on ants, and sleeping cats.

I handed the child to mother Tala, who almost dropped it in her excitement.

Mozaffar in himself was not the catastrophic event. It was the plan inspired by his birth, and put in motion afterwards, that would be so devastating for me.

"Come, come, daughter. Leave Şelale outside," my father's favoured consort bid me enter the library. It had been just over a week since she became a mother. Her cheeks glowed with health, and if her figure was any plumper, it was indistinguishable beneath the folds of fine fabric she wore. No longer chiming with silver charms or lacquered in bright-red rouge, she had softened somewhat. The more natural she was, the younger she looked, as though she had given birth to half a decade.

"Mother," I acknowledged.

Closing the door on Şelale, I went to sit in the chair opposite her, at the table with the wooden globe embedded in the centre.

"Your father thought it time that we had a little talk."

I couldn't think what the topic might be, so I remained silent.

"Here." She pushed a plate of baghlava towards me, sprinkled with almonds and pistachio, dripping with honey.

"No, thank you," I replied.

"A little tea, perhaps?" She smiled and poured me a glass anyway.

"Am I in trouble?" I asked, unable to think of any other reason why I should be summoned.

Shokuh laughed and poured herself a glass. "You don't have to be," she replied, fixing me with her eyes. "It all depends."

"On what?"

"How you feel about marriage."

The icy winds of the Alborz screamed through my veins.

"I'm not old enough to marry," was my first objection.

"You're twelve now, Afsar. There are women who have been married for years by your age. Your father can't keep you forever. Besides, until you marry, what hope have your sisters?"

I felt like a piece of wood caught in the metal vice of the carpenter's shop. She held me in her grip, tightening and squeezing so that I would bend.

Well, I would rather break.

Before I could open my mouth to object further, she tapped her glass against the tabletop, jolting me to attention.

"The first thing that we need to establish is that this is not optional," she told me. "It does not matter if you do not want to marry, you shall marry. What is optional is who you marry."

"You're jealous," I said, as soon as I regained the power of speech. "You were jealous of Azin, so you had her killed. You are jealous of me, so you are marrying me off."

She touched the back of her head and laughed. "Oh, my dear girl. For too long you have thought yourself special, different to the rest of us, when in fact you have simply been spoiled. Your father is mine now, as is everything in his kingdom. Which includes you."

"I won't let you do it."

"You don't need to. Your father has agreed. It is long past time you had a husband. You've grown wild these past few years. I'm sure you'd rather please him by doing as he asks than disappoint him with your frankly average poetry," she said, pulling a scrap of paper from her sleeve and throwing it on the table.

I recognised it as verse I had written a few weeks previously. My cheeks burned hot with shame.

"Or, worse, with your reputation as a girl who goes walking at night, looking for village children to torment."

My heart turned to stone and fell to the floor. I could hardly believe my ears, that she of all people would know this.

"So," she continued, "it really is quite simple. Whether you marry a prince or a frog is entirely up to you, for there are plenty of both to choose from."

In the moment it took to reach for my tea and dampen my parched mouth, a glimmer of a decision formed.

"I know who I wish to marry," I told her.

"Oh?"

"Vachon. I wish to marry Vachon."

"Your father's servant? Impossible."

"He's not a servant. He's a master mason, he builds palaces."

"He's a magician, he performs tricks."

"He would treat me well."

"We would be a laughing stock. It is impossible."

"Then I shall–"

"Then I shall choose for you," she said, tapping the glass so hard against the table that it shattered.

I sobbed into my pillow that night. How low I had come, to consider Eirik as a husband, not because he was attractive or rich, but because I knew that we were well suited. He would never demand anything of me, he would protect me, and we would enjoy the same pleasures and pastimes together in married life as we did unwed.

Eirik was my only friend, because I did not need another.

When morning came, my eyes were still red and full of grit. I dismissed Şelale and refused all food. I felt sick from head to toe. Of course I had known that this day would eventually come. I was not completely naïve. Yet knowing did not lessen the shock.

The way things had been left with Shokuh, I was convinced she would marry me off to Uncle Taqi's fourth son. Fourth eldest and four-eyed, wearing wiry glasses and walking with a limp, acne-ridden and buck-toothed. I would rather follow Azin to the ground than suffer such humiliation.

My one hope was that my father would have someone in mind for his beloved daughter, and that Shokuh would agree with his choice in order to please him.

Still, I was not reassured enough to keep a meal down.

I remained in my room for almost a week, brooding and stewing. I raged into my mirror, pulling my hair and spitting, wondering whether my father's reptilian bride would be able to marry off a disfigured girl? Scarring my face almost seemed an acceptable price to pay for my freedom.

I threw a pot of mica at the wall, where the clay exploded in a shower of glittering powder. I half expected Eirik to step out of it.

"What happened to you?" he asked, finally arriving on the fifth day. "You look half starved."

"Fat lot you care," I glared. "Why are you here?"

"Şelale told me to come. I can see why."

"I'll have her whipped."

"Is she the one you're angry with?"

If my eyes could have sliced him open, he'd be holding his heart in his hands. How dare he suggest that I needed him, or that I had been waiting for him to come. How dare he suggest I was that weak.

"Go away," I screamed.

"If you please."

He turned and started walking back towards the balcony. Hardly thinking, I reached for my dressing table and picked up another pot, throwing it with blinding force at his head.

His hand shot up, knocking the pot out of the air and releasing the kohl inside. Through the puff of soot, a black lark appeared. In its confusion it flew into Eirik, as though looking for a safe place to hide. With one swift movement, he captured it and broke its neck.

"Is this what you are trying to do to me?" he asked, eyes ablaze as he held the silent creature up to my face. "Have I disobeyed you? Must I be punished?"

I was so shocked by the speed of his brutal act that I could think of nothing to say.

Throwing the bird at my feet, he stepped away. He had come to me wearing a sleeveless brown jacket and wide şalvar embroidered with gold thread. I could tell that he had come from the building site as a thin film of brick dust dulled the tanned sheen of his arms. In his smooth leather mask, the one he wore for everyday appearance, he could have stood still and been mistaken for a wooden carving.

"Where were you?" I asked.

"Working. You think your father keeps me for free?"

I went to sit on my bed. Suddenly I did not have the heart for an argument. I was tired from refusing food, and close to tears at the thought of my dreadful fate.

"Did Şelale tell you why you should come?"

"No," he replied, taking the chair the Darougheh had once occupied.

"I am to be married."

I could forgive his lack of expression as masks cannot frown, but I found it harder to accept how level his voice remained. Here was I, my entire life mapped out in misery, my mind screaming like that little bird against his chest – looking for a safe escape – and there he sat, completely unaffected by my announcement.

"I see. Who is the gentleman?"

"How should I know? You think my life is that important?"

"I take it this was not your father's idea?"

"His div wife. That monster has waited to get rid of me from the day she set foot in this palace. She did away with Azin because she was pretty, and Ezzat because she was mean, and now me – because I am loved more than she is."

"If so, why not simply ask your father for a reprieve?"

I held his stare.

"Well," he continued, "it need not be the end of the world. We simply wait until the wedding night, then slip a little opium into his drink. We sprinkle a dash of pig semen and blood on the bed whilst he sleeps–"

"Blood?"

"Of no consequence," he shrugged. "Then we rub *golpar* on his prick and in the morning he'll be too sore to contemplate anything. In fact, he'll be so sore he'll never put it anywhere near you again. Best of all, he'll be too embarrassed to tell anyone. You'll have a marriage made in heaven. A man obliged by law to protect you, feed you, and see to your happiness, and one who will never bother you in the bedroom."

I thought about this for a moment.

"I would still have to move away. The wife joins her husband's harem."

He sat up a little in his chair.

"How long do we have to think about this?" he asked.

"I don't know. They haven't set a date."

"Because they haven't yet found you a husband. In the mean-time," he said, getting to his feet, "would you like to see something? I have a small surprise for you. I think it will put a smile back on your face."

I took his hand and allowed him to help me to my feet.

I had not visited the construction site since before mid-winter. It had become something spectacular in my absence. Columns of white marble towered before the cliff, smooth as bird eggs against the brittle thorns of their rocky nest. The entrance floor was nearly complete, artisans already at work fitting tiny tiles of lapis and malachite against an oceanic template.

Ladders and pulleys had been erected within, setting wide wooden joists at the top of imaginary staircases leading nowhere. Men hung from the scaffolding like monkeys, shouting to one another and throwing tools between platforms. Most wore loose robes with the sleeves tied back so that they wouldn't catch in the ropes, but others, men who looked darker of skin, perhaps Indians, wore nothing but loincloths and turbans, their sweat-streaked muscles glistening beneath the sun.

"Come," Eirik beckoned, watching me stare up through the vaulting theatre of his creation.

"I've never seen anything like it," I said, stepping carefully over discarded bricks and mixing palettes.

"That, over there," he pointed to a pillar of white stone beyond the main wall, "is a flying buttress. You see them on all the great cathedrals of Europe. And this," he traced his finger around an imaginary structure in the sky, "it will be a large domed inner courtyard with an oculus at the top, like the Pantheon in Rome."

"What is the Pantheon?" I asked.

"It's a temple, with an eye in the middle looking up to Heaven. When it rains, the water falls straight through and makes the marble shine. It brings the whole thing to life."

"Don't the people get wet?"

"No, the curve of the dome gives them shelter. And here, I plan to build troughs in quarter sections around the sides, for lighting fires in. We'll have tropical plants, and scented ones like frangipani and night blooming jasmine."

I hung on every word as he walked me across the vast space, imagining walls and halls and high, patterned ceilings. He talked of things from my father's palace that I could imagine, but far more about sights in Europe and Asia that I could not. If I am truthful, I was jealous. Jealous that he could paint pictures of wonderful things, and even more jealous that he could bring them to life. The simplest things that I could imagine, such as having a stallion of my own and riding it to the coast, were impossibilities; falling stars that burn bright and then die, leaving trails of smoke in place of wishes. Yet Eirik, he could dream the grandest dreams and make them truths.

"This way," he said, as we approached the far side of the foundations nearest the cliff.

At first, I thought we were going to walk around the back to the rope lift. I thought that he wanted to show me the latest plans he had been working on, but I was wrong. Glancing around to make sure that no one was paying too much attention, he removed a tile in a supporting column to reveal a lever. Pulling it, a larger panel opened in the floor between us.

"After you," he motioned.

Without hesitation, I descended the narrow staircase into darkness. As he followed above, the panel slid back into place and I could see nothing.

"Keep going," his voice came through the dark, dank air. "You'll know when you reach the bottom. It is not yet tiled."

Sure enough, my slipper found bare earth. I took a couple of steps forward so that he could stand beside me. A moment later I heard him strike a flint, then bright flame illuminated the space. He took the lead and I followed, ducking slightly along that tight corridor carved out of the ground and supported by wooden joists. We didn't have far to travel before we stopped again. This time he drew an iron key from around his neck and used it to unlock a door to the left. It revealed a second staircase, only this time it was little more than mud, descending once again into total darkness.

"I don't want to go down there," I told him.

"It isn't far, and then it opens out again. I promise, you will like what is on the other side."

I shook my head and took a step back. The shadows cast by his torch made it look as though hands were reaching out of the opening toward me.

"Afsar, don't you trust me?"

I looked back at him. The light from the flame disappeared in his eyes as though swallowed into a bottomless pit. For one brief moment I doubted he was even human.

"Very well," I said.

I went first, all the while holding my hand up so that he could grasp it from behind for safety, in case I slipped. The steps were so barely defined, it was almost a slope. Down and down and down it went. I swore I could hear the beating heart of the demon at the centre of the earth.

After what felt like a night and a day, my foot met solid ground once again. As before, I stepped forward so that Eirik could follow me. He held his torch to the wall and a bright string of flame shot along the tunnel, over a door at the far end, and back towards me. I shied away as it whooshed past my shoulder.

"Clever, isn't it?"

My eyes stung with the brightness of the light.

"It's a special fuel that burns very slowly. I can write words with the wick, or draw pictures, and they will burn for hours."

"How do you snuff it?"

"You can't. You have to wait for it to burn out. I only did this to gain your regard."

I swear he was smiling behind that mask of his.

"Help! Help me!"

My head snapped to the door at the far end.

"Help! Let me out!" someone called in a high, girlish voice.

"Who is it? Who do you have in there?"

"*Moi?*" Eirik asked, innocently raising his hand to his chest.

"Help me. Please let me out."

"Eirik, I don't like this," I said, backing towards the stairs.

"Afsar! Don't leave me!" the voice came again. "Don't leave me down here in the dark!"

I turned on my heels, desperate to return to the surface, only Eirik grasped my wrist to prevent me.

"Wait!" he said. "It's okay, Shahzadi. There's no one there."

"Don't lie to me!" I tried to pull away.

"I promise you. There is no one there."

"I heard them!"

The high-pitched voice came again from behind the door.

"You heard me, Shahzadi? Then get help!"

Confused, I stopped struggling.

"Or come closer, my dear," teased the voice, "and see what lies beyond."

Slowly, I understood.

"It is you. That is your voice?"

"Of course it is," Eirik replied. "When I promise you something, I always mean it. There is nobody there."

"*Heyvoon!*" I erupted, slapping his face so hard his mask came away. "How dare you trick me like that!" I was so angry, the ugliness of his face didn't even shock me.

He went to replace his disguise.

"Leave it off," I ordered. "That is to be your punishment, and mine. You for being so obnoxious, and me for being so stupid."

He laughed at this, but did not argue, tucking his second face into his kamar-band.

The door at the end of the corridor opened into a large room, carved into the side of the cliff. It felt cooler, but the air was less damp. The floor had been strewn with sawdust from the joiners' workshop, making it soft and springy underfoot.

"What is this place?" I asked, entering further inside.

"A present."

He stood back, allowing me to explore for myself. I found that I was drawn towards a chamber at the far end. It was a perfect hexagon made of glass, so that you could walk the perimeter and view the interior from every side. In the centre stood an exquisitely intricate tree, twisted from metal. Its burnished silver branches wound in on themselves, hiding pears and pomegranates that were only visible from certain angles.

"It is beautiful," I whispered, trailing my fingers across the glass as I walked its circumference.

"Ah, but do you know what it is for?"

I shook my head.

"It is for your entertainment."

"In what way?"

"In such a way that the Rosy Hours may continue, long into the evening."

I frowned, assessing the object more practically.

"You put people in here?"

"Anyone you like."

"And you can watch them."

"The floor is under-heated. There is a panel on the third side, you could drop a scorpion in if you wished—"

"There's a lasso!" I said, spotting it for the first time. I hadn't seen it at first because it had been wound from silver cord and twisted around the trunk.

"Do you notice the height of the branches?"

"The height of a man standing on a stool."

"Or a girl, or a boy."

"This is incredible!" I repeated, now that I fully understood what it was. "It's Ja'far's box, only better. A thousand times better."

"That is where I took my inspiration from. The way that you offered him that choice – to die slowly or to take his own life – such a splendid cruelty. I could not believe that I had never thought of it myself. You had outdone me, Shahzadi. Shown me a glimpse of what we could be if our games were combined."

I felt a flush of hot pleasure sweep through me. Nobody had ever complimented me for my intelligence in such a way. He intoned each word as though I were truly something original. No longer a fat grape on the edge of a platter, but the main meal itself.

"Then I have one adjustment to make."

"Anything."

"It shouldn't be made of glass."

"No?"

"Mirrors. They need to be able to watch themselves die."

I assumed that Shokuh had left me alone because the intricacies of palace life demanded more attention than finding her least-favoured daughter a crippled husband. Eirik's opium plot, whether he was joking or otherwise, had ignited a faint glimmer of hope that perhaps the horrors of marriage could be mitigated in part. If all else failed, perhaps we could string my future unfortunate from the metal tree and escape across the mountains.

Perhaps Eirik could build a palace of his own down there, beneath my father's house. He was so skilled with trapdoors and secret panels that no one would ever be able to find us. We could easily go for years unnoticed, living off stolen food and entertaining ourselves with our toy box.

In truth, Shokuh had not been ignoring me. She had simply been waiting.

One week before Ramadan, I was summoned before Mahde Olia in the main hall. She sat cross-legged on the floor, her ancient frame curved forward, elbows supported against her knees. Beneath her thickly-patterned robes of red and black, I imagined the leather wings of a dragon to be folded. I even wondered for a moment whether she herself might be the great dragon who returned the sun to the sky at Nowruz.

I removed my shoes by the archway as a sign of respect. In the silence of the hall, my soles sounded as though they were clapping against the tiles, applauding one of Eirik's magic tricks. The only sound louder was that of my heart.

I sank to the floor, cross-legged before her.

"Grandmother," I said, pressing my forehead to the ground.

"Eldest child," she replied, as I straightened.

A long period of silence followed. She reached out a finger and placed it beneath my chin, moving my head from one side to the other, examining my face. She took a strand of my hair and tested it with her thumb to see whether it was soft or strong. She even pulled down my lower lip to study my teeth.

When she was satisfied, she sat back a little.

"You are twelve years of age now, Afsar. Your mother believes it is time for you to marry."

Another uncomfortable silence passed, of which my grandmother was mistress.

Then she asked me, "How do you feel about this?"

There are defining moments in life when you must decide who you are. Every fibre of my being resented the thought of marriage. I hated the way that my body was changing, and the thoughts that these changes inspired in men. Shahab had been something sent from another world. I did not believe there would ever be another like him in my lifetime, especially not the lifetime that Shokuh had planned for me.

Yet, I was a daughter of my father's house.

A daughter of the Lion.

As I stared into my grandmother's eyes, I understood the weight of centuries. All of the decisions women had made, not because they wanted to, but because they had to. Those were the decisions that brought us to this time and place, that dictated the fate of generations. Men may fight their battles with sword and armour, but women's wars are won with words and deeds.

"I would very much like to be a wife," I said, quietly. "Nothing would give me more pleasure."

A slow smile spread across my grandmother's lips. Seeing the pleasure in her eyes brought a sort of pleasure to my own heart. A watery pleasure, one that paled beside the oil paint of Shahab's kiss, or the tightening of a Punjab lasso around my neck, but a pleasure nevertheless.

"There will be no wedding for you," came her words.

For a moment, I thought that I had misheard.

"You will never be a bride."

With that, she pushed herself to her feet and walked away, leaving me sitting there on the floor by myself.

At first, I felt relief. It was as though the executioner's sword had missed, screaming above my head but leaving me free to resume my life. My grandmother had overruled my father's wife. I had been spared.

The realisation was slow to dawn that this was not an act of kindness.

"What are you doing?" I asked, entering my room two days later to find Şelale packing the contents of my dressing table into a leather case. All of the wooden chests had gone. "Where are my clothes?"

She jumped with surprise, turning as though not expecting me to be there.

"Sultana," she said, her eyes puffy with tears.

"What is going on?"

"I do not know how to tell you this."

"Are you leaving?"

She held the back of her hand to her nose, to hide her crumpled chin.

"No, Sultana. We are leaving."

A wisp of laughter escaped my lips. "Stop being so silly. Put my things back immediately."

"It is an order. I cannot disobey."

"An order from whom?"

"Your grandmother."

A felt a cold prickle seep down my spine.

"You are to live at Shirgah, in the old River House."

"But that is a ruin!" I cried.

"They tell me there are some rooms restored. There is a tower, with supplies and a cooking hut." Her voice trailed off, aware of how insubstantial her words sounded. "We are to leave in the morning."

♦ 7 ♦

I exploded into my father's study. The door swung back, cracking against the wall in my rage, but my father was nowhere to be seen. I searched the halls, I shouted at servants, imploring them to find him, but no one could tell me where he might be.

Eventually, I went to the lounge. This was a room that I had been reluctant to enter since Shahab's murder. There, I found Shokuh and Mahde Olia partaking of tea.

I stood in the doorway, demanding to be noticed.

Shokuh looked up, calmly. "What do you want, Afsar?"

"I want to see my father."

"That is impossible. He is abroad, talking to the Russians."

"He would never allow you to send me away."

"Don't be so dramatic, child. It is only the other side of Sari, and you will be as comfortable there as you are here."

"This is my home. It always has been, long before you arrived."

Shokuh placed her cup on its saucer and rose. She was taller than I was, an imposing figure in her black silk and bright rouge. Before she could speak, my grandmother spoke for her.

"This was my home long before it was yours," she said, turning in her chair to look at me. "You should show more respect for your mother."

I was beyond anger now, my lips capable of speaking my thoughts so clearly that they would get me in trouble.

"And who has shown respect for me?" I asked.

"Those born without respect, gain no respect."

I did not understand her answer.

"You are excited," Shokuh said, taking another step towards me. "It is hot today, perhaps this has tired you. The Darougheh will see you to your room. You need to rest for your journey tomorrow."

I had been so blind with disbelief that I had not even noticed the Darougheh standing by the door.

"I am not tired, and I do not want to sleep," I said. "I want to see my father."

"And I have told you, that is impossible. Affairs of the country take precedence over the affairs of a spoiled little girl. Now, you will go to your room or I will have you carried there."

Her words were like water in a sink. Everything around me was spinning so fast, yet I was standing still. My vision blurred for a moment, and I thought perhaps I might faint from the hatred boiling up inside of me. If only my lasso had been in my hands, I dread to think what I might have done to my mother at that moment.

I felt the Darougheh's hand fall lightly against my arm. Turning to him, I allowed myself to be gently led from the room.

When we arrived at my quarters, Şelale was not to be seen. The space felt much larger now that all of my familiar belongings had been removed. All of the clothes and the toys and the trinkets that had occupied this room since I was old enough to remember – all of the things that made this my room – were gone. I did not recognise it any longer.

The Darougheh did not leave.

"What have I done?" I asked, turning in circles in the centre of the room, looking for an echo of the life I had always known. "Why do they hate me?"

Hot tears spilled down my cheeks as I collapsed on the floor. After a moment's hesitation, the Darougheh came forward, kneeling to scoop me up in his strong arms. He took me to the bed, where he stroked my hair as I cried against his chest.

When the worst of it was over, the sharpness of my fury blunted, I stared up at him and asked the same question.

"What have I done?"

"Ah, Shahzadi." His green eyes stared ahead at the opposite wall whilst he spoke, his hand still stroking my hair. "I do not think it is possible for anyone to love you more than your father did. I promised him – we all did – that it would never come to this. That your life would be a comfortable one, and that you would be happy. Unfortunately, he is no longer here to protect you, and old wounds are slow to heal."

"My father is dead?" I straightened in alarm.

"He has been dead a long time."

For a moment, I thought perhaps I had fainted after all, that this was a vision, or a dream. The words the Darougheh spoke could not be true, and so I reasoned that if they were not true, and if this was simply an apparition, there would be no harm in hearing more.

"Who was he?" I asked.

The Darougheh's eyes eventually met mine. He sighed in the way Shusha had sighed the day that he left, as though he were breathing out centuries.

"My child, you are twelve years old, and the Shah is twenty-two. He would not have been capable of fathering you. No, his first child was Mahmoud. Shah Mohammad was your father, and you were the last of his children."

This revelation was a shock, but one that I could survive. I was still a daughter of the royal dynasty. No longer the Shah's daughter, but his sister!

"Who was my mother?" I asked.

On this matter, the Darougheh remained quiet.

"Please," I begged.

"I took an oath, Afsar. You are not to know these things."

"I didn't hear them from you. I heard it from a stable boy."

"No stable boy would know this."

"Şelale?"

"Not even her. She was hired after you were born."

"There is nothing happens beneath the roof of this palace that one of my mothers does not know."

He laughed at this. "Well, perhaps Bousseh knew. Perhaps she told you a story once, and it has only now come to make sense."

"Was she there when I was born?"

"She was."

"What was the story she told me?"

"Perhaps she told you that your grandfather was a difficult man to love, because he found it difficult to love others."

"Shusha told me once that Shah Mohammad's brother stole the throne from him."

"That is correct. Because of that, he did not trust easily for the rest of his life, not even his wives or his sons. There were only two women he trusted implicitly. One was Mahde Olia, and the other was his final mistress, Nasrin."

"Named for the wild rose?"

"Indeed, wild and untamed. She was the daughter of a tribal warlord in the snowy Alborz. Your father claimed her as a trophy after defeating her tribe's attempts to steal grain one harsh winter."

"She did not run away?"

"No," he shook his head. "She became the love of your father's life. He doted on her."

"Do I look like her?"

"As though I were staring at her reflection through the river of time."

"Which is why I am despised by Mahde Olia?"

"Everything she had worked so hard to obtain, privilege, power and influence, he gave to your mother without question. They called her a witch. They said she must have enchanted your father."

"Was she?" I looked up, afraid of his answer.

"I couldn't say. Those people up there in the hills, they have strange customs. It was enough that people thought it."

After a moment, I asked him to tell me again how my mother died. He repeated the story I had always been told, that she had succumbed to fever after my fifth birthday, and that Shah Mohammad had pined for her until his death two years later.

"Did she die of fever?" I asked him.

"I do not know what you mean, Afsar."

"Did she die of fever, or did somebody decide that she should die?"

"We do not speculate on treason," he said, his voice hardening.

"Were you with her when she died? Did you know the physician who attended her?"

"That is enough." He stood from the bed. "This conversation has come to its end."

I called out to him before he reached the door.

"Darougheh, if you are my friend, answer me one last question before you leave."

He turned, but did not speak.

"Darougheh, what did *you* think of my mother?"

I watched his eyes consider me for a moment, light from the lamps dancing across them.

"I thought she was the most beautiful creature that ever drew breath."

I watched as that grey dawn broke on the morning of my exile. Sleep had not come for me after the Darougheh left. Instead, a hundred different histories sabotaged my mind as over and over I tumbled in the memories I thought I had known.

Everything seemed different now.

The man I had called Father for so long was not my father. The woman I had called grandmother was not even my blood relation. All these years I had looked up to her, wanted to be like her, wanted to impress her, and all that time she had secretly hated me.

Not so secretly any more.

If I had ceased to be blind in my adoration, I would have seen the signs long ago. When I unpicked the soiled carpet of my mind, I discovered a thousand wrinkled noses, the flat tone of her voice when she spoke to me, the missed stitches as her eyes passed over my face without stopping.

Silly Afsar. Seeing what you hoped was there when all the time it wasn't. Little, lost, motherless child.

I had been seven when my grandfath–, when my *father*, died.

He had been a big, broad bear of a man, lacking my brother's refinement. He dressed in black, trimmed in red, and dripping with silver. He had a brittle, black beard and a bellowing roar which echoed through the halls of the palace.

I do not remember him as someone who spent much time with me. I do not remember him as someone who held me, or played with me, or loved me. Though his presence remained large, he was forever a distant man.

Could he really have been my father?

If he had loved my mother so completely, if everything the Darougheh had said were true, then why had he not loved me equally? A room full of clothes and toys is no substitute for a dead mother. If I came from her, and I looked like her, then why would I not replace her in his affections? Why would he choose death over me?

These thoughts had not loosened their grip by the time Şelale came to my room. She knocked lightly, not wishing to wake me from the final moments of peace that she hoped sleep might bestow.

"Come," I said.

She entered to find me sitting on my balcony overlooking the forest, wrapped in a thick blanket to protect me from the chill.

"Sultana," she said softly, coming to sit beside me. "Will you let me wash you and dress you? There is still time before the carriage arrives."

We walked through our ritual as though in a trance. The sun rose, but the sky did not adopt its brilliance. As I felt the sponge trace the curves of my adolescent body, I heard thunder in the distance. She oiled out my hair and pinned it with every adornment she had not already packed. I looked like a peri by the time she had finished. A beautiful angel, sent to work off my mortal debts.

"It will not be so bad," she told me. "Everything you could miss of this place, I have already put on the carts."

"What is there to miss?" I replied.

A covered *vis-à-vis* awaited us in the forecourt, blue with a black awning. I told Şelale to sit with her back to the driver as I hated to travel backwards.

No one came to wave goodbye. Shokuh must have issued an order, though I doubted she would have gone to the trouble of explaining herself. That is what hurt the most. I was being sent away because of their wretched jealousy, their spite, and their inability to bear the fact that my mother had been most loved amongst her people. More so than the great Mahde Olia. They would spread lies about me, I knew it. They would say that I had been sent away for some indiscretion. They would call my character into question. They would tell the world that I was no good, that I was spoiled inside.

Well, perhaps I was. When infamy calls, you are a disappointment only if you do not answer.

As our carriage made its way to the road that led out of Sari, it was joined by two heavy carts which were piled high with my belongings, and with provisions for my exile. After talking with the Darougheh, I had come to the strong suspicion that my mother had been poisoned by a jealous rival.

I wondered what delicacies Shokuh had sent for my own kitchen.

The town of Shirgah was founded where the rivers Talar and Keselyan meet, surrounded by towering mountains. Shusha once told me that in ancient times it was called The Place of Bloody Thorns, because the undergrowth grew so thick that it scraped the skin from the hunters who went to find food for their families.

Later, it was renamed for the cow and the lion who fought a deadly battle there. The lion belonged to a powerful Shah who wagered that no animal could beat it in battle. He offered a reward of much riches to anyone who could prove him wrong.

One day, a local farmer came to the square and declared that he had an animal that could beat the lion. When the Shah arrived to take up the challenge, he held his own sides and wept with laughter. All he could see was a single calf tied to a post.

"Is this a joke?" he asked.

"No, master," the farmer replied. "Your lion will bow down before this calf."

The whole crowd shook their heads in disbelief as the Shah released his lion. It saw the calf immediately and began to move towards it, creeping on its belly, low to the ground.

The lion got so close to the calf that it could have reached out with one paw and opened its belly. Just as it was preparing to pounce, a sound began to rise from the parted onlookers. The lion was so startled that it forgot the calf and turned to see a giant black cow appear. The cow lowered its head, stamped the ground with its hooves, and charged.

The lion and the cow fought for a night and a day, round the village and up and down the mountains. The cow was eventually so tired that she could not move one more muscle, so the lion left her standing in the square whilst he went to claim his prize.

As the lion prepared to pounce for the second time, the cow summoned the very last of her strength. She kicked the lion in the head, killing it.

Then she collapsed beside her calf and died of exhaustion.

"Well," said the Shah. "Your animal was not victorious over mine, as they are both dead. However, I shall allow you to keep your calf as a prize."

The crowd were so outraged at the Shah's lack of honour that they shouted and booed until he was forced to give the farmer his cow's weight in gold and a big house to live in.

As we approached my own dwelling, I closed my eyes and tried to imagine that it was the great mansion that the Shah had bestowed upon the farmer.

It was far from it.

We had travelled six hours or more, and I felt sick from the motion of the carriage. Shirgah was not so far from Sari, but the carts were as slow as Ezzat's wit, and the weather had broken halfway. On top of it all, one of the wheels on my carriage had hit a rock and splintered, forcing us to stop to replace it. Every hour that passed on that road had brought with it some fresh hell. I had always dreamed of what it might be like to escape the confines of the palace, and now I longed to crawl back to them.

The old River House was built on a flat piece of land at the point where the two rivers met. It had once been a summer retreat for the wives of royal princes, though it had fallen out of fashion long ago. People preferred to take their holidays by the coast. I knew of it only because Ezzat had once visited with three of my brother's other wives, imagining that it was still a luxurious retreat. They complained about it for weeks afterwards, whilst my brother, the Shah, laughed and told them they should have listened to him when he said that it was not worth the journey.

It was a big house that smelled of dust and decaying water weed. The once-costly marble tiles were chipped. One or two were completely shattered, cracks spreading like spider-webs, waiting to catch bare feet upon their sharp edges.

On all three sides the house was hidden from the rivers by a jungle of overgrown trees. Had there been groundsmen to cut back the progression of time, there might have been a very fine view. As it was, neither beauty nor sunlight reached my eyes.

As the light faded and the men unpacked the carts, Șelale did her best to clean. With a pail of water she had collected from the river, and an old scrap of cloth she had found discarded there, she got down on her hands and knees and tried to wipe away the decades of dirt.

I wanted to tell her to stop, that no amount of scraping and rubbing could wash away the disappointment of this place. Instead, I bit my tongue. If it brought her comfort, then so be it. Besides, what else was there for us to do except play nard?

The men Shokuh had sent with us were little help. They did not unpack anything, they simply left the chests and sacks strewn throughout the rooms. When the carts had been unloaded, they returned to them and left. We listened to the slow rumble of wheels, that hollow, empty sound, an echo of our own abandonment.

Two men remained, dressed in shabby robes with little more than a *shamshir* between them. I feared they might cut their fingers on its sharp blade, trying to work out which end to hold.

Their names were Hesam and Hafez, and by the look of them they were probably brothers. Both shorter than my own brother's guards, and olive-skinned like the traders from the West. When I asked why they stayed, they told me that the Shah would be angry should anything happen to me.

I wondered who had told them this. Did Mahde Olia somehow fear that my brother might uphold his promise to protect me against all harm? Even against her? I doubted that. I was no longer under any illusion. My brother had many more tasks to attend to in running his country than to pamper a half-sister no longer in sight.

Between the backwards-forwards motion of Șelale's rag against the tiles, I told her my conclusion.

"They are here to kill me. When I have been gone long enough that nobody remembers me, she will order them to kill me."

After all, Mahde Olia had ordered my brother's senior advisor to be murdered in a bath house.

I found a table with a chipped vase and dragged it to the centre of the room. The oil lamps burned so dimly that everything seemed to have a softer edge to it. The light was impossible to read by, but good practice for my lasso. If my grandmother were to order my assassination, they would come in the early hours or in the evening, possibly in the dead of night. I realised that I should practice hard at every opportunity so that my rope would not miss when I needed it most.

On my first attempt, I caught the vase off centre. It fell to the floor where it smashed.

I took it as a sign that my life was in danger. They had banished me as an adult, but really I was still a child, with all the nightmares and fears of a child. I saw faces in the shadows, and flashing sabres in the reflection of the lamps in the mirrors.

As my heart began to pound in the silence of my first Shirgah night, I knew with certainty that Shokuh and Mahde Olia had conspired to burn me alive in that godforsaken house. The smoke from the firewood rose to suffocate me, its funerary flames licking at the foundations of my ruined sanctuary.

"Sultana," Şelale spoke from the doorway. "This is Sheyda."

"What of it?" were the words that left my lips before my eyes came to rest upon her. She was nothing really, not to look at. Her feet were bare and she wore a simple *kameez* of cheap purple cloth with a full brown skirt to her ankles. There was no lace or gold thread to decorate her attire. From the back, she would have seemed quite ordinary. Yet it was not from the back that I first saw her.

Sheyda's eyes defined her. There was nothing unusual about their size or shape, but they were the darkest bistre-brown you could imagine, and she had a crescent moon birthmark of the same shade riding high on her left cheek.

"She is your cook, Sultana. She has been sent from the village to live here. She has built a fire in one of the sheds and would like to know what you will take to eat?"

"What can she make?" I asked, never lifting my eyes from the girl.

"I can make whatever you would like," she replied. "We have fish from the river, or perhaps lamb with boiled plums? I can make āsh. We have some pickled vegetables, which I can present in parcels with vine leaves and sweet rice?"

"Make me whatever you like, only make it from local goods. Cook nothing from the supplies that were brought with us from Sari."

The girl nodded and left to go about her work whilst Şelale began picking up the pieces of broken pottery around the table.

"Who is that girl?" I enquired.

"I know nothing more than you do," she replied. "She was sent from the village to see whether we had work for her. She knows the local suppliers and we need a cook, so I showed her to a place where she could make a fire."

I didn't bother to ask how she had known we were here. The town was hardly half the size of Sari and we had entered it with a veritable camel train in tow. You would need to have been blind and deaf not to have noticed us passing.

"If you don't care for her, Sultana—"

"No, she may stay."

When Sheyda returned, she brought a simple plate of rice and fish, with a cup of sweetened milk.

"Taste it," I told her, as she placed the dishes on the floor before me. I watched carefully as she sat cross-legged, facing me. She reached out and pinched a little of the rice between her fingers, her soft pink lips closing around them as she sucked at the white grain.

"And the fish."

When she had eaten of the food and sipped the milk, we sat for a moment more in silence. I looked at her, as it was my right to do so, yet the strange thing was that she returned my stare with equal calm.

When I finally dismissed her, I ate my meal and retired to my bedchamber.

That night, I dreamed that I had awoken in my old bedroom at the palace near Sari. It was the sound of the fountain in the courtyard that had woken me. When I descended the steps I found myself surrounded by colour. The water flowed like liquid crystal, crisper and clearer than I ever remember it being. Sunlight hit the mirrors, reflecting green and red and blue like a thousand jewels. It was so very beautiful.

I woke softly as though rising from the depths of an ocean. Perhaps I even smiled, until I saw the motes of dust glitter in the dawn and remembered where I was. The sound of water had not come from the rose-scented fountain of my youth, but from the rivers that met beyond the trees.

My heart felt heavy as I swung my legs over the side of the bed and sheathed my feet in kidskin. The air was staler here without the breeze from the Caspian Sea. The mountains muffled the wind and even the birdsong seemed muted.

"Good morning," Şelale said, appearing at my door. "I have warmed water on our kitchen fire."

She placed the wooden tub on the floor and I stepped into it, allowing her to pull my nightshirt over my head.

"What is the point?" I asked her.

"Sultana?"

"The point. The point. What is the point of getting up, of getting dressed, of anything? Who is going to visit? Who are we going to entertain? Who cares whether we sit here and starve?"

She looked at me, startled. "You shouldn't say such things."

"There is nobody here to care whether we live or die."

"What if your father should call?"

I almost told her that unless he could rise from the dead it would be unlikely, but I was not ready yet to disclose my secret. Shusha had not taught me diplomacy as such, but he had taught me that sometimes the best you can say is nothing.

After she had pinned my hair with silver, and scented me with jasmine, I made my way to the back porch to await breakfast.

"You shouldn't sit there," she said, following me like a lost dog. "Sheyda's cousin works as a groundsman at the mosque. You should wait until he clears the scrub. There may be snakes."

"Let there be snakes. I'll snap their spines and then at least we'll have fresh meat to live off."

Şelale laughed, and I smiled.

"I know it looks hopeless now Sultana, but they will send for you soon, you wait and see."

"I have no choice but to wait," I replied.

I felt as though I had been waiting my entire life for my life to begin, first stuck inside a royal palace, now stuck inside a ruined shack. The closest I had ever come to living was on the nights of the full moon, when Eirik and I would sneak into Sari to play at being paupers.

Sheyda appeared on the porch with a plate of dried fruit and a cup of spiced milk. She placed them beside me and tasted them without being asked. First a plump fig, its tiny seeds cracking like grains of sand between her teeth, then the milk, its cardamom scent reminding me of infancy.

As she ate, I studied her face more closely. It was rounder than my own, though her cheeks were still well defined. That crescent moon looked as though it might be waxing with her own fortunes, for I doubted she had ever laid eyes on the daughter of a Shah before, yet alone served one.

"How does it taste?" I asked.

"Good—" She hesitated, uncertain how to address me.

"Good, Shahzadi."

She repeated my words, bowed her head and made to leave.

"Wait," I instructed. "Tell me what the villagers say of me."

I expected her to stumble over her words whilst she thought of something that would please me. Instead, she stood tall where she was, her eyes rising to meet mine behind heavy lashes.

"They say that you are an exalted daughter of the Shah, here to rest before your wedding."

"When do they say my wedding will be?"

"Nobody talks of a date."

"And who shall be my husband?"

"Nobody talks of a husband."

"And what do they really say of me?"

Her tongue flickered quickly across her upper lip, the only sign of nerves she had shown.

"They say that you have been banished by your father because you refuse to marry."

I held her gaze for a moment longer, then turned my face away.

After she had gone I filled my mouth with fruit and milk, for I was famished.

That night the dream came again, and the night after, and the night after that. Every night the same, standing there beside the scented fountain, each time the colours a little brighter. I felt a sense of joy I could not describe. I had never really stopped to look at that fountain since I was a child. It had simply become a place to pass through between my quarters and the grounds of the palace. Yet, in my dream, it was a palace all of its own.

On the evening of the fourth day, I decided to explore the house, wrapped in a thick woollen shawl as the heat of summer had been washed away by the rivers. The house was not big, but it was much bigger than my quarters at the palace. There were perhaps eight or nine bedrooms on the upper floor, a large room that might once have been a kitchen to the rear, two or three spacious rooms for entertaining guests, a parlour, and perhaps a library, for there were several collapsed shelves.

It was from one of the upstairs windows that I chanced to see Sheyda with Hafez. She had firewood in her arms and appeared to be trying to pass him to get to the cooking hut. Each time she went to pass, he would lean to one side to prevent her.

"Please," she told him, "I need to build the fire or it will go out."

He laughed. "I can keep you warmer than that fire."

"Perhaps, but I cannot boil āsh on your butt."

I covered my mouth with my shawl to stifle my laugh.

"Come now," he said, trying to wrestle the firewood from her arms. "Let me help you with that."

"Thank you, but I can manage. If you truly wish to help me, let me pass."

"What's the hurry?" he asked, cutting her off once again.

"I told you, the fire will go out and I have food to prepare."

He leaned in close to her, taking a strand of her hair from beneath her scarf and twisting it around his finger.

"Five minutes of your time, that's all I'm asking. Then I will light the fire for you and even chop the vegetables."

I felt cold inside. I didn't want him to touch her.

When she shook her head and told him no, I realised that I had been holding my breath.

That night I had the dream again. In the courtyard, the sound of the water seemed louder than before, and the colours glowed so brightly they were blinding. It was the strangest of dreams. I felt completely myself within it, as though I was not aware that I was dreaming at all.

When I approached the water to look at my reflection, the colours faded. I thought perhaps a cloud had covered the sun, but when I looked up it was still shining brightly in the sky. As I stared, I felt something soft around my neck. My fingers felt for it and found there a fine silk sash.

"You left without saying goodbye," Eirik whispered in my ear.

I awoke bathed in sweat.

Eirik was there, at the end of the bed!

I sat up rubbing my eyes, but when I looked again there was only an old hat stand with Şelale's blue maghnaeh hanging from it.

I reached for the glass of water by my bed and took several long sips.

"You should have said goodbye," he repeated, resting against the wall behind me.

I shrieked, spilling water across the sheets.

"I returned and you were gone," he said.

"There was no time," I hissed, struggling to lower my voice. "That div, Shokuh, had been planning this for months, I'm sure of it. They packed me off without any warning. Where were you, anyway?"

"With your father."

"And where was he?"

"There was a conference with the Russians about the Turks. Your father isn't popular at the moment."

It made no sense to me at that time. How could it? The politics of an unstable alliance had little place in the mind of an exiled Shahzadi. Although, put in that context, they probably ought to have.

"How did you find me?"

"The Darougheh was worried about you. He suggested I come to see how you are settling into your new home."

"It is hardly a home," I snorted.

"You have clearly never been destitute," he replied, coming to sit beside me on the bed. He was dressed in black şalvar, shirt and long cape, his mask moulded into sharp cheekbones with a smooth forehead, like the African carvings Uncle Taqi collected alongside his suits of armour. His lips and eyes were traced with brass which shimmered in the half-light.

"I'm going to make them pay, you know. They will be sorry for this."

"For what?" he asked.

"For sending me away, of course! For sending me away from the palace and imprisoning me in this ruin."

"Oh, Afsar," he said, getting to his feet and walking to the window. "You disappoint me."

"I disappoint you?"

"I thought you had more imagination than that."

I rose from the bed to join him.

"Look," he said, placing his hand against my back and gesturing to the darkness. "What do you see when you look into the night?"

I stared for a moment, listening to the sound of the rivers raging against one another beyond the line of trees that were barely visible.

"Nothing," I replied.

"Really? Nothing at all?"

I stared harder. "Perhaps the stars, I can see one just there, and the edge of the porch below."

He tutted and shook his head.

"Why, what can you see?"

"I can see the lights of Tehran from here. Can't you see them, glistening in the dark?"

I frowned at him for a moment, returning my gaze to the night. There were no lights.

"Can't you smell that squid frying in oil beneath Ferdowsi's statue, and the gypsy women with their tambourines and their *qalyan* pipes? Suck in the smoke and blow out a serpent."

Before my eyes a wisp of bright green smoke trailed from between his fingers!

"What are you talking about?"

"You are not a prisoner, Afsar! They have not imprisoned you. The opposite is true. They have given you your freedom. You are constrained only by your own imagination."

"We could go to Tehran?" I whispered.

"We could go anywhere you like. Who is watching?"

Eirik had performed the greatest conjuring trick I had ever seen. One moment I was confined within a box of bricks and mortar, the next I stood looking down on it from afar, the greatest escapologist the world would ever witness. All that it had taken was a subtle twist of perspective, a moment's deft legerdemain of the mind, and I was free.

The elation that followed this realisation caused me to forget myself. I turned to him without thinking, and placed my lips against his cold ebony. He drew back, surprised, and touched his fingers to the spot still warm with my breath.

"Eirik, you are a master!" I laughed. "Why did I never think of it that way? When shall we go?"

"I cannot stay tonight. I have things to do for your father. Next full moon I will return and we shall go then."

"Almost a month from now?" Disappointment rang plain in my voice. "How will I amuse myself until then?"

"I'm sure you will think of something. Use your imagination, not your eyes." His voice rose to that girlish squeak he often used to make fun of my mothers. "'Perhaps a star – oh, there's the porch!'" he mimicked. "Look beyond what things are, to what they might be."

After he left, I sat by the window with my eyes closed, listening to the rivers. No longer did it simply sound like water crashing against water. It sounded like a song. A story. One that started high up in the mountains with the goats and the tribespeople, falling down from the hills like a star falls to earth. Past the palace of a Shah's daughter – a witch – imprisoned by Zahhak's serpents, Shokuh and Olia, destined to be forgotten by time. Then on, on, faster and faster, a chariot of horse-drawn currents frothing white foam from their mouths. On to the capital, through the back streets and the squares, on through the jungles and the rice paddies, flowing beneath the bridges that ancient elders built. On to the Caspian Sea, and across it to Russia and Europe and America.

All the world was a possibility, beginning with me.

When Şelale came to wake me that morning, she found me asleep in a chair by the window with a smile on my lips. I never had that dream again. Instead, my visions were filled with the river and the lands beyond.

"I have warmed the water," she said, placing the tub and towels on the floor. As she did so, a little of the water rose too high and sloshed onto the tiles. "I'll get a cloth."

"Don't bother," I said. "Send that new girl with it."

She paused at the door to look at me.

"Did you not hear what I said?"

When Sheyda arrived, cloth in hand, she looked more in need of a wash than I did. She wore a short bell-skirt of brittle blue fabric, which puffed out above her knees, displaying thin, soot-smudged legs where she had been kneeling by the fire. Her hair was held back with white cloth, her neck and kameez as grubby as her shins.

"You sent for me," she offered.

I beckoned her to come closer. As she approached, she brought with her the thick, ashy scent of burning wood. It was intoxicating, calling up memories of nights by the fire, of tales told and warm sugar burning on the embers; of men jumping high flames on Sizdah Be-dar, the day of chaos.

"Undress me," I told her, stepping into the tub.

Taking the hem of my night shirt, she lifted it over my head, her face ending level with mine. Suddenly I longed for Şelale, for I felt more than naked in Sheyda's presence. In her brown eyes I saw my entire self reflected.

I took a moment to draw breath as she folded my garment and placed it neatly by the pillow on my bed.

When she returned, she knelt to collect the sponge from the water. She rubbed it with a bar of sandalwood soap and began to move the suds in circles lightly up my legs. I thought that I would melt.

As she reached my thighs, she stood so that she could continue more comfortably. When she had finished cleaning my breasts and my neck, she walked around me to clean my back.

"Am I doing this correctly?" she asked, her lips hovering near my ear.

I had no words. I could only nod.

She returned to the front and knelt to rinse out the sponge, staring up at me from the floor. She must have seen it in me. My whole body must have blushed.

Rubbing the sponge against the soap, she stood for a final time, sliding it between my legs, pushing it gently back and forth to clean my most private place.

I could not help myself. A sigh left my lips.

As I closed my eyes, her own mouth met mine.

Our kiss was so fleeting that I thought perhaps I had imagined it. When I opened my eyes she was already bending to rinse the sponge. She spread one of the towels on the floor for me to step onto, and the other she wrapped around me, folding it over the curves of my body.

No longer naked, I thanked her for her service and dismissed her.

For the first time that I could ever remember, I oiled my own hair and dressed myself.

Gradually, Sheyda began to take over more of Şelale's chores, shopping at the market, taking items to be mended, sweeping my room and making my bed. In turn, Şelale spent more time in the cooking hut, preparing meals with a distinctly Turkish flavour.

It was never a formal agreement among the three us, but it suited me best.

"It is understandable," Şelale told me one night over a game of nard, "that you should want someone of your own age to talk with."

I enjoyed Sheyda's company. We spoke little, yet I felt somehow different when I was in her presence. As though a part of me had been missing and, all my life, I had restlessly been trying to locate it. When Sheyda was with me, I no longer believed this. I felt at ease.

One evening I played a rusty old qanun she had found at the market. I played it so badly that it obviously wasn't the state of the instrument that was to blame. But it didn't matter. She laughed, and I laughed, and the palace at Sari felt a thousand lifetimes ago.

Eirik came for me the day before the full moon. He arrived in a fine black carriage drawn by four equally black horses. I did not recognise it as one of my father's, but I was too excited to think of where it came from.

"I very much admire what you have done with the place," he said, noting the animal carvings and the embroidered wall hangings that Sheyda had helped me to choose from the market. "You are settling in?"

"I am exploring the potential of things," I said with a smile, taking his arm and sweeping him through the first of the main rooms to the porch at the back.

"Still no view of the river, I see?"

"My maid's cousin can't come. They say it would be bad luck for him to work for a single, unmarried woman. Even a rich unmarried woman. Şelale has sent to Sari for someone."

"Maids and cousins and groundsmen. So much is changing."

He smiled behind his leather mask. I could tell by the way it lifted a fraction.

"Come, my dear, we must pack. It will take the best part of the day to get there."

"My servants are at the market. I wasn't expecting you."

"No matter, we'll write them a note."

"They cannot read."

"Then I'll paint them a picture."

"But I will need a maid with me," I said, "to help me dress."

"That has been taken care of. Go and pack what you need. Don't bring too much, just a night gown and whatever it is you need to make your hair do that," he said, flicking one of the silver butterfly clasps that held my braids in place.

"I wouldn't know what to pack. Şelale always arranges my–"

"Şelale, Şelale, Şelale," he mimicked. "Anyone would think you were in love with the woman. Just make your best guess. Anything you don't have we can buy."

I flushed hotly and went upstairs to my room.

Partly I wanted to be slow in picking my things, in the hope that Sheyda would come home. It was not simply that I needed her to help me dress, but that I wanted her to come with us. Since that night, when Eirik had planted the seed of possibility in my mind that I might one day get to see our capital city, I had imagined it over and over again, but always Sheyda was by my side. We walked through the royal quarters of the Arg, through the Rose Garden Palace, the seat of my family's power, and lost ourselves in the silks and the scents of the grand bazaar.

In all of those imaginings, I found it hard to think where Eirik might be. Yet it was Eirik who was about to make these daydreams manifest. The allure of adventure finally outweighed my fondness for my maid.

Eirik held my hand whilst I mounted the step of his carriage. I happened to notice that the pattern of silver swirls on the outer panel formed a skull. Two more silver skulls, like ornate handles on walking sticks, were facing forward on either side of the coachman's chair.

It was a dramatic statement.

The journey to Tehran was long and tiring. We left that morning and did not arrive until it was dusk. Eirik drove the horses hard. We stopped only to water them, and once to buy skewered meat from a tradesman. It had not rained in many days, so the road was solid, but the motion of the carriage made me feel faint and I slept as often as I could.

When we finally reached the outskirts of the capital, the first thing that hit me was the smell. Whereas my fantasies had been filled with rose gardens and grand palaces, the reality of Tehran proved to be festering drains and potholes you might drown in. It would be at least another decade before my brother, with his love of engineering and design, would think to develop the city.

As the carriage swayed through the sewage, I felt as though my stomach might escape through my mouth. The horses shied at a group of children spitting pips from the gutter. I heard Eirik's whip crack, forcing them on.

Slow terror began to build in my heart. Where had he brought me? Peering from behind the curtain, I wondered whether he had driven that carriage straight to hell. I saw a woman hitch up her skirt and urinate on the ground. There was another woman suckling a child in plain view, her teat in the infant's mouth. I saw a squid merchant throwing scraps to a creature so riddled with mange that I couldn't tell whether it was a dog or a cat. Every alley we passed seemed to hold down it some new depravity. I saw people passed out from opium pipes, others arguing in the way only wine provokes, and women and men pressed up against walls in positions of pleasure and sin.

I watched all of it.

Everything.

Allowing the curtain to fall into place, I sat back with a smile. Eirik guided me with impunity through those streets of immorality. It was not as I had imagined. It was better.

When we finally came to a halt, I feared to look in case he had arranged for us to stay in a tent made of pigskin. I need not have worried, though. When the door to the carriage swung back, it opened onto a quiet, cobbled courtyard lit by the rising moon.

It was as though we had somehow passed over into the shadow lands, for there was not a single person to be seen. As Eirik reached up his hand to help me to earth, I wondered whether all that I had witnessed from the carriage had simply been one of his illusions.

"Where are we?" I asked.

"In the Arg."

The Arg was the ancient citadel of Tehran. My brother's palace was said to account for more than a third of it. The rest was a web of beautiful gardens and grand houses built to impress foreign dignitaries.

"Come," he said, leading me towards one of these towering abodes. A grand entranceway arched like a brushstroke towards the stars, framed by pillars on either side with a round window of stained glass above, watching us approach.

A boy appeared from this entrance and went to the carriage to fetch my case.

"I've never seen anything like it," I said, as we ascended the steps.

"It's a mixture of Persian and Venetian architecture. The house belonged to the Ambassador to Florence until recently."

"What happened to him?"

Eirik shrugged. "No one is entirely sure. There are constant whispers of war and unification from his part of the world. Perhaps he had more pressing business to attend to."

"How lucky for you."

And lucky he was indeed, for his apartments were magnificent. The entrance hall comprised black and white tiles like a chess board, with red roses blooming between ceramic diamonds that separated the pattern and confused the eye. The walls were hung with fine white-gold damask, falling in drapes from ceilings of dizzying height, where a crystal chandelier hung like a princely crown. I stared at it a fraction too long, and when I looked away all the world was dancing with little black dots.

In Persia we favour wide, open spaces with archways, rather than passageways, yet the upper floors were carpeted in thick crimson and joined together by narrow corridors. These town quarters were at once claustrophobic and enticing, as though one were living inside a chocolate box, each passageway a flavour leading to a new surprise.

"Your room," he said, pushing against a heavy wooden door to reveal a canvas of emerald green. In the centre stood a four-post bed with velvet curtains to match the ones at the window. The floor was evergreen, and the wallpaper was a touch lighter with gold *fleur-de-lis*.

Even the porcelain washbowl was green, with a green bar of soap to match.

"It has been a long journey, but I am afraid there is no time to rest. We have an appointment, and you must change."

"Into what?"

"You will see."

He bowed and retreated, leaving me there on my own in that strange room.

I was not alone for long.

A parade of pretty girls entered. The room was so green that I had not noticed the green dress lying on top of my green bed. The first girl, with ringlets of blonde hair and bright blue eyes, went to the bed to collect the dress. Another, with hair the colour and scent of apricots, entered with a tray of powders and potions. A third, who looked a little like my sister Fakhr, brought with her a tub of water and towels.

Before I had time to protest, they had stripped me of my road-worn attire and were sponging me down as delicately as one might stroke a rare bird. They dabbed me dry and oiled me with a fragrance I could not quite place. It was rich and warm like sandalwood, but dark as *neroli*. It caused the blood to stir against my cheeks.

"What is this?" I asked, as the golden-haired girl bade me step into a mass of ribbon and wire.

"A crinoline, my lady."

As she rose, it unfolded like a picture in a pop-up book, imprisoning my legs within a bell-shaped cage. The Indian Green dress, trimmed with black lace, came down over my head until it hung, suspended above the crinoline.

"Hold to the bedpost," she instructed me.

As I did so, I heard the snap and pull of cords tightening. Two panels of fabric at the front of the dress placed such pressure against my chest that my bosom lifted two or three inches. I gasped for breath and turned on the girl.

"What do you think you are doing?"

"Dressing you, my lady," she replied, as sweet as Turkish delight. "It's all the fashion in Europe."

She took my hand and led me to a full-length mirror on the wall. The transformation was astonishing. I had never seen myself look so much like a picture from the heathen continent. My figure was not my own. It pinched in at the waist and widened out at the hips. My buttocks must have seemed like those of a hippo from behind. The sleeves of the dress were short and tied with lace, falling from my shoulders as though I were half undressed. There, between them, were the mounds of my small breasts, precariously perched like two eggs about to fall out of their nest. My neck was exposed further as the apricot-scented girl began to pin my hair with pearls.

"I can't possibly wear this," I protested. "It's indecent."

"Welcome to the royal city," she replied with a smile.

"Are you ready, my dear?" Eirik appeared in the doorway dressed in black trousers, tighter than the flowing şalvar of the East. They were like two pipes that clearly defined the separation of his legs, as my cage had forced my lower body to become one. His feet were thin and painted, shiny as butter and slightly raised at the back. On top, he wore a crisp white shirt with a long black coat, and around his neck a funny little bow such as a woman might tie in her hair. To cover his face he wore an elaborate mask of mother of pearl, which caught the light in a million different ways. He framed it with a black wig which he had oiled back and tied with a ribbon. From the front, it gave the glossy appearance of a skullcap.

Seeing him so strangely dressed put me a little at ease about my own appearance.

"For you, *belle dame*," he said, handing me a mask of my own.

It was only half a mask, one made of black lace which framed my eyes. To the left, a construction of wires formed the wing of a raven, its elegant tip pointing to heaven. He helped me to fasten it, tying the cord and moving a silver clip so that my hair completely covered it.

"Also, this." He flicked his wrist and a matching lace fan appeared in his hand. He snapped it open and placed it between my own fingers. "I believe we are ready," he said, holding up my hand and turning me around.

"I can't possibly go out like this, Eirik."

"You can and you will, my dear. Don't you trust me? Before the night is out, you shall have all the Arg enchanted."

♦ 8 ♦

Opulence and wealth are only words until you see them incarnate. Then, they are more than words. They are the making of memories; of the dreams of kings and queens. Whilst half a town lies scrabbling in the gutter, drowning in its own effluent, the other half revels in its affluence, its tummy tickled by the bubbles of champagne served in fine crystal flutes that sing beneath the fingers of teasing drunks.

It was the night of the full moon. The fullest I had ever seen. The streets were lit with silver, and the gardens of my brother's palace were carpeted in white rose petals.

"Remember," Eirik said to me in the carriage as his serving boy drove us to the ball, "nobody knows who you are. For one night, you may be anyone you choose."

"What if I lose myself?"

"Then I shall find you."

His gloved hand squeezed mine as our carriage joined a procession of others, up to the gates of the Golestān.

A twist of nerves took me. "They will want to know who I am."

"Tonight is a masquerade, my dear. No one knows who anyone is, that's half the fun. If anyone should ask, simply smile and tell them you are a friend of the Comte de la Mort Rouge."

I repeated this carefully so that I would remember.

"I want you to forget all you have been taught about decorum and etiquette in your rural palace, Shahzadi. You are in the capital now. The rules are different."

And they were. Oh, how they were!

Dignitaries from around the world had gathered at the Rose Palace that night. I heard accents from Turkey, Russia, England, and many more that Eirik had to whisper the history of. The costumes were like nothing I had seen: charmeuse satin, shot silk, *ciselé* velvet and chiffon.

The women wore dresses much like mine, their bosoms prominent, their backsides angled like the billowing sails of a ship, which gave them the impression of gliding across the floor. I came to see that I was an anomaly. A dark-skinned, dark-haired woman in a sea of milk and honey.

"The chasm of concubines," Eirik said, passing a door leading to a room with a sunken circular centre. The enclave was filled with cushions and Iranian women. "Quaint *double entendre*," he smiled.

"Who are they?"

"Who do you think? More of your father's wives."

I stared again. Those women sprawled across the cushions looked nothing like my own mothers. The plump women back home at Sari who spent their days drawing on their eyebrows and darkening their upper lips with coffee – they would not know where to look.

My brother's wives at Tehran were svelte, like Shokuh. They wore rouge on their lips and their cheeks, covering their flesh sparsely as though any moment they might perform the seductive steps of *raqs sharqi*.

"He is not my father," I whispered, but Eirik did not hear me.

That night we danced.

We danced until my feet were sore. We danced strange dances, held in tight embrace. We rose and we fell like we had that night in my room near Sari. We danced chaotic dances, with roses clenched between our teeth as he told me the Spanish do. There were dances with clapping, and dances with archways formed of arms, and dances with swords crossed on the ground and scimitars held aloft. There were dances with hops and dances with skips, dances with eyes and hips and fingertips.

We played games with our eyes blindfolded, and others where we hid behind furniture and curtains. I was found once by an older man with silver hair and the mask of a fox. He discovered me behind a Moroccan screen, pinned me to it and kissed me!

He tasted pleasantly of peppermint and tobacco.

I kissed him back.

We were not the only animals. The palace was a menagerie that night: butterflies, dogs, cats, bears and lions. Every beast you could name, even a snow leopard complete with skin and tail. So many masks, and some who had simply painted their faces to represent masks.

I had heard stories of the Arg at Tehran, but neither the stories nor the paintings I had seen could have prepared me for its magnificence. It was so large that given an entire year I doubt I would have seen every room.

I had sworn after my experience with Uncle Ja'far that I would never touch a drop of alcohol, yet the alcohol they served that night did not taste sour like wine. There was a thick, clear liquid that tasted of peaches. I enjoyed it so much that before long I had consumed several glasses.

Not being used to it, my head soon softened with laughter. Almost everything anybody said was funny, even when I could hardly understand the language they had spoken in.

"Impressive, isn't he?" a tall jester asked. His mask was adorned with silver bells, chiming from the ends of folded coils of stiff musical scores. "Such a pity about his face."

I had been standing by an open window, trying to catch the breeze. My new companion was referring to Eirik, who stood across the room speaking to a group of women and one portly gentleman whose wobbling jowls threatened to snap the cord of his mask.

"They say it was an accident with acid," he continued.

"They do?"

"Yes. Doesn't bear thinking about."

"Indeed. Who do I have the pleasure—"

"Ludovico Ghorbani, at your service."

Looking back towards Eirik, I saw that he had gone, swept away by a sea of apricot silk and sparkling silverware.

"Walk with me?" Ludovico smiled.

In one of the gardens a giant bonfire had been lit. Pillows and rugs lay around it where people reclined in various attitudes, fanning themselves and feeding one another dried fruit.

"Ludovico, that is not an Iranian name," I observed, watching tiny sparks float from the flames.

"My father is Iranian, my mother Italian."

"Would I know of him?"

"I doubt it. He's a philosopher, but we spend most of our time in Milan nowadays."

"Did you know the Ambassador to Florence?" I asked. "The Comte de la Mort Rouge lives at his house now."

"I'm sorry, the Comte– You mean Vachon?" He laughed as he reached for a handful of salted almonds.

"I am not allowed to call him that anymore."

"Why not?"

The story was too long to repeat, and it brought with it memories of Shahab.

"Your eyes, they are become sad," he whispered, leaning closer and kissing my cheek. "Does he mistreat you, this Comte de la Mort Rouge?"

"Why would you suspect such a thing?"

"Please, do not think that I speak out of turn. I cannot doubt the brilliance of the man's mind. All who have seen his palace at Sari, and he allows few access, say that it is one of the greatest feats of architectural genius in the modern world. Nobody doubts his ability, though perhaps there are a few who might question his capacity for human affection. Can love come easily to a man such as he?"

"What such a man is he?"

"My lady," he said, drawing close again so that my eyes had nowhere to look but his own. "He is a killer."

"All men are killers."

"Perhaps so," he conceded, reaching for a grape and placing it in his mouth. "I do not mean to distress you, but he did not gain the nickname Red Death for his murderous love of pomegranate wine. They say he is the Shah's finest assassin."

"Surely that is his Darougheh?"

"Ah, no, my lady. A common misconception. The Darougheh is the public face of the Shah's force. Vachon is his invisible hand, for which it is rumoured he is paid many times more what the Darougheh is worth. If you are his mistress and can stomach what I have told you, you would be wise to stay with him. He is a very wealthy man."

The fire cracked, drawing my attention. When I had been allowed to call Eirik by his name, he had been a travelling magician with a circus show. His friends had been freaks and deformations. He slept each night in a tent and washed in the river. Since I had been forbidden his true name, it had apparently become one of national renown, whispered by firelight at masked balls. Along with a reputation, he had gained a carriage and an Ambassador's house in the royal quarters of my brother's capital.

Whereas I had been banished to obscurity.

"Tell me, what are your father's philosophies?"

"He had the heart of Aristotle, but the pragmatic acceptance of Machiavelli."

"I do not understand."

"Well, Aristotle was a Greek. They invented the concept of democracy, whereby the populace consent to be governed. He believed that true democracy occurs only when those with the least, rather than those with the most, hold rule. Machiavelli was a Florentine. He saw democracy outstripped by wealth and power every time, and concluded that although love and consent are admirable, given the opportunity, it is always better to be armed and feared."

"Was he right?"

"They both were, but moral rightness is secondary to might, which would make Machiavelli the most right of the two."

I laughed.

"He wrote an entire thesis on governing nations. It's a shame the Shah can't read Latin."

"Why would the Shah have need of a Florentine philosopher?"

Ludovico reached for a slice of dried mango. He tore off a strip with his teeth and chewed thoughtfully.

"This dynasty has run its course. The Shah has made all of the fatal errors of statesmanship. He has strengthened his enemies, deferred to them, and not only invited foreign forces in, but allowed them to walk out with half of his country's resources."

I felt cold hearing this. Nobody had ever spoken so honestly to me, for everyone had always known who I was. Suddenly, I longed for Shusha's kind smile and quick mind. Someone to explain to me what this man was telling me of my own family's failings.

"Which foreigners?" I asked.

"He refuses to pick between the Turks and the Russians, so neither despise him but neither will help him either. He's auctioning off every asset to the French and the English, and even my mother's people, for whatever price they are willing to pay him. Where do you think the money for nights like this come from?"

"The Shah is rich," I replied.

"Was rich. Half the female population of the country has joined his harem. Since murdering his friend and former advisor, few statesmen trust him, and no one can abide his mother."

"You talk liberally beneath his roof."

My companion laughed. "That is why we spend most of our time in Milan. Our family possesses the fault of liberal thinking. We are tolerated because of our wealth. Though wealth is worth little behind bars, where we have long suspected we may all end up."

"That does not frighten you?"

"Of course it does. Sadly, philosophy leads us to contemplate the implications of our lives beyond merely our own lifetimes."

"Oh, so you are a philosopher also?"

He smiled and took another bite of mango.

"Enough of philosophy, let us talk of beauty. It is far more engaging."

"Whose beauty might we talk of?"

"I don't know," he said, glancing around. "That lady over there, perhaps?" He inclined his strip of mango towards a woman in a peacock-feathered dress with a mask of equal splendour. "Or perhaps that one over there?" He raised his chin towards another woman in a snow-white gown, her bosom as wide as watermelons. "No," he said with a sigh. "I would rather talk of yours."

"How do you know that I am beautiful when you cannot see my face?"

"Your eyes are beautiful, and your voice. Your figure is beautiful, as is your hair. What could possibly be imperfect in the small space between your left ear and your right?"

He pulled himself up and traced a finger along my jaw.

I held his wrist to prevent the progress of his finger to my lips.

"Many things may be uglier than you imagine."

His eyes held mine, uncertain what to make of my warning.

"My dear, there you are."

Eirik appeared beside us.

"This is Ludovico Ghorbani, my love."

The change in Ludovico was instantaneous. He sat almost to attention in the presence of the Shah's finest assassin.

"He is a philosopher."

"My father is," he stammered.

"Oh?" Eirik settled beside me, reclining like a cat.

"He was teaching me the difference between Aristotle and Machiavelli. Do you know of them?"

"Love is a single soul within two bodies."

"Very good," Ludovico smiled.

"Was that Aristotle?" I asked.

"It was indeed. It would seem that the Comte de la Mort Rouge knows his philosophers."

"The Comte de la Mort Rouge knows many things," I informed him.

"And you," Eirik asked, addressing him with a lazy glance. "What do you know?"

"Ah, our friend Ludovico knows about politics," I answered.

Eirik sat up to study him more closely.

"Will you excuse me? I need to refresh myself," I said, allowing Ludovico's hand to help me to my feet.

There were so many things strange about that night. The fact that I was walking through the halls of my brother's palace, that his palace was filled with people from every corner of the world, in every conceivable dress and skin tone, and that no one had the faintest idea who I was.

It was some sort of decadent dream I dearly wished would last forever.

The bathrooms, like the walkways of the gardens, were decorated in beautiful mosaics. Unlike the gardens, which were clad in chips of burnished bronze and sunrise, the bathrooms were the colour of the sea, tiny slivers of mirror providing the frothing foam between waves.

There were women in the bathrooms to help liberate me from my cage. Each of these women were dark of skin, hair and eyes. They were young, some even younger than I, destined for a life of servitude or perhaps pleasure. They attended to me well, yet I could feel their gaze flick between one another, asking themselves who I was, this Iranian beauty dressed in a *farangi* gown. What part of my heritage had I forgotten? Which of Allah's vows had I forsaken?

The dress acted as a tent when I squatted, affording a great deal of privacy whilst I pissed into the white porcelain bowl, though it made cleaning myself impossible, and necessitated help from one of the women. More than that, it was uncomfortable. It made breathing difficult, and I longed for the loose, comfortable clothes of my own kind.

As I returned to the gardens, I overheard a group of women by one of the pillars.

"Are you sure that's him?" a girl asked her confidantes, warm skin glistening like starlight beneath the candles.

"Absolutely, I would know him anywhere. He is the only man who never removes his mask."

They huddled together, peeking around the pillar to the spot where Eirik sat.

"What happened to him?"

"I heard the rumour that a bear drew its claws across his face."

They gasped in unison.

"Was he handsome?"

"If he was, he is no longer, though he is very, very rich."

They dissolved into giggles.

It was only when I returned to the fireplace that I realised Eirik was sitting alone.

"Where is our friend?" I asked him.

"Ah, Monsieur Ghorbani has gone for refreshments."

"You did not like him?"

"*Au contraire*, I found him fascinating. Wherever did you find him?"

"He found me."

"Of course he did."

Eirik took me by the hand and raised me up.

"I can't dance any longer, my feet are sore with it."

"One last dance to remember a wonderful night?"

I could not resist him. We returned inside to the main ballroom. Although long past midnight, there were still a hundred couples spinning and weaving beneath great chandeliers that looked like entire icebergs suspended from the ceiling, melting their frosted teardrops on those below.

We sailed across the floor. I was a quick learner, mastering the steps of the Viennese Waltz with far more grace than I had learned to pluck the qanun, thankfully for Eirik's toes. He was a masterful teacher. He could predict with absolute certainty when my foot would fall misplaced, then, using only the strength of his arm around my waist, he would correct my position. He danced for both of us and in so doing created the illusion of two figures spinning perfectly as one.

Elegance married with Grace.

As we made our way through the gardens towards the courtyard, I was overcome by another fit of giggles.

We paused by a rose-scented fountain, its heady perfume casting memories of a forgotten jinn's lair across the rainbow-coloured reminiscence of my mind.

"What is it?" I asked, staring into his nacreous face.

"You are beautiful when you laugh."

I saw it then, something in those eyes black as coal.

His sacred spark.

History is a dark and unforgiving thing. All that history is can never be altered or undone. That is the nature of history. It is set. Immutable. Absolute.

There, on that night, I was granted a glimpse of history unwritten.

I laughed, and turned away.

Alcohol had a far more pleasing effect than I had anticipated. I felt warm and pleasantly sleepy. I removed my mask in the carriage so that I could rest my head against the curtain.

"What do you think of your father's fine city?" he asked me.

"I see why he would keep me from it all these years."

"Why is that?"

"Because I would have danced until dawn every night and become a foot shorter than I am."

He laughed and drew back the curtain with one finger to display Tehran in all her nightly splendour. The Arg was surprisingly silent beyond our window. Guards around the old moat must have been doing their job of keeping out the commoners. It struck me then how little difference there was between our two halves of society. The peasants wore rags and the gentry wore silk, but we all drank, danced and fornicated.

"I prefer the night," he told me. "If I could sleep all my days and only wake at night, I think I would be happier. The daytime is for work, the night time for wonder."

"You would have no one see your face?"

"It is more than that. There is a silence in darkness that gives life to all thoughts. I compose my best work at night. Cathedrals of sound that enshrine the beating heart of humanity within their walls."

"Music?"

"The purest of all architecture. Buildings are naught but clay and mud, which time eventually reduces them to once again. Scores, now they are designed of an altogether higher material. The universe itself is built on the chords and harmonies of gods."

"I thought you did not believe in God?"

"When we talk of men, no. But of music, oh there are angels and demons and gods aplenty. Divinity itself is defined between the lines of a manuscript. You must let me prove it to you."

"There is only one divinity that I know of."

"Ah." He allowed the curtain to fall back into place, eclipsing the moon-drenched streets. "Do you miss them, those rosy hours?"

I curled my feet up beneath me on the cushioned bench, pretending to fall asleep.

"Afsar, you cannot hide your desires from me."

After a moment, I switched places to join him on his side of the carriage. He opened his arm to allow me to nuzzle my face against his neck. There was a sweet smell about him, as though he had been kept in a box of *papier d'Arménie*, of which he would later become so fond.

"I miss the way we were. The nights we spent in Sari, the days we watered our lawns with Bábí blood."

"Poor, sweet Afsar. You find yourself without a playfellow."

By the time our horses drew to a halt outside Eirik's apartments, I was no longer feigning sleep. He must have carried me to my room, for I have the strangest memory of hands undressing me. Not his – these were far too soft. All the time, whilst my clothes were being removed, voices rose and fell like the tides of the sea. I could not make out the words, or perhaps they were sung in another language, yet I recognised it as the most painful of *ghazal*, a song of love enduring heartbreak, enduring death itself.

I believe I wept as sleep returned to swallow me. I wept for my sad situation, to be born of mountain blood, and a girl at that. I wept for the loss of a mother I barely remembered, and a father more distant than the Russian Empire. I wept for the loss of Shusha and the knowledge he took with him, for all the things I did not understand and had never been taught. I wept for the poems I no longer wrote, and the brothers and sisters I had despised, yet in losing had lost parts of myself.

At one point the song rose to such delicate pathos that I felt as though a cord had been pulled from my privates to the crown of my head. The very fabric of my being burned with flames of grief; the blistering pain of mortality, blissfully contrasting oblivion.

I breathed in the dragon of the dawn, and it ate my soul.

I woke in the early afternoon. Light through the open curtain fell hazily against my arm, the air rich with sickly-sweet smoke. As I rose to rub my eyes, I discovered myself entangled amidst many limbs. The blonde girl, and the dark one, and the one with hair the colour of apricots, they all lay beside me, dressed in thin cotton, their tresses undone and spilling across the sheets.

I slept a little while longer, my head foggy from the night before. One of the girls eventually rose and opened the window to let the air clear. She returned and offered her hand to help me rise. As I stood, she pressed her lips gently against mine to welcome me to the waking world.

After they bathed me and combed out my hair, they dressed me in loose şalvar of rose-petal pink, held with a kamar-band of gold weave and complemented by a white silk kameez.

I followed the sound of a violin to a music room on the lower floor. The walls were tiled with Persian calligraphy where the words had been drawn as musical notes. Stark black on white, the entire room confused the eye much as a disharmonious chord confuses the ear.

Perhaps that had always been the point, as Eirik played with his eyes shut.

He was a fine musician, and the music was pleasing, but it did not move me in the way I had been moved the night before.

When he noticed me watching, he placed the violin on a table and came towards me. "Shahzadi, did you sleep?"

"As though I slept in the arms of Allah."

"Good. You will need your strength. I have a surprise for you this evening."

We breakfasted late on goat's cheese, quince jam and sweet tea.

He left me then, whilst he went out to attend to business. The girl who reminded me of Fakhr entered the room with a nard board, but I had no wish to play.

"I do so hate the sound of the counters, don't you? So repetitive," I said.

"I had never thought of it," she replied, "but if it displeases you then of course it must go."

I returned to the music room and found that it contained more than a violin. There was a santur and a qanun, but also many others that I did not recognise. There was something that looked like a long black serpent, twisting in waves. Another looked like an Iranian *chang*, only far taller and cast in bronze.

"It's called a harp," the honey-haired girl explained, demonstrating the sound by plucking the strings.

"It's beautiful," I said. "As are you all. Tell me, where did your master find you?"

"He found us here in Tehran, my lady." She smiled as she ran her fingers along the harp's frame.

"Yet I hazard you are not from Tehran? You speak Farsi with an accent."

"Ah, *merde*. One tries so hard to better oneself."

I recognised the word from the building site. Eirik used it often.

"You are French, like your master?"

"I am, my lady. Gabrielle is from Portugal, and Pelagia," she indicated the dark-haired girl, "from Greece."

"And how did you find yourselves here, being found by the Comte?"

"It was simple, really. We each came as the servants of our mistresses. The Comte has a love of singing. He would often frequent the houses of noblemen living near the Arg, especially when they entertained renowned performers from Europe and the Americas. One evening he bid the servants sing, and our voices impressed him so much that he bought our freedom."

"Yet you are not free, are you? You are still in the service of your master."

"Forgive me, my lady, but this is not service. This is pure pleasure. We have every freedom afforded us, to do as we please. Can you say the same?"

The directness of her question offended me. How could a common servant dare question the happiness of a Shah's daughter?

Before I could reply, a knock at the door caused the girl, whose name I never did learn, to leave me. A moment later a familiar figure appeared in the doorway.

"Ludovico!" I cried out.

"Forgive me, am I early? The invitation was for six and it is not yet quarter to."

"I did not know you were expected at all." I went to greet him, placing my hand on his arm.

He seemed taller in the daylight, his sun-blessed Iranian skin smoothed across what I could only assume to be a square Italian jaw. His hair was a mass of shaggy curls, and throughout the evening he would raise his hand to sweep them from his eyes.

"The Comte de la Mort Rouge, is he not at home?"

Those same dark eyes that had held mine in the firelight only the night before now flitted momentarily between the music room and the hall.

"No, he has business. He did not say when he would return."

"Ah, then I have the pleasure of your company all to myself?"

"Will it suffice?"

He took my hand to his lips. "More than suffice. It is an exquisite privilege."

I caught my reflection in his stare and my breath stilled for a moment.

"My lady." Gabrielle appeared behind him. "The table is set."

Just as I had not been prepared for our guest's arrival, I was even less informed of our dinner plans. The dining room had been arranged in the European fashion: a long wooden table dressed in strips of ivory and gold damask. Down the centre sat six red glass jars, each with a candle in, though the skylight above still allowed a little light. Behind Ludovico hung a large portrait of a woman I did not recognise, and, behind my chair, there was a huge bevelled mirror almost twice my own height.

It seemed absurd sitting facing one another from opposite ends of such a long table, yet he assured me this was quite common in the great houses of France and Italy, reminding me that, after all, the Comte was a Frenchman. He asked how I would rather dine, and I told him that my family preferred to sit together on the floor, eating from a central dish. This was changing though, as my brother increasingly paid attention to Western fashions, and hoped one day to visit those countries.

Eirik's three servants drifted in and out like wisps of smoke, lingering only to pour wine or place something new and exotic before us.

"Your brother must be an important man," he said, taking a sip of his wine.

I realised that I had said too much, shrugging as I reached for my own chalice. This was a trick that I had learned in my brother's harem – that a gentleman will allow a lady her secrets.

We continued to talk as the light faded from the sky, replaced by rose-red candles which cast shadows against the wall. Bowls of spiced lamb were served with baqala beans, and I remembered Mahmoud attempting to stab Fakhr with the pen that I later stole from him. All because she would not share her beans.

After the meat, came fruit: pomegranate, melon, dates and figs, decorated with almonds and sugared ginger that sparkled like diamond dust.

We laughed a lot those first few hours. Ludovico proved a quick-witted philosopher, and had travelled far. He told me of the five-day war that had threatened his family's estate some years ago. How his father had led them out through the vineyards on the backs of mules, dressed as peasants. When they returned, they found their rooms filled with women from Milan's brothels, who had thought the place abandoned and were preparing to set up shop. Ludovico's father, being an *umanista* and not a moralist, reasoned that what was good for the troops was probably also good for his family. He allowed them to work under his roof until the troubles settled, taking a percentage of their earnings for bed and board, and employing two of them afterwards as cooks.

"What of your mother?" I asked, open-mouthed and incredulous.

"Oh, she learned to sleep with plugs of wax in her ears."

"She did not mind her husband cavorting with his harem of common women?"

"His harem?" Ludovico frowned and then laughed. "Oh! You misunderstand me. My father was not sleeping with them, he merely allowed them to ply their trade with the soldiers. No, in the West there are no harems. Men take only one bride."

"Only one?"

"Yes. It is a very different way of life."

"Your father agreed to this?"

"In order to marry my mother, yes."

"What would cause such a foolish union?"

He smiled at me in the way Shusha used to smile at me before informing me that I knew nothing of politics.

"That is simple, sweet lady. Love."

He held my eyes until I felt myself blush. "Have you ever been in love?" he asked me.

"Perhaps. Once."

"What happened to your love?"

"I have a jealous friend."

"Ah, the Comte de la Mort Rouge?"

"Indeed."

"Then the Comte de la Mort Rouge was not your love?"

"Oh, I love him, but in a different way."

He took a sliver of ginger on his thumb, sucking it between his lips.

"Tell me," I asked, "how do men in Europe display their wealth if not through their wives?"

"The fewer wives a man has, the greater his wealth tends to be," he smiled. "Take the Shah of Iran, for instance–"

"Yes, let's."

"He has more wives than he can count, and hardly anything left to show for it."

"What do you mean?"

"He sells off his country's wealth to foreign powers in order to fund his pursuit of pleasure."

I took a sip of water to disguise the thoughts raging through my mind.

"It is a shame he cannot sell wives, for he would find himself master of many assets. Though, with the harem fashion for dark moustaches and *synophrys*, they may fetch far less on the Western market."

"You are saying the Shah's wives are ugly?"

"Well, I have seen two of his harems, and neither were stocked with the type of wives he keeps at Tehran. Certainly few with your beauty, my lady."

"You think I am beautiful?"

"I think the Comte is a lucky man indeed."

"Are you married?"

"Me? No," he laughed.

"You would prefer to keep your wealth instead?"

"I have been afforded enough in life to be granted the rarest of gifts. I do not intend to waste it."

"What gift is that?"

"The freedom to marry for love."

"The Shah marries for love. It just happens that he loves many."

"I hold more of a classical notion of love."

"And how might an Italian prove this love of his?"

"First, he would bring the one he loved a gift."

Ludovico rose from his seat and came towards me, taking another piece of crystallised ginger between his fingers.

"Something as sweet as she."

He sat on the table beside me and fed me the ginger.

I allowed it to melt on my tongue before swallowing.

"It is sweet. Yet ginger has a bite, does it not?"

"It has spice."

"What next?"

"Then, he would ask her to dance."

He held out his hand and I accepted.

"Without music?"

"If they were truly in love, they would make their own music."

He took me in his arms and began to hum a simple tune as we waltzed. I tried to add my own voice to his, and then laughed as he spun me beneath his arm.

"Oh!" he exclaimed, stopping suddenly.

I followed his gaze to the mirror.

"What is it?"

"Nothing. Only I– nothing."

He shook his head and smiled, taking me once again in hold as we resumed our dance.

"How long before she falls in love with him?" I asked.

"Oh, days. Sometimes years. But always, he is patient."

"Love does not happen in an instant?"

"Love that happens in an instant is lost in an instant. Love that is cultivated will continue to grow for a lifetime."

"This is your philosophy?"

He threw back his head and laughed.

The candles flickered in their cradles.

"There!" he shouted, spinning me towards the mirror. "I saw something!"

I stared for a moment before suggesting that it was merely our own reflection.

"No. I saw something."

"What was it?"

"I–" Aware of my eyes on him, he shook his head and allowed his shoulders to drop.

"This is how they woo their women in the West?" I mocked. "Oh, those lucky Western women. Is it some sort of game?"

"You know, my lady, the hour is late. I thank you for the exquisite meal and your charming hospitality, but I must return to my family now."

"I do not understand. You are afraid of your own reflection?"

"I tell you again," he snapped, "it was not my reflection." He turned towards the door.

As he did so it swung closed, its lock sliding into place.

"What is this?" he asked, pulling at the handle to no avail.

I felt a thrill through my bones. I did not know what game this was, but I knew that something spectacular was about to happen, and I knew that it was Eirik's doing.

The candles on the table went out, plunging us into complete darkness.

"Leaving so soon?" a voice came from the mirror.

Slowly, an image began to take form, as though rising up from the depths of a moonlit pool.

Eirik was dressed in a long dark cloak, a human skull for a face.

Ludovico's laugh was nervous. "Good Comte, you arrive at last!"

"Indeed. I have been observing your little soiree."

"Why did you not join us sooner?"

"I was rather enjoying watching the foolish designs you possessed towards my good lady."

"I assure you, I have no such designs. I merely wished to make her smile."

"You think she does not smile when she is with me?"

"You were not here."

"You are wrong, monsieur. I have been here all along."

Ludovico looked to me, but my eyes were fixed on Eirik. His mask reminded me of the silver head on his carriage.

"Tell me, my errant guest: loved or feared, which did Machiavelli reason it was better to be?"

He swallowed before replying. "Feared."

"Indeed. Then I shall be feared."

The image in the mirror faded and I let out a scream as the floor beneath me disappeared. I landed on a soft hay mattress, Eirik's finger pressed to my lips to silence me.

"My dear, I hope you have not grown too fond of him."

"If I had, would you release him?"

A lamp flared into existence and I noticed that he was dressed entirely in red, with black epaulettes, and that the mask he wore had been carved of ivory to give the true appearance of bone.

"Come," he said. "Let me give you the grand tour."

It was that night that I realised the true extent of Eirik's genius. All of his skills of deception and misdirection had been transposed onto that house. Absolutely nothing was as it seemed. Behind every bookshelf sat a secret passage, beneath every chandelier a trapdoor lay in wait, within every fireplace lurked a set of stairs. Most impressive of all were the mirrors. Each one throughout the house acted as a window to the room beyond.

Ludovico had found the door to the dining room unlocked after my sudden disappearance. He managed to make his way into the hall, only to make the unfortunate discovery that the front door did not yield so easily to his touch. By the front door hung another tall mirror, and behind its opaque surface, Eirik and I stood watching, mere inches from his face. If it weren't for the glass between us, I could have reached out and touched him.

"You are absolutely certain he cannot see us?" I asked Eirik.

"Yes, but he may hear us if you speak above a whisper."

In this way we followed our guest from room to room. In places where there were no mirrors, Eirik had drilled spy holes through the eyes of portraits, and removed bolts from the fixtures of chandeliers. There was nowhere within the house for Ludovico to hide from us, even as he thought himself to be completely alone.

Oh! The games we played that night.

As Ludovico made his way desperately from room to room, searching for his escape, we vested fresh horrors upon him at every turn. In the bathroom, Gabrielle, her skin as white as milk, lay motionless in a bath of goat's blood, looking for all the world as though she had opened her own veins.

When he returned to the dining room, he found Pelagia's silver reflection hanging from a rope in the mirror. In the music room, a large black serpent complemented its musical namesake, devouring a suckling pig in the centre of the room whilst the harp appeared to play itself.

It was as though the house were bewitched. A beautiful theatre of brutality, bringing to life all the worst nightmares of the mind. As Ludovico stumbled from one ghastly vision to the next, he began to sob, crying out to Eirik that he was sorry and that he would leave Tehran immediately and never return if he would but spare his life.

He did not know Eirik as well as I did.

Nor, for that matter, did he know me.

The scenes that we arranged were merely an appetiser in our grand banquet of murder. With every cry and every plea, the pleasure grew. It reminded me of that prickling sensation, when the evening breeze would brush against the back of my neck on our walks into Sari. Soon, it grew to the thunderous sound of my heart clamouring against my breast.

Eirik felt it too.

Our nostrils flared, our movements becoming quick and agile. We transformed into hunters, stalking our prey. Great, inhuman hunters, with the darkness of the jungle flowing through our veins.

The final scene brought Ludovico to his knees. We whispered it to one another as we followed him, staring between reflections. He knelt by the front door, pawing like a dog wishing to be let out by its master. The candles on the walls flickered and began to go out one by one. I learned that Eirik did this by manipulating the wicks, which were joined behind the wall to a dial. When the dial was turned the wicks sank and were snuffed.

Eventually, only the light directly above the door remained lit, Ludovico curled beneath it, reduced to a whimper.

That is when Eirik revealed himself.

He appeared at the far end of the corridor, dressed as the Red Death, and began to stalk his quarry.

"Please, please, Comte, I beg of you. I never meant to insult you. I never meant to take advantage of your hospitality. Please, please, let me go."

"Ah, Prospero, how quickly your courage fails you."

"Has someone hired you to do away with me?"

Eirik's laugh was terrible, as chilling as nails down a chalkboard.

"No, monsieur. This is simply for pleasure."

Such a coward he was. In all the time Ludovico spent travelling the house, he never once looked for anything to use as a weapon. Now, he folded in on himself like a snail sheltering from the lark's beak.

"Stop!" I cried, showing myself at the top of the stairs. "Don't hurt him!"

The hope in his eyes was almost enough to convince me of his ardour. If he hadn't truly loved me before, at that very moment he loved no one better.

"I thought you were dead," he cried.

"No, my love. No."

I ran down the stairs and cradled him in my arms, pretending not to notice that he wiped clean the mucus of his nose against my kameez. He clung to me, struggling to contain his terror. When his breathing calmed a little, he peered around looking for Eirik, but Eirik was gone.

"Where is he?" Ludovico asked, his voice atremble.

"Who, my love?"

"You know who! The man who would have me killed!"

I frowned, placing my hand beneath his chin so that he was forced to look into my eyes.

"Oh, Ludovico, my poor, dear soul. Something in the food must have upset you. You've been shouting at your own shadow for an hour or more."

"I have?" He wiped tears from the sides of his eyes and sat up a little.

"Every time I tried to approach, to calm you down, you screamed and ran to another room."

"I did?"

"You did." I nodded with such perfect innocence in my expression that he must have thought me an angel. "Come, let me sit you down."

He allowed me to lead him like a lamb. We entered the dining room. All of the candles were lit and the food sat perfectly in its place. As I lowered him into his chair, I noticed that his eyes kept darting to the mirror as though expecting it to talk to him.

"Here," I said, pouring water into a crystal goblet, "you must drink something."

He took it from me and held it to his trembling lips. "Such terrible visions," he murmured. "Such awful, awful nightmares."

"Hush, it is over now. I will have the cook whipped for whatever has harmed you."

"Yet you," he brought his eyes back to me. "You have not been affected?"

"No." I shook my head and plucked a piece of ginger from the plate, popping it into my mouth to prove that I was not afraid of the food.

He shook his head and took another gulp from the goblet, and then another.

"Perhaps it was something in the water?" I smiled.

The poison was slow to take effect. As it did, he found he could no longer hold the glass, so I took it from him and placed it on the table.

"I cannot feel my legs," he complained, trying to rise from his seat and failing.

The paralysis spread up his body until even his head fell backwards, his neck unable to support its weight. The last words he spoke before his tongue failed were, "Help me."

Unoriginal words.

As those rosy hours had once taught me, most people seek help in their final moments. Few ever receive it.

We gorged ourselves that night on every dark fantasy. Before, our pleasures had always been rushed. A life stolen silently on the moonlit road from Sari, a public execution conducted in full view of a roaring crowd. The only time we had ever been at our leisure had been Ja'far in his little wooden box. That had been over a year ago now, and the possibilities we had glimpsed those weeks had collected and grown within our minds like a breeze stirring into a gale.

Oh, Ludovico. Poor Ludovico.

I woke next morning swathed in white cotton sheets, the green cover lying on the floor with my discarded dress. The blonde maid and the apricot maid lay naked across me, their hair spun like a shroud, covering my blood-stained breast. Eirik sat in a chair in the corner, his fingers steepled against the lips of his ivory mask. I thought he was asleep at first, before his eyelids opened and his onyx orbs came to rest on mine.

He left then, silently, and I fell back into a long doze, waking only when my companions began to stir from their slumbering depths, yawning and rubbing their eyes. By the time they had bathed and dressed me, it was no longer morning. Our games had lasted late into the night, sleep demanding our company longer than usual.

We breakfasted in the garden on dried figs and honeyed milk whilst the maids attended to matters indoors. I did not ask after Ludovico's body, and Eirik did not offer such information. All that I needed to know was that we had shared in each other's waking dream last night. The daybreak had washed away all of our sins, banishing them like shadows. We had transformed ourselves as easily as Eirik had changed his mask from shell to leather, from unique to ordinary.

"I've ordered you a carriage," he told me, as we watched small birds chase one another through the branches of the plum tree.

"I don't wish to leave."

"I know, *ma chérie*, but you must. Your staff will begin to miss you, and what if your father should send someone to check, and find you gone?"

"You know he is not my father, don't you?"

He stopped chewing and took a moment to dab the corner of his mouth with a cloth.

"I did not."

"I am still the Shah's daughter. Only, not this Shah."

"Then he is?"

"My brother."

"And you are?"

"A witch."

He laughed at that, quite abruptly.

"Do I disappoint you?"

"Afsar, you could never disappoint me."

He smiled, placing his hand over mine.

"I thought you knew everything? The man my brother sends to spy on his own spies?"

He poured another glass of milk from the jug. "I do not go looking for secrets where I expect there to be none."

"My mother was a tribeswoman from the mountains. A witch. That is why I have been banished from the palace. My father loved my mother most of all, and Mahde Olia could never stand that. She still can't. She hates me. Shokuh is less personal, and despises me simply for breathing. They have conspired to be rid of me, and now I am forgotten."

"I have not forgotten you."

"No. You have not forgotten me, but everyone who matters has."

"I do not matter? I dress you in silk, adorn you with diamonds, deliver a night of dark dreaming and passion, fill your soul with the music of life, death and destruction, and I do not matter?"

The anger in his voice caused me to recoil.

"I did not mean it like that—"

"Yet that is what you said."

Our eyes locked, my wide brown worlds meeting his bottomless voids.

"I am sorry," I whispered. "You do matter. You are my only freedom."

"And you are my only friend."

"I am?"

"Afsar, look at me." He removed his mask. The sight of his ravaged face was no longer as shocking to me as once it had been, yet nevertheless I would have preferred he kept it on. "Do you think anybody else would willingly sit down to breakfast with this?" He pointed to himself.

"But you are wealthy beyond counting. You can buy as many friends as you like."

"How many friends have you bought?" he asked me.

I found that I could not answer. It was true that my value was in my name, rather than my possessions. Still, I had only one true friend I could think of. "That is beside the point."

"It isn't as easy to buy friends as you thought, is it? And what if I wanted more than friendship? What if I wanted love? You cannot buy love, not for all the riches of Persia."

He spoke so freely of love, yet I wondered whether he truly knew the meaning of the word. How could a boy who had never been shown love, grow into an adult capable of recognising it?

How could a girl, for that matter.

♦ 9 ♦

I thought about our conversation on the long journey home to Shirgah, my feelings changing direction with each jolt of the wheel against the rocks beneath.

I found myself lost in the intoxicating beauty of Ludovico's death. The desperation in his eyes, the silent scream caught behind his paralysed tongue, the hammering of his pulse against the pale slant of his neck as Eirik played the most heart-soaringly hypnotic tune on his violin.

The moment when life finally left him.

Eye to eye. Lip to lip.

That final breath.

Occasionally reason surfaced to ask a question, to search its own doubt over whether Eirik had truly never known that I was not his master's daughter? Whether there was more to our games than simply the pleasure of it? Whether, as I suspected over breakfast, he wanted more of me than I was willing to give?

Could I love a man with a face like that?

I had thought to marry him once.

It was past dark by the time my carriage began its climb back into the mountains. The temperature dropped, dry dust giving way to thick forest and the screech of night creatures on the prowl. I did not manage to sleep at all on the way back, my mind too alive with all that I had seen: the brilliance of the crystal chandeliers at my brother's palace, the coloured silks of his guests' attire, and the crimson of Ludovico's blood glistening in the candlelight.

I was exhausted when I returned. Shirgah was asleep, and I asked the coachman to muffle the horses' hooves with cloth. In that thin mountain air sound travelled quickly, and I did not want everyone to know my business.

When we came to the gate of my house, Hafez was asleep on the ground, his head resting against the wall. The driver cracked his whip above the guard's ear and he shot to his feet as though pulled up by a rope. His hand reached for his knife but stopped the moment he realised what had happened.

"Shahzadi?"

He came to the side, squinting up at the window.

"Open the gate, Hafez."

Once the carriage had come to a standstill in the courtyard, he opened the door and offered his hand.

"Why are the lights off?" I asked.

"We were conserving oil. It is harder to purchase here than by the coast."

I glanced around at my dark sanctuary. It seemed to be sitting there, expectantly awaiting me. The house no longer looked like a prison from the outside. Now that I had seen how easy it was to fly to exotic lands and return, it felt more like a nest. Perhaps Eirik had been right: it was not exile, but freedom.

"Fine," I sighed, turning towards the door. "I am tired and wish to sleep. Send Sheyda to me."

As I climbed the stairs to my chamber, I heard the carriage turning in the yard. By the time I had reached my bedchamber, the muffled clack of the horses' hooves had been replaced by the rivers outside my window, beating against bare rock in the moonlight.

When Şelale entered my room, she found me sitting on the bed, my eyes hardly open.

"Ah, çocukcağız," she crooned, coming towards me. She took a soft brush from my table and sat beside me, unpinning my hair and collecting the ornaments in her lap. "Where have you been? We were worried."

"Why are you here?" I asked, placing my hand over hers to stop her. "I told the guard to send Sheyda."

"Sheyda could not come," she said, removing her hand from beneath mine and continuing to brush out my hair.

I was so tired, and Şelale's familiar scent was so comforting – those hands that had brushed my hair a hundred thousand times since I was a girl – that I had not the strength to argue.

When I could no longer fight sleep, I rested my head against her chest, the brush replaced by the soothing flow of her fingers as she began to hum a Turkish lullaby that she had once taught me the words to, but which I had since forgotten, like so many things that had once seemed important.

The next morning I rose from the depths through a net of seaweed and maiden's hair, until my captor revealed itself to be nothing more than my own bed sheets. Sunlight streamed through the open arches of my windows, and I discovered myself to be still half-dressed.

The sound of a peacock brought me to the window. In my absence of only three days, someone had chopped back the grass and straightened the edges of my garden. A handful of plump peahens were scratching for grubs whilst a single white cock, its mating plumage wilted after the season, looked on abashed.

On the steps Şelale was shelling peas into a silver bowl. As I drew level with her, I saw the boy on the other side of the lawn, turning over sods of earth with a bent slice of metal.

"Who is that?" I asked.

"Your new gardener. He arrived from Sari the first morning you were gone," she said, her words clinking from her mouth like peas into her bowl.

"Eirik left you a picture."

"It is not the same." She looked up at me, hurt shining in her eyes. "I did not know where you had gone. You should have waited to tell me. What if something had happened to you?"

"You knew I was with Eirik. I couldn't have been safer."

"Are you sure, Sultana? I have heard those rumours, too."

"What rumours?"

"About what the grand *monsieur* Vachon gets up to in your father's employ." She mimicked the French in his accent, drowning it in disapproval.

"Well, that is not your concern."

"No, it is not. I am here to brush your hair, to feed you, to watch you grow day by day into a woman, but never to worry about you."

"Nobody asked you to do those things."

"Your father did," she sighed, plucking the peas from their pods with increased fervour.

"Well, he seems to have ceased worrying about me since." I stared out at the lawn again, my eyes moving from the boy to the peacock, and then to the trees at the furthest point. "Where is Sheyda?"

"She is no longer with us," Şelale replied.

"Where has she gone?"

"I do not know."

"You must know!" I said, my voice barely concealing my anger as I knelt down, grasping my servant's wrist. In her surprise, she almost dropped the bowl of peas.

"When I woke yesterday, she was gone. I had to prepare breakfast on my own. I lit the fire, swept the porches, washed the clothes, hung them to dry. No one came to help me. Those guards of yours, they just stood and stared."

"She must be visiting her family."

Şelale shrugged, reaching for a fistful of pods with her free hand.

I loosened my grip and watched for a moment. Şelale's brow furrowed in concentration, pretending so hard not to notice me there; pretending too hard.

"You know something," I said. "What are you not telling me?"

Her fingers paused, one white nail embedded in green flesh, poised to slit it from top to tail.

"I know nothing, Sultana. I swear to you. Perhaps it is Hafez you should be talking to."

It was the strangest sensation, as though Allah had torn the stars from the sky and placed them behind my eyes. Such a loud roar as the sky ripped, it eclipsed the mighty sound of the rivers as they crashed head-to-head like duelling bulls. Oh, and the pain, as breath left my lungs, refusing to return.

For the first time in my life, I fainted.

When I came to, Şelale was seated beside me on my bed, her face lined with worry. I realised that she had aged in the short time we had been in Shirgah. The cool air did not suit her. It had frozen the glow of her radiant skin, paling the high bones of her cheek like frost on the mountains.

I blamed the long ride from Tehran, the hardship of the road, the lack of water, lack of food. I blamed the change in temperature, in altitude, in company.

Lies flowed from my tongue like saliva, for I could not admit the truth even to myself.

I knew what men were capable of doing to women. Ja'far had attempted to do it to me, and, had it not been for the Darougheh, he may very well have succeeded. I had seen that same look in Hafez's eyes the day he stopped Sheyda from entering the cook hut. I had not taken it seriously then, for who could have believed that anyone would get the better of Sheyda? She was wise, and clever, and born of the village, where women knew how to take care of themselves and were not wrapped in rose petals like silly daughters of the harem.

Yet she had not been able to take care of herself, and I had not been there to save her as the Darougheh had saved me.

I told Şelale to leave me. Once she had gone, I rolled over on my bed and stuffed the corner of my pillow into my mouth. I screamed and screamed and screamed, for I knew that I was right.

I knew what had happened.

It is not enough to know in your heart. You must know with your eyes and your ears, also.

That evening, I called Hesam to me.

I sat cross-legged on the floor with a spread of dried figs, dates and nuts around me. When he arrived, I asked him to sit with me. Then I asked him to eat with me, and he accepted.

"I never did ask," I began, my voice light as a Caspian breeze, "you and Hafez are brothers?"

"Cousins, Shahzadi," he replied, reaching for a handful of salted almonds.

"I thought there was a resemblance."

"Our fathers are brothers."

"And you worked at the palace together, near Sari?"

"Yes. We grew up in Sari. When we came of age we went to the palace to ask for work, and the Darougheh accepted us."

"Did he choose you to join me in exile?"

"Yes," he smiled. "He needed men he could trust."

His words buzzed in my ears like a hornet. It stung my heart to know that the Darougheh himself had been fooled by these men. How could someone who had saved me from disgrace, choose those who would inflict it on others?

It made no sense to me.

"Where is your cousin tonight?" I asked.

"He has gone to the mosque. It will soon be Hajj, and his brother is making the journey to Mecca. He has gone to make offerings for his safe return."

My eyes narrowed as I watched him reach for a slice of apricot, unaware that he was anything other than completely welcome in my company. How far I felt from Sari now, where the only men allowed to be alone in my presence had been my tutor and my brothers. In exile I had been forgotten in every respect: in honour, in title, and in morals.

"Do you enjoy living here?" I asked.

"Yes, Shahzadi." He looked up, the nagging seed of doubt planted. Was I about to dismiss him? "Though–"

"Yes?"

"Well, it does get cold at night," he smiled.

"Yes." I smiled back.

He reached for another slice of apricot and began to chew.

"However do you stay warm?"

"Two kaftans," he replied. "One cotton, one wool. They sell them at the bazaar."

"And your cousin, how does he keep himself warm?"

Hesam looked uncertain, pausing to swallow before replying, "The same."

"You may pour yourself a cup of water if you like."

He reached for the jug and did so.

"Would you like one?" he offered.

I shook my head.

The knot in his throat bounced up and down with each gulp as he strained back his neck. When he was finished, he wiped the back of his hand across his lips and placed the cup down with a satisfied sigh.

"Tomorrow," I told him, "before you switch places with Hafez, I want you both to come to me. I cannot have you going cold out there in the night."

It is remarkable how stupid people are. You invite them to sit with you, to eat with you, and they never ask themselves why. They never think to themselves: *I am a servant, and she a Shahzadi, why should she even notice me?* No, not men like this. Somehow they think it is their right to eat with me, to sit with me.

I repaid their stupidity tenfold.

"How did you do that?" I had asked of Eirik, after our game with Ludovico. "It is like magic, the way he sat so still; the way his eyes followed us, yet his muscles did not so much as flinch when your blade went in."

"A sort of magic, yes," he had replied, wiping Ludovico's blood from his knife. "Would you like me to teach you the spell?"

I kept it hidden in a ring he gave me. A silver skull, like the ones on his carriage. A tiny catch inside causing the jaw to open when you twisted it in just the right way.

"Be careful," he told me. "Never lick your fingers afterwards. No sorcerer can lift this curse, once it is cast."

Fire had flickered in his eyes, and I knew in my soul that the enchantment would be final.

With no more than a sip of water, Hafez and Hesam fell beneath my will.

That was the easy part.

In my mind I saw a grand display. Using black and gold cord for lassos, I would suspend Hafez in the centre of the room, wrists and ankles splayed as though caught in a spider's web. Naked. His genitals lank between his legs, his chin dipped upon his breast, staring down at his shame. When Sheyda arrived she would see him that way and she would not be afraid. Indeed, she would laugh at such a pitiful sight and, seeing that he could no longer harm her, she would slice off his testicles and force them down his throat until he choked upon them.

Even as a fully grown woman, I would not have had the strength to string up one of Hafez's arms, yet alone his entire body. Instead, I had to straighten out their bodies where they had fallen, slowly rolling them like barrels to the side of the room. When they would roll no further, I drew tables across them. Then I threw thick blankets over the tables and placed trays upon them, to make it look as though they were altars. I dressed Hesam in red, the colour of Mehrgan, the festival of the harvest which had just passed. Hafez I dressed in blue, the colour of the goddess Nahid, for I had no doubt that she would know what to do with him.

Then I waited.

I waited all afternoon, sitting in the centre of the room and checking occasionally with my hand pressed to their nostrils, making sure there was still breath left in them. I worried a lot that they might die before their time, that all of my effort would be for nothing.

It was not until the sun began to set, casting the mountains as dark puppets against an orange lantern, that Şelale returned. At first I thought she had failed, she came so meekly before me, her sandals soiled in mud and the hem of her skirt dark from walking by the river.

I opened my mouth to ask, but my question was answered before the words left my lips. Sheyda appeared beside her. My Sheyda. Her beautiful moon-crescent cheek cresting a galaxy of emotions from fear to fury that drifted so subtly across her face that none but I would ever notice.

I could see the frown forming on Şelale's brow. Two tables had materialised in her absence, and she was about to ask why. In the freedom of my exile, without the eyes of many mothers following me from room to room, Mecca was lucky if it saw the bend of my knee five times a day. Yet here was I, lauding Zoroaster's name in brash colours and cut flowers that thickened the room with scent as they died.

"Şelale," I stopped her before she could take a step towards them, "I need you to do something for me. An important errand."

"Another?"

"It has been six months since Shahab passed." Her face softened at the mention of his name. "I cannot go to the palace myself to plant a fig, so you must go for me. You know what he meant to me, and I would trust no one else with this duty."

"Of course I will go, çocukcağız."

"I need you to leave tonight."

"I will leave at first light."

"You will leave now. I cannot bear to think of another day passing without the burden of death made lighter for him. Take a cutting from the fig that stands guard by my gate, and plant it there with prayers to Allah."

"If you want me gone, I will go," she said, knowing me well enough to understand when my will was unbendable. "What if someone should see me and ask of you?"

"Do your best not to be seen. Cover your face. If you should be discovered, tell them that I am well. Tell them of my devotion to prayer. Tell them—" I struggled for words. "Tell them that I am absorbed in a life that is gracious and good."

She hesitated, reluctant to leave. It would soon be dark and even though Sari was only a few hours away, stories of bandits plagued the minds of law-abiding travellers.

"The roads will be peaceful with the moon so bright."

"Very well," she said eventually.

I motioned Sheyda to sit with me and eat from the food which had been made safe. She sipped sweet milk and chewed a handful of almonds whilst Şelale packed her belongings into a woven bag and prepared her horse. I waited until I heard the gate close behind her, and then a little longer whilst she cut a branch from the fig tree. Only when I heard the sound of her horse's hooves fade in the mud did I speak.

"You left me," I said.

A flash of fear shot through Sheyda's eyes. "I am sorry, Shahzadi, I did not mean to dishonour you."

"I want to know why."

Her cheeks flushed as she stared down at the food in her hand. "I do not wish to tell you a lie, but I cannot tell you the truth."

"I can guess the truth," I told her.

I rose to my feet and walked a little, circling out and each time returning. She sat with her head still bowed, and this hurt me. Had I ever whipped her, or teased her, or threatened her in any way? No. So why would she not look at me?

"Come," I said, offering my hand. "Let us pray to Nahid."

She came with me to the table draped in blue.

"Light incense," I instructed, rolling a cone of scented paper and placing it on a bowl for her to ignite with a match. "The goddess of the waters knows our innermost thoughts, and washes them clean in her rivers of joy."

"I would like to be clean," she said, as the cone of paper fizzled and turned to coils of light grey smoke.

"That would require a sacrifice," I said.

She looked at me, once again uncertain, as though I might draw her own blood before the altar. I shook my head.

Taking hold of the front of the blanket, I drew it up as though raising the curtain of one of those European theatres my brother was so fascinated by. In that moment, I think I understood his obsession a little better. Raising the curtain was like opening a door upon all of the possibilities of the future. Until you looked behind the curtain, anything was possible. Once it had been lifted, you knew what was probable.

Sheyda let out a gasp, covering her mouth with her hands.

"It's all right," I told her, reaching out to stay her.

I lifted the cloth further, folding its edges over the ends of the table so that Hafez's body was fully exposed. His head faced towards us, his cheeks stained with tears as his unblinking eyes tried to keep from drying up. I should have covered them. It looked too much as though he were crying, and I did not want to give Sheyda any reason to feel remorse.

"He is not dead," I told her, "but he cannot move."

"How did you know?" she asked me, kneeling to see him better, a look of fascination replacing her shock.

"It almost happened to me, once."

"You, Shahzadi? Who would dare to lay their hands upon the daughter of the Shah?"

"The uncle of the Shah," I confided.

Her horror was gratifying, a validation of how wrong Ja'far had been in his actions; how wrong Hafez now was.

"A friend, a very close and dear friend, made me a gift of him. He gave me back the control that was robbed from me, and now I do the same for you."

I took one end of the table and drew it back across the floor until Hafez appeared like a log in the forest, lying there, waiting for the woodcutter to come. I reached into my sash and pulled out my dagger, placing it in Sheyda's hands and curling her fingers around the handle.

"He will know, but he will not feel the pain," I told her.

This may not have been true. I could not say whether Ludovico had felt pain. All I knew was that he did not move, because he could not move. I didn't want Sheyda to hesitate, though. I did not want her to take the vengeance she was owed and then regret it.

Walking to the next table, I drew back the red blanket to reveal Hesam.

"I don't understand," she said. "Hesam did nothing to me."

"Are you sure?"

"He was not even there."

"They are cousins. He should have prevented it."

I saw her expression falter, fascination melting to doubt. Quickly, I replaced the cloth to hide him from view.

"You are right," I said. "Justice only to those who deserve it."

"I don't think I can–"

"Look at him," I said, guiding her gaze back to Hafez. "You do not have to tell me what he did, but look at him. He came here today to eat with me as though he had a right to, as though I should be grateful for his protection. As though I needed it."

"He cornered me, in the cook hut. I couldn't escape. I couldn't–"

"It was never your fault. There is no blame on you. There is no blame in you taking what you are owed, taking back your dignity and your honour."

I reached my arms over Hafez and pulled him towards me, rolling him away from the wall until I could slip my feet between it and his back, turning him over and over towards the centre of the room.

"Come, Sheyda. I am your mistress and I give him to you. Hurt him as he hurt you."

She came towards me, the knife held by her side.

"I don't know if I can–"

"It is like slitting the throat of a goat. He's no better than an animal," I told her. "Look at him, each beat of his heart offends the ears of Allah."

"He held me down..."

I could see tears forming in her beautiful eyes and my own soul wept with her. I wanted to take the knife for myself, but this was her kill, not mine.

"Like a goat or a calf," I repeated.

She stared at him for a moment, spellbound as though gazing at the most beautiful jewel found in a puddle of mud. She raised the blade to his throat and pressed it gently a few times, testing how soft his flesh was without drawing blood.

"Just like a stray dog in the village, he spreads diseases and madness," I encouraged.

She pushed up his shirt to reveal his chest, smooth and unmarred by the wiry hair that older men seemed to sprout in later years.

Again, she pressed the blade tentatively against his skin, as though testing for weakness.

He could not scream, and he could not move, but his eyes betrayed fear.

I know, because I was looking.

Gently, I moved myself behind Sheyda, bringing both her hands to the hilt and placing my own over them.

"Together," I whispered.

This time the blade did not stop. The tip pierced his flesh, sinking deeper as a ruby well sprang from his skin. It grazed against bone, a rivulet of red cascading down his chest, pooling on the floor and soaking into his clothes.

Sheyda came to life. I lost my balance and fell to the floor as she jerked backwards. Her arm raised and raised again. Stab. Stab. Stab. Again and again and again. The sound of her exertion bubbled up through the spit on her lips and she cried out as she sank the blade deeper and deeper.

She began to sob and scream in equal measure until eventually she collapsed, exhausted, across the floor.

I sat there for a long time in shock. It was as though I had seen myself kill for the first time. Not the little Indian girl, she had been more of an accident, a spur-of-the-moment decision. But the first time I had killed close-up. Seen death face-to-face. It was thrilling, but the sort of thrill that leaves your flesh ringing and your mind reeling, as though you do not know what to think because there are no thoughts left in the entire world.

"Sheyda," I whispered her name as I rose, placing my hand gently on her shoulder.

She did not move, yet neither was she crying. I expect she felt the same as me.

Slowly, I slid my hands beneath her and pulled her towards me. She did not resist, though my foot slipped in the blood as I helped her to stand. There was so much blood, not only on the floor, but on our clothes, our hands, our faces.

I helped her up the stairs to my bed. I went to the cook hut and lit a fire. I boiled water, then stripped down and washed myself there, my fine clothes lying stained upon the earthen floor. I used a lump of laundry soap to scrub my skin, and rinsed the smell of copper from my hair.

Tipping the pail, I watched the dirty water soak into the ground, turning the dust to clay beneath my feet. I boiled more water, less this time because my arms were not as strong as Şelale's, and walked naked across the courtyard and up the stairs to my room.

Sheyda rose and allowed me to undress her. I stood her in the pail and used my own sponge to wipe her down. The blood on her face had started to dry. It took the appearance of a macabre *mehndi* pattern, and was particularly difficult to remove. I wiped so hard in places that her skin flushed pink.

Once she was clean, I dried her and dressed her in one of my night shirts. I pulled another over my own body and we lay there on the covers. I held her as she slept, feeling the rise and fall of her breath beneath my arm.

I knew then that I would never feel more satisfied with life than I did at that moment. I held my treasured companion beside me, alone in our private fortress, our enemies vanquished.

That night the rivers beyond the trees sounded as though they were singing. The violent clashing of water sounded more like a rebellious song of righteous defiance. It told of victory and of vitriol; a poem started long before the first page of the *Shahnameh* had been conceived.

It told me that I could love.

It was three weeks later that the Darougheh arrived.

Those were a strange three weeks, a sort of twilight era where everything had been turned on its head. My house, once comfortable and protected, now lay vulnerable. A servant occupied my room whilst

I went about the chores. I had watched Şelale enough throughout my childhood to have a rudimentary grasp of what the cooking pot should contain, and how to chop goat meat and vegetables. I could manage nothing more complicated than stew, which we ate with rice from the bag as I could not make bread.

The first batch of rice I attempted had to be thrown away. I did not cook it long enough and it hurt my teeth to chew. The second batch was cooked too long in too much water, it carried no taste and had the texture of mashed yam. Still, I kept trying until I got it right. There were four sacks of rice in the cook house, so we were in no danger of running out.

Sheyda remained in my room, on my bed. Each morning I would take her tea and sit and brush her hair. She said very little to me, neither 'good morning' nor 'good night'. She relieved herself in my bedpan, which I would take outside and empty at the bottom of the garden into the river. I assumed that must be what Şelale did with mine, though I had never asked her.

In the evenings I would sit and play the rusted qanun with little metal picks attached to my fingers on rings. Şelale had bought them at the bazaar, and it was easier than using the wooden hammers that Shusha had favoured. My fumbling almost began to sound like music. She would sit up in bed, listening to me. Whenever I would pause, she would raise her eyes to mine as though asking me to continue. We passed entire nights like that, with me playing and occasionally reciting some of the poems I had once liked to write. I had not written poetry since Shokuh had told me how little she thought of it, but I did not feel ashamed in front of Sheyda.

When I came down one morning to find the Darougheh standing at the back door, I half expected him.

"Shahzadi," he addressed me, with a slight bow.

He had come dressed as though he were marching to the Russian front, his head covered by a thick karakul hat, and his body weighed down by a heavy grey coat. It was cooler in the mountains, but perhaps he felt the cold more than most.

"Why have you come?" I asked. "Has my brother's bride finally decided to be rid of me once and for all?"

His moustache twitched at this suggestion, and a slow smile spread beneath it. Whenever the Darougheh smiled, it always reached his eyes. The lines there made him look older, like Shusha. Yet when he stopped smiling and his skin smoothed, there was still enough black in his hair to make him look young again. It was as though he were magically able to transform himself, a trick even Eirik would have been proud of.

"No, Shahzadi. Even if that were the case, she would never ask me to perform such an act. I am a servant of the Royal Dynasty and you, my child, are its progeny."

"Are you saying that you would protect me against her?"

"I am saying that I would protect you even against yourself."

He held my eyes, and I lowered mine first.

"Ah," I said quietly.

He came into the room, his shadow cast before him in the bright morning light. I watched as he ran his fingers over the side table, lifting them and rubbing the dust between their tips. He did not say anything, so I continued to watch as he admired one of the hangings on the wall, a bright orange tapestry shot through with gold thread. He continued his explorations, and I followed behind him, into the room where we had killed Hafez.

"Oh child," he sighed, more in disappointment than admonishment. "What have you done?"

What I had done was to get down on my hands and knees the next morning with a pail of scalding water and wipe away the blood. I scrubbed until my knuckles were raw. The water was changed five times and still it had not come clean. The tiles sparkled, but the grout had absorbed the colour and turned a telltale shade of brown, webbing out from the centre of the floor.

I did not answer.

He turned to me, studying me closely without expression. After a while he shrugged and shook his head.

"Was it Hafez?" he asked.

"How did you know?" I replied, full of surprise.

"Because I sent you two men, and only one came back."

"Oh. I wondered what had happened to him."

Whilst I was on my knees scrubbing at the blood-soaked tiles, it had not escaped my attention that Hesam was missing. I had left him beneath the table overnight, and resolved to take him water in the morning. I had not decided what I would do with him, but Sheyda had saved his life and I did not wish to upset her by killing him, at least not in a way she might notice.

When I lifted the cloth, he was gone.

I searched the downstairs rooms and the garden, but I could not find him. It didn't occur to me that he could have gone very far, unless Eirik had been wrong about his poison. Perhaps he had never kept a person alive for so long after using it. Perhaps the curse did lift eventually, and Hesam had simply wandered off.

I knew in my heart that this was an insubstantial explanation, but I had other tasks to attend to. If he had escaped, and if he had regained the power of speech and told his story to anyone, they might come to the door. If they did that, they would certainly discover the pool of blood on the floor. It had been more important for me to clean the house than to search for him.

When nobody came knocking that night, or the morning after, I assumed that he had simply vanished. It suited me to think that way, and to immerse myself in Sheyda's needs.

"Ah, Afsar, Afsar, Afsar. You did not *think*, did you?" This sudden explosion of anger caused me to draw back. "You should never have been left alone like this."

"You do not understand–"

"I do not need to understand, Afsar. All of the understanding in the world would not save your neck had anyone found him. Don't you see, child? Nobody would have been interested in your explanations. Nobody would care that you were the daughter of the Shah. Nothing would have protected you from the people's anger."

"The people's anger?"

"Where are the rest of your servants?" he asked, lowering his voice.

"I have none," I lied. "Şelale is away on errands."

"You have no other staff?"

"None."

He stared at me, unconvinced.

"We live a simple life here," I told him. "I have learned to dress myself in exile. I enjoy it, even."

"What about the cooking and the horses?"

"I can cook a little. Şelale taught me. As for the horses, my guards have not been gone long enough that they grow restless. In fact, that is where Şelale has gone," I added quickly, "to find help for them. Why do you ask?"

"Hesam was found entering the palace at Sari. My men stopped a cart pulled by an old man. Beneath the cloth they discovered his body with a sign around its neck." He reached into his coat and handed me a dirty piece of parchment. Scrawled across it in black paint read the words: *Victim of H.I.H. Afsar.* I felt my throat tighten. "We took the man to the rack, but he would not speak."

"What does it mean?"

"It means that someone is watching you."

"The Bábí!" I cried. "It must be the Bábí. Since those Rosy Hours, I have felt as though someone were watching me–"

"Haven't you heard, Shahzadi? Your brother exiled the Baha'u'llah months ago. The Bábí can no longer call Iran their home. Their marriages will be annulled, their books will be burned, and any who resist will find themselves chained in the Síyáh-Chál at Tehran. You no longer need to fear the insurgence. They have left like lambs."

I fell speechless for a moment. My brother had triumphed over the infidel, the enemies of Allah, and I had not known of this.

I felt a sudden sickness in my heart. I missed Shusha. I missed my schooling. I missed palace life, where everything was known by everybody all of the time.

My house in the hills could not have felt more abandoned than it did at that moment.

"If not the Bábí, then who?"

"I do not know Shahzadi, but I intend to find out. Meanwhile, you must play your part. From this moment on you must live a life utterly beyond reproach. Do you understand? You must give nobody cause for suspicion or reason to doubt your honour–"

"That is it, though! It was to protect my honour that I killed him."

"Keep your voice down," he instructed.

"Hafez was like Ja'far," I hissed. "That is why he had to die."

The Darougheh paled.

"He tried to do the things my uncle wished to do, so I killed him for it."

"Oh, child," he said.

"Now do you see?"

"Yes, I see, and I blame myself." He turned away for a moment, his hand reaching up to his face, his palm pulling down across his mouth as he turned back to me. "Here is what we shall do. I will return to Sari to continue my investigations. I will send two eunuch guards to replace the last two, and a maid to help you dress yourself–"

"No maid," I interrupted. "Şelale is enough."

"Then you must send her away on no more errands. It does not look well for a young woman to remain unchaperoned in a remote house. It invites trouble."

I nodded my consent.

"We will crack this mystery once and for all," he continued. "I will not have your safety threatened, but in return you must do nothing to threaten it yourself. Do I make myself understood?"

"Yes, Darougheh."

"And, Afsar."

"Yes?"

"Find a rug for the floor. Those bloodstains will never wash out."

You may not believe me, but I fully intended to keep my word. I knew that he was right. I had become so absorbed in my own freedom, in the absolute power I held over my diminutive realm, that I had ceased to be cautious. The mystery of Hesam's disappearance served as a cold reminder that no one is without enemies.

So it was that several weeks passed, and life resumed normality in my household. Şelale returned from Sari, having planted a fig on Shahab's grave to ease his burdens in death. This had not entirely been a distraction, for I had truly wished to do that for Shahab myself. It simply happened that circumstances required my servant to go in my place.

She brought with her news from my many mothers. She had been careful to remain veiled and out of sight, but gossip flowed like a river around the palace walls and she was easily able to bring some home in a cup for me to drink.

It was true that the spiritual leader of the Bábí had been exiled to Iraq, his movement broken after a bloody battle in the South. I was surprised to find myself feeling slightly sorry for the man. A beast from the darkest depths of *Duzakh* he may have been, but to be cast out from your family and your home was a punishment I could sympathise with more than most. Still, I was glad that he was gone, and that the sanctity of Islam remained untarnished within our glorious country.

Other news came that my mothers were restless among themselves. Since Shokuh had borne the Shah a son, he had been neglecting his conjugal duties. Many of the mothers desiring offspring were becoming increasingly belligerent towards her, refusing to acknowledge her as his favoured wife. It was also said that my brother's affections had shifted, and that he was showing an increasing interest in Monir, the daughter of an esteemed architect.

My heart soared to hear this, for I was certain that my exile would last only as long as Shokuh's hold over my brother. Mahde Olia may have hated me just as much, but as Mother to the Shah, her duties were many and widespread. If she visited Sari more than twice a year it was unusual, and whilst she was there I could easily keep myself out of sight.

There was a strong sense that Shokuh's days as head of the harem were numbered, and I for one was not in the least bit sorry.

Although I was glad for news of Sari, I was less enthralled by Şelale's return. In her absence, Sheyda and I had lived in some sort of heaven. With nobody watching us, the lines between my privilege and her poverty seemed to blur.

We slept beneath my cotton sheets, ate the simple stew that I was able to prepare, washed one another and took it in turns to comb each other's hair. I taught her how to pick the strings of the qanun and she took to it more naturally than I ever had. She played songs from the village and taught me the words in a dialect so thick I could hardly understand them.

When Şelale came back, all of that had to stop. Once again I was the only one to sleep beneath my cotton sheets, cold in the night from the lack of Sheyda's heat, whilst she knelt in the mud of the cook hut, preparing complicated meals with ingredients she walked each day to the bazaar to collect. I dearly wished Şelale gone, and I did not have to wait long for an excuse.

I woke late at night to hear cursing outside my window. In the dark of a new moon, I could just make out Şelale's shadow below, her face illuminated by a single oil lamp. She was hissing at something and jabbing it with the end of a broom. At first I thought it was a cat, until a loud cry went up and I realised that it was the snow-white peacock.

"What is it?" I asked, appearing on the garden terrace beside her. "Why are you tormenting the peacock at this late hour?"

She muttered something beneath her breath and turned to me, wiping a strand of hair from her eyes.

"He is the worst kind of man, that one," she told me. "Something has attacked the hens. There are two of them dead over there, and where do I find him? Stuffing his fat gullet with my peas. Look," she said, indicating a brown hessian sack. "I left them here to dry and he has swallowed nearly half of them!"

I was about to berate her for leaving peas where they might so easily be eaten. Had it not been for the peacock, I was certain a rat would have found them.

"Where is that stupid boy?" she went on. "The garden is his responsibility."

This caused me to stop, my mind instantly awake.

"My gardener?" I asked.

"Yes, Aram. Where is he? Good for nothing, ungrateful..."

She continued to describe him in ever more inventive terms, yet I had stopped listening, my eyes staring out across the lawn, wide in the starless night.

Where was he, indeed?

I had forgotten that I even had a gardener. He was such an unassuming thing, digging gently around the borders and neatening the edges of the grass with oil-silenced sheers. I could not recall seeing him in days, and the plants were looking sorrier than they should.

I placed my hand on Şelale's arm to quiet her.

"I need you to return to the palace," I told her.

She shook her head as if to protest.

"Not tonight," I smiled, trying to appear calmer than I felt, so that she would do as I said with less fuss. "You can go in the morning, but I need you to find the Darougheh." At the mention of his name she stopped resisting and listened quietly. "It is very important you find him. You must give him a message. I need you to tell him that it was – what was his name?"

"Aram?" she ventured.

"Yes, tell him that the note was from Aram. Tell him he was my gardener, and tell him the boy was from Sari. Tell him everything you know of his activities and his past, anything he told you when he started working here."

"I know very little," she said. "I did not hire him, he simply arrived one day from the palace. I thought perhaps your father had sent him, or that maybe Shokuh's heart had softened."

"It doesn't matter." I waved a hand to silence her. "I need you to find the Darougheh and to tell him that. It is very important."

She nodded, though her expression told me she wished she had left the peacock alone instead.

The next morning Şelale was gone, leaving Sheyda and I as we were.

One more blissful week we enjoyed before the Darougheh's eunuchs arrived, closely followed by Şelale and the Darougheh himself. It was like throwing a stick only to have it returned by a pack of hounds. Yet that final week was ours. It sparkles in my memory like a precious stone. We talked late into the night, drinking honeyed wine until we laughed ourselves to sleep. My laughter and hers, it was like a kind of madness had come over us. The story of our lives flowed like wax, and just like wax it hardened at that moment where we plunged the knife into Hafez.

"I can't believe he has gone," she confided, curled up in my arms as we sank between the feather pillows. "You gave me my freedom. You gave me back myself, Afsar. I owe you everything."

"I don't want anything from you," I told her. "Only–" I hesitated, unable to ask for what I most desired.

I did not have to. She raised herself up on one arm and pressed her rosewater lips against mine.

A kiss that lasted a moment; a moment that lasted a lifetime.

"I never dreamt," she whispered, "growing up in a house with straw for a roof and goats for company, that I would ever serve in a house so fine, let alone sleep in a bed so soft."

"Or that you would love a Shahzadi?"

"Oh," she smiled. "I think I loved you even before I met you."

"How is that possible?" I asked.

"You are part of my soul. I am part of yours. I have known you all my life."

That was how brilliant our flame shone that last week, before the storm descended.

◆ 10 ◆

The eunuchs were strange creatures. Men who could hardly be said to be such, they held a special place in my brother's guard, attending to the safety of his harems and any other public office where temptation of the opposite sex might lead to corruption. After what I had told him of Hafez, the Darougheh would take no more risks with my virtue.

Their names were Adel and Majid, and instantly I preferred them to my previous guards. They were both somewhat rounder across the cheeks than my former, angular-featured guards, which made them appear more honest. Majid had a beard, which Shusha had once explained meant that he was castrated later in life, whereas Adel was fresh-faced like a baby. Shusha also told me that people joined the Shah's ranks in this way for many different reasons.

Some were born to it, castrated at an early age, often by poorer parents. Eunuch pageboys were much in demand, receiving both an education and a plentiful supply of food. Others, like Majid, had made the decision later in life, usually after falling on hard times.

I knew that one of the harem servants at Sari had chosen to become a eunuch after the woman he was desperately in love with had decided to marry another man. When my mothers were short on entertainment, he would sometimes sing sad songs about it. He knew that he would never love another as deeply again, so he decided not to love at all.

Majid and Adel were far more self-sufficient than Hesam and Hafez had been. They knew how to cook, and would even wash their own clothes, so Sheyda never had to lift a finger for them. Despite their soft voices and their gentle mannerisms, they were both big, broad men. I felt safe with them guarding my gates, and suspected they were some of the Darougheh's finest.

Then, one evening the Darougheh returned on horseback from Sari, with Şelale riding beside him. They clattered into the courtyard, the Darougheh shouting for me even before he'd dismounted. They entered my house red-faced and sweat-drenched.

"Afsar, you lied to me!" he roared. "Where is your maid?"

I was halfway down the stairs, and almost tumbled the rest of the way as he pushed past me.

"No, wait!" I called, but it was too late.

He caught Sheyda coming out of my room, carrying an armful of clothes for the wash. They fell to the floor as he grabbed her wrist, pulling her back down the stairs to stand trial in the centre of the room.

"I'll have your name," he bellowed in her face.

"Sheyda," she cried. "My name is Sheyda."

Her face went deathly pale and her legs faltered beneath her, but he pulled her to her feet again.

"Where do you come from? Who are your family?"

"I'm from Shirgah. My family live here, by the mosque."

He held her head back by her hair, scrutinising her frightened eyes.

"What is this about?" I demanded, crossing the space between us.

Eventually, he let go and she sank to the floor.

"Your gardener must have had help. This Aram of yours does not exist, yet there are some who remember a servant leaving for Shirgah at about the right time. By all accounts he was only a boy. How can a boy lift a dead man onto a cart?"

"Dead man?" Sheyda asked, staring between us.

"I don't know anything about that, but I know that my maid had nothing to do with it."

"How do you know?"

"Because I did lie to you. Because it was not me that Hafez tried to attack."

The Darougheh's head snapped around so fast I thought it might fly off.

"He violated you?" he asked Sheyda.

The colour of her cheeks matched the colour of the bloodstain beneath the rug she sat upon. That pretty moon of hers rising against a sunset. All she could do was nod.

"Why didn't you tell me?" he asked.

"Would you have taken it so seriously had it been my maid rather than myself he attacked?"

"It would have shown the man's character, and I would have had him dismissed," he said, seeming to calm a little. He offered his hand to Sheyda, who allowed him to help her to her feet. Instead of letting go of her hand, he clasped it firmly, causing her to gasp. "Unless they were in this together? A conspiracy?"

"A conspiracy to get himself murdered?"

"No, unlikely," he agreed, letting go of her at last. "Still, you must not keep things from me, Afsar. How am I supposed to protect you when you do not tell me the truth? Things you might not think important may prove to be very important."

He stayed that night. Şelale cooked *fesenjän* with duck they had shot on their journey. Sheyda ate hers in the cook hut with the eunuchs, whilst the Darougheh and I shared a plate on the garden steps. At first we had little to say to one another: a girl of almost thirteen and a man more than thrice her age. The aromatic spices in the dish slowly began to loosen our tongues, and the cardamom toffee Şelale produced for dessert sweetened his words.

"You are much like your mother," he eventually said, when he was certain we were alone.

"In what way?" I asked.

"Infuriating."

I expected him to smile as though this were a joke, but he did not.

"She was guided by her own desires, rarely aware of the consequences of her actions or the envy of others. Her enemies were powerful, influential women, yet she lived her life as though she had none. Whatever she wished to do, she did. Your father indulged her and on occasion even encouraged her."

"Who is here to encourage me?" I observed.

"You do not need encouragement. You are perfectly capable of hanging yourself."

I opened my mouth to protest.

"Don't," he said. "I am old, and I have no energy left to argue. Please just listen to me, Afsar. Life is not kind, but it is not kind to anybody. You have been born into far greater comfort and privilege than almost anyone else in Iran. It may not seem like it to you, but take it from one who has walked through the gutter, who has seen pestilence and starvation, seen what it can do to desperate men and women. You need never know that, ever. I pray that you shan't. So I urge you, stop courting disaster—"

"I was defending my honour! You would not allow a prince to touch me, do you assume I should let a commoner put his grubby hands upon my maid?"

The Darougheh flinched with the bluntness of my words. "That is not it, child. You lie to me again. You forget what I know of your night-time walks to the village. Perhaps this was defence, but there is more to it than that. There is bloodlust in your veins, it pumps through the heart of your family, but in you it is more obvious than in others."

I felt my cheeks burn beneath his stare. I had never thought myself obvious in my pleasures. Eirik and I had always taken great care to cover our tracks.

"You cannot simply make people disappear, Afsar. Your father at least has the excuse of state to mask his pleasure in killing. Did your tutor teach you nothing of politics? He who kills in the name of his people is a hero. Those who simply kill are villains. You cannot afford to be a villain, Afsar. You have no family to protect you now. Shokuh's pride is injured by your brother's new flirtation. She is looking for any opportunity to hurt him, and stoning you would be an effective way of doing that. As for Mahde Olia, she would do it for her own pleasure alone."

"My brother would never allow it!"

"Politics, Afsar. Politics. Your brother is sorely compromised. He may have chased off the Bábí, but he has the Turks, the Russians, and the British bearing down upon him. His harems drain the public purse, and he sells Iran's assets to pay for them. Cheaply, I may add. He is a young Shah, with dreams of modernisation his father – *your* father – would baulk at. He is losing the confidence of the traditionalists, and angering the economists and the nationalists. You, Afsar, are a tiny drop in the vast ocean that is his empire. If his people demanded it – if you gave them reason to demand it – he would serve you up to them sooner than lose their respect. He cannot afford not to."

His words rang in my ears. I had never considered that my brother had weaknesses. He was the Shah of Iran, one in a long line of Persian rulers whose birthright it was to govern the people of this ancient land. In knowing that, I had never once suspected that in order to govern them he might have to appease them. How little of the world Shusha had ever really taught me.

"I mean nothing to him," I murmured, staring out across the lawn.

"No, child. You mean a great deal to him, but there are only so many times he can save you. Or I, for that matter."

"You speak as though I am already saved."

The Darougheh reached out his thick, weathered hand and took another piece of toffee. Sucking it thoughtfully, he asked, "Did you ever wonder how your friend rose so swiftly to prominence in your brother's esteem?"

"Eirik?"

"Eirik, Vachon, the Comte de la Mort Rouge. Whatever name he chooses to go by this week. Doesn't it strike you as odd how a travelling circus performer is suddenly placed in charge of building the Shah a palace?"

"He is my brother's assassin. I imagine that comes with some rewards."

"A lofty promotion for one so young. Don't you think that strange?"

I glared at him, for I could tell that he knew something I did not. He refused to look back, sucking on his toffee, watching the white peacock strut across the lawn.

"You speak as though you do not like him."

"Oh, very much the opposite. I have great admiration for the boy. To be born with the misfortune of his face and not only to have survived, but to have prospered. That is a feat unimaginable to most. A builder, a magician, a musician, an assassin. Any one of those skills would be sufficient for one man, yet he has perfected them all. It beggars belief."

"Then you have answered your own question, have you not? How did he rise so quickly in my brother's esteem? He is talented and ambitious."

The Darougheh nodded. "Of course. That must be so."

I felt that he was holding something back, but pride would not allow me to ask him. Instead, I asked about Hesam's body, and the cart pulled by the old man.

"Do I take it your investigation has gone cold, now that you have interrogated my maid?"

I expected him to bristle at this, but he shrugged calmly.

"No. We know where your suspect is. We are keeping a close eye on him to uncover his plans."

"I thought you said the old man would not speak?"

"He was very old. His heart gave out within a few moments of the rack being tightened. Overzealousness on the part of my men. Still, after removing the body we released the horse. It walked all the way home."

"And where was that?"

"The stables to the west of the palace walls."

He watched my brow furrow as I tried to recall who lived there.

"The groundsmen," he reminded me. "The cart was met by the head gardener, Vafar. He even lifted the cloth at the back as though expecting to find something."

I felt my throat go dry.

"Vafar was..." I couldn't finish the sentence.

"Shahab's father. Indeed."

"And my gardener, who was he?"

"Possibly a cousin, or a younger brother. We'll ask him when we find him."

"This is what you meant by the 'people's anger,' isn't it?"

He ran his tongue around the inside of his cheek, sucking the sweetness from his teeth.

"Sitting on top of the Peacock Throne, the world can look very small beneath, Shahzadi. Your brother flies like an eagle above his people, who swarm like ants below. But you must never forget for one moment the strength there is in numbers. If you poke a stick into a termite nest, you can expect them to tear down your house."

The Darougheh left for Sari again the next morning, convinced that Sheyda was neither a spy nor a threat. The mountain air cooled, and soon we were all wearing thick robes and layers of cotton to keep winter at bay. In the evenings we could see our own breath against the sky. I longed for the balmy air of the Caspian shore. I remembered the nights I had lain awake there, cursing the way my sleep-drenched clothes clung to my body with their pungent salty scent. If I had known then that I would one day be shivering in the hills of Shirgah, I would never have dared to complain.

It was on the eve of the mid-winter festival that Eirik clattered into our courtyard, standing tall at the front of his silver-skulled carriage, its black lacquer reflecting the moon back upon itself. He leant back, hauling on the reins of his horses to bring them to a standstill, whilst I watched from the window above.

He came dressed in black, wearing his nacre mask with the ruby-encrusted lips. The candles in the doorway cast dichroic shadows across it, like an opal held to the light. For a moment his face reminded me of the jinn's lair so strongly that I could smell its rose-scented waters. A sickly-sweet smell that caused my heart to curl in on itself. It had been months since I last saw Eirik, since our night in Tehran. I thought about him most days, but less and less since Sheyda and I had become close. It was as though they occupied two separate parts of me: Sheyda the light, and Eirik the dark.

"Shahzadi," he said, kneeling and bending his head in an unnecessary display of respect, as though mocking me.

"Get up," I instructed.

"What?" he said. "You are not pleased to see me?"

"Of course I am, but it's cold and it's late and I'm tired. You could have warned me you were coming."

"Warned you? Do I look like an invading army?"

Şelale appeared in the doorway behind me, carrying a tray of dried fruit for the guards.

"This is what happens in my absence," he addressed her. "The little princess loses all her joy. It is clear, I must never leave again."

I felt my skin bristle. The days when we played together at the palace in Sari seemed very far away, his words now ringing with a familiarity they no longer had any right to possess. The Darougheh knew something of Eirik that I did not, and I wished then that I had let him speak of it. With people like Şelale, time did not seem to change them. I could imagine that if she went away for a week, or maybe even a year, I would still recognise her. We would soon fall back to the way we were. If I ever chanced to see Shusha again, that is how I imagine we would be – just as we were before. Yet with Eirik, it was different. In the short time I had known him, he had, as the Darougheh himself pointed out, risen from a travelling vagabond with nothing to his name to one of my brother's most prominent henchmen. Every time I saw him, he had changed. He grew taller, both physically and in confidence, no longer stooped and treading in the shadows, but bold and upright.

The strangest image crossed my mind then, of a tick I had once seen in the ear of a cat. The cat used to come and sit with me when I read on the bench by the lawns. It was a white cat, which is why I did not notice the parasite at first. It was tiny. Yet, as the days passed, it grew and grew and grew, becoming fat on the cat's blood. Sucking its nutrients, its life force, its moisture. Nothing the tick ate had it found for itself, yet it continued to grow off what another had provided. At that moment, with his pearl-white face and his blood-red lips, that is exactly what Eirik reminded me of.

Şelale simply bowed her head and looked to me for a sign that she might continue through to the front of the house.

Once she had gone, I asked Eirik why he was here.

"What sort of a welcome is that?" he asked, offended.

"I explained, it is late."

"And I have travelled a long way."

"Perhaps you should have waited until morning."

He stood there, perfectly still. "Do you know what day it is?"

For a moment I had to think. Since being left by myself the days seemed to blur into one another. I lost track of them too easily. If it weren't for the call of the mosque, I might even lose track of hours. I watched my guards unfurl their prayer mats towards Mecca, but Şelale and myself had grown lax in our observance of *Şalāt*. You had to be pure to pray, and I had not felt that in a long time. If I opened my mouth, I doubted Allah would hear me.

"It is *Sadé*. The whole of Shirgah is ablaze, yet here you are huddled away in your empty house with a Turkish servant for company. If you're cold, come and warm yourself."

Eirik's special gift lay in illusions. They were more than simply magic tricks or being able to make his voice leave his body. It was in making you feel as though everything around you was a fabrication, that you could simply reach out and change what you did not like.

That night, we all went to the centre of Shirgah. All except Adel, who stayed behind to watch over the house. We dressed ourselves in velvet robes with hoods to hide our faces. Not that anyone would recognise me, as I never ventured out of my fortress, but it added to the sense of mystery, and it helped to keep us warm.

Eirik had been right about the fires. Sadé is the festival of flames. The second ruler of the world, Hōšang, uncovered the secret of fire when he threw a rock at a snake. It missed the snake, but struck another rock, creating sparks. These sparks embody the light of God, and are present in all of his creatures. In the depths of winter we celebrate His fire, because that is when we are most grateful for its heat.

Shirgah was a village compared with Sari, its inhabitants half as many and half as rich. Yet they came in their very best costumes: bright scarlet dye and gold trim, silver ankle charms that sang as the women stepped in elaborate patterns, lifting their arms and flicking their wrists, mimicking the flames. Their laughter was infectious and even Sheyda managed to smile.

Eirik joined the other men from the village, walking barefoot across a bed of brightly glowing embers. When he reached the other side, he performed four perfect backflips, returning to the start of the trail. The crowd gasped at this, and almost fainted at what happened next. He raised his hands slowly, palms up to the sky as though summoning serpents. The embers flared, blazing bright and golden, before dying down to the ash once again.

The crowd applauded and shouted for more, and Eirik was only too glad to oblige, for he did so love to be the centre of attention, provided he could hide his true face.

Sheyda and I watched for a while as he threw his voice, causing words to fall from little girls' mouths that their parents had never heard them say before, reciting passages from the *Shahnameh* as though they had written it themselves.

After the initial silence of surprise, in which the spectators' eyes grew wide and their lips O-shaped, there always followed laughter and applause. He could juggle almost any object, eat fire from a stick, and twist perfect balls of crystal between his fingers as though they danced with him.

After a while we left him there, performing to his adoring public, whilst we went in search of food. We bought kebabs from a trader and crouched on the ground to eat them, whilst we watched young men daring each other to jump higher and higher over the bonfire, adding an extra log each time.

"Who is your friend?" Sheyda asked, sucking meat juice from her thumb. "I have seen him here before, but I do not know his name."

"His name is Eirik," I told her. "He works for the Shah. I know him from the palace at Sari."

"What does he do for your father?"

"Many things. He is an architect, and an entertainer."

"Why does he always wear a mask?"

"His face is ugly. He was damaged at birth."

She looked sad for a moment, and then asked, "Do you love him?"

Her question caught me by surprise, and I almost fell backwards on my heels.

"Of course not! How can you ask such a thing?"

"Why else would he come here, if there was not something between you?"

"We are friends, that is all."

"Friends? One man, one woman?" She laughed at this, and my cheeks burned hot like embers beneath the ash.

"Did you love Hefaz?"

Her laugh dried in her throat.

"What men feel is not always the most important thing," I told her. "What about what women feel? I love you more than I love him."

She stared for a moment, uncertain whether to trust me.

"I am glad," she whispered.

The next day, Eirik ordered Şelale to pack up a pannier of food and the two of us, as well as Sheyda, rode out to find the waterfall on the road to Zirab.

Zirab was a larger city, through the jungle to the south. By the fireside the night before, one of the women had told Eirik of a singing well hidden beneath a waterfall on the road leading out of Shirgah.

"It drums when danger is approaching, and sings when all is well," she had told him.

"You hole yourself away in your home," he said to me that morning. "You should be out exploring. There are so many things to see, Shahzadi."

It was little use arguing with Eirik, or trying to explain that the Darougheh would prefer I never leave the house again. He had seen half the world already, and although I knew now that I was unlikely ever to leave Iran, I still felt a deep urge to follow him. Whenever I had in the past, there had always been great adventures.

That particular day was warmer than usual, as though summer were throwing an unlikely shadow. After ten minutes on the road, Sheyda and I had already opened the front of our overcoats and found ourselves mopping our brows with the tails of our scarves.

The heat did not let up as we entered the jungle, though its thick canopy offered some relief. We moved slowly so as not to exhaust the horses, the light through the leaves almost trance-inducing, causing us to fall silent, the thud of our beasts' hooves against the earth measuring out our own heartbeats.

"These trees are ancient," I told my companions. "They once belonged to the *Verkâna.*"

"The Kingdom of the Wolves," Sheyda echoed, smiling as I turned to look at her. "We know of them here," she continued. "It is a bedtime story our mothers tell us as children, that we must never go walking through the trees at night, otherwise the wolf people will snatch us away."

"Baron Bisclavret," Eirik joined in. "He was a French nobleman who was half-man, half-wolf. There were many like him in France at one point, stealing children in their sleep and attacking women and young men as they walked the streets after dark."

"Really?" Sheyda asked, her expression like a child. "Where is France?"

"A long way from here."

"Further than Tehran?"

Eirik laughed and waved his hand to indicate much further.

It was at this point that his horse veered off the path and disappeared into the fern. At first I was afraid he had performed a disappearing trick. Then we saw that there was a deer trail leading down a steep gully. I leaned back in the saddle and allowed my hips to swing loosely from side to side so that I would not be pulled over my mount's head if it lost its footing.

At the bottom of the gulley, we could look up at the trees lining the path we had previously been on. It was as though someone had covered our ears with pillows, the sound of the birds seemed muted from below, the sunlight dimmed.

"This way," Eirik called, his horse several lengths ahead.

As we continued, a low rumbling replaced the silence, becoming a roar as we turned a bend in the road. We found ourselves confronted by a sheer cliff towering before us. It was as though a giant had thrust his trowel into the earth and scooped out a hole, exposing a rocky, semicircular scar to the world. Plummeting down this grey rock was a jet of pure, crystal-transparent water.

Dismounting, we walked towards it over ground made uneven by head-sized boulders. We had to strain our necks to gaze up, and the further we looked, the greener the walls of the waterfall became, painted with moss and overhanging vines.

Beneath, where the water had kissed its reflection over generations, it left a dark circle, as though it fell straight to the centre of the earth itself. This must have been what the woman meant by a well beneath the waterfall. I listened carefully, trying to decide whether it sounded as though it were singing or drumming, yet this was like placing your ear next to a miquelet and trying to decipher the words it spoke as you fired.

"It's incredible," I whispered, my voice washed away in the ringing chasm.

I felt tiny in its presence, as though the sound alone could crush me. A deliciously fresh breeze blew off the surface of the pool. At first it felt like a tonic to the warm weather, but soon my skin grew rough with goose bumps. Still, none of us hurried to leave.

Sheyda walked all the way up to the pool, her leather sandals slipping across the stones. When she reached it, she drew back her scarf and cupped her hands together. She drank from them before cupping water over her face and head. Watching from a distance, it looked like a holy act.

We stayed until we were deaf, transfixed by the might of Allah.

When we eventually reached the road again, Eirik did not turn right towards Shirgah, but left towards Zirab. I know not why, but I did not question him, still swimming within the raging white of my mind.

It soon became clear that he was intent on finding the top of the waterfall. After some time there was a second deer track trailing between the trees, level with the main path. It was like a reversal of before. This time it was the sound of the falling water that seemed muted, and the birds that sang loudly. Here, the river eddied over a flatbed of smooth rock, swelling and thinning to create a number of bathing pools, some shallow and sun-warmed, others deep and cool.

As though thinking with one mind, we stripped to our kameez, and Eirik to his şalvar, and threw ourselves beneath the surface. We were children again, unaware of the difference of our bodies, or the separation which society demanded. We cupped our hands and ped-alled our feet, dousing one another in water, laughing like siblings.

It felt so free. As though the whole of the rest of the world had ceased to exist beyond the trees. If I could have built a hut out of wood and twine and lived there, I would have. The type of day you can catch in your hands and keep forever.

It was the next morning that Sheyda was sick for the first time.

She had a bed of her own downstairs, near Şelale's, but most nights she would sneak upstairs to my room after the Turk had finished her chores and turned in. By then I found it difficult to sleep when she was not there. We would curl up together, face to face, her breath against my cheek. Some nights we even shared the same dreams.

That morning, I was woken by the sound of her retching. She was flat on her stomach across the bed, her fingers clawing up bunches of bedding, her head drooped over the side, vomiting into our bedpan.

"Sheyda!" I cried, kneeling forward to stroke her back.

After a moment she wiped her mouth with the back of her hand and took several deep breaths. Tears were streaming down her cheeks.

"What is it?" I asked. "Have you a fever?"

She shook her head and crawled back to her pillow, pressing her face flat against its cool cotton. I stroked her hair gently, cooing like a dove to calm her, but soon she was back across the bed, emptying her stomach on the floor. I was so afraid that I ran to find Şelale, shouting at her to bring towels and a pot.

I sat in the corner, twisting my nightgown between my fists as I waited to learn what was wrong, all the time praying that it was not poison or disease. She looked so pale, her forehead jewelled with sweat. I remembered her drinking from the pool, and thinking how the water disappeared beneath the depths as though reaching to the centre of the earth. What if it truly did? What if it reached all the way to hell and she was being punished for tasting such wickedness?

If that were the case I would go to hell myself. I would seek out Iblīs if need be, and make him give her back her health.

But it was worse than that.

As the days passed, a pattern started to emerge which told us that Sheyda's illness was nothing to do with anything she had eaten or drunk.

"She is pregnant," Şelale announced a week later.

I had not slept that entire week, sat in a room that stank of sour vomit and sweat. It reminded me of Sarvar, these two years past, the metallic smell of blood and despair as Bousseh wiped her face with a cloth. The moment Şelale gave her diagnosis, fear closed around my heart like a vice, squeezing the air from me. Could it be possible that Hefaz might yet have his revenge? I had killed him for what he had done to Sheyda, yet might he still call her to him from beyond the grave?

The news broke her. She refused all food for a week, sobbing into the sheets as though trying to suffocate herself. Her cries were worse than her silence, the blood in my veins turning to saltwater as though her tears ran through them. There was nothing I could think to say to comfort her, and no one I could kill to release my pain, for the perpetrator was beyond my knife.

Eventually, Şelale managed to get her to take a little broth. She cared for Sheyda as though she were a daughter, feeding her only food that would not aggravate her sickness, pulling back the sheets when she flushed and tucking them back in when she shivered. Sheyda would not allow us to call for her true mother as she was too ashamed of what had happened. It was not uncommon for a woman to be forced to marry her rapist, as even that was considered better than to have no husband at all. As the sire of Sheyda's child would never be able to marry her, she had become like me, an exile.

Once she started to take food, I spent most of my time in the gardens, walking endlessly between the river and the terrace. Since the boy had disappeared, the garden had once again become overgrown. At the far end, next to a tiny rosebush choked by vines, I discovered a circle of white feathers, as though someone had dropped a bag of

flour on the ground. It occurred to me that I had not heard the peacock for several days. Either something had stolen into my garden and
attacked it, or Şelale had put it in her broth.

"A sad end," Eirik said, appearing beside me in his brown leather
mask.

Sheyda's sickness had so consumed me that I'd had forgotten Eirik
was even there. I assumed he had taken his leave, returning to his building site at Sari, or his fine house in Tehran. I did not know whether he
was referring to the peacock or to Sheyda, so I remained silent.

"You know," he continued, "it would do your friend good to get
some fresh air. It's unhealthy to remain in bed for so long. Let me build
her a shelter where she can sit and enjoy the garden, shaded from the
sun."

I stared at him for a moment, uncertain why he should care.

"Where?" I asked.

He thought for a moment, casting his eye across the grounds.

"There." He pointed to a part of the lawn in the east, which caught
the best of the morning light but which the trees protected at noon.
"A perfect place, wouldn't you agree?"

I could not see what he saw. To me, it was simply another patch of
garden. Where he saw a magnificent pagoda, I saw only grass and sky.

"Do you really want to do something to help my servant?" I asked
him.

"Of course," he replied. "If it helps you."

"Then get rid of the baby," I said urgently, placing my hand on his
arm. "You can do that. You can make anything happen. Perform your
magic and make it vanish. Make it never have happened."

"I cannot do that."

"You – you can do anything. You can make men silent and still
whilst you remove their organs in front of their eyes. You can build
palaces with passages that lead to the ends of the earth. You can
appear in mirrors. You can make music like the angels. You can speak
from the other side of the room and lasso a needle from twenty paces.
Yet you tell me you cannot make one tiny, unborn infant disappear?"

"I will not do it," he said quietly.

"You can but you will not? You dare to defy me in this matter?"

Tears started to prickle the sides of my eyes. I went to slap him,
but he caught my wrist.

"Shahzadi, life is sacred."

I snorted my disdain. "You're an assassin, a murderer. How can you stand there and tell me such a thing!"

"Everything will die, but first it must live."

"Oh!" I cried. "Really? Even if it is born as ugly as you?"

He released my wrist and lowered his gaze.

"How many nights have you lain awake wishing you had never been born, I wonder?"

"And yet, here I am, so I could not have wished it that hard."

I bit down on my tongue until I could taste blood. "Fine. If you will not save her from her fate, then you may as well build her a shelter from whence she can view it."

"Very well."

He bowed slightly and withdrew, leaving me to the salty taste of my own turmoil. What sort of friend was he that he could not do this one favour for me – for us? This Prince of Conjurers, this King of Stranglers, who stood quietly by as Sheyda's terror grew within her. At that moment, I hated him with all my heart.

The next few months passed beneath a layer of brick dust and gold leaf. Each morning I would wake by Sheyda's side, scouring her still-sleeping body for any sign that she was showing. As long as her belly remained flat, I could fool myself into thinking she was simply recovering from a bout of food poisoning. Any day now she might open her eyes, smile at me, and ask for money to go to the bazaar. Soon she would resume her duties alongside Şelale, and we would laugh, play nard, and sing to the qanun just as before.

After a few indulgent moments of delusion I would rise, rub my eyes, slip on my gown, and pad down the cold, tiled steps to the entrance hall, where I would find the front doors wide open and Eirik up to his armpits in sand.

It had taken him a week to build a gazebo in the exact spot he had first mentioned. It was only a simple structure, with six pillars made from white ceramic flowerpots stacked upside-down, one on top of the other. The roof sloped in a wide circle, like a brass cymbal used as a hat, only there were ridges around it in the pattern of a spider's web, between which the blue tiles draped themselves. When it rained, the water ran between these ridges and cascaded over the ends of the roof. It was quite beautiful in its way.

The floor of the structure had also been tiled in white, painted with peonies and lotus. In the centre he had placed a woven gelim and a set of big, comfortable cushions to sit upon.

Still being angry with him, I had not watched much of the building process, yet I had been aware of a steady stream of boys and young men coming to the garden to help dig the foundations and mix cement. Had I not been so angry with him, I'm sure I would have marvelled at his ability to organise everything so efficiently. This strange, masked man, who spoke a dozen languages fluently yet always with an unplaceable accent, who could walk into an unfamiliar town in the foothills of Iran and return with everything he needed to build Sheyda's surprise.

I could not do that, and I was the daughter of a Shah.

Not content with his ornamental creation, he went on to order the garden landscaped, and soon there were herbs and spices growing all around the back steps and the cook hut. The roses were gathered up from their forlorn, abandoned places, and rehomed in a designated rose garden beneath my bedroom window. Jasmine and honeysuckle entwined anything they could climb, as well as trailing the supports of the gazebo. It was not their season to flower yet, but already I could imagine warm summer evenings on the terrace, bathing in their heady scent.

Once the garden had been righted and the lawns clipped, he turned his attention to the interior. Many of the chipped tiles were replaced, and a constant pile of cement mix and gypsum appeared at the front door. Over the days and weeks that followed, the interior of my house began to sparkle. Crystal chandeliers, reminiscent of those at the Arg in Tehran, hung from the ceilings like the teardrops of angels. Carefully positioned mirrors reflected light between the rooms, so that even on a cloudy day they seemed larger and brighter than ever they had before.

At first I thought his attentions purely decorative. After our argument we spoke little to one another. Every day I hoped he would simply leave. Instead, he refurbished my house. I chose to take this as an unspoken apology.

The more I watched, though, the more I came to notice other changes. He wasn't simply altering the way that my house looked, he was altering the very way that it behaved. Bookshelves appeared, lined with books I had never read, mantelpieces gathered ornaments I would never have bought, and paintings hung at strange angles from the walls.

There was a trick or a spring attached to almost everything. If you twisted the head on the ceramic cat above the mantelpiece, a brick at the back of the hearth grumbled aside to reveal a secret storage space. A large silk hanging in the parlour revealed a safe, complete with a dial mechanism and secret code. The bookshelf, of course, was not a bookshelf, but the disguise for a door that allowed you to move instantly between two rooms.

Eirik was building me a palace. It was nowhere near as spacious or grand as my brother's at Sari, nor even as clever as his own house in Tehran, which seemed to have been built twice: once on the outside, for the eyes to see, then again on the inside, behind the mirrors and walls. Yet it was fascinating, and I was fascinated. Trying my best to hide my interest in his work, I took to pacing around the house instead of the garden, passing the rooms he was working on, noting the items he removed and replaced.

From time to time he would leave Shirgah. A messenger would arrive by horse, looking flustered and hot. They would thrust a piece of paper into his hand and ride away again without pausing for breath. When this happened, he would disappear without a word, sometimes for a few days, sometimes for weeks on end. He would always return, though.

By the dawn of the New Year, and my thirteenth birthday, I had practically forgotten my animosity towards Eirik. It seemed almost amusing that he had once been so angry at me for taking a life from this world, whilst I was there now, angry at him for not.

Sheyda was round as a plum by this point. Afraid that someone might recognise her in the town, we stayed at home on Nowruz and Eirik performed a special show for us. As Adel and Majid could not leave either, they were roped into acting as his assistants. He played on their sexlessness, wrapping their faces in colourful scarves so that only their eyes were visible, then conducting entire conversations between the two, throwing his voice into their bodies. It was hilarious. Both Sheyda and I were in tears before long, rocking back and forth, begging him to stop. Even the eunuchs flushed behind their veils, Adel's fat stomach bouncing up and down as he laughed.

Then Eirik told them to pretend that he was a male intruder in the royal harem, and they were the Shah's angry wives. He charged them with capturing him and throwing him from the building, a role which my guards relished. They rolled up their sleeves and ran towards him, the tails of their scarves trailing out behind.

Eirik allowed them to chase him for a while, jumping over chairs and sliding under tables to evade their outstretched arms. Just as it looked as though they had him cornered, he turned on them. A flash of light appeared, followed by another and another. Adel and Majid drew back as an assault of fireballs streamed towards them. All of a sudden there was one big flash. When we blinked, he was gone!

"Thirsty work," Eirik said, walking in through the door behind us. "May I have a glass of water?"

The water he turned into wine, scarves he turned into serpents and then back again, the air he filled with doves. He plucked gold from ears and made time stop simply by clicking his fingers at the clock. He had us bind him with rope, and within seconds he had freed himself. Then he did the same to Majid and we all laughed as he fell over himself, struggling like a pig at market.

We cried our delight and clapped our hands. Throughout however, I had the strangest feeling he was performing for Sheyda rather than myself. When he bowed, he bowed to her. When he smiled, he looked around the room, yet his eyes seemed to rest a moment longer on hers. When he flourished his hand at the very end, producing a blood-red rose, he presented the flower to her.

Why should I have cared, though?

Sheyda's happiness was mine also.

Those months of waiting would have been interminable had it not been for the news filtering in from our neighbours, the Ottomans. What I did not know of politics, Eirik undertook to teach me. He hired an elderly woman of letters to come from Zirab twice a week, hiding behind the curtains whilst she entranced Sheyda, Şelale and myself with her animated retelling of the unfolding drama.

Some time the year before, probably not long after my brother was embroiled in his conference with the Russians about the Turks, those two great empires had declared war upon one another. In recent months my father's friends, the British, with their female Shah, along with Eirik's kinsmen, the French, had waded in on the side of the Turks. This was cause for great mirth on our part, as the Russians had sent us nothing but plagues and invasions throughout history, and the thought of them humbled through a Turkish-European alliance was pleasing indeed.

Eirik explained that in order for my brother to maintain former peace treaties with the Russians, and to placate his main investors, the British, as well as the ancient origins of his own bloodline, the Turks, he had wisely decided to keep his nose clean of this conflict. It meant that we could sit unconcerned in my little house in the hills, drinking spiced tea and eating dates, whilst the latest news dribbled from between Afrouzeh's gummy jaws.

One of the stories that most amused us was that of İskender Paşa and Ömer Paşa, two of the greatest Ottoman generals leading the campaign. What made them so funny was that neither were Turkish. One was a Polish freedom fighter who fled to Turkey as a wanted criminal, and the other was an Austrian soldier and Orthodox Christian. Both of them had converted to Islam in order to join the Sultan's army.

We laughed hard about this. It had always been a joke in Persia that the Turkish had others do their fighting for them, and when they couldn't find people to stand between them and the cannons, they would use their horses. I suppose I laughed so hard because I dearly needed the distraction.

In a rare display of confidence, Şelale pointed out that the founders of my own dynasty derived long ago from the Oghuz Turks.

"We kept the brains, but left them the horses." I smiled.

Afrouzeh laughed and rocked on her heels. It was one of the few times I had been in the presence of a learned woman. I wondered, in another life, one in which I had been encouraged to pursue knowledge rather than power, whether her face might have been mine some day. It was leathered like Bousseh's, and when she smiled the lines reminded me of a map of Persia before the cartographer painstakingly applied gold leaf.

"And what of your story?" I asked her. "Your face is awfully brown for someone who spends her time in the libraries of noble houses."

The old woman's smile vanished and she fell still, her arms drooping between her legs as though I had asked her when she expected to die.

"I was not always a woman of letters," she confided. "I was born in the fields, the daughter of a farmer. One summer a man came to our village from Fath-Ali Shah's court, looking for new wives."

"You married the Shah?" I asked, incredulous.

"No. I married the man who came looking for wives." Her face creased up again and a mischievous glint shone in her eye.

We all fell about laughing.

"Anyway, he was clever and I was bored, so I learned quickly," she concluded.

That night I could not sleep. Sheyda's belly had swelled to the shape of a watermelon. She would rise many times in the night to urinate, and because of this I had asked her to return to her own room downstairs. In the grey-blue light formed by the full moon reflecting off the mirrors in my room, I tossed and turned thinking about the life I might have had if only I had been born Afrouzeh and not Afsar. The poems I might have composed with all the ink that sat in my old room in Sari, turning to dust whilst waiting to be used.

Eventually, I knew it was no use. The only way I would be able to close my eyes and sleep soundly would be in Sheyda's embrace, even if it meant curving my spine around the protrusion of her midriff.

I pulled on a silk robe and went to open my door. Then, remembering a modification Eirik had made to the house, I turned and instead unlocked the door to my closet. Twisting the brass key in its lock, I pulled both handles open.

There was nothing in the closet, making it easy to step inside and feel along the wooden panel at the back. Pressing both of my palms flat against it, one at the top right corner and the other near to the centre, I heard the click of the mechanism as the whole panel sprang back. Then I slid it smoothly aside, wondering how the wall was able to swallow it.

Behind the closet was a set of steep winding steps leading down into darkness. I returned to my room and lit an oil lamp. Even with this in my hand, it was impossible to tell exactly what was beneath. The steps smelled damp and clay-like, as though the cement had been denied the sunlight it required to dry properly. Tentatively, I placed one foot on the top step, half expecting my toes to sink into it, but they did not. The steps were solid enough, so I took another, and another.

When I arrived at the bottom step, I had a moment of claustrophobic terror. The walls were all around me, with barely room enough to hold my lamp. There appeared no way out, and the panel of the wardrobe had clicked back into place as I descended. It meant that no one could follow me, but I worried that I might not be able to get out again, either.

There appeared to be no escape.

I forced myself to take a breath and to think like Eirik. He would never build a secret passage that led to nothing. There had to be a door somewhere. I felt around the curve of the wall in front of me, squinting in the lamplight, scrutinizing the masonry. I found what looked to be a regular crack running up one side and along the top of my head; yet it was far too straight, too uniform. So there was a door, I just didn't know how to open it.

I tried pressing the bricks in turn, but none of them moved. I tried digging my nails between the cracks in the hopes they would widen, but only succeeded in breaking one of my nails. Cursing, I stepped back, and accidentally kicked one of the bricks in the bottom step.

Instantly, the wall slid aside.

I stepped out, dazed, into the white-tiled room beneath my own chamber. The staircase had been disguised as a supporting pillar, like the one at Sari which led to the underground dungeon. I held my hand over my lips to stifle a laugh, and watched as the door slid smoothly back into place. It was a miracle of engineering, as Uncle Taqi would probably have described it. I wondered fleetingly whether my mother's magicians up in the mountains would ever have been able to make somebody appear and disappear with such ease.

A large oil painting hung on the wall, depicting the Safavid ruler Shah Abbas the Great. There was a bridge named after him in Shirgah, and the painting had been bought from an artisan who plied his trade beside it. The nose and the chin looked oddly disproportioned, but the strangest thing about it was the way he had painted the eyes. They stared straight ahead, which gave the impression that the deceased leader of Iran was watching you as you crossed the room. It had been amusing at first, yet glittering in the spotlight of my oil lamp his wide pupils seemed eerily alive.

I left the room as quickly as I could, opening the door silently and padding with bare feet through to the room immediately opposite. This one had no door, only a tall archway carved from marble. This was the room with the bookshelf that allowed you to pass between the walls. I found the correct title and pulled it towards me, then stepped through into the study. More bookshelves had accrued along the walls, so that the trick one didn't stand out as being odd.

I ran my fingers across the desk and wondered why it was that I had not taken to writing more poetry. Why shouldn't I? Now that I had been cast into obscurity here in the provinces, who would ever know if my fingers were stained with ink and half my allowance spent on paper?

A sound made me look up, instinctively placing my hand across the front of my lamp to dim its brightness. I peered out of the window, wondering whether someone were outside, but the sound came again, from the room next door.

Turning to the adjoining wall, I almost dropped my lamp in surprise. My heart hammered against my ribs as though trying to fly free of me. Thinking I had seen a ghost, I came to realise that it was just my own reflection. Above hung a mirror at a slight angle, so that I looked up to see myself looking down. I suppose the mirror must have always been there, though during the daytime I had never had cause to notice it.

I closed my eyes and listened, finally aware that the sound I had heard was that of voices. The low rumble of a man and the whisper of a woman, conversing in the next room. It surprised me, as I had not thought anyone else to be awake at that time.

Placing the lamp on the desk, I silently lifted the chair beside it and carried it to the mirror. It was a struggle as the chair was carved from heavy wood and I had to lift it so that it would not scrape against the tiles, but I managed it through sheer obstinate will. Living with Eirik for so long had taught me to be suspicious of everything. Even ordinary objects took on second uses, such as the ring he had given me, packed with paralysis, and the wine glasses he had brought from Shiraz which were so finely polished, with such a silvery sheen, that you could see behind you whilst you drank.

The fact that I had never noticed the mirror before meant that it was probably an important object, one that undoubtedly had a second use.

I was right.

The mirror hung at an angle, out from the wall. At the bottom, where the mirror touched the wall, was a small silver plaque. I had to stand on the chair to reach it, and I had to return for the lamp to read the inscription. Etched in wide swirling letters were the words: *Truth is Merely a Reflection.* The sort of riddle Eirik delighted in.

I placed my finger over the inscription and slid it to one side, revealing a peephole into the room beyond. The view on the other side formed a perfect tableau of intimacy. Against the far wall, Sheyda and Eirik sat pressed against its cool plaster, surrounded by sweetmeats and dried fruit, small glasses of tea beside a steaming silver *samovar.* It looked as though they had been talking for hours, so relaxed they seemed in one another's company.

"...stank almost as bad as the sewers," Eirik was telling her, his face covered by the habitual leather mask which had come to represent his face in ordinary company. "Yet what could we do? He was the foreman of the Cathedral. None of us would have had employment if we'd told him what we really thought, so we simply had to tie our belts to the scaffold in case we accidentally leaned back too far, trying to avoid his breath."

Sheyda let out a giggle as if he'd tickled her very soul with a parrot feather.

"It is good to see you laugh again," he said.

"You have no idea how much better I feel. Honestly, if mothers ever warned their daughters what sickness pregnancy brings, I swear, the human race would come to an end."

"Are you prepared for the cramps of labour?" I heard him ask.

"No, but what choice do I have? There is only one way out for this child."

"I pray, after all this pain, you are not disappointed with the result."

She stared at him for a long moment, one hand resting across the bulge of her belly.

"Was your mother disappointed with you?"

A bitter laugh issued forth in place of an answer.

"I do wish you would let me see," she whispered, her fingers reaching for the edge of his mask.

"No." He stopped her hand, wrapping her fingers in his.

"What worries you so? You are my friend now, Eirik. We laugh together, we eat together. I would not turn away from a friend because of the misfortune of their face."

I saw his fingers relax a little, but they did not release hers.

"The shock. It might not be good for the child."

"The shock of a child was not good for me," she replied, "yet somehow I managed."

He smiled then, letting go of her hand.

I was both fascinated and enraged by what I was witnessing. Eirik showed his face to no one except me.

Not unless he was forced to.

Yet poor, sweet, Sheyda – I was desperate to see her reaction. I had always thought of us as sisters, as more than sisters, two halves of one peach. Would she, like me, revel in the horror of him?

She drew in her breath, but she did not draw back.

"Ah!" Her hand went to her mouth, though not to cover it, simply to rest her fingers on her chin, as though catching her thoughts before they could tumble from her lips. "Poor Eirik," she sighed. "You have always looked this way?"

He nodded.

"I have a cousin," she continued. "Your face reminds me of him. He was three years old when a candle caught the drape of his crib and set light to it. He was very badly burned, but he lived. That is what it looks like, a little. Only you have trapped some of the heat from the flame beneath your skin, there where it is red..."

She reached out to touch his face, but he drew back.

"You have had to live your whole life with this face?" she asked again.

"I was a bitter disappointment," he said, almost smiling.

"Is that why you cultivated such beauty in your music and in your magic?"

"Could you imagine if I were both ugly *and* uninteresting?"

"I am not sure about ugly, now that my eyes have had time to adjust. I feel a stab inside me, but perhaps that is because it looks so painful. Does it hurt?"

He shook his head. "Do you pity me?" he asked.

"Yes."

"That is what hurts."

There was silence for a moment, and then she placed her hand back across her belly and rubbed it soothingly.

"You are right," she said. "I am in no position to pity anybody."

"You know, I have a very beautiful house," he told her. "In the Arg in Tehran, where all of the dignitaries from around the world have their houses. I could take you there, if you like. Once the infant is born."

I felt ice water flow down my neck.

"I would like that," she replied.

I realised she had missed the subtlety of his meaning.

"I have maids, they would take care of you. Dress you in the finest fabrics and prepare any food you care to name. You would never have to lift a finger again."

I saw a shadow cross her face, the crescent moon drooping in its sky as she finally understood what he was proposing.

"Oh," she replied. "Are you–"

"I would make a good father, Sheyda. You would be safe and protected. I am feared throughout all of Iran, nobody would dare speak ill of you or your child. Why would they? He would have two parents. He would be legitimate."

"I – I don't know," she said, struggling to sit upright. "That – that's very kind of you, but I – I need time to think, to–"

"I understand," he said, placing his hand over hers, on top of her swelling abdomen. "Please, it is only an offer of kindness, from a friend. Take all of the time you need to decide. We can leave whenever you are ready."

I could not tear my eyes from what I was seeing. Their voices were drowned by a sharp ringing in my ears. For a moment, I thought I might faint.

What Sheyda had not heard, I had heard plain as day: the desperation in Eirik's voice. I had not known before, though it should have come as no surprise.

He was hopelessly, inconsolably lonely.

All of his trickery and public exhibitionism, his confident words in a thousand different languages, they were all a mask like the one that covered his face. He could move among people, from Shahs and Daroughehs to the lowliest builders and merchants, yet he could never be at one with them. All the time he watched the adoration and respect in their eyes, knowing how quickly that would crumble should they ever catch a glimpse of his true face. No amount of talent or loyalty could earn him love.

He craved a family, and as I had rejected him he sought to claim my one happiness as his own.

That in itself was enough to stir the lion in my royal blood.

Then to hear Sheyda squirm like that, "That's so kind of you! I need time to think." Her answer should have come hot and fast to her tongue. What was there to think about? She loved me, as I loved her. Me, and only me. What man could come between us? Especially one with a face like a corpse.

I had suffered these common rats aboard my ship for too long.

♦ 11 ♦

The night that Sheyda's baby came, Eirik was away on an errand. Şelale saw to the birth herself, for she had learned well in my brother's harem under the regular tutelage of Bousseh.

At first I thought it nothing but a bad dream. I was standing by the fountain in the courtyard at Sari, its dancing light colourfully confusing my eyes. The scent of the rosewater seemed overpowering and the heat of the day caused it to bead from my forehead. I was sweating scented petals. As I gazed upon my wet hands, the light started to fade until blackness swallowed me and all that I could hear were screams.

It was a prophecy.

When I opened my eyes, Sheyda was thrashing against me, her small hand wound around white cotton sheets, restraining her bundled fist.

I took her gently by the shoulder and rocked her awake, softly speaking her name over and over.

"It is only a nightmare," I told her.

A flood issued from between her thighs. At first I thought she had wet herself, and drew back in horror. I was thirteen years old, a virgin. What did I know of childbirth's early stages?

Some call it a miracle, bringing life into this world. To me it was nothing but a hot, sticky mess. I loved Sheyda, but not at that moment.

That creature that grew within her had sucked out her desire for me, leaving only a husk in her place. A vessel. I was damned if I was going to take orders from Şelale to help bring it into the world.

I sent the eunuchs to assist her whilst I took myself away to the gazebo on the lawn. In the darkness it was stripped of colour. The black lines that formed the peonies looked more like snakes, slithering their way across the tiled floor. I traced them with my fingernails, feeling the cool glaze slip beneath their tips like scales.

Hours went by as midnight crawled towards morning. Far off in the distance the muezzin called first prayer. Soon after, the slovenly light of a sleepy sky folded over the mountaintops. I wanted to meet it with the flat of my palm, to push it back into yesterday, and the day before, and the day before that. To push it right back before Hafez raped Sheyda, back before my exile to this godforsaken village, back further still, before my brother met that cur of a wife, Shokuh. Right, right back.

Back before I ever met Eirik.

Back to the day when I still believed my brother to be my father. To the day he first heard of the circus at Kabul. When he turned to me with a smile and asked: "You'd like that, wouldn't you?" Only this time I would turn to him and pout my lips, I would stamp my foot in stubbornness and tell him "No. I would not."

Eirik would never have come to Sari.

I would never have been exiled.

Sheyda would not exist in my life.

All of this would be over, because it never would have begun.

Suddenly I felt an overwhelming sense of homesickness, a messenger pigeon that has lost both its message and its direction.

Purposeless.

"You look sad, Shahzadi," a soft voice said.

At first, I thought Eirik had returned early from his duties, and that this was one of his conjuring tricks; yet when I reached out to touch Shahab, my fingers passed straight through him.

"How can this be?" I asked him, my eyes widening in astonishment.

"We are friends, Shahzadi. That does not change in death."

"So you are dead?"

He smiled but did not answer.

I blanched in the half-light as I remembered how he had died.

"Do you blame me?" I asked.

"Never. I was not quick enough."

"I did not plead hard enough on your behalf."

"I would not have wished my last memory of you to be one of such anguish."

I relaxed a little, growing accustomed to speaking with a ghost. There was kindness there, in his familiar gold-flecked eyes. I had not realised how much I had missed him.

"Why are you here, Shahab?"

"You called to me. Perhaps you needed a friend?"

"I do not know what to do," I confided. "Love is not a constant, it ebbs and flows. The thing you think you love most one moment, you doubt the next. Nothing lasts, Shahab. Nothing is pure in this world."

"What I felt for you was pure."

I stared at him hard, half expecting him to disappear like smoke. "Oh! Were it that you could live again." I took a sharp intake of breath which stabbed at my heart, causing my eyes to prickle. There was a weight pressing down upon me, yet I refused to yield.

"You should go home, Shahzadi. You do not belong here."

"I cannot."

"You are the Shah's daughter," he said. "There is nothing you cannot do."

And with that, he was gone.

I thought about this for a long time, convinced beyond any shadow of a doubt that it truly was Shahab who had sat before me. My dearest, wondrous Shahab, with hands as rough as the earth, who, with a single kiss, had made me feel as though I were falling like a star.

He had come to me as a friend. Being dead, there was nothing I could offer him that he could take, so what other reason to find me than love?

Pure love.

My resolve was set. The words he spoke had been my words, only I had not heard them when they came from my own lips.

I needed to go home.

My exile was at its end.

Sheyda's birth was not an easy one. By that afternoon, when the child filled its lungs with Allah's breath and screamed for the first time, there was a pile of blood-soaked rags outside the door. Şelale emerged as pale as snow, thick smudges of kohl beneath her eyes.

Despite her weariness, her lips parted in a smile when she saw me.

"A boy," she announced. "A healthy baby boy."

Perhaps Allah was trying to redress the balance by replacing father with son.

"Sheyda will need to rest. She has lost a lot of blood. I cannot give her medicine for it might affect the baby, so she must sleep as much as possible."

"Who will nurse it?"

"She will, awake or asleep," she said, smiling again as though this were some beautiful, mystical strength imparted by motherhood.

My stomach twisted at the thought of Sheyda taking her rapist's child to her breast and nurturing it as though it had a right to live. Would she love it? Of course she would. She was a simple slave from the hills. She wouldn't know what else to do.

I was not entirely right. She did feed the baby, but she cried all the while. I watched once or twice through one of Eirik's spy-holes. After what I had heard her say to him, I refused to visit in person.

Yet I was there. I did see.

She would cry and nurse it, pass it back to Şelale and then curl into her pillow and fall asleep. She slept for hours, and so did the child. It was the quietest infant I had ever witnessed. Perhaps she cried because it had been born with a thick shock of curly black hair, which reminded her of its father. Perhaps every time it touched her, she remembered his touch. Only the child was gentle, where he had been rough.

"You should go to her," Şelale said one day, finding me beneath the gazebo, tracing the snakes around the peonies. "She asks for you."

"What has she named it?"

"She hasn't yet. She is still recovering from the ordeal. Perhaps when her strength returns. Why don't you go to her and help her to decide a name?"

"I will," I assured her.

That night, three days after the infant was born, I went to her room, careful not to wake her. I wrapped the child tight in its swaddling and lifted it clear of the cot.

Smearing the smallest amount of poppy paste around the inside of its gums, I slipped it into a padded bag beneath my cloak, and went to wake Adel.

I found him by the front gate. He was not even asleep, and stood to attention as he heard me approach.

"Shahzadi." He bowed his head.

"Saddle my horse."

"It is the middle of the night, it is not safe to—"

"I must ride for Babol immediately. It is a matter that affects the Shah's safety."

"Then let me take a message for you."

"No, this information cannot be trusted to anyone else, even one as faithful and devoted as yourself, though I will let you ride with me. Saddle my horse and bring him to me, so that I might tighten his girth whilst you saddle your own."

"Very well," he said, though his brow furrowed in reluctance.

All the same, Adel brought Nisfey Shab to me, his bridle in place, the girth of his saddle loose beneath his black barrel chest. He scraped the ground with his hoof whilst I struggled to pull the buckle tighter.

Heaving the metal gate back, I did not wait for Adel. As fast as I could, I stepped into the stirrup, swung my leg across Nisfey Shab's back, and fled. I could not risk Adel hearing the baby cry. I had to stay ahead of him. My horse was a thoroughbred Arab, one of the two Eirik used for his coach. I knew that it was faster by far than any of the other horses Adel could have chosen. With the baby at my front and the wind at my back, I raced north.

In little over an hour I had reached the town of Shahi. It looked different riding alone in the dark than it had from the safety of my carriage that hot afternoon of my exile. My horse didn't like the look of it either, and the infant stirred in its pouch and began to bawl.

"Hush," I told it.

I fidgeted for the little tin of poppy paste in the side pocket of my bag, forcing a little more into its raging mouth. Soon it fell silent again, though I was already afraid someone might have heard.

I decided to circumnavigate the town rather than go through it. It had not rained for many days and the road had turned to baked clay. There was little chance Adel would be able to identify my prints amongst the others, not in the dark. He would carry on to Babol in the west, whilst I took the turn for Sari in the east.

I arrived in Sari in the thick of night, long before first prayer. I rode past the palace to the town. When one of the guards stopped me, I drew back my hood and asked to be taken to the Darougheh.

"He is sleeping," he told me.

"Then wake him."

"I cannot wake him—"

"Wake him or wake tomorrow to find your head on a spike outside the Arg at Tehran."

The guard blanched and bowed to the ground. I could not give him my royal title, otherwise he would have to arrest me for breaking my exile, yet years of God-given authority had taught me how to direct people to act without question. It was easy in a land where women seldom commanded men. Any woman with the courage to do so must be somebody important.

"Forgive me," he said, taking the reins of my horse and leading me dutifully through the quiet streets to a large house near the local jail.

I dismounted and followed him to the stable, where the stable boy took the horse and my guide took the angry stare of the Darougheh's servant for waking him at such an hour.

"Afsar! What on earth are you doing here?" the Darougheh asked, rubbing sleep from his eyes.

He stood in the doorway, dressed in a long blue robe, hastily fastened at the waist with a sash.

It was at this point that the baby stirred again, a soft gurgle issuing up from its drug-drowsy stupor.

"What do you have there?" He waved his servant away and came towards me. "Open that bag."

"Please," I said, clutching it tighter to me. "You have to swear that you will help me."

"What?"

"You loved my mother once, didn't you?" He stood there, frozen like the mountains she had come from. "You would have done anything to help her, I know that. Now I am here, and I need you to help me as you would have helped my mother. I am in the most terrible danger."

"What are you afraid of?"

"Here," I said, stepping forward and revealing the contents of my bag.

Watching his face closely, I saw a flicker of a smile cross his eyes before they hardened in realisation. There was kindness in him, beneath his sense of duty.

"I did not tell you everything, when I confessed to killing my guard."

"That does not surprise me."

"At first, I told you that I had killed Hafez because he had tried to do to me what Ja'far had intended. Only I lied. He did not try. He succeeded."

The Darougheh swore, his cheeks flushing red.

"Then why did you tell me it was your maid he attacked?"

"You were holding her so tightly, I thought you might suffocate the poor woman. I knew she wasn't a spy, because she was the one who pulled Hafez from me. She tried to protect me. I couldn't let you interrogate her, so I told you the one thing I knew you would believe her for. I did not know at the time that I was with child, and that I would later need to admit my deception."

"Why should I believe you now, Afsar? Your words fall in riddles from your mouth, my ears grow tired of hearing."

"Please, you must believe me. I have nowhere else to turn. Hafez was on top of me. When my maid pulled him from me, I slid the knife into him. This child is the result of our bitter union. Şelale managed to persuade Sheyda to say that the child was hers. They both swore to protect me until death, and would never tell the truth. But it is not her child, it is mine. You are the only one I can confess my shame to. The only one I can call friend."

His eyes shone in the light from the oil lamps, staring at me as though staring back in time. "Oh, Afsar," he said finally.

"Please, give my son a life. A proper life."

He pulled aside the edge of the bag and gazed down with unbridled compassion.

"What is his name?" he asked.

"Dariush," I replied.

It was a name I had thought of on the long ride from Shirgah. It was a noble name, belonging to a great Persian Shah. It had come to mean *keeper of good*, and I hoped that deep down, in whatever remained of my soul, he might find there a tiny spark of goodness left, and hold it for me.

"I cannot keep him," I explained. "Every time I hold him I am reminded of what was done to me. But I would not see him harmed, either. You are a good man, Darougheh. Say that you found him in the arms of a dying woman. Say he was abandoned outside your door. Say that you found him being raised by dogs in the gutter, and that your charity and your mercy took hold of you."

"Do not fear, Shahzadi. Your secret is safe with me. I blame myself for what happened. To do your bidding is only part recompense for what I owe you."

He reached down and lifted the boy up in his hands. "He is so fragile," he whispered.

I could see from the moment the Darougheh held Dariush, that he loved him. I knew that the child would be safe and cared for. Under his tutelage, the boy was destined for a life far brighter than Sheyda could ever have given him.

The Darougheh sent his servant to locate a wet-nurse straight away, whilst I slept in his warm bed, exhausted by the journey.

I did not wake again until the following evening.

The Darougheh sat at a table in the European style, Dariush resting on his knee. In daylight, the infant seemed even smaller than I remembered.

"He's been restless all morning, wondering where his mother went."

I smiled, knowing that he was probably missing the opium more than me.

"His mother has given up her title," I reminded him.

I sat at the table and picked at a platter of dried fruit. "I do not wish to return to Shirgah," I told him.

"You have few options."

Sucking the remains of a fig from my fingertip, I rose from my seat and went to stand behind the Darougheh. Leaning forward to stare at the child, my uncovered hair fell loosely over his shoulder. I could feel his body stiffen.

"You are a kind man," I said softly. "You have always been kind to me."

He made no movement.

"I would ask you one more favour." I kissed his cheek.

"Afsar–" he said, turning his face towards mine.

I kissed his lips. I blush to think how brazen I was. My words had not been false, he was the kindest man I had known in my entire life. Which made my actions all the more cruel.

His hand met my face, entangling my hair between his fingers as he kissed me back.

The baby cried out below, causing him to hold me away, then draw me close again, resting his forehead against mine.

"What peri bewitches me?" he sighed.

"I will repay your kindness a thousandfold if you will do for me one last service."

"Do you not understand, child? You do not have to buy me." He released my hair as he pushed my face away for a second time. "My loyalty is given freely, it always has been."

A flood of shame raced through my veins, turning my cheeks hot.

"I am sorry," I said.

"What is it you want of me?"

I returned to the other side of the table and resumed picking at the dried fruit.

"Is Shokuh still my father's favoured wife?"

"Heavens, no," he snorted. "She remains his favourite ornament, the one he keeps on show for official engagements, but they have not been close now for a long time. That honour falls to Monir, or sometimes Saeedeh, who he has made a whore of by refusing a formal marriage."

I marvelled at the level to which women would sink for a powerful man.

"And my grandmother?"

"I have not seen her in these parts for months. Relations have soured somewhat between your brother and Mahde Olia. He has not forgiven her for the death of his friend and former Prime Minister, Amir Kabir."

I recalled my brother crying in his office so long ago and wondered for the first time whether the cruelty he inflicted on Shahab had simply been an expression of the anger he could not vent on his own mother. Perhaps we had been caught in the whirlwind of her royal tempest, as Ludovico Ghorbani had been in mine. Savage acts are bred of savage feelings. They will find their way into this world one way or another.

"Do you think you might arrange a meeting for me with Mother Shokuh?"

The Darougheh's brow arched, but he did not look particularly surprised. "You think now might be a good time to ask her for permission to return to the palace?"

"If you were to campaign on my behalf, perhaps she might agree. My brother never wanted my exile, he was simply trying to placate her. Now that he is no longer showing her any interest, perhaps she would consider granting my request as a means of regaining some small esteem in his eyes? Besides, I imagine that after the way she treated everybody, she must be short on female allies. The harem can be a viper's nest for queen hornets who fall out of favour."

Within a week, the Darougheh had arranged a meeting for me with Shokuh. To make it appear that I had arrived from Shirgah, he arranged for his servant to slip me out of the city on the Western road, where a small carriage waited. His guards met me along the road to the palace, so that when we arrived it appeared as though I had an escort.

Shokuh had changed since I last saw her. Although her figure remained svelte and elegant, she had draped it in silk the colour of wood smoke, adorned with a few silver bangles but not much else. Before, her dresses would have been garishly bright, or if they were grey they would at least have been dripping with pearls and rubies. Either motherhood or marriage had not been kind, and her mood showed in the downturn of her mouth.

"Mother," I said, humbling myself before her by pressing my lips to her feet.

"Get up."

Despite this inauspicious greeting, things did not go at all badly for me. When she stared into my eyes, she must have recognised something of herself. A woman whose high hopes and dreams had been trodden on, mostly beneath the boots of men. Her own ambition had coiled on her like a snake, biting its own tail.

"So," she said eventually, as we sat sucking halva on the plush saffron carpet in her quarters. "You wish to return to the palace?"

"I realise now," I said, swallowing every inch of my pride, "that my actions were wholly disrespectful and wrong. I beg you, mother, to understand that I was only a young woman. I did not understand the importance of sorority."

"And now?"

"I have learned well from the lesson you have taught me. Time by myself has caused me to think hard on my actions. I realise that, as women, we must rely on one another for our security and our happiness."

My words must have touched her, possibly because I knew that the other women in the harem had largely abandoned her.

"I do not know whether I still wield the authority to recant your exile."

"Perhaps if you asked the Shah, he would consider your actions merciful and it would set his heart aglow for your maternal grace. It is only your word that has sent me away. Surely your word could bring me back?"

"You assume that I want you back."

"I assume nothing," I said quickly. "I only hope."

She sighed and thought for a moment.

"Very well," she said. "If there is space within the harem, you may return."

This revelation shook me. I had always assumed that I would be returning to my own private quarters, set aside from the rest of the palace. The idea of being squeezed into a single room in the main harem filled me with revulsion.

"Perhaps I might return to my former rooms?" I asked, trying to keep my voice steady.

"Impossible. Those are my son's rooms now."

I had to make a quick decision. Return to the palace under whatever amnesty might be offered, or remain in exile in the hills of Shirgah, forgotten by my family and by history.

There was no choice to be made.

I quickly settled back into life at the palace. Although I was not allowed to return to my old room, the quarters afforded me within the harem were not so small. My brother did indeed smile upon Shokuh recanting her decision to banish me. I learned from Mother Tala that he had even graced her with a visit the night after she had met with him to discuss it. Apparently this had become a rare event, worthy of note.

My brother also came to visit me. He swept me up in his arms and spun me around as though I were still a small child. His wide, generous smile beamed out from beneath his moustache.

"Ah! My eldest daughter!" He laughed, kissing me on both cheeks. "I trust the country air has been of benefit to your health?"

"Not as much as the sunshine of your being." I laughed.

He spoke as though I had simply decided to take a sojourn to the provinces, rather than enduring harsh punishment thrust upon me by one of his, now lesser-loved, wives. I did not tell him that I knew about my mother. As long as I maintained the pretence of a daughter, he would maintain the pretence of a father, with all the indulgence and protection that entailed.

It was clear that my new quarters were due in no small part to his guilt. He knew that I knew that my disappearance from palace life was entirely down to Shokuh's jealousy, and he also knew that she wasn't much liked by his other wives, or even himself come to that. It was a terrible father, or even brother, who would throw over his own flesh and blood for a fancy.

He made up for this with expensive furnishings, half a dozen handmaids trained in the arts of hair, makeup, and jewellery selection, an increase in my allowance and not a single mention of marriage. It was as though I had been born again. No longer an impatient young girl, cosseted by a Turkish slave and tutored by a decrepit old moraliser, I was a woman now, and a woman with more opportunity than most. My bloodline was royal. I lived as a person of means. I ate the finest foods and walked through the perfectly manicured lawns and rose gardens of my brother's palace. I rode the fastest horses, listened to the loveliest music, and slept each night in the arms of the most beautiful servants.

The confidence that comes through knowing what it is to kill another person, not out of defence, but purely for pleasure, infused me with a certain glow that seemed to attract others to me. As confused as it sounds, people would come to me to ask my opinion as my brother's eldest daughter, beg me to speak on their behalf, or simply offer gifts in the hopes that I might one day smile upon their needs.

If my exile had caused me to see my old home through fresh eyes, my removal from the palace, and then my return, had acted as a memory trick on the courtiers. It was as though they had completely forgotten the girl who kept to herself and practiced lasso with her common companion. Instead, they saw a mighty dynastic daughter, as powerful and resonant as the legendary Simurgh.

I came to relish my new position.

Adel had called on the Darougheh shortly after my meeting with Shokuh. He had spent almost a week searching for me at Babol before continuing on to Amol. When he found no trace of me there, he realised he had been duped and decided to try the other direction. The Darougheh assured him that I was safe and that he had done his duty admirably, but not to look for me further.

"What should I do?" he had asked. "If she is not to return to Shirgah, then what is left there to guard?"

"Indeed," the Darougheh had replied. "Organise with Majid to have her belongings brought to the palace."

When he came to tell me that my possessions had been sent for, I panicked a little. What if Adel returned to Shirgah to find Sheyda inconsolable. I did not doubt that, in time, she would come to see the loss of her child as a relief, but I did wonder whether there might be a moment's hesitation before accepting her circumstances. Perhaps, in her confusion, she would try to convince herself that she could have been a mother to it. Perhaps she might mistake its thirst for milk, and think that its cries had been those of love. Nothing is able to feel love before it is old enough to understand need. We all need, but it takes intelligence to love, and infants do not yet have that.

I worried that she would learn where I had gone and decide to come after me. Then I reasoned that she would not have the strength to do so, or the wit. Sheyda was an enchanting girl, in her way, yet she was also a girl who thought France was a region of Tehran. How could she ever find her way to Sari, yet alone to my front door?

No, it was Şelale who posed the threat. Only she knew her way back to the harem, and she was owed wages for the past month of my disappearance. Perhaps she would demand more to stay silent about the child. Şelale had never tried to blackmail me or coerce me in the past, though who could tell what a Turk might do if it thought its star were rising.

I pre-empted this problem by spreading the rumour that Şelale had stolen from me. I placed a substantial pouch of silver with Farzan at the treasury, with instructions to the harem guards that, should Şelale show her face, she was not to be admitted but to be paid what she was owed and escorted from the palace grounds.

I did not check with the treasury, so I was not sure whether she ever claimed that money, but I felt a strange sort of relief in knowing her part in my life was over. I suppose, of all the people who lived and worked at Sari, Şelale had been the one who knew me best. She had raised me, almost. Washed me down, brushed out my hair, taught me how to speak and how to dress.

You cannot live your life constantly reminded of what you once were. There comes a point at which you must cast off such crutches of youth and learn to stand proudly upon your own feet. It is impossible to stand proudly when there is always one pair of eyes in the room who have seen you crying, seen you when you were small and incontinent, seen the mistakes you made and the vulnerabilities you nursed.

Life without Şelale was a breath of clean summer sky.

Although I would never have admitted it to myself at the time, a little part of me felt comforted in the knowledge that Şelale would have money, and that she would return to Shirgah and use it to make Sheyda well again, and hopefully they might build a new life together, somewhere peaceful and unknown. Perhaps Sheyda might even return to Turkey with her, and they might find employment in the home of another family, one kinder and more benevolent than my own.

And that is how my life was for many months. Shirgah faded from oil to watercolour in my memory. At night I would sometimes wake, believing the twisted sheets to be Sheyda's arms around me, or the shadow of the door to be Eirik come to sing me a lullaby, but in waking hours they fell from my mind as leaves fall from an autumn tree, leaving room for new growth.

I played the role of First Daughter impeccably. I made time to walk with my brothers and sister. Fakhr and Mahmoud were coming up to ten years of age, and growing taller by the day. Their vocabulary expanded with their height and soon my sister was reciting the *Shahnameh* to me whilst her brother loosed arrows on the lawn.

I am sure that Shokuh came to dislike me just as before, yet she no longer had grounds to banish me. Instead, she watched from her window as I grew in popularity amongst the other women of the harem.

In the evenings I had taken to writing poetry again. Instead of burning them as before, I showed them to some of the other women, and eventually to the Shah. He was pleased with them, and showed them to his friends. I began to make a name for myself. Prominent figures in the political arena would sometimes write to me to request a poem for their wife's birthday or to please a loved one.

Over those months I felt a swelling of contentment within me. It was as though a miasma of foul thoughts had rested over my youth, suffocating me with desires I could not satisfy. Now, three months after my fourteenth birthday, I felt as though I had come into my inheritance. As though my thoughts finally fitted within my skin.

It was shortly before Nowruz 1234, and a little after the Gregorian New Year of 1855, that my brother, the Shah, threw a huge party at his magnificent palace in Tehran. He had recently become friendly with a German named Paul Julius Reuter, a banker from London. With the approval of the Queen of England, he and my brother were to establish the Imperial Bank of Persia.

My brother was incredibly excited by this prospect.

"It will make us players on the world stage," he kept repeating. "The world will know Iran and our wealth!"

Our subjects seemed a little less convinced, and several small protests took place. Had Shusha been with us, I'm sure I would have understood better, but as far as I could comprehend some of the more traditional minds in society were accusing my brother of selling Iran's assets to the Europeans.

One or two executions followed the protests and my brother dismissed the claims as "closed minds opposed to progress."

The party was to celebrate the foundation of the Imperial Bank, heralding a bright new chapter in Persian history. For the first time, my brother invited me to accompany him on a trip outside the palace at Sari. The enthusiasm I showed him was real. I had been to Tehran once before, but in disguise, for amusement. This time I would enter the great Arg as though I owned it.

My gown had been ordered weeks in advance, woven of dusky rose silk as soft as petals against my skin. To impress his guests, my brother hired a European designer to dress his wives and brothers in the height of London fashion for the night.

Shokuh wore a red taffeta gown with a wide, box-pleated skirt and silver trim. To protect her modesty, a matching shawl had been fastened across her shoulders, where the droop of the collar exposed them. I cared little for modesty, and instead draped my naked flesh with diamonds, matching those encrusting the hem of my full crinoline.

A French hairdresser was brought to the palace. Under the watchful supervision of the eunuch guards and Mother Arezoo, he twisted and heated our tresses into unfathomable shapes. Tala's coarse hair was forced into corkscrew curls which framed her face. Mother Nazu's hair looped around two tall ostrich feathers that made her look like a ceremonial horse. Shokuh refused to let him touch her, and I must admit to feeling apprehensive when my turn came.

"*Et voilà!*" he exclaimed, angling the hand mirror so that I could admire his work.

He had allowed my hair to fall freely, weaving in raindrop pearls and pinning two strands at the back with a filigree silver clip.

Elegance incarnate.

"As beautiful as the Empress Eugénie," the Frenchman's interpreter translated.

Shokuh fidgeted the entire afternoon whilst we prepared ourselves at the Arg. We were not the only contingent of wives shipped in for the occasion. There were many women I did not know, as well as many with fine features and beautiful figures that I recognised as belonging to the harem at Tehran. Three times I saw Shokuh's maids re-attach her shawl where she had pulled at it in frustration. I almost felt sorry for her.

Thankfully she had been asleep as our carriage passed through Shirgah on its journey to the capital. I held back the curtain with the tip of my finger. Although the road did not pass by the River House, I recognised the small bridge that we would have taken to get there. It felt as though I might have been watching in a dream, as though Shirgah itself was but a dream, that sense of things happening again that Eirik called *déjà vu*. A place that felt familiar, yet one that I had never visited. A doll's house of a town where, in my mind, I played out scenes: white feathers on the lawn, murdered men beneath tables, long hot nights in the arms of a girl with the moon on her face.

Soon we had passed through, its scattering of houses fading to obscurity in the distance.

Guests started to arrive in a steady stream from late afternoon. They wore dresses as varied as the languages they spoke. I slipped my way between the rooms of the palace, looking down from a thousand angles at the fine carriages as they pulled up alongside the fountains in the courtyard.

As light began to fade from the sky, glass jars twinkling with candles were strung between the buildings and around the arched entrances. They were coloured red as cherries and yellow as honey. Musicians positioned themselves around the fountains, their music and the sound of flowing water marrying together in an enchanting refrain.

This was a rare occasion, where women of my brother's provincial harems were allowed to meet and mingle without a chaperone. His guards were there, but seemed almost casual in their duties, smiling, laughing, and eating from the plentiful supply of silver trays that passed before them. There was a sense of possibility that permeated everything and everybody.

When I finally decided to descend the main staircase to the throng below, I took the edges of my ample skirt in each hand, lifting it so that my dainty slippers could meet the step below unimpeded. I had seen pictures of European ladies doing this in books from the West. It seemed that ladies in Europe did a lot of walking down steps in impractical dresses, sitting at candle-lit tables with excessive cutlery, balancing towering wigs on their heads.

I was disappointed by the lack of wigs. It must have been a fashion that had fallen from favour, for all of the foreign women wore their hair naturally, their faces blushed by the heat rather than whitened with powder. Still, they made an impressive spectacle. Half the jewels on earth sparkled beneath my brother's chandeliers that night.

I had drunk two glasses of strong wine when I spotted her.

At first I thought it could not possibly be, standing at the foot of a white marble staircase as wide as a polo field, resting her back against the volute. There were several young men beside her, dressed in waistcoats, morning coats, and cravats. How brazenly she laughed with them as she reached for a passing flute of champagne.

Concealing myself behind a pillar, I tried to convince myself that I was wrong, yet I would have known her body anywhere. No woman, however practised, could draw a beauty spot so delicate with the fumbled cosmetic sticks available from our pharmacists.

Sheyda had changed completely. Her eyes, already the defining feature of her face, now seemed exquisite, framed with kohl and glittering mica. Her lips shone as though she had just bitten into a pomegranate, and her hair had been brushed to the point where it reflected back the light from the crystal chandeliers above. Her dress was made of blue velvet, hemmed with rhinestones. The diamonds across my throat dulled in comparison.

For a moment, I could not breathe.

"Afsar, there you are!" the Shah roared in my ear.

He was dressed in clothes that could hardly contain his divine royal glory. The coat he wore seemed to glow red from within, as though stained by his own blood. Its chest glittered with gold leaf and dripped with Caspian pearls which were strung in double ribbons across either shoulder, crossing beneath his ribs and over the top of a blue moiré sash that ran from left to right. Just below his stiff, high collar he wore a medallion the size of a woman's fist. It was cast in silver, with a ferocious lion gazing out from the middle; a symbol of the Order of the Lion and Sun. On his head he wore a tall black hat with a white egret feather that splayed as it rose, as though his bright thoughts were fountaining from the centre of his mind.

"Father," I smiled, kissing his cheek. "What a beautiful display."

"I know." He laughed, his dark eyes glistening. "Come, there is someone I wish for you to meet."

Leading me to a small group of people not far away, I was instantly struck by the woman before me. She was nothing like any other woman I had seen my father talking to. Her hair was spun of raw gold, and her eyes seemed almost translucent, like a cloudless summer sky.

"Monir, I would like to introduce you to my eldest daughter, Princess Afsar."

"So pleased to meet you," she said, bending low so that the skirt of her ivory dress crumpled against the floor. "Your father has mentioned you many times. I am honoured to finally make your acquaintance."

"Indeed." I smiled, holding out my hand for her to kiss. She looked a little uncertain for a moment, and then shook it.

My brother laughed loudly at this confusion of customs, as did his white-haired, white-skinned, overweight companion.

"Afsar, this is Mr. Bernard Frothampton. He is a scholar of Mughal Architecture, of all things, but has kindly taken a rest from his studies in order to grace us with his presence."

It suddenly occurred to me that this was the architect's daughter the Darougheh had told me about.

"Monir?" I asked, returning my gaze to her.

"Oh!" the grey, fat man exclaimed. "Yes, this is not our first trip to the East. Monir was born here, in fact, in Tabriz. We named her after my wife's friend, an Iranian lady who made us very welcome when we first arrived."

"That is quite an honour," I said.

"My father and I work together," the woman explained. "He draws the blueprints for his building plans, and I bring them to life through watercolours."

The man nodded. "Yes, my brain is full of angles and trajectories I'm afraid. Necessary for construction, but a little boring on the old eyes. Thankfully my daughter has a far better sense for beauty than myself. Without her, I doubt I would have won half the commissions I have."

"It's my job to show people a glimpse of what my father's buildings could look like, if they were built," she added helpfully.

"Monir has quite an incredible talent," my brother interjected, speaking to me whilst beaming at her. "You almost feel as though you are standing in front of wonderful structures called straight from the designs of her father's mind."

"Are you building something now?" I asked.

"My father helped to design the facade for the new bank," she replied.

Monir and her father continued to make small talk, explaining at great length how they had been lucky enough to make the acquaintance of Mr. Reuter, who was granted the royal commission to establish the bank, and how he had introduced them to his architectural colleagues, and to the Shah himself. It sounded rather like the type of good fortune story one might find themselves living after making a wish on a jinn's lamp. All the while, I found myself staring at this woman's features: her tiny, upturned nose, her finely-arched eyebrows, almost invisible against her pale complexion, her glowing golden hair, and the sapphire necklace that underscored her eyes like the ocean does the sky.

Could my brother really love such a fragile, fluttering person? She was certainly no Shokuh. There was no authority to her voice. Even her shoulders sloped inwardly a little, as though she were waiting for you to reach out and topple her over with your pointed finger.

I began to surmise that my closest flesh and blood was simply an admirer of variety. He collected wives like cooks collect exotic flavours, to taste them and see how they work in combination with one another. Still, I doubted he would ever forge an alliance stronger than friendship with Miss Frothampton. The English simply didn't work within our marital customs. Polygamy gave them indigestion.

It was only when a new member joined our intimate group that the spell was broken.

"Ah, Vachon!" my brother exclaimed.

My heart ceased to beat as though the Hidden Imam had just revealed himself to the room.

"Shahanshah," Eirik acknowledged, bowing to my brother.

"Bernard, this is the genius I was telling you about."

"The palace at Sari?"

"The very same."

I listened to another monologue from Mr. Frothampton, brimming with adulation for the great achievements he had heard of yet never seen. The gadrooning was widely talked of, reminiscent of the Rococo period, and how had he managed to stabilise the *muqarnas* at such a width as had been reported by friends of friends, who he must have met personally, and might even have been able to talk about had Frothampton shut his mouth long enough to draw breath.

What amazed me about the man was that, through all of this talk of buildings and the beauty of design, he didn't once seem to think it odd that the man before him wore a facade of his own. Eirik was dressed in sumptuous black silk, starkly at odds with the vibrant parade around him. It was as though he had dressed to pull all of those other colours towards him, and then extinguish them as night extinguishes day. Beneath his morning coat he wore a starched white shirt and a coal-coloured cravat. His face was covered with a simple black leather mask, without frills or fancy jewels. As such, it seemed almost natural, as though everyone's face should match their dress.

When Frothampton finally ran out of words, he introduced Eirik to his daughter. Ever the gentleman, Eirik took her hand and kissed it, at once turning her cheeks as red as her lips. My brother cleared his throat beside me and enquired after his own wife.

"You are married?" Monir asked, disappointment thick in her voice.

"In a manner of speaking," Eirik replied.

"That makes no sense, man. Either one is married or one is not," Frothampton interposed, clearly touching on a matter of some personal importance.

"Then let us say that I am married." Eirik smiled.

Perhaps he had thrown his voice to magical effect, for Sheyda suddenly appeared beside him.

"And this must be your charming wife?" Frothampton continued, oblivious to the wry smile on my brother's lips, or the wary eyes of his eldest daughter, taking Sheyda's measurement from the top of her head to the tip of her toes.

"Indeed." He stood back a little so that Sheyda could fully insert herself into our company.

I reached for a glass of champagne as it passed, but did not have time to lift it to my lips, my brother taking it from me with a cautionary scowl.

"Shahzadi, have you met before?" Eirik asked, forcing me to offer my hand.

Sheyda took it, and kissed it. All the while looking up at me with those wide, world-swallowing eyes of hers.

"No," I said softly, the back of my throat too dry for words.

"If you'll excuse me," my brother announced, setting off across the room to greet new arrivals.

There was a lull in conversation. Sheyda remained staring at me, yet I could not meet her gaze. Instead, I watched Eirik smiling at Monir, whilst her father stared longingly at Sheyda.

Eventually, Monir's curiosity overwhelmed her. "Forgive me for asking," she began, "but–"

"A building accident," Eirik replied, saving her the indiscretion of vocalising her thoughts. "It was many years ago. I was hit by a falling grotesque."

"Oh, my!" she exclaimed, placing her hand across her ample bosom. "Was it terribly bad?"

"I'm afraid so, madam. I can never again show my face in polite company."

"My dear man," her father joined in. "The sacrifices we make for our art. Though yours, I must admit, seems greater than most."

"Have you been in the employ of the Shah long?" Monir asked.

"Three years."

"And already you have built him a palace?"

"I'm surprised you've heard of it."

"Everyone in Persia has heard of it. They call it The Box of Tricks." She laughed.

He laughed too, and it sounded as false as the chink of fool's gold in a whore's purse.

Instinctively, I looked to Sheyda to share the joke. We had always been of one opinion on the people we met. Those I thought silly, she thought silly. Those she found funny, I smiled at also. Yet she was no longer looking at me, her attention transferred to Monir.

I studied her profile for a moment, tracing the familiar line of her jaw with my eyes, feeling her skin beneath my fingertips as I did so, remembering our secret intimacies.

Her eyes flashed back to mine, pulling at me, and I looked away, startled.

What was in her mind? There we were, acting like strangers when I had robbed her of her most personal property. I had wondered once what Şelale might say to me had she been free to say anything. Now I felt supremely grateful for the laws of etiquette which meant that Sheyda must remain silent.

"Forgive me," I said, excusing myself to go in search of another glass of champagne.

When I finally found it, my hands were trembling so hard I could barely lift it to my mouth for fear of spilling it. A thousand questions swarmed through my head. How had they both come to be here together? How was Sheyda so transformed? Last time I had seen her, she had been a simple village girl with callused hands and mud between her toes. Yet here she was, not simply dressed as a noble woman, but behaving like one too.

There was only one explanation, and the sour taste of it rose with the bubbles in my drink to burn my heart.

I was too afraid, and too ashamed, to remain in the ballroom.

It was clear to me that Eirik had returned to Shirgah to find Sheyda alone, without her baby. She must have told him what had happened, the details no doubt provided by my Turkish servant. He must have propositioned her a second time.

"Be my wife, and I shall protect you," he must have said, promising her fine jewels, beautiful clothing and more children.

She said yes.

She said yes, because I had left her no choice. In my arrogance and my anger, I had punished her, and in so doing, punished myself. *Oh, Afsar! You stupid fool!*

I hid in an upstairs room. There was a writing desk, and a circular paisley rug of dark green and gold which looked like leaves floating on a river at sunset. It comforted me a little to lose myself in the pattern, to avoid losing my mind.

I could not tell which was worse, my hatred at her for accepting his offer, or the horror at myself for forcing her hand. My notion of her leaving for Turkey with Şelale had been ridiculous. People acted according to human nature, not according to the plays I wrote for them in my fantasies. If Şelale had collected the money I had left her, she would keep it. Sheyda was not her daughter, nor even her family, and money is money. She could not have afforded to share it. Even had she offered, what woman is stupid enough to accept a six-hundred-mile journey over rough terrain, when she has the offer of a comfortable marriage before her?

No. Not just comfortable.

Eirik had given her more than she could have dreamt of, even when she slept in my arms. He had unleashed her beauty, then bound it again in blue silk. He'd made her the envy of every man's eye, and presented her before me as his possession.

He was gloating.

Anger boiled in my veins, turning my sorrow to stony resolve.

◆ 12 ◆

Nowruz that year had been quiet as my brother spent his time almost exclusively in Tehran, seeing to his new bank and mediating between the Turks, the British and our old enemies, Russia. His wives, who at first had been overwhelmed by the opulence and extravagance of their husband's palace there, began to compare their own quarters at Sari and found them wanting. As such they were often grumpy, and although they made the best of the occasion with sweets and bonfires, they could not help imagining the tiered cakes and sparkling chandeliers that the Shah was enjoying without them.

My birthday went largely unmarked. Had it not been for Shokuh's insistence that we pitch a marquee on the lawn and gather there for a picnic, I might have been able to fool myself that it had never happened.

Shokuh had taken me into her confidence by that point. Although she never told me outright that she was unhappy, she would regularly seek out my company during the daytime, to walk in the gardens or recite verse to one another in the library. That spoke more to me of her loneliness than anything, as no woman usually seeks to be in the presence of a person they so recently couldn't place far enough away.

This made it difficult for me to escape by myself, and it wasn't until several weeks after the party in Tehran that I was able to leave the palace grounds. It was a stiflingly hot afternoon, and Shokuh had been struck down by a migraine, most likely induced by dehydration.

Despite the heat, I covered myself in a full veil and long coat so that it would be harder for anyone to recognise me. I took one of my sister's horses, a fat bay mare, rather than risk being seen on Nisfey Shab.

I rode to the building site against the cliff, holding my breath in the hope that I might find Eirik there. When I arrived, I was shocked to discover that the forest had been cut far back from the foundations. Perhaps they had needed the wood, or perhaps Eirik had simply thought it prudent that the Shah should have a clear view of anyone approaching.

Although I had to strain my eyes to see, I remained beneath the cover of the trees until I was sure that he was there. Dozens of men swarmed across the grounds like ants, their thick loincloths knotted at their muscular thighs, their arms bulging as they carried heavy bricks and tools from one site to the other. I was afraid that if they saw me, they might try to take advantage.

The building itself had grown tenfold since last I had seen it. The little room in the cliff where we once stood to watch construction had been eclipsed by a large dome. You could no longer see inside the building from the outside as all of the external walls were in place. Hands worked tirelessly with chisel and hammer to chip out miniature tiles for the mosaics.

I had given up hope of finding Eirik, when I saw him walk out of the main entrance. He stopped a few paces from the door and looked back, hands on his hips, as though admiring a beautiful canvas. In a way, I suppose it was his canvas, the bricks and mortar his paint.

Spurring my horse forward, I cantered up to him and swung to the ground. A few of the workers looked round in surprise, though soon they returned to their tasks.

"We need to talk," I told him, wasting no time on pleasantries.

"You may talk, and I may choose to listen," he replied, "but I have very little to say to you."

"Somewhere private."

He looked at me for a moment, his figure as transformed as Sheyda's had been. Only, instead of a villager becoming a princess, Eirik had changed in the opposite direction. The dashing European gentleman had turned into a desert savage, his loose brown şalvar and leather waistcoat barely covering a body which, over the past three years, had come to resemble that of his workers. His tanned muscles glistened in the sunlight. Only his face looked empty of life, its frozen features forever untroubled by mortal emotion.

Without a word, he began walking back inside the building. I followed him, rivulets of sweat cascading down my face and back, soaking into my clothes and leaving dark, damp patches. The shade felt like a dark tide washing over me, cooling my burning flesh.

We walked between rooms that had not been there when I last visited, yet despite the unfamiliarity of it all, I still recognised the pillar as we approached it.

Looking around to make sure that no one was watching, he slid back the hidden panel and pulled the lever. A low rumble revealed the steps down into the stomach of the building. They had been compacted and scattered with shale to firm them, though they did not look well used.

Taking a deep breath, I started my descent.

We stood before the glass cabinet, with its one-way looking glass and its fruit-blooming metal tree. I tore off my coat and veil so that I could finally breathe.

"I want you to give her back to me," I said. "I don't care what it takes, but you will release her into my service."

He said nothing for a moment, and then walked to the opposite side of our dungeon, where a small pipe dripped steadily into a wooden trough. He reached down a sponge into the water, squeezed it, and then came towards me. Dabbing it against my brow, then lightly across my lips, he spoke very softly in my ear.

"You think she is my possession?"

"She is your wife."

He drew away, a funny sort of smile beneath the philtrum of his mask.

"No, she is not."

"She refused you?"

"Try not to smile, Shahzadi."

"Why did she refuse you?"

His laugh reminded me of flint being struck, the spark dying as quickly as it is lit. He took my hand in his, our fingers interlacing as he held them aloft, flattening his palm to press against mine as they slowly descended.

"Perhaps I reminded her too much of her scorched cousin."

His hollow eyes met mine, and I froze.

"If you are going to spy on people, Afsar, at least close the spy-hole once you are done. Or were you expecting a servant to do that for you?"

"I–"

"She refused me for the same reason you did. Because of this."

He tore off his mask, exposing me to the full horror of his face. Its uneven, blemished skin like boiled rice; those tough spikes of hair beneath his wig that reminded me of rats' tails. I recoiled, but he held me tight.

"Look at me until you love me," he instructed.

I opened my eyes little by little, plucking the wings from the butterflies that had risen in my stomach, until all was silent and still.

"If she will not accept you, why do you keep her?"

"Why shouldn't I?"

"She is not a pet, Eirik."

He shrugged as if to say *Isn't she?* then returned the sponge to the trough.

"As long as she is willing to play the part," he said, "I am willing to clothe her and feed her. In time, she will come to realise that she cannot do without me."

"That is not love. That is desperation."

"The distinction being?"

"Love is given freely. The other is a ransom, paid in pretence."

He thought on this for a moment, crouching down and running the cool sponge across the back of his neck. Once he had finished, he turned to me.

"You speak as though you have known love."

"Have you ever considered there may be other reasons than your irrefutable ugliness that prevent her from becoming your wife?"

"Such as?"

"Perhaps she already loves another."

He turned to the chamber, walking slowly around it, fingers trailing the glass until his eyes met mine in the faint reflection.

"You think one woman can feel for another as one woman feels for a man?"

"I know we can."

"And you think she loves you more?"

I smiled triumphantly as he turned to face me.

"Then why should I let you leave this room?"

My smile faltered.

"After all, with you gone, I would have no rival to my affection."

"Are you threatening the daughter of the Shah?"

"No," he said, taking a step closer. "I am threatening you." He took a strand of my hair between his fingers and twisted it gently. "Besides, who is here to know? Would you run to your sisters in the harem and tell them what I have done, and where you have been, alone, unchaperoned?"

Caught in the spider's web, I knew that this was no idle threat. Eirik was right, I could tell no one of my exploits beyond the harem. Women had suffered imprisonment and worse for such crimes. Despite the cold realisation of my mistake, I could not help but feel a slight glimmer of admiration for the way in which his mind worked.

Looking into the depths of his hollow eyes, I lifted my hand and allowed my fingers to lightly touch the uneven whorls of skin by his temple. My intestines twisted at the smooth, warm sensation where I had expected to feel the scales of a snake. After a moment, the tingling subsided and I looked afresh at this strange, devilish monster.

He let out a soft breath that stroked against my cheek.

"How would you kill me, if you were to kill me?" I asked. "Would you poison me, leave me paralysed in a ditch? Or would you lasso me from your sculpted tree?"

"How would you like to die?" he asked, moving behind me, placing one hand across my waist and the other at my throat.

"In such a way that I did not know I was dying, but thought myself in the throes of ecstasy."

"*La petite mort*," he whispered in my ear.

I turned my face to his, our lips softly meeting.

His grip relaxed as his mind filled with thoughts as far from killing as mine had come from fearing him.

"You are trembling," I said, gently taking his hand from my throat and holding it in my own.

I kissed him again, lost in the thick scent of sweetgum and *khansar* that clung to his skin from the *qalyān* houses. It felt as though a little of the smoke from the water pipes remained, as though I were inhaling him as he breathed against me. The sensation of his lips pressed to mine was enough to blind me to his features. Neither did it evoke the ghost of Shahab's kiss, those many moons ago. I wanted for nothing and no one else in his embrace. It was like kissing myself.

"This is the cruellest thing you have done to me yet, Shahzadi," he whispered.

"I thought it one of your conjuring tricks."

"Then we have enchanted each other."

I knew that if we turned towards one another, we would be lost.

"There is still the problem of your wife," I said, stepping away.

"I will not give her up," he replied.

"Neither will I."

That night I stole a goat from the stables and led it out into the woods beyond the lawns. I faced it towards Mecca, straddled it, and slit its throat. As its legs gave way beneath me, I held it tightly, feeling it thrash out its panic in my arms.

I had not killed since Hafez. Being so close to Sari, where Eirik and I once owned the starless night, the urge felt overwhelming. It was as though a storm had been building inside me since I took Sheyda's child. The pressure needed to be released before it crushed me.

I clung to the corpse of the goat until it felt cold. My black robes had soaked up the blood, its metallic smell acting like lavender on an infant. I felt suddenly tired, and would have liked to curl up there and sleep.

The crack of a twig brought me back to myself. I knew that it could only have been a deer, for nothing larger haunted my brother's estate, yet the realisation that I was lying there, in the dark, hugging a dead goat was rather sobering. I thought it best to make my way home before I was missed.

I cannot explain to you the desire to kill. It was not the destruction of a thing which drove me, nor the sense of ultimate power that comes from holding sway over another's life, though that is undeniably what compelled me to it in the first place. However, power is like any sweet, once you have had your fill, it no longer holds its attraction. You take for granted the privileges you are born to. Kill enough, or eat enough halva, and you soon grow sick of it. No. For me, there was something else behind my lust for blood. It felt familiar. As though I had come home.

Every lesson I had learned of any value had been taught to me by Death. From the moment of my first kill, I had learned that enemies bleed red like the rest of us. I had learned the price of betrayal when I killed Ishya, and the agony of loss in losing Shahab. I had learned that Death spared neither infants nor mothers, nor the pretty or the handsome. Some nights I still saw that final look on Azin's face, the mild surprise to see me watching as she stepped from the roof of the palace. I had learned that Death is effective against those who threaten us, turning the green lawns red with encrusted rubies, bled from the Bábí during those Rosy Hours. Also, I had learned to wield it as revenge against those who had harmed us, like Hafez.

Everything I knew, I knew because of Death.

Killing felt like an affirmation of those lessons.

Shusha had abandoned me, but Death never would, and with each killing I knew that there would always be more to learn.

Once within the grounds of the harem, I stripped off my outer garments and bundled them beneath my arms so that they would not drip. I placed them in a chest beneath my bed, and resolved to throw them into the fire at *Haurvatat*, at the end of the month. A fitting sacrifice to the water god for bestowing wholeness and perfection.

I had just finished washing my hands when one of the eunuchs escorted the Darougheh into my quarters. I hastily poured the contents of the bowl into the small drain that ran along the wall behind my chest of drawers, its terracotta colour masking the red.

"I'm sorry for disturbing you at this time, Shahzadi."

"Please, come in." I gestured to a cushion on the floor and made to join him.

We both looked at the guard, but he stood stoically by the door. I had never been chaperoned so closely when I lived in my own quarters, before I could be considered a woman. Now that I had moved to the harem proper, there was hardly a moment of the day when somebody's eyes were not on me.

"I did not expect to find you awake," the Darougheh told me.

"I find it hard to sleep here. Sometimes I hear my mothers snoring through the walls." I laughed. "I sit and write verse instead."

I saw his eyes flick to my clean hands.

"Indeed," he said.

"How is Dariush? I hope he is not the reason for your visit?"

"No, the child is in perfect health."

"Then please, tell me what I can do for you."

"I hope over the years I have proven my loyalty Shahzadi, and that you will take anything I have to say in the spirit of friendship with which it is intended."

"Of course, Darougheh."

"I hope also that you know me professionally, and understand that I take my job very seriously. The safety of the country is my utmost concern. As such, I have eyes and ears everywhere."

"One would hope as much." I smiled, though caution was beginning to play on me. "Please, say what must be said."

"One of my men came to me earlier today, to tell me that he had seen you at the building site, talking with Eirik."

"I do not recall that," I said quickly. "How did he know it was me?"

The Darougheh sighed and looked up at the ceiling for a moment.

"Have we not had this conversation before, Daughter of Greatness? Did we not once speak of how small the common folk look from such lofty heights? You may look on them as little more than ants, but I assure you, ants have the memories of elephants when it comes to protecting their nests. My men study the faces of the royal household rigorously, precisely so that they can recognise them if they are in disguise, or should they choose to ride another's horse."

My cheeks flushed.

"I know," he continued, "because it is my job to know the whereabouts of the Royal wives and daughters, that you did not have permission from the Shah to be there."

"I had business with Eirik."

"You are a woman, Afsar. You have no business of your own."

"He invited me!"

"And you were not at liberty to accept."

I glared at him in silence for a moment.

"Did we not also have another conversation once? One in which you promised me that you would do nothing to pull disaster down upon yourself?"

"I do not exist to make your job easier."

"Oh, I know!" He laughed. "I do know that, Shahzadi. I have known it for a long time."

I saw the funny side of this too, and smiled. "I am sorry," I said. "But you cannot expect me to go from being the mistress of my own household to a prisoner in this palace."

"Sadly, I am afraid that is exactly what is expected. It is the price you pay for being allowed back into the fold."

The humour drained from me as I stared at him with gritted teeth.

"I know this will not be easy for you–"

"It will be impossible. Eirik is organising a party there next month."

"Really? The palace is far from complete."

"He wishes to invite the Frothamptons to view it."

"Then you must do as any woman of the harem must, and write to the Shah for permission to attend. Ask nicely and he is unlikely to refuse you."

He did not refuse me.

In fact, my brother saw this as a sparkling opportunity for me to befriend the Frothamptons and report back to him on their experience of the new palace, and any suggestions they might make for improvements.

They arrived at Sari the night before, and were hosted by the Darougheh. He hired a wet-nurse to attend to Dariush so that his cries would not wake them in the night.

Early that morning they arrived at the main palace. We ate breakfast on the lawn with Shokuh and Arezoo, the most senior of my brother's wives, and therefore those charged with the duties of hospitality. My other mothers were confined to quarters so as not to overwhelm our guests with their bountiful womanhood.

I dressed formally in dark blue silk with gold detail, my wrists and ankles chiming with silver bangles.

"This is such a treat," Monir chirped, like a skittish songbird. "We so rarely get to see the provinces, do we, Father? We spend so much of our time in the stuffy libraries at Tehran and the Matenadaran at Yerevan."

"Armenia is a long way to travel for books," Shokuh said, sweetening her words by offering a pot of cream for Monir to spread on warm *lavash* bread.

"They are some of the oldest in the world," Bernard informed her, as though Shokuh herself had been deprived an education. "It's quite a journey, though always worth it."

"I saw the Matenadaran once," Arezoo interrupted. She rarely spoke, content simply to listen to the stories of a world she had once travelled extensively as the daughter of a wealthy Sultan. She only spoke now to deflect the barely concealed contempt that radiated from Shokuh in the general direction of Monir. She was, after all, the usurper of Shokuh's former glory. "The books there were very beautiful, and very old."

After exchanging pleasantries, we left my brother's wives to their gossip and took a carriage to the construction site.

"Magnificent!" Bernard said. "This truly is a chocolate box of architecture. Just look at those lines, Monir. How do you think it's resting? Supported by the cliff or free-standing?"

"There must be some form of support," she said, pulling a pencil from her hair and reaching beneath the carriage seat for one of the sketchbooks she had brought with her.

I watched Monir work whilst her father strutted up and down, whistling to himself and shaking his head. The scene was almost comical. I felt instantly sorry for poor Shokuh. These Western women were born of a different universe.

It was clear that my mother had nothing to fear from Monir. The woman was far too bright to find my brother's offer of being his four-hundredth wife appealing. How would she occupy herself in a harem – constantly redesigning the flower vases?

I smiled and smoothed out my skirt whilst I waited for them to resume their seats. Instead, they decided to walk to the entrance in order to take in its full splendour.

"Drive on," I shouted, rapping the side of the door as I closed it.

A few minutes later, the carriage drew up outside the palace. There was barely a road to it, since it wasn't yet open to visitors. The dry earth had been raked in a circular fashion, to indicate the position of a future fountain. It reminded me of one of the Shah's drawings, the way he would sketch out shapes in pencil before adding permanent ink.

Eirik appeared at the top of the steps, Sheyda dressed in green by his side.

She looked like an oasis in the desert. A Jericho rose unfurling in the dusty heat of the day. I drank her in whilst her master descended the steps to open my carriage door.

"You are alone?" he asked, surprised. "Have you murdered them?"

"They are busy murdering themselves in the midday sun."

"It's an English custom, I believe."

From the top of the steps we could see the Frothamptons some way off.

"What is she doing?" he asked.

"It looks as though she has dropped something. Possibly her pencil."

"Her pencil?"

"She's attempting to draw whilst she walks."

"*Merde*, it will take all day at this rate. You, and you," he clicked his fingers at two of the workers who stood nearby, watching with us, "take a tarpaulin and stretch it out over them. If they don't get shade, they'll combust."

We awaited them in one of the front rooms, which was almost complete. Many of the white marble tiles had been laid, and an array of colourful cushions had been positioned over a circular rug in the centre of the floor. Eirik called for tea to be brought, and we sipped in silence whilst muscular, tanned men went about their business, treading sand across the floor and sweeping it up in an endless expenditure of effort.

"How have you been?" I asked Sheyda, lifting my eyes to hers whilst I blew to cool my tea.

These were the first words we had exchanged since I stole her child.

"I am well, thank you."

I sipped from my cup but found it hard to swallow, the liquid making an audible glugging sound as it forced its way through my constricted throat. How could she sit there and thank me after what I had done to her? She seemed carved of the same marble the craftsman was chipping his tiles from.

"I am glad," I replied. "And how is married life?"

"It suits me well, thank you." There was something strange in the way she spoke. Her words were carefully pronounced, as if she had been trained to bury her rural accent. The smile on her face remained sanguine yet pertly symmetrical, as though someone had measured it out and told her not to move, posing for an invisible photographer.

"Do you enjoy living in Tehran? It is a glorious city, is it not?" I asked.

"It is indeed. I enjoy it very much. And you, you find life at Sari satisfactory?"

"Yes," I said, taking another sip of my tea. "I feel as though I am home. You must come to visit some day."

"That is very kind of you to offer, thank you."

The third thank you in as many minutes. Was this Sheyda, my servant and my lover, or some imposter he had pulled from a party at the Arg? I glanced at Eirik, but he was fidgeting with the edge of his şalvar in the way one might if they were deliberately trying to avoid someone's gaze.

"Tell me, what news of Şelale? I have not heard from her in months."

For the first time, Sheyda's smile faltered, her pretty lips curving down at either side. Before she had a chance to answer me, the Frothamptons appeared in the doorway, scarlet as pomegranates with cheeks just as puffed.

"Ah! *Bon, mes amis.* Welcome, come in." Eirik clapped his hands and a tray appeared with a jug of water containing slices of lemon. "Drink up, you need to replenish your fluids."

They didn't need encouragement, emptying their glasses like fish.

"Is that really you, Vachon?" Bernard asked, squinting up at him from the cushion he had collapsed onto, patting his forehead with a handkerchief.

I could tell by the flex of Eirik's jaw that he was trying to fathom Frothampton's question.

"Yes, it is I," he said, uncertainly.

"Only, I wouldn't have recognised you in those clothes, old chap!"

Looking between the two, I understood what he meant.

The Frothamptons were dressed much as I'd seen Europeans dress in books about Africa, wearing *khâk*-coloured material as though they had simply lain down in the dirt and rolled about in it. Shusha used to tell me this was for camouflage – that people would be less likely to see them coming if they dressed in this colour – yet it looked so drab. Had I been forced to wear it, I would dearly hope that no one would see me. It baffled me that Westerners made such a bright display at their formal engagements, yet their armies skulked through the undergrowth as though they had no pride at all. How embarrassing it would be to die dressed like that.

In contrast to their cream and dirt-coloured attire, Eirik wore şalvar and a waistcoat cut from green silk, to match his wife's dress. Underneath the waistcoat was a long-sleeved, white shirt. He looked incredibly elegant. Though, it dawned on me that the only time the Frothamptons had met him previously, he had been wearing one of their morning suits and a cravat. This must have come as some surprise to them, especially as they seemed to consider him a fellow member of their civilised continent.

Eirik's own failure to grasp the reason for Mr. Frothampton's question probably came from the fact that he was the only one in the room, and quite possibly Iran, to be wearing a mask. Who else was it possibly going to be behind that lacquered *papier-mâché*, the colour of moss?

"You find me in my work clothes," he offered.

"By Jove, you'd never catch me on a building site in trousers like that! Liable to get caught in anything by the look of them."

"I can assure you, they are quite practical."

"Do you find the natives open up to you more when you dress as one of them?" Monir asked, leaning forward with her paper and pencil as though about to make notes.

I glanced at Sheyda. As the only other 'native' in the room, I desperately wanted her to return my stare so that we might look away quickly and stifle our giggles. Had it been the old Sheyda, the Sheyda who had loved me once, before I had broken something inside her, she would have done.

Eirik cleared his throat and suggested we take a turn about the palace.

As they strode ahead, down the corridor that smelled of brick dust and wet cement, I put my hand on Sheyda's arm and turned her towards me.

"Please, come with me," I said, searching her eyes for something once remembered.

She offered no encouragement, but no protest either. I took her by the hand and led her through the downstairs rooms. When we came to the familiar pillar with the hidden panel, I released the trap and we descended.

"What is this place?" she asked, as I guided her through the final door into the underground room with the glass chamber.

"Somewhere we can talk, privately."

She stepped out into the room, turning whilst her eyes roamed the ceiling and the walls, taking everything in beneath the soft glow of the oil lamps.

She moved to the water trough and dipped her fingers into it. "Do you remember that day we went to the waterfall, on the road to Zirab? We stripped off our clothes and splashed in the pools like children."

"I do," I said, feeling my throat once again tighten, as though Eirik's lasso were around it.

"That was a good day, Shahzadi. We laughed a lot that day. I still remember it sometimes, when I close my eyes to sleep."

"Do you miss our life together?" I asked, taking a step towards her.

"It's that first day I remember most."

"That first day?"

"The day we met. There I was, stood in the doorway in my rags, not even any shoes on my feet. I was so nervous to be standing before the royal daughter of the Shah. Şelale introduced me. Do you remember?"

"I think so, a little."

"Do you remember what you said?"

I shook my head.

"'What of it?' That's what you said. 'What of it.'"

It felt as though someone had thrust a knife into my heart and twisted.

"Oh, my love." I closed the gap between us, opening my arms to gather her to me.

"Don't," she said, stepping away. "Please don't. If you touch me, I think I might cry."

"You hate me."

"No, it's not that—"

"How can you not, after what I have done?"

"I don't hate you," she repeated, taking my hands in hers. "I understood that you took the baby for good reasons. That you wanted to protect me." Her voice trailed off, and I felt bound to answer her unspoken question.

"It died," I told her. "I didn't kill it, but it died on the journey."

"And that is why you did not return?"

There it was, my lie all laid out before me.

"Yes. I was so ashamed. I could not bear to see the look on your face when I told you."

I expected her to scream, to bite her teeth into my arm and claw at my face.

Instead, tears filled her eyes and she smiled.

"*Allahu Akbar*," she whispered. "I thought I had disgraced you."

"Disgraced me? In what way?"

"By having the child. I thought that is why you took it, to purge me of my shame."

My heart was breaking. "No, never! The disgrace was entirely Hafez's. Do you not remember? He paid in full."

"Yes, but still, I thought perhaps you had not forgiven me."

"I forgave you entirely, for there was nothing there to forgive. No, it was not that."

Her smile once again faltered.

"Then it was something?"

"Yes. It was something."

Her eyes became wide as she pressed her forehead to mine, caressing my cheek with her hand.

"Tell me, Shahzadi. Tell me what it was, and let me make amends."

"It is so simple," I told her. "You loved him more than me."

At that moment, she became aware of his presence.

Eirik had entered the chamber by a separate door, hidden within the wall. I did not know where the entrance lay, yet I had seen him arrive about the time I felt my own heart die.

Her hand tightened around mine, even as she turned to him. "My love," she said, greeting him through habit before she could prevent the words from leaving her lips.

She turned quickly back to me with eyes that implored my understanding.

"I don't," she said quickly. "I don't."

Eirik stepped towards her, their matching outfits like two figures on a wedding cake.

"What was that, oh moonlight of my life? You do not what?"

"She does not love you," I replied, filling the silence between them.

"Is this true?" he took another step towards her.

"No! I do not love you *more*. I do not love you *more!*" Her eyes could no longer hold back the flood. "Please, Vachon!" She released my hand and went to him, holding her hands to his mask, pressing paper where there should have been skin. "I love you, I do."

"Not in the way a wife should love a husband, though."

"I'm sorry," she sobbed. "You have been so kind to me, and I have tried, I have tried so hard."

He took her hands from his face and lowered them.

"That is a shame," he whispered, "for I have loved you without trying."

Had my heart still been beating, I would have found this all too much. We were destroying her, the two of us, and it was within my power to end her suffering. Instead, I simply watched, waiting for the next heartfelt revelation as though watching one of those ballets my brother so enjoyed. A love story in costume and in character. Me, the silent audience to a choreographed tragedy.

As she crumpled against his chest, he looked to me. Those bottomless eyes flickering as though the screaming souls of *Jahannam* burned within them.

"What have you done with our guests?" I asked him.

"There was something in the water. They drank too fast, and now they are sleeping it off."

We continued to stare at one another as Sheyda slid down his body to the cold, hard earth. She clung to his ankle, her face pressed to his shoe, lips parted as though in prayer.

Slowly, I crouched down beside her, lifting her chin with my finger.

"It is okay, Sheyda. I do not blame you. He offered you a life. With me, the best you could ever have hoped for was to be my servant."

"I *love* you," she cried.

"Therein lies the sadness," I replied. "For I love you, and he loves you."

"Then it is what I feel that should decide!"

Eirik knelt beside her, too.

"Unfortunately," he said quietly, "that is not quite how this game is played."

"Game?"

Her eyes flicked between us, uncomprehending.

"I am a deliberate deceiver, as Ellis Bell might say. A Judas, a traitor, and a worthless friend."

I saw him smile, and spoke to draw her attention away.

"I have never lied to you, Sheyda. I have always loved you more than him, but I am afraid I cannot love you better than him."

"I don't understand."

"Your mistress and I have known one another a long time," he explained. "We have shared loves, and inflicted losses. We have both known sacrifice, shall we say?"

"Until now, our slate has held even," I continued. "What he loved most, I stole, and what I loved most, he vanquished. Then came you."

"Do you not see?" he asked. "Whichever one of us you choose, we are both lost."

I felt the animal in him rise: the flare of his nostrils, the glistening of his eyes, the flex of his muscular arms. That familiar, bestial excitement preceding a kill. The tiger within me rose to meet his dragon, and I could no longer control the words that came from my mouth.

"We are one and the same," I said, as we stood together. "You were a glimpse of the daylight, but I belong to night. I belong to him."

"And I belong to her."

"No!" Sheyda cried, clawing the earth where she sat. "No, no, no... Afsar, it isn't true."

Although my heart was dead, I knew that I deceived Death itself. It wasn't true. Sheyda had been my greatest joy, and my greatest weakness. Though what could I do? The goodness I had loved in Sheyda would forever now be tainted. She could never love me again as she had when she thought me to be pure and kind. Like Eirik, I had removed my mask and she had recoiled. If I chose her over him, for the rest of our lives she would only ever fear me, never love me. Whereas Eirik knew me for all that I was, and he did not turn away, because we were mirror images of each other.

I heard Eirik's dagger hit the ground. For one brief moment I imagined what my life would be if Sheyda took the blade and slit his throat instead of her own. Yet Sheyda was the sweetest of all things on this earth. Even as we crushed her hopes beneath our careless feet, she could only ever find fault in herself.

Her wretched sobs turned to cries of agony as she plunged the blade into herself.

I turned my head to look, but Eirik held me there in our embrace, his lips firmly pressed against mine. It was not until I felt the warmth of her blood seeping through my slippers that I finally pulled away.

Blood.

There was so much of it.

I could see my own reflection on the floor.

Sheyda lay slumped, both hands wrapped around the hilt. I do not think she was entirely dead, or perhaps the rise and fall of her chest was simply an illusion of the candlelight. Perhaps I was not yet willing to accept that she was gone.

"There is something profound in destroying one's own future, don't you think?"

I understood what he meant.

I had taken something genuine and turned it into a possession, a cheap trinket, to do with as I pleased. Sheyda held the whole of me those nights in Shirgah. Nothing should ever be allowed to possess you entirely. It can never be safe for you or for them.

"What now?" I asked.

"Let us bathe her, and lay her out beneath the tree. It is cool enough down here that she will keep until we can afford her a proper burial."

He went about collecting a bucket from the trough, whilst I stared down at my poor, dead love and wondered whether I had made the right decision.

There was something about Eirik, though.

It was as though he were an illusion, misdirecting your eye with his genius for trickery, so that all the while you failed to notice that he himself did not exist. His flesh was merely a conduit for a hundred different demons. When he laughed, when he sang, when he murdered, each of these acts were governed by the force of nature itself, bubbling up from the centre of the earth to inflict its will upon the poor clay vessels it encountered, cracking them like pots, strewn as porcelain figurines beneath the wheels of an unstoppable, runaway cart.

One with silver skulls at its helm.

I helped him to undress her, careful to avoid getting blood on my clean garments. We laid Sheyda's body out and sluiced it down, bucket after bucket, until most of the red had seeped into the earth or disappeared down the small drain by the wall.

I paused to kiss the crescent moon on her cheek before closing her eyes.

"It was the right thing to do," I agreed.

The Frothamptons awoke several hours later with no recollection of how they had come to be asleep in an upstairs room at the palace. Eirik played on their own embarrassment to convince them that they had been overcome by heatstroke from their arduous walk. He thought it best to let them rest. His own wife sent her apologies, for she was also feeling unwell and had retired to her room.

They were ridiculously grateful to Eirik for the ease at which he overlooked their social transgression. After completing their tour, we returned to the palace at Sari to eat a fine meal and listen to their insipid suggestions for improvements to what was already a perfect design. The thought that someone as bland as Bernard Frothampton, or as practical as his daughter, could ever have the imagination to improve upon Eirik's work was simply laughable.

My one regret is that I spent my last evening despising their company. Had I known then what was to come, I would have laughed at every joke, found pleasure in every morsel of food, and given myself without restraint to the joys of companionship, regardless of whose company I found it in. Yet we can never see our own grave until we are standing in it.

The hour was late when the Frothamptons finally retired. I yawned and stretched by the dying embers of the fire, watching smoke curl like fingers into the night's sky, reaching for the stars, amongst whom one extra now shone.

"Wait for me by the fountain," Eirik instructed, as he went to bid farewell to our guests.

Void of sunlight, there were no colours dancing in the courtyard, only the sound of cascading water and the thick, heady scent of rose petals.

I closed my eyes and breathed in deeply.

As I listened, the sound of the water built to a crescendo, subtly at first, then intensifying to a staggering roar. I was transported back to the drumming well at Shirgah, staring down into the bottomless waters that seemed to lead straight to Jahannam.

I gasped as Eirik pressed against me, his hand once again at my throat, his other against my hip, reaching down to scrunch my silk skirt into his fist. My panic melted to desire. We had been damned from the moment we first met. There was no reason left to fight, or to deny it. His lips brushed against my neck and I pushed against him in pleasure.

He led me to my old quarters, up to the room that had once been mine. Shokuh had never used it for her son's room, she simply had not wanted me to have it. Everything looked the same, only empty. The floor was coated in a thin layer of dust, merely another neglected room in a palace full of rooms.

There was a bed.

He undressed me in the way Şelale once had. Only, instead of washing me down, he drenched me in kisses, over every sacred part of my body.

When we were both naked, I removed his mask.

His features no longer held horror for me, as I knew my own soul to be an uglier thing than his face. I wanted to look upon him, to see my friend as he had always been beneath his many disguises. The part of him that remained constant. That had loved me, taught me, and forgiven me.

The pain as he pushed into me was replaced with the sensation that he filled me entirely. I could no longer distinguish myself from him, nor tell where I ended and he began. Though we occupied separate bodies, our mind and our spirit had been poured of the same poison.

We clung to one another in the dark.

♦ 13 ♦

It was a little after midnight when we woke to a clamorous disturbance outside. Eirik untangled himself from me, kissed my lips and went to the window. The shadows cast by the moon drew the contours of his muscles, causing me to reach for him.

"Wait," he said, holding up his hand.

"What is it?"

"They are calling your name."

I pulled myself up to listen, and sure enough there were shouts from the harem: "Afsar! Where is the Shahzadi, she must be found."

I did not recognise the voices.

"Get dressed, quickly!" Eirik ordered, already pulling on his own shirt.

Whilst I was struggling with my skirt, he produced a chiffon scarf from one of his pockets and threw it at me, ordering me to cover my face with it and wait there for him to return.

The shouts in the courtyard were getting louder. I could hear my mothers crying out, their own voices joining the cacophony like hens protecting the coop. I was too afraid to look out of the window, so I pressed myself against the corner of the bed. I realised that Eirik had forgotten to put on his mask when he left. It felt as though he was gone for an eternity.

When he burst back through the door I half expected to see a blood-crazed bandit, come to carry me away.

"Come with me," he barked. "There is no time to lose."

I shrieked as he grabbed my wrist and yanked me towards the stairs. Instead of crossing to the main palace, we slunk like cats behind the fountain and out through a small doorway that I had barely noticed before. On the other side of the wall, we crossed onto the lawn so that our feet made no sound as we ran.

By the time we reached the woods, my legs were weak beneath me and I thought that I might faint. His black stallion, the companion of Nisfey Shab, stood tethered to a tree. It sensed our urgency, rolling its eyes and stamping its hooves as Eirik swung into the saddle, reaching down to lift me in front of him.

"What is happening?" I asked.

He kicked the horse furiously and it took off along the path through the woods. Air filled my mouth and I could ask no more.

It soon became clear to me that we were riding for Shirgah. That is when I became afraid. It was an emotion I rarely felt, for I had never had cause to fear much in my life. Even when Eirik slowed the horse, I kept my face pressed to his chest. I did not wish to ask my question a second time, for in my heart I knew what was happening.

We must have been discovered somehow. The only reason I was not in chains was because I had spent the night with Eirik in my old quarters. When they went to search my rooms at the harem, they had found my bed empty.

I had embraced darkness and it had saved me.

When we arrived at Shirgah, the old house was deserted. Adel and Majid no longer stood guard at the gate, the cook hut was empty, and the lamps were all off. It did not feel like the house I had once known. The shadows seemed longer, and the hoot of an owl made me fear that the ghost of Sheyda had followed us, the crescent moon in the sky looking down in scorn.

Eirik carried me from the horse to my room, where he rested me upon the bed. He took the veil he had given me and wrapped it around his own face.

"Don't leave me here!" I cried.

"I must return to Sari. I need to know what has happened."

"I'm afraid to be alone."

I expected to see compassion, but instead he turned away.

"Never fear the night, Afsar. It is the daylight that illuminates our sins for the world to see."

"Have we sinned?"

Instead of answering, he left, locking the door behind him. I ran to it and tried to turn the handle, but it would not open. I heard a rumbling sound behind me, and turned to see the chest of drawers roll back. It was positioned beside my bed, on the opposite side to the fireplace. Eirik crawled through from the room next door.

"This way," he beckoned.

I followed and he showed me how to open a door which had been disguised as a stuffed fish mounted on the wall in a glass cabinet. Behind it was a black tunnel dropping vertically to the room below. A length of rope disappeared down into the depths. By winding a wheel set into the back of the door, the rope drew steadily upwards to reveal a wooden tray.

"The door to your room is no longer visible from the hallway," he told me. "It looks like part of the wall. Each morning and each evening you may crawl through the escape I have just shown you, and pull up this rope. There will be food. When you have eaten, send down your plates and your chamber pot."

"How will I know that the food is safe?"

"The food will be safe. Trust me. But you must never leave your room at any other time. Not even to look out of the windows. For as long as you remain hidden, you will be safe. Nobody knows you are here. I will return when I have news."

For three days I remained holed up in my room, crawling behind the chest of drawers twice a day to collect meagre rations of bread and cheese.

On the fourth day, I pressed my ear to the wall as had become my habit. Hearing it was silent, I pushed the chest of drawers aside and crawled through into the adjoining room. Only, when I lifted my head, I discovered that I was not alone.

"I knew you would return, Sultana."

I rose to my feet and stared at Şelale, her clothes tattered and her feet caked in dirt.

"They asked me to go with them to Tehran, but I refused."

"Did you not receive the money I left for you?"

"What money?"

"Şelale, why have you not returned home?"

"My home is by your side, Sultana."

Something did not feel right, but I watched whilst she went to the stuffed fish and drew up my breakfast, the plate resting on top of a clean chamber pot.

We returned through the hole and I pushed the chest of drawers back into place whilst she laid out the food on the floor. We sat together on cushions, sharing that pitiful meal.

"How have you survived here for so long?" I asked.

"Vachon gave me permission to sell what they did not take with them. It has been enough to buy food and charcoal. The rest of the time I hunt in the river and the woods outside the town."

"Why on earth did you not go with them?"

"After you left, Sultana, things here were very difficult. Your companion tried to starve herself to death. At first I thought it was a mother's grief over the loss of her child, but soon I came to realise that another kind of love flowed through her veins. An unnatural attachment."

I looked down, unable to swallow my food.

"I tried to help her to recover from her affliction. I went to her family, but they did not wish to know. There were rumours that our house was a place of witchcraft, and that the Shah had banished you here for immorality. Even though they knew nothing of the child, they feared taking her back after she had been living here for so long. They felt she might be cursed, and that she would bring bad luck upon them."

"Ignorant peasants."

"There was a doctor, though. He lives up in the hills. I had to walk more than a day to get to him. He agreed to help her in return for a donkey and a modest sum of money. He came to the house and performed healing rituals to drive out the devil in her. He tied her to the bed to prevent her thrashing. Then he cut her in many places across her back. He affixed heated glass jars to the cuts, which filled with her blood. I have never seen anything like it in my life. Yet it seemed to calm her, until Vachon returned."

"He found her that way?"

"The anger on his face! He cast the doctor out without pay, and washed her wounds clean himself. He tended to her for a month or more, coaxing her to eat and nursing her back to health."

"And you?"

"I was flogged. He brought men from the village. They stripped me and beat me."

I could not imagine such shame. I found it hard to meet her gaze, yet still she continued to stare through me. I should have apologised for leaving her there. It was her nature to care for others. She just hadn't known which course of action to take. She had sought out a doctor to help Sheyda. How was she to know whether his methods were right? Yet she was also a servant, and for that reason her failings were not mine to apologise for.

"He can be cruel, your Comte."

"Yet you stayed?"

"Sheyda spoke to him on my behalf. He allowed me back into the house, and announced that they would leave for Tehran. He offered me a position in his household, but I declined. How could I leave for Tehran when you might yet return?"

"Did he ever ask of me?"

"No, not that I heard. He became devoted to Sheyda."

"Did he ask after the child?"

"Neither of them did."

The weight of this struck me hard. Eirik must truly have loved Sheyda to invest his time in her as he had. Undoubtedly he had known that I was responsible for the disappearance of the child, and no doubt he assumed I had killed it. Perhaps he would have done so himself, for it was nothing but a burden on the girl.

It was at that moment that I heard hooves on the gravel outside. A short while later, the chest of drawers slid back and Eirik's sweat-drenched face appeared. He held his leather mask in one hand, wiping at the sweat with the same chiffon veil he had taken the night he left. Looking up, the light from the window caught the full awfulness of his face. Şelale shrieked and drew back.

"Oh, shut up," he snapped, more annoyed than surprised to see her there.

"Eirik–"

"They are coming for you, we must leave."

"Coming for me?"

"They know. Everybody knows. One of the gardeners at the palace – your lover's father, Vafar, of all people – found a goat slaughtered in the woods. He started ranting like a lunatic, telling people that the Shah's daughter was a murderess. Of course, nobody believed him except his closest friends and relations. He gathered them up and stormed the harem looking for you. That is what happened the night we left Sari. It didn't take long for the Darougheh's men to suppress their rebellion. The next morning, Shokuh had Vafar hanged for treason. Only, just after the rope dropped, two of his sons stormed the platform with a box they claimed they had found in your quarters. When the box was opened, it contained a blood-drenched robe!"

I must have gone white, for he knelt down beside me and held my face in his hands.

"Afsar, you have doomed yourself!"

I could not speak, so he continued.

"Shokuh and Arezoo tried to have them arrested, to stand trial for theft before the Shah, only the crowd began to rally round them. One of the brothers was your gardener, Aram. He told them of the murder of your guards. How he had watched you butcher Hafez, and how he had sneaked in early the next morning to try to rescue Hesam, expecting him still to be alive. He painted a picture for the crowd of a lake of blood, and a poison that rendered its victim conscious but unable to scream. That is when the Darougheh stepped in. He ordered his guards to contain the crowd, but one of the women panicked and tried to run. His men shot her."

"I don't understand," I said. "Why didn't they shoot the brothers?"

"Would that they had. They did not shoot them because they were afraid of inciting a riot. The Darougheh mistakenly thought he could calm the situation. In the silence that fell after the gunshot, Aram continued to tell the story of his time here at Shirgah. He told how he had loaded Hesam's body onto a cart bound for Sari, to provide evidence of your wicked crime, and how that body never arrived. The crowd began to chant your name, Shahzadi, demanding you be brought to justice."

"This cannot be true!"

"It was then that the crowd turned on the Darougheh. Who else could make evidence like that disappear? The crowd were outraged. The Darougheh's men were reluctant to open fire as many of the crowd were family of the guards. In the end they had no choice, though their hesitation meant that they were soon overpowered, and the Darougheh fled for his life. I was watching from the upper floor of the palace. Shokuh, flanked by Mother Arezoo, took the platform. The crowd quieted to hear what she would say."

"She forsook me."

"She served you up like a plate of lamb kebab. Re-forming the guard, she charged the Darougheh with finding you."

My eyes grew wide with horror as the obvious dawned on me.

"They searched your palace?"

"We had been there less than two days before. People remembered seeing us. It was an obvious hiding place. When they arrived there, one of the younger workers had been paying closer attention than the others. He had been in the employ of Vafar, who was paying for information about me since the incident with the lasso. I thought I had been so careful, yet somehow he found the secret staircase. He had never dared enter before, but with that lynch mob at his back he had no such qualm. He sprung the mechanism and within the hour they had carried the body of Sheyda to the surface."

"You never had a chance to dispose of her?"

"I planned to after our night together, but instead we came here. By the time I returned to Sari it was already daylight and a large crowd was gathering around Vafar, the crazy man shouting about a goat. Things escalated too fast, there was no time."

"So now they have a body and my blood-soaked cloak."

"They are coming for us both. They may have found your cloak, but the torture chamber was my design."

"How long do we have?"

"I left as soon as the crowd began to repeat Aram's suspicion that you had fled to your old place of exile. They cannot be more than an hour behind me."

"Well then, we will stay here. We will lock ourselves inside and wait until they leave."

"It is too late, Afsar. After storming the construction site, they are wise to all of my tricks. It won't take them long to discover the traps that open these secret doors."

"There is only one thing for it, Sultana. You must go to your father. You must beg the Shah's protection," cried Şelale.

"Şelale is right," I said. "I must go to the Shah. I will tell him that I sacrificed that goat to Allah in his name, and that I had not washed my robes yet. I shall tell him I know nothing of the body at the palace, or how it came to be there. Let him blame the worker who opened the trapdoor. He was an apprentice builder, he knew where the mechanism was, so it's reasonable to assume he built it and tried to place the blame on you. With Eirik gone, he was hoping for promotion. He wanted your job."

"Do you know how ridiculous that sounds?"

"It's all a misunderstanding. The locals will see that when he explains it to them. They just need a reasonable explanation to replace the mad rantings of Vafar, and the Shah will look for any reason to defend me—"

"No, he won't."

"The Shah would not condemn his eldest daughter on the rumours of a few of his subjects. One of them has already been hanged for inciting an uprising. He has to defend me, or pardon those who speak against the royal family. He would never do that. I've known him all my life. He would never believe them over me."

"You underestimate the gravity of the situation. It is not merely a few of his subjects. It is half the population of Sari, such was the disturbance after the Darougheh's men opened fire."

I laughed, for I had already talked myself into the sanctuary of my brother's arms. "So, the termites have come to tear down my house, have they? Well, let them come. They will soon learn the meaning of humility by the time the Shah is through. Sheep do not threaten lions."

"Come," Şelale said. "Eat up now, you will need your strength for the ride. Should I go ahead and warn your father of events? Perhaps he can send his guard to escort you safely to the capital?"

"You are not listening to me," Eirik snapped. "The Shah will not protect you."

"Don't talk such nonsense—"

"How do you think I gained my position?"

"What?"

"Look at me, Shahzadi. I am a travelling circus performer building a royal palace. You think that sort of fortune God-given?"

"You are also an accomplished assassin. I assume silence brings its own rewards."

"Silence, yes, but not over matters of state. It was far more personal than that."

"I don't understand."

"Did you ever wonder how Ishya came to be in the tiger's cage?"

I froze. It had been a question which had haunted me in that space between wake and sleep almost every night for half a year after it had occurred.

"I followed you that night," he explained. "I wanted to see what games you would play in Sari without me. Instead, I watched you murder my closest friend by pushing her from a tree."

"You were watching?"

"That is the night I realised how alike we are. After I recovered from the shock, I asked myself why you might do such a thing. People kill for one of three reasons: fear, revenge or pleasure. Although I am certain you took pleasure in it, I doubted that to be your main motivation, and I knew that you could have nothing to fear from a little Indian girl. So the only conclusion I could draw was revenge, borne of jealousy."

"The same reason you killed Shahab?"

"And believe me, I took a lot of pleasure in that."

I flinched.

"You had killed her so carelessly and simply walked away. The fact that nobody saw you was nothing short of a miracle. I had two choices: bury her and weep out my grief alone, or use the situation to my advantage."

"To teach me a lesson?"

"That most of all, though also to advance my own status."

"To what ends?"

"Oh, Afsar. You wander through your life as though everything exists for your gratification. You never truly stop to *look*. To see the sacrifices people make to get to positions they are not born to. All around you, every day, people think through plans and carry them out, strive, fail, die for their dreams, and occasionally succeed. Life is nothing but a high-risk gamble where people bet their lives hour after hour for the hope of winning more than they already have. I am no different. I was born with absolutely nothing. Less than nothing. Had I only been born empty-handed, perhaps I would never have become so invested in the game. Yet born with this handicap," he pointed to his face, "is it any wonder I had to run twice as fast, to compensate for my burden?" He paused to wipe the beads of sweat that had formed at his brow. "I saw an opportunity and I took it. After I lay Ishya out in the tiger's cage and doused her in goat's blood, I went to the Shah and told him what had happened. I told him there had been an accident. That you had been playing with the girl, but that your game had become rougher than intended. He understood what I meant, and was grateful that I had provided a plausible solution to the problem. He appreciated that I had preserved the jewel in his family crown from having her lustre tarnished."

"When he shot the tiger, he knew that it had not killed her?"

"Now you see what a debt of gratitude attaches itself to my name?" He grinned. "I had proven myself loyal and quick-witted. The Shah is a business man, albeit poor at balancing his own books. He respected a boy trying to better himself, especially one with raw talent in deception. I carried out the tasks he gave me with efficiency, never expecting any sort of reward. The more time I spent in his company, the more I was able to delight him with my tricks, and later with little model palaces build of card. He was looking for a way to repay the debt without losing face, so he feigned such astonishment at my architectural vision that he commissioned me to build him a palace."

"You took advantage of me!"

"No more than you took advantage of me. At least I saved your life in doing so. Had anyone discovered Ishya's body and suspected you, even the Shah would not have been able to offer you protection. What shame you would have brought to the royal household. It is for that reason that he cannot save you now."

"Because he already knows me for what I am."

We all fell silent for a long moment.

"I know you for what you are," Eirik said eventually. "And I love you for it." He held out his hand to me, helping me to stand. "Come with me," he said. "Let us leave Iran."

"And go where?"

"Anywhere. The whole world awaits you, Shahzadi."

"I would no longer be myself, though. What weight would my life carry without my royal name?"

"Better a living woman than a dead princess."

I smiled. "I do not think that I could survive."

"Of course you can! Think of it. The mighty pillars of Rome, cradle of the Roman Empire, the Danube and the glory of the Taj Mahal. We could follow the Silk Road all the way to China and have tea with Emperor Xianfeng."

I laughed. "Don't tease me."

"I am not teasing you. All of this is possible. Simply say 'yes'. Say 'yes' to me. Accept me, *love* me, Afsar, and we will conquer the world together."

A shiver ran through me.

"I do love you," I said.

For that one simple moment, it was true.

Eirik was my friend. The only true friend I had ever known. More than that, he held a mirror up to my soul, and told me that my reflection was beautiful. Sheyda had loved me too, yet she had never honestly known me. In Eirik, our darkness bled into one another, twisted and tightened, like the binding of a rope that can never again be separated.

Our lips met, his hands cupping my face. There was an urgency in him that suggested our love was running out of time and that we should savour it before the last grain of sand fell from the hourglass.

He bit my lip as his teeth clashed together.

As he fell to his knees, his arms wrapped around my neck, pulling me with him. At first I did not understand what had happened. From deep within him came a deafening roar. My hand felt the handle of the knife protruding from his back.

"What have you done?" I cried, staring up at Şelale with eyes as wide as the sky.

"Run, Sultana. We must leave. This monster's soul is as ugly as his face. He will have us all hanged!"

"What have you done!" My voice rose to a screech as I felt hot, thick blood on my fingers.

"We will go to your father. We will make him understand. It was all this demon's fault, Shahzadi. You have not been yourself since he arrived. Your father will protect you."

She was ranting like a woman possessed, shocked by her own actions.

It was at that moment we heard the sound of hooves on the gravel outside.

"Who is it?"

Şelale ran to the window, pressing her face to the glass.

"I cannot see!"

We sat there in that room, as quiet as mice. Şelale crouched in the corner, twisting her hair between her fingers, whilst Eirik lay in my arms, his mouth stuffed with the edge of my bed sheet to stifle his screams.

Moments later we heard heavy footsteps climbing the stairs, followed by the frantic sound of scratching against the wall.

"Shahzadi! Shahzadi, are you there?"

"The Darougheh," I whispered. "He knows there must be a door there. Şelale, let him in."

For a moment she looked as though she did not understand me, then slowly she uncurled herself and pushed back the chest of drawers, disappearing through the hole in the wall. A moment later she reappeared, followed by the Darougheh.

"Afsar! Thank goodness you are safe," he said, crawling towards me on all fours. He stopped when he saw the pool of blood on the floor. "What is this?"

"It doesn't matter, but you must help him. Please!"

"Shahzadi, something terrible has happened—"

"I know. I know all about the uprising. Eirik was there, he saw."

"I am supposed to bring you back to Sari, to stand trial on the orders of Mother Shokuh."

"How quickly the dog turns from licking the hand of its friend to biting," I said bitterly.

"You must go with him, Sultana. Beg forgiveness for your sins. If Shokuh has ordered your arrest, she will be able to annul it. Tell her about this demon. Give him to her, pledge yourself and kiss her feet. She will forgive you. She will send the crowds away."

I could hardly believe what I was hearing. Had my servant become completely deranged?

"She will string you up alongside me," Eirik said, pulling the sheet from his mouth.

"I fear you are right," the Darougheh concurred. "I too believe she would play a trio on her strings, and that I would be the surprise performance."

"I did not take you as a musical fellow," Eirik said, grimacing as he struggled to sit up.

"My dear man," the Darougheh replied, taking his weight from me, "there is much you and I never learned of one another. Now, I fear the hour has grown too late for sharing secrets."

"But you are the law in Sari!" I cried. "How can you fear such a stupid woman?"

"I could not control my men, Shahzadi. Two of them panicked and opened fire. They should not have done so, and their failing was my own."

"So they fired a few shots, what of it?"

"They killed a woman."

"Only one? Worse than that has happened in the past, or have you forgotten those Rosy Hours?"

"I have lost the respect of the people, Shahzadi. They have given their ear to Shokuh, and she is busy whispering her orders into it."

"They do not respect you because they do not fear you! Fire upon a few more and they will soon remember their master."

"When a dog turns rabid, it no longer thinks of fear. The only thing that fills its mind is the kill. They will not rest until their lust for blood is sated."

Eirik caught my eye and I felt a sinking sensation. I knew that thirst for blood only too well, and I knew that the Darougheh spoke the truth. If he dragged me back to Sari, Mother Shokuh would see us all hang, and the crowd would love her for it. Perhaps even my brother would love her for it. Who was I to him, after all? An unwanted child with witchcraft in her veins, who held little value and great risk. The people would hail her the Saviour of Sari, purging the palace of evil. My brother would seek to bask in her light, such was his desire for public approval and the need to distance himself from my own scandal.

"Come, there isn't any time, we must get him to a surgeon."

"I only have one horse," the Darougheh said. "I trust Eirik's is in the stable?"

Eirik nodded.

"Then we must go now."

Without pausing for breath, the Darougheh pulled Eirik forward, grasped the hilt of the blade and pulled it from his body. Eirik screamed so loudly that I thought he would faint.

"*Ça me fait chier!*"

"I could not have put it better myself," the Darougheh smiled, before ordering me through the hole in the wall.

He placed Eirik on his stomach with his arms above his head, then pushed him through until I was able to grab him firmly by his sleeves. As I pulled him through the hole, he left a streak of blood behind on the floor. Usually the sight of suffering excited me, yet his suffering only made me afraid. To me, Eirik was invincible. He was the Prince of Conjurers, the King of Stranglers. He could not be weak, for if he were fallible what hope was there for the rest of us?

On the other side, the Darougheh helped him to stand, then together we manoeuvred him down the stairs to the front of the house. He sat, slumped against me, whilst my father's Chief of Police went to retrieve the second horse. Every second felt like an eternity as we waited for him to return, our eyes scouring the trees beyond the gate for any sign that the mob might have arrived from Sari. With the house surrounded on all sides by the raging waters of the two rivers, the gates proved the only escape to the main road, and from there to the countries and continents beyond.

The Darougheh's own horse lifted its head as he returned with Eirik's black stallion. With more strength than I thought possible in a man of his age, the Darougheh swung into the saddle, reached down, and pulled Eirik up in front of him. I wasted no time in mounting the black horse, but unlike the Darougheh I did not reach down for Şelale.

"Not you," I said, as she stood there with her arms outstretched. "It is because of you that we are in this mess."

"Sultana, I only wanted to protect you–"

"Protect me? The only thing I need protecting from is you."

"Sultana! I raised you from an infant. Have I not been your faithful companion these many years?"

"You got above yourself when you decided to stab my friend in the back."

"We don't have time for this," the Darougheh shouted. "They will be here at any moment."

We spurred our horses through the gates. Although they sped like the offspring of Areion, they were not fast enough to outrun the Darougheh's prophecy.

Everything happened so fast.

The road was in sight, just up ahead of us. From there, the route through the jungle to Amol. Then along the coast to the mighty Sassanid stronghold of Zanjan, where my brother had finally executed the Báb. Within four days, maybe five, the border with Azerbaijan.

That is where my mind was when the spear hit. So far ahead of my situation that I had not even considered whether Eirik would make the distance, where we would find a surgeon, or how long his recovery might take. In my heart, I had already fled Iran.

It was nothing more than a sharpened stick, thrown through the trees by a man whose face I never even saw. It did not hit my horse directly, but glanced between its front legs, causing it to trip. I was thrown across its head, flung between the ferns and the decaying leaves of the forest.

Too shocked even to feel pain, my natural desire to survive forced me to my feet. I caught the reins of the frightened beast as it made to pass me, following its injured master. I remember staring into the Darougheh's wide expression. The world fell perfectly still, as though we were the only two people in it. His green eyes sparkled like Panjshir emeralds, caught by the fading light of the day. They held within them all that he was: his loyalty, his cruelty, his resolve and his kindness.

Most of all his kindness.

"Go," I mouthed. "Save him."

People broke through the trees between us, and he knew that I was lost. Had I not given him the order to save Eirik, he would have wheeled his horse around and died defending me. Yet duty is more powerful than honour in men of his making.

By the time I had clawed my broken body back into the saddle of my terrified horse, there were a dozen other horses coming towards us. Pigeons must have carried news from Sari ahead of the arrival of my captors. The people in the road were merely the vanguard from Shirgah, reconnoitring ahead of Sari's *Savaran*.

I kicked my heels and fled back to the house. Şelale stood there in the courtyard, exactly where I had left her, the dust on her cheeks turned to clay by her tears. When she saw me, her face lit up as though she thought I had changed my mind and come to fetch her.

Her smile did not last. As I fell from the saddle, she saw the pack bearing down on me and screamed. Half-carrying, half-dragging, she threw me through the entrance, heaving the wooden doors shut behind us and slipping the bar into place. I was almost at the top of the stairs by the time she had completed this futile task. I looked down, waiting for her to follow, but instead she folded her arms and stood there, a resolute pout on her lips, those bovine eyes of hers determined to protect her calf.

I crawled through the hole behind the chest of drawers and slid it back into place behind me. Cocooned in the room that didn't exist, I covered my ears with my broken hands and sobbed with terror.

It did not take Aram and his brothers long to discover my secret room. It would have remained invisible, and perhaps I would have been able to hide there until they left, if it had not been for Eirik's blood on the floor. Thick streaks that seemed to disappear beneath the wall. It was obvious, even to an ignorant groundsman, that there had to be a hidden door.

It did not take them long to find the mechanism.

When they entered my room, it was empty.

At the bottom of the stairs, hidden inside the fake column, I felt strangely safe. That place which had once seemed claustrophobic felt more like freedom. They were clever enough to crawl through the chest of drawers, but they never did find the false back to my wardrobe.

Pressing my ear to the plaster, I could not hear anything in the room beyond. It was a risk. If I sprang the door and the room was not empty, they would catch me for certain. Yet, if the room *was* empty, then perhaps, just perhaps, I could make my escape across the back garden. I could throw myself into the river if necessary, and swim to the opposite shore.

A loud bang from the room above hardened my resolve. I had just made up my mind to chance my escape when I heard voices all around me. Having found the upstairs room empty, they were searching the downstairs rooms. I had left it too late.

"Find the bitch," I heard one man shout. "She's here somewhere. Sniff her out."

Soon after more voices joined the call for my execution.

"Beneath the rug in the hall," one announced, "the tiles are laced with blood."

"That must have been her slaughter room," another spoke.

"Where she murdered her guards?"

"And who knows who else!"

I have no idea how much time passed, or how long I was imprisoned in that confined space, nose full of the smell of freshly dug graves. There was no light to measure the hours, and my fear was such that every beat of my heart seemed to echo throughout history.

Eventually, silence fell.

I left it a long time, in case the men came back.

By the time I made up my mind to move, my body was hardly capable. Pain seared through every fibre of my being, yet enough desire to live remained that I forced myself upright.

Listening one last time, I pushed back the heel of my shoe against the step.

The mechanism clicked, but the door did not open.

I tried again. A second time, and a third.

My breathing began to quicken in panic.

That is when I smelled smoke.

## ♦ Epilogue ♦

I do not know whether the Darougheh came back for me. Whether he watched from the trees as the house burned. I do not know what happened to the ashes, whether they were swept into the violent currents that had kept me awake all those many nights of exile.

All I know is that my name was Afsar.

I was she, and no other.

That name belongs to me.

In years to come, scholars in the pay of my brother would remove me from the records. Some denied my existence, others claimed that I died in infancy. Those that could still remember me told their children I had been married abroad, or that I had died without children of my own, and therefore without purpose.

I was erased from history, eclipsed by Eirik's own legend.

The stories they told of him were heard throughout Persia and the Ottoman Empire; in fact, his name survived them all. They remembered him most as an architect. A man who built magic palaces. Those who visited my brother's new site at Sari soon forgot the rumour of the woman found in the basement. Sheyda's name, like mine, evaporated with her final breath.

No, they were far more intrigued by the hidden doors and the Shah's ability to walk between walls like a ghost. One moment there, the next gone. Materialising in mystical mirrors beneath chandeliers that appeared to cast out black light.

"Of course he had to die," people would proclaim. "He threatened to build a replica for the Khan of Afghanistan! Could you imagine?"

"The Shah blinded him, you know, for his insolence. Yet the creature could still build by feeling where he placed the bricks. He was guided by a jinn who took pity on his face."

"There was only one way the Shah could ensure he never built another palace like it."

"And the Darougheh of Sari?"

"Ah! A trick. A trick."

The legend goes that the Darougheh had been sent to kill Eirik on the Shah's orders, and that he had brought back a body. It was strung to a horse and paraded about the streets until its face was unrecognisable. Yet the Shah was not convinced. He sensed the deception and feared the reprisal of his prize assassin.

It is said that he confiscated the Darougheh's possessions and stripped him of his title, and that the man left town penniless, taking nothing with him but his horse, and an infant son whose mother was unknown.

My life blazed brightly for a moment, and was extinguished.

Whatever you might think of me, of what I was and what I did, know this:

My story was only the beginning of his.

### *Aknowledgements*

For my mother and father. For bookshelves and ABCs, for paperbacks, hardbacks and comics; for the power of words. Also for Marilyn, Merrick, my brother William and nephew Damian.

For a few good friends and the ghosts of the bottles of wine we have drunk: Martine, Ruairí and Cathryn in particular, who know me inside out and back to front, and for Joanna – Moma Zuba – for providing a safe place to land these past few months.

In the writing of this book: Mahna, for his lullabies, and Mohammad Ali Kazembeyki for an obscurely titled work which provided so much insight.

Finally, with the deepest of gratitude, to Salomé Jones at Ghostwoods Books for believing wholeheartedly in this story, and for her unwavering support and hard work. This is her book as much it is mine.

## *Mailing List*

For advance notice of upcoming releases and special member-only offers, please sign up to our occasional mailing list at:

**http://www.gwdbooks.com/mailing-list-sign-up.html**

We have a very strict policy of not being annoying email jerks. We'll never spam you, sell your details to anyone else, or broadcast any third-party offers.

If you enjoyed *Those Rosy Hours at Mazandaran*, please do consider leaving a review or spreading the word a little. It makes an immense difference.

Lightning Source UK Ltd.
Milton Keynes UK
UKOW02f0210220915

259002UK00002B/112/P